THE ENCHANTERS

THE LOSERS CLUB
Beverly and La Cienega

Groovy Locale of
THE ENCHANTERS

April 1962

JAMES ELLROY

THE ENCHANTERS

HUTCHINSON
HEINEMANN

1 3 5 7 9 10 8 6 4 2

Hutchinson Heinemann
20 Vauxhall Bridge Road
London SW1V 2SA

Hutchinson Heinemann is part of the Penguin Random House group of companies whose
addresses can be found at global.penguinrandomhouse.com

Penguin
Random House
UK

First published in the US by Alfred A. Knopf, a division of Penguin Random House
LLC, in 2023
First published in the UK by Hutchinson Heinemann in 2023

www.penguin.co.uk

A CIP catalogue record for this book is available from the British Library

ISBN 9781529151268 (hardback)
ISBN 9781529151275 (trade paperback)

Text design by Betty Lew

Printed and bound in Great Britain by Clays Ltd, Elcograf S.p.A.

The authorised representative in the EEA is Penguin Random House Ireland,
Morrison Chambers, 32 Nassau Street, Dublin D02 YH68

www.greenpenguin.co.uk

To François Guérif

Let me not be put to shame, Lord, for I have cried out to Thee; but let the wicked be put to shame and be silent in the realm of the dead.

—Psalms 31:17

CONFIDENTIAL MEMORANDUM

From: Lt. J. T. Meadows, Jr./#294883
Public Disorder & Intelligence Division
Los Angeles Police Department

To: Former Chief Daryl F. Gates
Dana Point, California
(by secure telefax)

Subject: Surveillance of memorial service for Fred
Otash & related observations on events of
summer 1962 (as previously discussed)

10/10/92

Sir:

The ceremony took place yesterday morning at Forest
Lawn, Glendale. Given your recent media notoriety (and
coerced early retirement), I understand your reluctance to
attend in person. Given my father's participation in the events
of summer '62—along with your own—I was honored to be
both your designated surveillor and your choice to author the
following brief.

Forty-three people attended the graveside service. A
Lebanese minister read a New Testament passage and cited
the "colorful life of the freewheeling Freddy O." A mourner,

former *Mirror-News* scribe Morty Bendish, told Channel 5 News anchor Tony Valdez that he "wrote the pastor's spiel, which Freddy himself dictated to him." It should be noted that Mr. Bendish was a suborned LAPD informant during the events of summer 1962.

The "spiel" was a sanitized biographical riff on the late Mr. Otash. It noted his 1945–1953 LAPD service and later "reign" as the "undisputed King of the Hollywood Private Eyes." The "spiel" failed to acknowledge Mr. Otash as a freelance extortionist, scandal-rag dirt digger, strongarm goon, perpetrator of divorce shakedowns, doper of racehorses, informant for Chief William H. Parker, procurer and dope conduit for President John F. Kennedy, and agent provocateur for Attorney General Robert F. Kennedy, in the combined LAPD/Justice Department operation of summer '62. The pastor concluded Mr. Bendish's "spiel" by lauding Mr. Otash as both the "Hellhound Who Held Hollywood Captive" and "a role model for all those in the Lebanese American community." Many mourners openly laughed at this concluding statement.

Per the mourners themselves:

Most were Mr. Otash's neighbors from the Park Wellington Apartments, along with three former operatives of the long-defunct Otash Detective Bureau: Phil Irwin, "Rodent" Robbie Molette, and Nathaniel "Nasty Nat" Denkins, the longtime host of *Nasty Nat's Soul Patrol* on Radio KBLK. Irwin, Molette, and Denkins were peripheral figures in the events of summer '62, but several individuals who might be termed "major players" also attended the ceremony. They were:

The two surviving members of the LAPD "Hat Squad," retired sergeants Harry Crowder and Clarence "Red" Stromwall;

Assistant U.S. Attorney Edgar Chacón, a Justice Department investigator under Robert F. Kennedy in the summer of '62;

Roddy McDowall, noted TV and film actor, as well as an "underground" director of homosexual porno films;

Recording artist/nightclub entertainer Eddie Fisher, who attended the service with former major league pitching ace Bo Belinsky. Mr. Fisher is the fourth husband of actress Elizabeth Taylor. It should be noted that Mr. Otash and Mr. Belinsky

pulled a divorce shakedown on Miss Taylor in the summer
of '62;

TV and stage actress Lois Nettleton, who attended the
service with the sister of John and Robert Kennedy and the ex-
wife of the late actor Peter Lawford, Patricia Kennedy Lawford.
The women appeared to be close friends of long standing. They
left the service in a chauffeured limousine. I tailed the limo to
St. Vibiana's church in downtown L.A. They lit altar candles,
presumably for Freddy Otash, and had the limo drive them to
the nearby Pacific Dining Car restaurant. I surveilled them in
the cocktail lounge. They became inebriated and offered up
toasts to Freddy Otash. At one point, Miss Nettleton said, "We
should have loved him more."

In conclusion:

I consider it unlikely that the death of Freddy Otash will
serve to reignite the rumors of LAPD/Justice Department
collusion that flourished and spawned much speculation
thirty years ago. That unique merging of movie stars,
major politicians, a corrupt Hollywood element, and a
vicious criminal demimonde has largely faded from public
consciousness, and most of the more celebrated and notorious
participants are now dead or have vested interests in retaining
their silence. Freddy Otash was the only one who knew the
entire story, and now *he's* dead. And I seriously doubt that
he left any sort of incriminating evidence and/or narrative
accounts behind. There's also this: You were there that summer,
sir. You know full well that Freddy himself was the most guilty
participant in the whole mess, and thus had the most to lose by
hoarding defamatory documents.

Respectfully,
Lt. J. T. Meadows, Jr./#294883/PDID

PART 1
BAIT GIRLS

(AUGUST 4, 1962)

1

The drop ran eighty feet. The cliff was loose dirt and no footholds. We hauled shitbird up to the edge and showed him the view.

The Pasadena Freeway, southbound. Due north of the Chavez Ravine exit and downtown L.A. Steady traffic clocking through at 65-plus.

Shitbird was Richard Douglas Danforth/white male American/ approximate age 36. No green sheet, no wants, no warrants. He's a bleak cat with a pachuco haircut and Sir Guy shirt.

I held his right arm. Max Herman held his left arm. Red Stromwall jammed his head down and force-fed him the view.

Freddy O. and the Hat Squad. We're at it again. Bill Parker says, "Jump." We say, "How high?" It's a kidnap job tonight.

Harry Crowder and Eddie Benson watchdogged Suspect #2. They stood him up by their prowl sled. They fed him the threats, the car noise, the view. He's Morris Hershel "Buzzy" Stein/WMA/age 42. His perv sheet dates back to 1938. He's a stat rape-o and psycho snout diver. Danforth and Stein were bought and paid for. Kidnap was a gas-chamber bounce.

This gig was strictly rogue and ad lib. Here's the gist:

A B-film actress named Gwen Perloff got strongarm snatched. It was late a.m., today. She lived in a cheese-luxe building up from the Strip. Three men grabbed her on the sidewalk. They wore Fidel Castro masks. Multiple eyewits saw them. They shoved her into a double-parked vehicle and jammed south. Said vehicle might have been a '58 Dodge or a '56 Chevy Nomad. Miss Perloff plays second leads in horror and dance-craze flicks. She's a 20th Century–Fox contract slave. The Strip is county turf. The L.A. Sheriff's caught the squawk, *but*—

Fox kingpin Darryl Zanuck got tipped off. Some unknown woman called him. She finked Danforth and Stein and spilled one of their two girl-stash locations. Zanuck called his tight pal, Bill Parker. Chief Bill bootjacked the kidnap job. He dispatched Freddy and the Hats to a house off 6th and Dunsmuir. We grabbed Danforth and Stein. Perloff was stashed elsewhere. Danforth and Stein refused to divulge the spot. Stein said there were three more snatch men still out there. *They* pulled the job, not him and Richie. Stein zipped it then. Harry and Eddie whomped him with sap gloves. Stein still kept it zipped. Ditto Danforth. That mandated the Death Threat and Freeway Drop Show.

I held Danforth's right arm. Max held his left arm. Red jammed his head down and force-fed him look-sees.

Max went *Where's the girl?* Red went *Give it up or you fly.* Harry, Eddie, and Pervdog Stein stood ten feet back from the drop.

It was August-in-L.A. hot and humid. Max and Red sweated through their shirts and suit coats. Danforth wriggled and squirmed. He dug his feet in and thrashed. Dirt clods skittered off the cliff. The fucking drop loomed.

I scoped Max and Red. They looked impatient. I clamped Danforth's arm. He buckled against me. My hand went numb. My legs fluttered. Max and Red ran six-four and 240. *Their* legs fluttered.

Red said, "You're wearing us thin, Richie. We can't keep this up all night. Tell us where the girl is, so we can walk away from here."

Danforth giggled and spit on Red's shoes. He said, "I'm having fun."

I slid on my brass knucks and kidney-punched him. He stifled a screech and dug his feet in. I looked over the cliff. Cars zigged by—fast, with no letup.

Max sighed. Red sighed. Max said, "Sink him, Freddy."

They dropped their hands. I shoved Danforth off the cliff. He treaded air for one split second. *"It's a put-up job"* came out garbled. I heard him hit a car roof. I heard brakes squeal. I heard wheels thump over him. Crisscrossed headlights lit him up. A pimpmobile Caddy dragged him against a guardrail and sheared off his feet.

2

We ran Code 3 to the Valley. Sheriff's black-and-whites blew past us. We two-car caravanned. I rode with Max and Red. Harry and Eddie took the pole slot.

We dumped Buzzy Stein with the DB guys at Highland Park station. Buzzy saw the drop show and finked a hostage pad in Encino. Gwen Perloff was stashed in a vacant bachelor crib off Woodman. The Fidel Castro dimwits hid her in a broom closet. Max called the lead Sheriff's IO. He ran the command out of the West Hollywood substation.

"Motel Mike" Bayless. Gloryhound cop and all-around nosebleed. He blew up four cholos at the Don José Motel, back in '50. The scalps went to his head. His wife and kids called him "Motel Mike." He named his dog Motel Mike Junior.

Six Sheriff's cars blew past us. The Ventura Freeway was all siren blare and hot lights. It vibed interagency grief. Bill Parker usurps a county job from Sheriff Pete Pitchess. Parker and Pitchess were film-biz suck-ups. Parker went rogue for Darryl F. Zanuck. Pitchess overplays the rescue. Old man Zanuck's shtupping Gwen Perloff. *That's* the key to this grief.

Max passed me his flask. I took two pops. It blew my sixteen days off the juice.

The jolt hit me. My brain waves sparked. I replayed the drop show. Danforth screeched "It's a put-up job." The snatch played unkosher. The Marie "The Body" McDonald job nudged me.

It's early '57. Marie's on the skids. The studios blackball her. Her nightclub act tanks. She concocts a jive kidnap tale. She says rough-trade boys abducted her and dumped her out near Palm Springs. She glommed brief headlines and saw it go *pffft*.

I brain-waved Buzzy Stein. He divulged the stash-hole location. He did *not* rat the Castro guys. He said *they* grabbed Gwen Perloff. The eyewit vehicle IDs did *not* comport with—

Max squelched my brain waves. "Danforth tried to escape. He took a wrong turn and went off the cliff. I stiffed a call to the Chief after I talked to Mike Bayless. He sent some AID guys out to clean up the mess. The Chief knows what's what, but he likes our revised version better."

Red laughed. "Motel Mike's a bullshitter. He planted throwdown guns on those beaners he blew up. You want the punch line? They weren't really righteous 211 guys. They tapped the till and swiped some beaver mags from a dirty-book stall, and took off running."

I lit a cigarette. "Here's what I don't get. Bayless works SHIT—the Sheriff's so-called Handpicked Intelligence Team—and we all know that intel is a big bug up Pete Pitchess' ass."

Max said, "Yeah. So, what's Bayless doing shagging kidnap calls out of the West Hollywood squad?"

I made the jack-off sign. Two more Sheriff's cars blew past us. We followed Harry and Eddie's taillight blinks and cut to the far right lane. We hit the Woodman exit and hauled due north.

Ventura Boulevard held us back. We ran a red light and hit residential Encino. Sirens overlapped somewhere northeast. We blew a string of stop signs and caught a string of Sheriff's sleds. We tailed them down a northbound alley. Said alley was narrow and way tight. We bumper-smashed trash cans and sent household shit airborne.

The alley dead-ended at Saticoy Street. Déjà vu ditzed me. I knew I'd been here before. My brain wires fritzed. I couldn't place the context. This summer was half booze-and-dope blur.

The Sheriff's cars swung east. Our two PD cars bird-dogged them.

The turf went downscale. Ranch spreads devolved to apartment blocks. Swinger joints. Schmooze pits. Stewardess crash pads. Fag cribs and bachelorette dumps for kept women.

And, *this:*

Eight Sheriff's cars clustered outside the Tiki-Torch Village.

We fishtailed on over and skid-braked. Six uniformed deputies blocked the streetside entrance. They packed pump shotguns. Jumbo tiki torches flanked wrought-iron gates. It was San Fernando Valley hot. The torches leaked propane. The air reeked. The sky pressed down, explosive.

The Hats plus Freddy O. We're here to observe. We killed one guy and locked one guy up. LAPD came in early. The Sheriff's came in late. Let's watch them save the girl.

We piled out of our prowl sleds and mingled. Max and Harry passed their flasks. The Hats plus Freddy O. got a good glow on. Eddie chatted up a Pan Am stew and got her phone number. A Mexicali stew told me the Tiki-Torch Village swung hard. Her shit-faced copilot confirmed it. He said four Sheriff's dicks were inside the complex, right now. It was some kind of kidnapped-starlet caper.

Somebody yelled, "No suspects inside."

Somebody yelled, "We've got her."

I climbed the back bumper of a Sheriff's black-and-white. It gave me a high and wide view. The shotgun deputies slid the gates open and stepped back. *Here they come, here they come.*

There's Motel Mike Bayless. He's tall and stupid-handsome. He's got too-hip razor-cut hair. He's waltzing out Gwen Perloff.

She's no starlet, she wears glasses, she's at least thirty-five. She's big and rangy. She's a schoolmarm knockout in a summer shift dress.

3

The dump job. The bent schoolmarm. Saturday-night kicks gone wrong.

I prowled my pad-office and inventoried my shit. I was up-the-ass antsy. I Man Camera'd my four rooms and muzzled my thoughts.

Here's the inventory:

I've got bug-and-tap gear, piled in boxes. I've got an LAPD-issue Teletype. I've got an evidence kit. I've got a forensic-shot Polaroid camera. There's four file cabinets—packed with dirt sheets and filthy snapshots. Plus a box of throwdown guns and two pump shotguns. Plus belt saps, handcuffs, and come-along restraints.

I took a USC night course, back in '46. Criminalistics for Police Officers. A Nazi professor named Hans Maslick developed the Man Camera technique. You observe interior-crime scenes and imprint minute details. You stare and study and lodge details in specific brain vaults. Your vaults never leak or spill their contents. I'm a self-taught eideteker and never lose what I imprint. I stare and study and hone my application of the technique. It rewires my brain circuits and often serves to curb my lust for booze and dope.

Man Camera. My work gear, out in plain sight. Here's a late-breaking flashback. That pimp Caddy drags Richie Danforth off a guardrail and severs his feet.

I dumped the gear back in my hall closet. I inventoried my personal shit and went in Man Camera tight.

My projector, pull-down screen, and film-can trove. Lois Nettleton in *Naked City* and *Alcoa Presents*. TV to Broadway. Lois as Maggie in *Cat on a Hot Tin Roof*. It's 1956. She's the lead's understudy. I've imprinted every soaring moment and gaffe.

Lois to Pat. One framed photograph. V-J Day in Kodacolor. Pat's USO hostess gown droops. My Marine dress blues gleam.

She's gawky working on regal. She can't outrun her star surname. She tried to then. She's past it now. Hollywood Boulevard erupts behind us. I've imprinted every anonymous face and the glint off every windowpane.

My reverie unraveled. The dump job schizzed me. We'd waltz on it. I knew that. Some types have just got to GO. Rape-o's, hot-prowl guys. Hostage takers. Kidnap-for-profit and sex-motive fucks. Bill Parker would frost repercussions. Local press geeks would cosign *El Jefe*'s PR line. Buzzy Stein would refuse to fink the snatch men. I cranked my lens in tight and framed two outtakes.

Richie Danforth flails and drops. *"It's a put-up job."* The crowd outside the Tiki-Torch Village. Cops and airline stews jazzed by the show. A Pan Am stew did samba steps with Harry Crowder. Eddie Benson scored fourteen phone numbers. I've got my high bumper perch.

Man Camera. Crane shot. Motel Mike Bayless and Gwen Perloff walk out. Gwen's unruffled and unmussed. It's ninety-three degrees at 10:00 p.m. She's been locked in a broom closet. There's no sweat pools on her mint green shift. There's no tape-gag residue. There's no wrist-restraint chafe marks. She's redoubtably composed.

She's an actress walking into a crowd. Some men whistle. Some hopped-up stews jump and wave. Motel Mike stands apart from Gwen. He's not consoling a distraught kidnap victim. He's establishing parameters. He's telling the crowd he's not poking the big, rangy dish.

I shut my eyes. It doused the room lights and reset my lens cap. It cut me loose to brood and think.

Gwen Perloff looked like a bait girl. She might play main squeeze in Darryl Zanuck's all-starlet stable. Zanuck was high up and bitched up at Fox. The big toga lox *Cleopatra* had Fox strung up and fucked-up and gouting money. It was Movie Debacle as Worldwide Sensation. Liz Taylor's shacked with Richard Burton. They swoon through Rome by night and screw in prop rooms at Cinecittà. Fox might sell their backlot to cover cost overruns. Darryl Zanuck's high up and bitched up and has shit stacked high on his plate. Then some woman calls him and rats out a sketchy kidnap deal.

I gnawed the *Cleo* rumors. Fox kingpin Zanuck, Fox starlet Gwen Perloff. I popped two Dexedrine for late-night pizzazz. I replayed the first Hats-plus-Freddy O. caper.

May '54. The Red Devil Bandit/aka George Collier Akin. He's a hot-prowl sadist/rape-o. He hits USC sorority pads. *HE JUST HAS TO GO.*

He wore a red rubber devil mask. He torqued his victims with monster film one-liners. We jumped him outside a coed rooming house. We had .45 Colts and Ithaca pumps with rat poison–dipped buckshot. The reverb blew out four downstairs windows.

My biz phone rang. I grabbed it two rings in. A Brit-voiced man babbled at me. I made the voice. It was Peter Lawford. He was half-gassed and far-gone panicked.

I heard *"dinner party"/"no show"/"found the body."* I said, "Calm down and make sense."

Lawford wheezed. My phone line staticked up. I heard *"late for dinner party"/"oh my God"/"Marilyn Monroe."* Gasps and garbles spelled it out. The line cleared. He went over/he saw the pill vials/there was no housekeeper extant—Freddy, she was *cold*.

I shrill-whistled. It fritzed up the line feed and made dipshit Lawford *eeeeek*. I heard coins drop. Dipshit fed dimes to a pay phone.

Lawford mewled and wheezed. I heard *"My wife, Pat."* That stopped me short. I said, "Go back to the house and sit in your car. I'll be right over."

Lawford pitched boo-hoo. *Freddy, you're a mensch. She was such a talent and such—*

I hung up and dialed Bill Parker's home phone. Spool clicks blurred to dialtones. The Chief recorded his calls. Local malcontents and dissidents dialed the boss for kicks and grins.

Parker said, "Who's calling?"

"It's Fred Otash, sir."

"Are you calling for reassurance? You shouldn't be. It's been settled. Mr. Danforth escaped and misjudged the drop off the embankment. Mr. Stein is in custody, and the Sheriff's will deal with the three suspects at large."

I lit a cigarette. "It's something else, sir."

"Let's not string this out. What 'something else' are we talking about?"

"Marilyn Monroe's dead. It looks like a pill OD or a suicide. Peter Lawford found her and called me. He's waiting for me at the house. I'm going out."

Tap-taps hit the line. I knew the ploy. Parker pencil-tapped the phone and bought response time. I clocked the taps at—

"Intel has extensive files on Miss Monroe and her movie-business and political chums and lovers, up to and including John and Robert Kennedy. Peter Lawford supplies his brother-in-law Jack with dope and girls, a reprise of your mid-'50s role as the young senator's pimp and supplier. You're a charter member of the L.A. cognoscenti, Freddy. How up-to-date are you on all of this?"

I gulped. "I'm up-to-the-moment, sir."

Parker said, "Really? As in?"

"As in a recent gig I had."

"You'll tell me about it? As in the next time we speak?"

"Yes, sir."

More tap-taps hit. They extended. I timed them off my watch. They ran two minutes and sixteen seconds.

"Go back to the house. Calm Lawford down and coerce him into silence. Enter the house and perform a full forensic. I'll post perimeter guards to keep civilians at bay. Meet the Hats at PC Bell in Santa Monica, tomorrow at 8:00. Pull Miss Monroe's phone records for this calendar year, along with her up-to-date toll tickets. Let's see what we can do about keeping this contained, and perhaps reaping benefit from it."

Nightclub traffic bottlenecked the Strip. Cars crawled past Ciro's and the Crescendo. I cut side streets south and Santa Monica to Wilshire westbound. Traffic thinned down to zero. I hit Barrington and San Vicente. Commercial Brentwood was shut down tight.

I hooked north on Carmelina. The swank level popped exponential. Grok the deep lawns and tall hedgerows. Dig the quaint Spanish cribs and outsize Spanish de-luxe.

There's Fifth Helena Drive. There's the Monroe crib. There's Peter Lawford's cherry Rolls parked in front.

Headlight blips hit me. I caught two blip sets, on and off. It was Parker's point men in civilian cars. They were stashed across the street and down from the Rolls.

I blipped back and pulled up to the Rolls, snout-to-snout. I banged the front bumper and hit my brights to jolt the cocksucker. The windshield lit up glare white. Lawford blinked and fumbled a cigarette. I killed my lights and stepped out of the car.

Lawford cracked his passenger door. I slid in beside him. Green leather and burled wood cocooned us. Lawford had the shakes. I passed him my flask. It was brim-full of jungle juice—151 rum and powdered Benzedrine.

He sucked on the nozzle. Don't light a cigarette—the shit might ignite.

I said, "Okay, she's dead. The key thing now is protecting some very important friends of hers, and we don't need to name names here."

Lawford went electric. Jungle juice hits you fast.

"I know who you're talking about, because they're my family. I resent the fact that you know them, and that you deign to mention them so casually."

I bitch-slapped him. He yelped. I grabbed the flask and took two good pops.

"I like Jack. I can do without Bobby, but that's a topic for another time and place. When what's-her-name's body is discovered, they'll need friends, and as far as this town goes, that's the Los Angeles Police Department, and I've been delegated to tell you that Chief Parker's friendship comes with a price."

Lawford broke a sweat. Hot night, jungle juice, manhandling.

"'What's-her-name' is the greatest female film star of her era, and the men you so blithely refer to as 'Jack' and 'Bobby' are the president and attorney general of the United States. And I happen to be married to—"

I bitch-slapped him. He yelped and blubbered. I tossed him my pocket square.

"Marilyn was nothing but a glorified bait girl. I know shit about her, Jack, and Bobby that you wouldn't believe. And don't start in on who you're married to, because that's when the hurt really starts."

He wiped his face and neck. He looked at me. Hot night, jungle juice, manhandling. Check his eyes. He can't decode my riff on Pat.

"Where's the AG? He was in the *Herald* this morning. Something about a speech in San Francisco."

Lawford wiped his nose. He trashed my pocket square in two seconds flat.

"Yes, he's up there. He's at the St. Francis."

I said, "Call him and get him down here. Bill Parker will want to talk to him."

Lawford wiped his eyes and kicked the ignition. I slid out of the car. The Rolls laid rubber, westbound. I whistled and signaled the point cops—I'm going in.

"Full forensic."

The Monroe pad, redux.

My evidence kit was suitcase-size and full-fitted. It held one Polaroid camera. It held thirty film rolls and eighty flashbulbs. Plus print gear and rubber gloves. Plus fiber-collection combs and sheaths and a crank-up fiber vacuum.

Spray cans. Ninhydrin to pull bloodstains and acid phosphatase to pull jizz. Stoppered vials to store liquid samples. Twelve rolls of Scotch tape. Good print-lift and dust-collection strips.

Lawford left the front gate and front door ajar. I knew the interior layout. I rolled on surgeon's gloves and flexed my hands. It was a work-in-the-dark job. I got out my penlight and bit down on the shaft. I was ripped to the gills. I clicked on the Man Camera inside my head.

The evidence kit was deadweight. I lugged it up the steps and inside. I kicked the door shut and threw the bolt. Man Camera plus penlight. Aim, point, discern, and imprint.

Fuck the slothful living room. It's standard Monroe disarray. Let's go case the stiff.

I walked to her bedroom. My light beam zigzagged a path. I clocked bare white walls, pulled window drapes, the dull-veneer wood floor.

There's the nightstand and pill vials. There's the bedside phone. There's Marilyn's left hand, hot to grab. She's curled prone beneath white sheets.

I ran a hand under them. She was nude/her skin was cold/the bed-covers trapped no heat.

I scoped the vials. Nembutal, Seconal, chloral hydrate. Instant dreamland. That shit promotes deep sleep.

Film scripts piled under the nightstand. Mouse turds close by. Here's an anomaly.

A clock radio. It's been upended and dumped on the floor. It's flush between the bed and the nightstand. The plug's still in the wall.

Say she's zorched and flailing. She's got options. More pills or the phone as a last-ditch yelp for help?

I knelt by the bed and penlight-flashed close-ups. Here's Anomaly #2:

Dried washcloth streaks. *Print-wipe* streaks. All along the top surface and the grab sides of the gizmo. Two pale blue fibers stuck to the top-surface streak.

I popped my evidence kit. I tweezer-pinched the fibers and bagged them. They looked like terry cloth. I powder-dusted the top and grab sides. The streaks stood out bold now. I picked up two rubber-glove prints. I diagnosed it:

Crime-scene obfuscation. Evidence of a professional print-wipe job.

The front and back of the gizmo were fabric/wire mesh. That meant non-print-sustaining. I sat on the bed and quadrant-scanned the whole radio. Note the print-wipe streaks on the dial. Note the dial needle stuck at All-News KLEZ. I goosed the dial and got sound. A newshound spieled through static skreek.

"... *daring kidnap in the shadow of the hip Sunset Strip. Starlet Gwen Perloff*—"

Static blur cut off the newsman. I jiggled the dial. I got *"one suspect fell to his death"* and line fuzz. I got *"suspect now in custody"* and blur, fuzz, hum, crackle, skreek.

I jiggled the plug wire. I got *"This updates our 9:05 broadcast. The three men remain at large."*

I hauled my evidence kit up on the bed and scooched the lid up against Monroe. I got out my Polaroid and spooled in a twelve-shot roll of film. I adjusted the flash attachment and screwed in a bulb. I hit the button.

The room blew up white. White glare lit the white sheets and white walls. I got the nightstand and dead white arm. I got the phone and the pill vials. I got white-blond hair on a white pillow.

I waited sixty seconds and pulled out the print. Pic #1: dead bait girl. I dropped the print in my kit and shot eleven more bedroom exposures. The clock radio, the nightstand, the pill vials. The whole room in wide-angle shots. Mid-shots of the bed. Peekaboos of the one exposed leg and disheveled white-blond hair.

Twelve bulb bursts. Twelve brain imprints. I must retain what I see.

I walked into the living room. I penlight-flashed the walls and floors and reloaded the Polaroid. I caught Anomaly #3:

Deep-pile carpets. Mashed-down foot impressions. Large male feet/ heavy shoes/deep fiber displacement. Footprints to and from a quarter-cracked eastside window. Tall-man footprints. This guy walked big.

I got out my measuring tape and unfurled it. I penlight-flashed representative footpaths and laid my tape down between imprints. 26", 25.4", 30". Tall Man had to run six-one or six-two.

I fed bulbs to my bulb strip. I shot the measured and unmeasured paths. I shot loose paint chips by the cracked-window ledge.

He entered through that window. The fibers had been foot-mashed *down*. They bounced *back* and smoothed out as I watched. Tall Man prowled the room tonight. The LAPD lab could develop a walking portrait off my pix.

I strolled the pad. I quadrant-flashed the walls and floors. I caught Anomalies #4 and 5 fast.

Bug mounts. Camouflaged as outlet plugs. Flush on the wall wainscoting. One per the living room/one per the spare bedroom.

They weren't *my* bug mounts. I pulled *my* mounts two weeks back. *These* mounts were now defunct. The connector wires had been snipped.

My mounts were oblong. These were square. I pulled *my* mounts. *These* mounts were not on the premises then.

I unscrewed the mounts and dropped them in my evidence kit. They looked like L.A. Sheriff's or FBI-issue. The Jap transistors gave them away.

Bug mounts meant potential tapped phone lines. The Monroe crib featured three extensions. Living room, spare bedroom, Marilyn's boudoir. I made the rounds and ran receiver checks.

I pulled the handsets off the phones and unscrewed the perforated tops and bottoms. I checked for stashed mini-mikes and got zilch. *But*— I saw left-behind circuit spacers. That meant the three phones had been tapped. The spacers were frayed and corroded. *My* spacers and mikes had been inset in the handgrips. Monroe bought the house in February and moved in March 10. My surveillance job began April 11.

I photographed the three spacer sets and replaced the receiver caps. I dropped the damp prints in my kit. I returned to Monroe's bedroom and worked up fibers and prints.

Hardwood flooring. Two throw rugs by the foot of the bed. One wood-veneer dresser. The flooring would not trap dry-constituent fibers. The rugs would. The dresser had good touch-and-grab planes that might sustain latent prints.

I blew off the floor and vacuumed the rugs. I filled half an evidence sheath with threads and unknown gack. I brush-dusted the touch-and-grab planes on the dresser and got useless partials, smudges, and smears.

Monroe was a hoarder. My prior B and E's taught me that. The dresser drawers deserved a toss. I might find all-new shit. It might be evidentially germane.

The bedroom was hot, *hot*. I was dexedrined and jungle-juiced. This prowl-and-seek gig eroticized me. I penlight-flashed the bed and saw that white-blond hair on the white pillow.

I opened the top drawer and viewed the contents. I inventoried nine pairs of nylon stockings and a red crocheted bikini. I photo-snapped said contents and counted off sixty seconds. I pulled the print and dropped it in my evidence kit.

The room heat spiked. I broke a sweat. A strong wind rattled the windows. I reached under the bedsheets and touched Marilyn's leg. It felt dead cold and hot-room warm all at once.

Drawer #2 contained assorted slips and Chanel No. 5 sachets. Hot-room air merged with perfume residue. I counted six sachets and slips. The slips were all pale pastel. The armholes were sweat-stained. It enticed me.

I picked up a pink brocade slip and held it close to my face. I crossed myself. It quashed an urge to touch the whole batch.

The drawer was jammed open. I jiggled it and shifted the contents. I saw an old black-and-white snapshot and a yellowed piece of paper beside it. The gist hit me, straight off.

It's an L.A. County morgue shot. That's Carole Landis, buck nude on a gurney. She's a bottle blonde, she's a pre-Monroe manqué, she quaffed barbs and booze in July '48 and left a woe-is-me note for her fans. She'd tried suicide before. As in four times. She was on Husband #4. She had a run of costar gigs at Fox and a sub-run of poverty-row quickies. Brit hearthrob Rex Harrison declined to dump his wife for her. She had a big spread in Pacific Palisades and a film career stuck in skidsville.

Skidsville to creepsville. The yellow paper displayed a note. It was fashioned in cutout/pasted-on magazine letters. The paper was old. The typeface was old. The note read:

I loved her before I loved you.
She was nicer. You're more desperate and pretentious.
I had to learn to love you. She made it easy.

I shot the note and the morgue pic. Flashbulb pop lit the bedroom some crazy new way. I counted off sixty seconds and pulled the print. I dropped it in my evidence kit.

I dusted the morgue pic. I brought up one partial and two smears. I photographed them. I dusted the paper backing and brought up bupkes.

The room heat *re*-spiked. The room went claustrophobic. I sheath-wrapped the morgue pic and note. I dropped the photos in my kit. I unjammed the undie drawer and rammed it shut. The jolt tripped a lever.

A wooden tray below the drawer slipped out and open. I crouched close. *Ich bin ein eideteker.* I saw and imprinted *this:*

Fuckee-suckee pix. Four in all. Black-and-white Polaroids. The nude Marilyn Monroe and a cruel stud with a big pompadour. There's white-out strips over his eyes. It distorts his identity. He's beefy-muscular. Monroe's Monroe. They're fucking, sucking, going 69. It's Kama Sutraville, baby. Note the sleazy motel backdrop. Monroe looks younger. The pix connote '58 or '59.

Dried jizz crusts. Some perv spritzed all four pix. Clusters of dead cells and blood-type markers. The lab can run tests, we can ID this freak—

MAN CAMERA

RECALL/IMPRINT/REWIND—

PART 2
BUG JOB

(APRIL 9–AUGUST 4, 1962)

4

The Losers Club. Beverly and La Cienega. It's a strip joint. It veers topical. Large-draw comics slum here. Lenny Bruce, Don Rickles, Mort Sahl. They're sanctioned to work raw. It's the Losers gestalt.

There's a big sign out front. It denotes the "Loser of the Week." Eddie Fisher begins his reign tonight. He's the designated schmuck and all-star attraction. I'm bodyguarding Eddie. We're perched in the greenroom. There's a full bar and a deli-nosh spread. Note the goblets crammed with goofballs and bennies.

Eddie said, "Nixon's been Loser of the Week twice. Rock Hudson got the nod last month, but nobody knows why."

I lit a cigarette. "Sheriff's Vice caught him blowing a quiff in the john at the Hamburger Hamlet. The nod's to the cognoscenti. The Rock's got a secret-life scenario going. He's not a signature loser, like you and Nixon."

Eddie yukked. "I'll take it, because it's getting me work, but Liz should get Loser of the Millenium. Her makeup man's an old pal of mine. I get daily reports from the set. All indications point to catastrophe."

He meant the *Cleopatra* mess and Fox in the shitter. The shoot's a cash drain and pure chaos. The Rome-to-L.A. cable lines buzz twenty-four hours. Liz Taylor rates Shrew of the Year to Eddie's Passive Putz. She's zonked on booze and pills and beset by mystery ailments. She malingers in swank hotel suites and eats herself fat. She's bonking her costar, Richard Burton. Paparazzi bird-dog them down the Via Veneto.

Liz and Eddie are splitsville. She's dumping Husband #4 and warming up #5 in hot-sheet flops on the Appian Way. Eddie's Mr. Cornuto and a revived nightclub sensation. He's done turn-away biz in Vegas and

L.A.'s Cocoanut Grove. Tonight's his Losers Club debut. He's embraced loserhood. There's six hundred Eddiephiles lined up outside.

I've got three operatives working the rope line. Horny women press envelopes and bribe cash on my guys. The envelopes contain mash notes, cheesecake pix, and snipped pubic hair.

Eddie sipped a scotch-rocks. "All the Liz tsuris and money tsuris aside, the picture is already a legendary dog in waiting. Zanuck is planning to reshoot it, with Lassie and Rin Tin Tin in the lead roles."

I yocked. Bo Belinsky walked in. He's the new pitching stud for the L.A. Angels. Women dig him. He's out of Trenton, Eddie's out of Philly. They're big new best friends. They party hearty and denigrate Liz nonstop.

Eddie and Bo embraced. Their "Love ya, *bubi*" schtick commenced on cue. I ditched the greenroom and ducked outside.

La Cienega was tight-packed. The rope line ran two blocks north. Nat Denkins, Phil Irwin, and Robbie Molette worked the crowd. They checked the prepay tickets for Eddie's ten, midnight, and 2:00 a.m. shows. They dispensed laughs and booted underaged kids out of line.

I counted heads and crossed myself. The Eddie gig was a money-maker. It's 100% open-end. The gig would last as long as Eddie's victim status held and Liz notched headlines in Rome.

I needed the work. I'd been tanksville for months. I'd been repossessing cars for Felix the Cat Chevrolet. I'd been working divorce shakedowns and sandbagging tomcat hubbies. Bill Parker shot me strongarm jobs too dicey for regular cops. It kept Robbie, Phil, and Nat part-time employed. The Eddie gig was a sinecure and a life raft.

Eddie's intro music trickled outside. I ducked inside. The crowd was shoehorned in tight. Check the SRO bar. Check the six-set tables with ten fans crammed in tight. Check the wall-to-wall standees. Check the cocktail girls in beatnik black leotards and berets.

They wore cleavage-clip buttons. They read *I'm Joyce, I'm June, I'm Jane—rip me!!!!!* The tables featured lava lamps and plastic back scratchers. Dipshit guys grabbed the scratchers and raked the girls' leotards. The girls dodged gropes and served drinks in tatters.

Eddie's combo weaved onstage. Tenor sax, trumpet, bass, plug-in keyboard. All junkies on work furlough from Wayside Honor Rancho. All in tight black suits and fruit boots and half on the nod.

They set up and tuned up. The crowd sent up *"EDDIE!"* chants. And there he is—

Now.

Eddie hopped onstage. He twirled a hand mike on a cord. The combo ran off-key riffs on the "Peppermint Twist." The crowd went nuts. Eddie twist-stepped to center stage. The crowd simmered down. Eddie jacked off the mike handle. The crowd went *re*-nuts. Eddie made like the Big White Bwana and went *Hush, my children—for now I shall speak.*

The crowd went hush. The Mahatma has spoken. Eddie said, "*So?* What's new with *you?*"

The crowd bayed. They stomped, hooted, whistled, shrieked. A cocktail waitress hopped onstage. Her leotard was sliced into slivers. The combo relaunched the "Peppermint Twist." Eddie grabbed the waitress. They did bump-and-grind twist steps in sync.

The *"EDDIE!"* chants reprised. The waitress hopped offstage and dodged gropes across the room. Mahatma Eddie went *Hush.* The crowd went hush. Eddie introduced his combo as the Four Muff Divers. The crowd yock-yocked.

Eddie said, "My label, RCA Victor, wants me to include 'Arrivederci, Roma' and 'After You've Gone' on my next album. But I told them, 'There's limits to my self-abasement.'"

The crowd *re*-yocked. Eddie said, "I've got a couple of tidbits, hot off the wire from Rome. My soon-to-be-ex, aka Liz, aka Cleopatra, was seen baring her soiled soul at a meeting of Nymphos Anonymous."

The crowd yocked on overdrive. Eddie jacked off the mike handle and pelvis-popped steps from the wah watusi. Boozed-out college kids and drink girls watusi'd down on the floor.

Eddie said, "More news from Rome. *La Repubblica* has reported that Richard Burton was seen poking an Italian greyhound near the Trevi Fountain—but it was a *female* greyhound, so I don't see anything wrong with it."

The crowd stomped and woof-woofed. The combo launched "Fly Me to the Moon." Eddie kicked the struts loose and crooned.

He's a nebbish and shaggy-haired twerp. Where'd he get that big baritone?

It's 3:00 a.m. now. It's the nightly debrief at Eddie's crib. It was Liz and Eddie's crib, up to *Cleopatra.*

It's some boss crib. As in sixteen rooms off Benedict Canyon. The pad bids Eddie to grieve and kvetch nonstop. He'll have to divest. Liz is okay on the cash and property split—as of now. She'll get wise and brown him up the dirt road—soon. They're jungled up with beaucoup kids from beaucoup gone-bust unions. They've got beaucoup land holdings. They've got studio deals and *Cleo* predecreed as dreck.

Oy, oy, oy. His rabbi calls him a "self-loathing Jew." He urges him to emigrate to Israel and join a kibbutz. The rabbi calls Liz "overprivileged *traph*" and the "poisonous fruit of the *goyishe* tree."

Oy, oy, oy. Eddie's gassed on all this turmoil. His nightclub career's *re*-thriving and the world's veering back his way.

The trophy den was debrief HQ. It featured green leather furniture and pix of Eddie with Cardinal Spellman and Congo strongman Patrice Lumumba. Two waitresses played backgammon and eyeballed hunky Bo Belinsky. They're June and Jane—RIP ME!!!! Losers Club losers obliged. They doffed their tattered leotards and donned low-cut bikinis. Eddie supplied them. He kept a big stash on hand.

Eddie and Bo read through tonight's mash notes and admired select snapshots. Bo tabulated phone numbers. I was bored. I sipped a scotch-rocks and futzed around with Eddie's pit bull, Roscoe. My guys worked crowd control, outside. Forty-some fans tailed us back here from the club. Eddie had his housekeeper bake up chocolate cookies. The fans were 99% women. My guys passed out cookies and racked up phone numbers, wholesale.

I was restless. I had Lois and Pat on the brain. Lois/Pat/Lois/Pat. I ping-ponged between the—

The phone rang. It startled me. Eddie picked up. He went *Who's this?* and listened. He muffled the receiver with a pillow.

He said, "For you, Freddy. It's Jimmy Hoffa. He sounds like a man with a bone to pick."

5

Jimmy Hoffa said, "The Kennedys. My sources tell me you go back with those shitheels."

The downtown Statler. A tidy junior suite. Coffee and crullers. It's a face-off. We're in two chairs crammed knee-to-knee tight.

"With Jack, I do. I'm sure you know the story."

Hoffa cracked his knuckles. "You pulled him out of some grief with a call girl. You had options. You chose the wrong one, and it queered your relationship with our future president."

I sipped coffee. "I presented my bill. Jack's people stiffed me with counterfeit money. It was a nice touch."

Hoffa slapped his knees. "What about his dogshit brother, Bobby?"

I went *Comme ci, comme ça.* "I've met him a few times. I'd say you know him a tad better than I do."

Hoffa goaded me. "Come *on.* Give me your interpretation."

I said, "The McClellan Committee. Bobby and Jack, back when Jack was in the Senate. Televised hearings, lockstep surveillance, government audits, indictments, rubber-stamp grand juries, public humiliation as regards your 'assumed' mobbed-up status. And now the little cocksucker's the attorney general of the United States, and crawling up your ass with renewed vigor."

Hoffa cracked his thumbs. "Did you smirk when you said 'assumed'? Like it's all just so obvious that everybody knows?"

I stifled a stage yawn. "Tell me what you have in mind. Yeah, I know the brothers. Yeah, I know how you feel about them, and you know what I do for a living."

Hoffa brushed crumbs off his lap. "Jack the K is ramming Marilyn Monroe, and now he's passed her along to his kid brother. I have this on good authority, but I can't reveal my source. I want you to build a derogatory profile on Monroe, Jack, Bobby, and any other extraneous cooze those whipdicks are slipping it to, not to mention whatever bedroom dirt you can get me on Miss Marilyn Monroe herself, who is well known to be the Whore of Babylon in Hollywood circles."

Tilt. Royal flush. Money tree. Three-cherry jackpot.

"You want full-time bugs and taps. Listening posts, monitor shifts, tape copies and transcriptions, summary reports, physical surveillance on Monroe and the other principals, and you want all this shit to rock around the clock, and you are keenly aware that it's going to cost you a great deal of money."

Hoffa went *harumph*. "You're a camel jockey, and you're out to bilk James Riddle Hoffa with no compunction."

I leaned close. Hoffa flinched. I ticked points, wham-bam.

"Me. My three guys for the day-to-day. Bernie Spindel for the installations. It's a hundred thousand for the job, and more if it extends past this summer. You cover salaries and all operating expenses. You pledge bail money and lawyers, if it comes to that. It's an audacious piece of work you want done, and you came to the only guy who can do it."

Hoffa shot his cuffs and scratched his balls. Hoffa cricked his neck and flicked lint off his suit coat.

"Okay. I'm sure it's a bargain by your Lebanese standards."

I said, "I'll send you up-to-the-minute bug-and-tap reels once a week, along with typed transcripts. I'll Teletype you summary reports every other week. I'll—"

Hoffa cut me off. "The Monroe bitch just bought a house in Brentwood. I want it hot-wired, de-luxe. Jack and Bobby tryst out of Peter Lawford's spread on the Coast Highway. I want it hot-wired. Lawford's married to one of the Kennedy sisters, I forget which one. . . ."

I said, "Pat. Her name is Pat."

Hoffa blotted his necktie. Hoffa snapped his waistband and buffed his gold watch.

"I want it ugly, Freddy. I want lots of sordid behavior, with an emphasis on sex."

Shitwork prep first. Vibe the terrain. Learn the entry/exit points. Scout listening-post locations.

I drove out to the beach. The Lawford estate backed up to the sand.

It was right at the L.A. City/Malibu line. A big landside bluff overlooked it. Boho cottages were clumped behind a paved access road. They supplied high-up/look-down access across PCH. That meant peeper range.

The access road took me up. Cars boomed north and south, below me. Street noise statics up bug-tap reception. The PCH boom was all-time bad.

I got out and perched on a guardrail. I screwed a zoom lens to my Rolleiflex and eyeballed the house. It was a big Spanish rancho. Add-on wings destroyed the lines and klutzed up the overall look.

It was one big spread. Seven thousand square feet. Two stories. Prime beachfront turf. I zoomed close and shot pix of doors, windows, roof ledges. I'm a seasoned peeper/burglar. All bug-tap jobs start with break-ins.

Flagstone walkways flanked the house, north and south. They led back to a beach-view swimming pool and lounge setup. I shot a north-side doorway. Pat walked straight into my lens.

She wore a madras plaid shirtdress and scuffed saddle shoes. Plus tortoiseshell glasses and a man's Rolex watch. Real camera meets Man Camera. It's almost seventeen years. I'm twenty-three, Pat's twenty-one. Hollywood Boulevard erupts.

The Japs pulled the plug. Strangers kiss in the street. I spot Pat, she spots me, our brain waves mesh. The kiss extends. A roving photographer takes our picture and seals history. I give him ten bucks and tell him what for. Send two copies to the LAPD Academy. I'll be there in three weeks.

Pat grabbed me and kissed me again. We went crazy telepathic. We walked to the Hollywood Plaza and checked in.

That night was it. We had that night and no more. We've sent each other Christmas cards, from '45 up to now. Pat married fuckhead Peter Lawford. I'm the "Hellhound Who Held Hollywood Captive" and her big brother's ex–bird dog and dope chute. Said big brother? He's the president of the United States. I've just been hired to put him down in the shit.

The Monroe house. 12305 Fifth Helena Drive, Brentwood. Clock it. It's 4.3 miles east of the Lawford beach digs. Call it. This is a West L.A. caper from the jump.

The Brentwood quasi-village was due east. It was upscale ginchy. Gas station, two markets, drugstore. Public library, espresso pit, French bistro. Major throughways boxed in Fifth Helena and the adjacent blocks.

Bundy to the east. San Vicente to the south. Sunset to the north. Extended greenbelt loomed west. Helena Drives two to five ran one long block and dead-ended. The immediate area was affluent and all residential.

That rendered park-and-sit-type surveillance untenable. I'd have to glom five service vehicles and paint-job them. PC Bell, Happytime Liquor, Luanne's Dial-A-Florist. Plus two beat-to-hell gardeners' trucks.

The house itself:

Whitewashed Spanish. One story. Modest for Brentwood. Big front yard, small backyard. Stucco retaining walls, all around. Tall hedgerows, front and back. An oak gate and tile steps to the front door.

I parked across the street and snapped photos. Note the front casement windows. They were all draped and unscreened. They were all cracked for ventilation. *Peep me, B and E me*—the pad screamed it.

I shot the back side of the house already. I got the screened kitchen door with the flimsy hook-and-eye latch. I got the unscreened service-porch window. Monroe had a part-time housekeeper. I read a *Herald* piece on the new house and her housekeeping regime. The housekeeper slept out most nights. *Peep me, B and E me, hot-wire me for sound.*

Nat Denkins knew a clerk at the Hollywood DMV. He slid the guy a yard and got Monroe's vehicle stats. She drove a '59 Buick Invicta. Phil Irwin braced a clerk at the Malibu DMV. The Lawfords owned five vehicles. Pat drove a '58 Bonneville ragtop.

Hearts and arrows. Freddy loves Pat, Freddy loves Lois. Carve up that palm tree by Marilyn's front door.

I popped two Dexedrine and chain-smoked. I perimeter-scanned the front of the house. The door popped open. There she is. I clocked it at 4:16 p.m.

She's huddled up in a white bathrobe. She's wearing This Look. Hey, that's my new front yard.

A car pulled up in front of me. It was a '60 Corvair, maroon over black. A big blond girl got out and looked around. She was sixteen or seventeen. Note the rear-bumper sticker: PALI HIGH, HOME OF THE DOLPHINS.

The girl walked across the street. She braced the hedgerow and stood on her tiptoes. She was tall. She cadged a damn good look.

Marilyn waved to her. The girl shrieked and waved back.

6

Derogatory Profile. Day #2. The real shitwork begins.

I traded up. Eddie Fisher to Jimmy Hoffa. Nightclub antics to a sex squeeze on the Worldwide Big Kahuna and his vindictive kid brother. The bait girl's The Blond of Our Era. It all bodes combustion. Something's got to give.

That's the title of Monroe's new flick. It's currently shooting at Fox. Scribe-for-hire Morry Zolotow fed me the gist. Monroe's zonked on pills. Monroe's chronically tardy. Monroe succumbs to mystery ailments. The shoot's behind schedule. Mogul D. F. Zanuck's pissed, director George Cukor's enraged.

I worked in my living room/office. Nat Denkins scored floor-plan drawings from the county structural outfit. I studied schematics of the Lawford and Monroe pads and brainstormed bug-and-tap mount installations. Robbie Molette's out at PC Bell. He's scanning phone-service records. It's crucial. Bell lists all phone extensions and notes their room-to-room locations.

Basic tap rules apply here. Individual taps assure vivid sound flow. That's interior shitwork. Add exterior grief. Car noise on Bundy and San Vicente could fuzz the Monroe feed lines. Surf hum and car noise on PCH could scotch the Lawford feeds. Listening-post locations were crucial here.

Rentable homes in residential Brentwood? It would backfire on us. Round-the-clock activity and goons on-site would arouse square-citizen suspicion. There were no available rentals on the Brentwood commercial strip. The Lawford feeds might necessitate two listening posts. A house on the east bluff, across PCH. A backup location on the Malibu Pier.

I brainstormed. I called Eddie Fisher and pink-slipped him. I told him I'm quits. I said something came up. Eddie said, "Yeah—as in Jimmy Hoffa." I pooh-poohed it and told Eddie I'd set him up with Art Ara-gon. Art was an ex–ranked welterweight and noted cad-about-town. He loved muscle work and oozed charm. Eddie swooned. I was relieved. I traded up. I dumped low-stakes Hollywood for high-stakes intrigue and six times the pay.

And there's Pat. She was twenty-one then. She's thirty-seven now. Her fuckhead husband pimps for Jack the K. He's usurped my old gig and the one-night love that still torches me.

Pervdog, voyeur, peeper.

That's me. I'll be across the coast road. I'll be up on that bluff. I'll be attached to a headset and crouched in the dark. Man Camera. Ongoing live sound. Who knows what I'll see and hear.

Monroe's garage opened out on Sixth Helena. I parked across the street. Big pepper trees shadowed my Chevy coupe. Nat Denkins was out shag-ging stakeout vehicles. Personal cars agitated local stiffs and magnetized fuzz. This was a meet-your-mark tail. The gig was *on* as of *NOW.*

The kickoff meet was last night, at Ollie Hammond's. I booked a pri-vate room. The crew showed up. Phil Irwin, Robbie Molette, Nat Den-kins. Plus Bernie "Bug King" Spindel. We boozed and noshed T-bone steaks. I laid out the five-point plan.

1) Bernie and I will hot-wire the Lawford and Monroe locations.
2) Nat, Phil, and Robbie will dig up three listening-post rentals. One in Brentwood. Brentwood's a tough go. Be assiduous here. Plus two Lawford-house rentals. One on the east bluff-side. One on the Malibu Pier.
3) I want active monitor shifts. That's one man per post and three shifts per day. I'll spell you, impromptu. Bernie and I will install voice-activated taps and room bugs. They'll transmit to low-frequency receivers. Room bugs are always problematic. You get dead air, ambient noise, and half-heard conversation. Make tape copies and hand-transcribe every-thing you hear, regardless. Verbatim log all bug-and-tap

tapes. Make one copy for Jimmy H. and one for our master file.

4) Phone taps will make or break this operation. Keep current on your tape copies. Keep current on your log transcriptions. This is a film-biz/political caper. These humps love to talk. I want every word taped and transcribed.

5) I want intermittent tail surveillance on Monroe and time-dated surveillance logs kept. I'll spell you there, impromptu. Jimmy's pledged bonus bread, upon wrap-up. As in, ten grand per man.

My guys salivated. I salivated. The caper was high-risk/high-compensation. We toasted Jack, Marilyn, and Camelot, aflame.

Sit-still surveillance. Time always slogs. 2:26, 2:42, 3:04. My ass itched. I smoked myself hoarse. The garage door cracked open at 3:09 p.m.

There's Marilyn. She's done up movie-star incognito. Dark slacks, tight jumper. Wraparound shades and an Hermès scarf.

She climbed in the Buick Invicta and nosed out. She punched the gas westbound and sideswiped three trash cans. Empty booze bottles and dog food cans flew. I tailed her and idled forty yards back. Marilyn cut left on Carmelina and right on San Vicente. That put her westbound. A median strip forced traffic one-way. It was grassed up and dotted with azalea shrubs.

Marilyn hit her left-turn signal and bumped her car up and over the abutment. The undercarriage dislodged loose cement and cracked her back bumper. She slid on wet grass and brodied through a line of azaleas. She bumped back off the cement and hauled eastbound.

I tailed her. I downshifted and eased over the abutment. I slid on grass and sluiced back onto eastbound San Vicente. I came up behind Marilyn. A male motorist drew up alongside her. He yelled something. She flipped him off. He cut south on Bundy. Dig his fuck-you-finger farewell.

Marilyn jammed to the curb and parked in a meter space. I parked behind her. She got out and jaywalked across San Vicente. She ignored traffic lights and passing cars and beelined to the Vicente Pharmacy. Clock it: 3:16 p.m.

She's back out at 3:21. She digs into a small paper bag and unscrews a pill vial. She smiles and pops two of something. She skips back across the street. She gloms her unsexy Buick and peels east.

I tailed her. She hooked south on Barrington and east on Wilshire. Big-boulevard traffic cloaked me. Marilyn drove hesitant-cum-dreamy. We passed through Westwood and the high-rise corridor. Beverly Hills traffic snared us. Marilyn parked in the cab rank upside the Beverly Wilshire.

She braced a doorman. She passed him her car keys and pulled off her shades. He went *Holy shit, you're Marilyn Monroe!* She laid a fat kiss on him. It looked like she shot him some tongue.

I pulled up and idled two car lengths back. I clocked Marilyn's hotel sojourn. It ran 6.4 minutes. She zipped back out clutching a pill vial and a cellophane-wrapped gown.

She snatched her keys from the doorman. He laughed and slapped his knees. She pulled on her shades, shagged her sled, and fishtailed out into traffic.

She drove east. She drove hesitant-cum-dreamy. She hopped lanes and tailgated. Horns blared. She kissed her fingertips and waved them out the window. She turned north on Doheny. I bird-dogged her in close.

She turned right on Elevado and parked, quicksville. I crawled up behind her. We're right at the West Hollywood/Beverly Hills border. I knew that space-age-mod building on the southeast corner. It was packed full of call-girl pads.

Marilyn breezed in the front gate. I got out and checked the mailbox bank. There's six units and six female occupants. In Unit #4: Hollywood denizen Jeanne Carmen.

Ex–call girl. Part-time carhop. Ex–Sheriff's informant. Noted pill pusher. Golf trick-shot artiste. Available for church picnics and bar mitzvahs. Close pal of ex-starlet Lila Leeds. Miss Leeds bait-girl'd Bob Mitchum's '48 reefer roust.

I dawdled by my car. Marilyn and Jeanne. The gabfest might extend. I'll trade you four yellow jackets for six black beauties. Marilyn and Jeanne. Two late '40s arrivistes. Phil Irwin worked Sheriff's Vice, '46–'53. He said Marilyn and Jeanne worked a hot-sheet hut behind Dave's Blue Room.

There's Marilyn now. She glides over to her beat-on Buick. She cranks a U-turn and hits Doheny northbound. I'm right behind her.

She tools west on Sunset. She's driving urgent now. We're right by the Beverly Hills Hotel. Marilyn blows a red light and peels south on Beverly Drive. She pulls up in front of a big Colonial job and parks at the curb.

She gets out. She dumps her scarf and shades and fluffs out her hair. She squares her shoulders and reapplies lipstick. She walks up a slate pathway and enters the manse.

942 North Beverly Drive. Double-deep, double-wide lot. Olympic pool, tennis court—

I snatched my reverse directories off the backseat. The Beverly Hills book ran light. Match the owner to the address. It's there on page 3.

Ralph R. Greenson, M.D. Practice in psychiatry.

I reclined my seat and set my Rolleiflex on the door ledge. I scanned the house, the grounds, the backyard. I circuited back and forth. I caught the payoff and zoomed in tight.

Marilyn and a burly man. Late forties, mustache, dark suit. They're sitting at a wrought-iron table. She's pitching a sob story. She's working The Method. Note her wringing hands and trembling lips. He's going *There, there.* Here's the kicker:

They're quaffing martinis. That pitcher's good for three each. Marilyn's one down already. She's orbing the pitcher. She's vibing *Cut loose, daddy—I'm coming out of my wig.*

I clocked the booze klatch. Fifty minutes, straight up. Psychiatric session. Mustache Man was Shrink Man Ralph Greenson.

He sipped his first drink. Marilyn siphoned the pitcher. She wept, she laughed, she posed. She stood up and did dance steps from some slave-girl-of-the-jungle flick. She motormouthed nonstop. Greenson went *Umm-hmn.*

He cut her off at fifty minutes, flat. He helped her up and weave-walked her out to her car. She hugged him good-bye and tumbled in behind the wheel. Shrink Man about-faced and checked his wristwatch. *Whew*—so much for *that.*

Marilyn's back in her car. She cranks the gas and peels rubber through a dicey four-way stop.

I laid tread. Zigzag traffic cut me off. Horns honked. Middle fingers shot out windows. Sit on it and twirl.

Marilyn vamoosed. It's Blown Tail #1. It won't be the last.

I went home. Phil Irwin was back at Fifth Helena. He called me and checked in. He said Nat and Robbie scored three surveillance trucks. His brother-in-law dolled them up. He quick-painted them. They were now predictable service vehicles: Acme Tree Men, Ajax TV Repair,

Citadel Florists. The paint was quick-dry. Phil camouflaged the back-seats and storage beds. He dumped in tree limbs, electrical parts, dead floral displays.

Per his Fifth Helena shift:

The housekeeper split for the day. Phil boom-miked a prior backyard chat. The housekeeper said she had plans tonight. Marilyn said she had party plans. She'd been popping black beauties and slurping Metrecal. She'll fit that Halston original with seams intact.

The wait dragged. I worked at my office-pad. I mounted corkboards on the living room walls and installed file cabinets below them. I went through stacks of old *Life* magazines and ripped out pictures. Monroe, John and Robert Kennedy. No-goodnik Peter Lawford, sans and un-sans Pat. Exterior pix of the Lawford house, exterior shots of Fifth Helena.

I pinned them to the corkboards. I pulled the Pat and Freddy photo out of the frame and pinned it beside a Monroe cheesecake shot. It's 1952. Marilyn wows our boys in Korea. Freddy and Pat storm Hollywood on V-J Day. It was some juxtaposition. I laughed my ass off.

Ajax TV Repair. It's a good ride for night stakeouts. TV's fritzed out twenty-four hours. Hollywood parties started late.

I pulled up behind Fifth Helena. I clocked in at 8:00 sharp.

The garage door was open. The Buick was parked snout out. I popped two Dexedrine and gargled 151. I inventoried my evidence kit and camera case and honed my lock picks on a pumice stone. I sizzled to break, enter, peep.

Time trek. I replayed my first brush with Monroe.

November '54. The infamous "Wrong-Door Raid." I was at the Villa Capri. *Confidential* owned me then. Every waiter, hooker, and car-park cat in L.A. fed me dirt. I schmoozed a bent plastic surgeon. He performed a dick-enlargement surgery on Montgomery Clift. I slid the doc a C-note and told him to scram. One table over: Sinatra and Joe DiMaggio. Joe was Monroe Husband #2.

The paisans quaffed dago red. DiMaggio sniveled. Marilyn was love-shacked with her hairdresser at a place in West Hollywood. He had a PI named Phil Irwin tailing her. He'd just reported in.

DiMaggio was outraged. Sinatra got outraged. Joe saw me at the next table and said join the lynch mob.

I smelled money. We three-car caravanned over to the love shack.

Phil Irwin was already there. That's how we met. It's now 11:00 p.m. We're outside a four-flat apartment house. Phil points to the downstairs left door. There's Sinatra, DiMaggio, Phil, and me. We're the lynch mob. We kick the door down. An old lady named Florence Klotz sits there, sipping tea.

Mrs. Klotz screams. Monroe's really *up*stairs. She's not shtupping her hairdresser. She's shtupping a Fox film editor named Timmy Berlin. They slip out a back door and scramble. Hence the "Wrong-Door Raid."

The Hearst rags played it up. The California State Assembly probed sleazoid scandal rags and blackmail-perpetrating detectives. I testified in closed session. Ditto, Phil Irwin. Marilyn divorced Joe. Phil went to work for me. Sinatra was married to Wife #2, Ava Gardner. He caught her muff-diving Lana Turner and went on a booze binge with Jackie Gleason. They got the DT's and wound up in Queen of Angels.

Time crawled. I chain-smoked. The garage light blipped on. Clock it: 8:42 p.m.

There's the car-door creaks, the headlight blips, the Buick nosing out.

She swung right by me. She took Sixth Helena down to Carmelina and turned north. I U-turned and came up behind her. Her left taillight blinked white. I scoped in on it and creep-crawled two car lengths back.

She veered east on Sunset. I tailed her. She drove plain hesitant tonight. Darting traffic got between us. I stuck one lane over and fixed on that light.

Sunset was hilly and curvy and high-swank underlit. The bum taillight supplied a tail beacon. We went through Brentwood and Westwood. We passed Beverly Glen and the Bel Air gates. We're in Holmby Hills now. Marilyn swerved into the right-hand lane and scraped her hubcaps on the curb.

She fishtailed and brodied south on Mapleton. It was all jumbo mansions with moats and king-size lawns. I saw a valet-park stand up ahead. Red-coat car jocks shagged Jags, Vettes, and Caddies double-quick. The car queue covered a half block. Marilyn pulled her sad-ass Buick up to the end of the line.

I pulled over and orbed the scene. Frat boys golf-carted guests up the big lawn. On-loan Playboy bunnies escorted them inside. The entry line stood one-hundred-deep.

Clock it. She'll mingle and misbehave. She'll get bored and split. You've got three hours tops.

———

My evidence kit weighed forty pounds. My camera case and bulb strips weighed ten. I parked on Carmelina and hauled the bags a full block.

I brazened a front-gate/front-door approach. The gate was open. The front door was jammed up. I slipped my Diners Club card through the latch portal. The lock bolts slid free.

My light touch worked. I made it inside. I left no tool marks or telltale scratches. I lugged the bags inside and locked the door behind me. *Darling, I'm home!*

Cool air hit me. Half-cracked windows stirred a breeze. I'd memorized the structural diagrams. I knew the floor plan and the phone-extension spots. I pulled out my penlight and bit down on the shaft. My eyes were my camera. The small beam was my swivel lens.

I dropped my kit and case and quick-prowled the premises. I flashed the wall-to-floor junctures. I noted ornamental wainscoting in the five main rooms. Wainscot ledges concealed feed wires with minimum paint camouflage.

My eyes and penlight lens worked in sync. I imprinted the wainscot strips and their proximity to phone-installation spots. I imprinted ceiling lamps and standing lamps and carpet pads to conceal room bugs.

I focused down. I tallied installation points. I tantalized myself with B and E foreplay. The mark's Marilyn Monroe. I'm saving the intimate prowl work for last.

I walked room-to-room. I unscrewed the three telephone handsets. I imprinted the internal circuitry and memorized spots to stash receiver mikes. I supplanted my memory with Polaroid snapshots. I went in lens-close and bulb-bright. I shot extreme close-ups of receiver housings and bounced light off the walls.

I tossed the wet prints and used bulbs in my evidence kit. Bulb glare induced double vision. I Murine-dosed my eyes. I re-toured the house and restored my 20/20 sight lines. I tracked penlight impressions, ad hoc.

The housekeeper's room. It's a monk's cell. Sight to scent. That's a lavender sachet. The kitchen. Sloth and disarray. Stacked dishes and dumped food in the sink. Mold spots on a standing rib roast. Black sink sludge. Backed-up pipes emitting a stink.

The master bathroom adjoined the kitchen. I smelled wet towels and soapy grime walking in. Note the bathtub rings. Note the plastic shower caps dumped on the floor.

I opened the medicine chest. There's Marilyn's stash.

Seconal/Nembutal/Biphetamine/Dexedrine/zonk-your-ass Dilaudid. Note the half-pint of vodka on the sink ledge. Note the toothbrush handle poking out the top. News flash: Marilyn Monroe brushes her teeth with Smirnoff 100.

I retrieved my camera case and bulb strips. I shot the kitchen and bathroom sloth. I shot the medicine-chest pharmacopia. I close-up shot the vodka jug and toothbrush.

My eyes fuzzed out again. I stashed the wet prints and used bulbs in my kit and walked back to the living room. The rugs looked cheap. The tacked-up wall photos spooked me. Drag queens at the Hollywood Ranch Market. A butch junkie shooting up at Linda's Little Log Cabin. Brain-dead tykes wearing Mickey Mouse beanies.

A liquor sideboard. Crammed with half-pints of Smirnoff 100 and paper cups. A big bowl on a pedestal. Piled high with hashish chunks.

I shot the living room. Six quick exposures, in and out. I'd been inside fifty-two minutes. My technical walk-through was solid. I had what I'd need to string wires and mount bugs and taps.

I wanted scent and sensation more than sight now. I wanted to touch things that touched her. I wanted to be where she got lonely and cut loose.

I lugged my gear into Marilyn's bedroom. I quadrant-scanned it, up and down.

Bland white walls. Wood-plank shelves. A nightstand by the bed. A white phone on top. Plus twelve pill vials and two vodka short dogs.

A king-size bed. All-white bedsheets and an all-white duvet. Soiled white pillowcases. Step in close, now. See if you can track her scent.

I smelled stale and recent exertion. I smelled mingled fluids, visible as dried stains. I smelled expensive perfume and cheap aftershave. I saw lipstick-stained and punched-down pillows. It denoted violent efforts to sleep.

I looked under the bed. I saw a large metal lockbox jammed between the floor and box springs. I pulled it out and flipped the lid latch. The box was stuffed with hundred-dollar bills.

Neat stacks. Thick stacks. All rubber-band cinched. I dumped the box on the bed and photo-shot green cash on soiled sheets.

I counted the money. It totaled forty grand. My Man Camera fritzed. My eyes burned and refocused within my penlight beam. I clenched my jaws and cracked a tooth on the shaft.

My legs spasmed. I steadied myself on a bed rail. My first thought: Steal the money. My second thought: Don't steal the money. My third thought: You're a detective. What does this mean?

I repacked the lockbox and repositioned it under the bed. I quadrant-scanned the walls and caught a sliding-door closet. I slid it open. An overweighted hanger bar dislodged and fell to the floor. Too-garish and too-dowdy garments collapsed in a heap.

I knelt down and examined them. I scoped pink muumuus, tweed skirts, low-bodice gowns in tiger-stripe velour. Op Art summer shifts, size 16. Sweatshirts and sweatpants with Big & Beautiful Boutique labels. Ankle-length duffle coats, sized for men. Bull dyke jumpsuits by Large Marge of Huntington Beach. See-thru raincoats with drawstring hoods—a hot item from Plus Size De-Luxe.

Monroe was five-four and svelte. This dreck couture was fat-lady capacious. My first thought: It's some Actors Studio exercise. Subsume your thin self and become someone both more and less. My second thought: It's more perverse and sinister than that.

I smelled her then. The perfume scenting the bedsheets saturated the clothes on the floor. Marilyn Monroe had capered in each and every one of these getups.

I reattached the hanger bar and rehung the threads in approximate order. I smelled like *HER* now. I flashed the west-facing wall. My beam caught a plank bookshelf sans books.

The shelf ran half the length of the wall. I walked up to it. My breath stirred dust up through my light beam. I ran my hands down the shelf. A sheet of white notebook paper stuck to my fingers.

I close-up flashed it. Block print covered the page. The style was pure high school girl. Curlicues and drawn hearts to dot the *i*'s.

Marilyn mixed numbers, dates, and abbreviations. I caught the gist fast. "Refs" meant refills. The "30s" and "60s" meant pill counts. "Biphet," "Dilau," "Nemb," "Sec" and "Chloral H" denoted fine shit. The dates ranged from 8/12/60 up to last week. Below the dates: "Nice Drs" circled by schoolgirl hearts.

"Internist/Engleberg"/four bursting hearts. "Gynecologist/Kaplan"/one heart cracked in half. "Won't write Rxs & too handsy, but cute." "Cardiologist/Brammey/Rxs on occasion. Ick! Had my *Playboy* spread framed on his desk."

I hovered over the shelf and penlight-scanned the full surface. I saw *this:*

Notebook Page #2. A block-print pharmacy list. The Vincente, the Roxbury, the Beverly Wilshire, Schwab's, the Mickey Fine. Plus phone numbers and hours of operation. Below that—an obvious lover list, with kooky artwork.

"Al"/"stuntman"/three sketched dicks going *Boing*. "Biff"/"pizza delivery boy"/one wilted dick and peanut-size balls. "George"/"gas station jockey"/four giant dicks spurting jizz. "Lou"/"car-park valet"/ two normal-size dicks and "Go-down guy—not bad." Below that: "Rick Dawes. Mean—maybe a fag." Followed by four illegibly crossed-out block-print lines.

Here's my guess:

Marilyn's pissed at Rick D. She expunged his telephone-answering-service names and phone numbers. He's a closet queen. Fuck him. He's out of her life.

Below that:

"L.A. Sheriff's" and the main switchboard number—MA-46682.

Non sequitur. Head scratcher. Big anomaly—Monroe and the county fuzz. I photo-snapped the notebook sheets. I counted off sixty seconds per and pulled the prints. I dropped them in my evidence kit.

My first thought: Where's Marilyn's address book? Where does she list her friends, colleagues, flunkies, ex-husbands, and lovers for real? My second thought: Where's her received correspondence and fan mail? Where's her hotsville missives from John F. and Robert F. Kennedy?

My first guess: Stashed on the premises. My second guess: She keeps her address book and all hotsville notes on her person. My third guess: She's mercurial defined. She dumps boring correspondence and fan mail. She keeps the good stuff in a bank vault.

I'd been inside for two hours and nineteen minutes. I couldn't dust for prints or vacuum fibers. I could quick-toss the premises and beat feet.

I allotted fifteen minutes. I checked drawers, pulled up rugs, quick-scanned the kitchen cabinets. I combed closets and looked for stash holes. I got late-breaking Non Sequiturs #2 and 3.

Under the bathroom rug. One Martindale's Bookshop bookmark. Scrawled on the back: *"Jack at White House"* and *"Bobby at Justice."* Plus two main-switchboard numbers.

Stashed in a hall closet. One triple-reinforced pillowcase filled with quarters, nickels, dimes.

I photographed the bookmark and coin stash. I was clocked down to three minutes. I checked a lo-boy bookshelf. Monroe dug the highbrow frogs.

Sartre, Camus, de Beauvoir. I flipped pages through five books. She'd bookmarked pithy passages and added margin notes. As in: *"use at party,"* *"drop as casual bon mot."* As in: *"pretend it's my quote"* and *"Jack will luv this."*

Phony Marilyn. She's desperate to impress.

I rescanned the bookshelf. It was all left-wing frog fare, save *this:*

The Sexual Criminal, by Paul de River, M.D. I knew de River, circa '49. He was a batshit crazy headshrinker jungled up with LAPD. He ran the jive-progressive Sex Offense Bureau. Ex-Chief Worton brought him in. De River headshrunk rape-o's, pud pullers, whipout men, transvestites, and lust killers. He geezed them up with his own dope concoctions and browbeat them in group therapy stints. Bill Parker replaced Worton in '50. He disdained de River and his humbug sex theories. He canned his ass off the LAPD.

I skimmed pages. De River theorized, bloviated, and gasbagged at great length. The book featured photographs. Sex fiends lolled in hard-backed chairs and gaped, insensate. Whiteout strips covered their eyes.

I recognized Otto Stephen Wilson. He eviscerated two women in downtown hotels and fell for Murder One. He mouthed off to me at the Lincoln Heights Jail, late '45. I beat the shit out of him. He sucked gas up at Quentin, fall '46.

The book sickened me. I tossed it back on the shelf. A slip of note-book paper fell out. Marilyn Monroe block-printed *this:*

"When all other forms of applied therapy have failed, it may be possible to contravene absent, passive, or self-destructively reactive behavior with the imposition of direct criminal action."

7

I worked it. My guys worked it. We disdained nomenclature. It was "the job," "the gig," "the deal." It wasn't "Operation Blond" or *"L'affaire Jacques."* It was a dirt probe. We excavated dirt for Jimmy Hoffa. We fed him bug-tap scraps, surveillance briefs, and unverified innuendo. We bombarded him with listless tape reels and transcriptions. He's charged to make data blips cohere and jell as evidence of moral turpitude and actionable criminal offense.

My 4/11 pad prowl served up Marilyn Monroe. Her sloth. Her dope addiction. Her all-star libido and urgent fix on the Kennedy brothers. She stashed forty grand under her bed. It played ambiguous. Film studios played money fast and loose. They dispensed cash to contravene IRS payouts. The forty grand might be innocuous. The forty grand might indict criminal malfeasance.

I corkboard-pinned my B and E snapshots and telefaxed duplicates to Jimmy. The job vibed slow burn and slow build toward ho-hum revelation. Deficient hygiene. Dope. Adultery. Financial misconduct. Camelot as sanctified shuck. I knew that shit going in. I'm an eyeball man. My need to see and sift dirt pushed me past easily foregone conclusions.

That first pad prowl torqued me. The forty grand. The coin stash. Monroe's zaftig threads. Paul de River's nutty book and Monroe's nutty critique of de River's nutty ethos. They were tangent leads to work solo. My immediate brief was to oversee the establishment of an electronic eavesdropping system and a compatible system of sit-still and mobile surveillance.

Jimmy H. shot me a twenty-grand bank draft. I paid my guys two weeks in advance and put them to work. They ran sound and frequency-reception checks near the Lawford and Monroe pads and rented two beachside listening posts within twenty-four hours. Post #1: a small house on the east bluffside above PCH. It's got good eyeball lines and direct-frequency bearings. High foliage obscures in-and-out foot and car traffic. Post #2: a small storeroom at the Sip 'n' Surf Lounge on Malibu Pier. It's got surfer girls and a private back entrance. That makes two Lawford posts. Plus two radio frequencies. That's two shots to blunt car noise/wave crash/bum-feed contingencies.

Phil Irwin scored a perfect Monroe post. It was a disused maintenance shack on a side street upside Brentwood Country Club. It featured three rooms, a crapper/shower combo, six wall outlets, and a roof antenna. It was one-half mile from Fifth Helena Drive and provided clear signal access. Plus a backyard and carport and a tree-cloaked rear entrance. The Brentwood CC groundskeeper and Sip 'n' Surf boss were ex–L.A. Sheriff's. Phil rated them A-OK.

Nat and Robbie ran the motor pool. We stashed our surveillance sleds in Robbie's garage. Nat and Robbie humped it. Jimmy Hoffa decreed a full-court press. He was mobbed up and unioned up, nationwide. He connived two grip jobs on the *Something's Got to Give* set. Nat and Robbie would work their listening-post assignments and full soundstage shifts at Fox.

They worked the prep for the shoot. They scrounged quick drift per Monroe's upcoming travels.

4/17. She'll fly to New York. She's off to schmooze arts poseurs Lee and Paula Strasberg. Plus *this*:

Jack the K's birthday bash. Mid-May, New York City. Scheduled for Madison Square Garden. Marilyn's set to sing "Happy Birthday" to the Big Kahuna. The Strasbergs are primed to pep-talk our girl and ascribe motivation. She'll be gone two full days. That's my shot to hot-wire and *re*-prowl her crib.

The days dragged by. We set up our equipment at the listening posts. We ran endless sound checks. I creamed to get back inside Fifth Helena. We rolled out at midnight on 4/18.

Bernie Spindel and I picked locks and entered. Phil, Nat, and Robbie triangulated outside. They perched in our camouflage rides. They curb-patrolled Carmelina, Fifth and Sixth Helena. They sustained walkie-talkie contact and eyeball-strafed for nocturnal fuzz.

Bernie and I laid wire. We were inside four hours and nine minutes. I looked under Monroe's bed. The cash box was gone. A Jackie Kennedy voodoo doll was propped up on a chair pillow. Marilyn pincushioned Jackie. She stuck a cocktail fork straight up the First Lady's keester.

We got in, we got out. We hobknobbed at the Brentwood post and ran sound checks. We heard dead air and got audible dial clicks. Monroe's calls went straight to her answering service. We left bogus messages. The operators' voices came through audible-plus.

4/19. Monroe returns to L.A. The soundstage was prepped and ready. The shoot begins 4/23. I prebribed gate guards and secured a three-month premises pass.

I roamed the lot. I bribed a crafts hut flunky and secured my own golf cart. I went unrecognized. My *Confidential* magazine/scourge-of-Hollywood days were long gone. I piled lumber scraps in the cart and played working stiff.

I tailed Monroe to Fox. I observed the soundstage setups. I observed *HER*.

She worked people. She used people. She possessed three modes of address. She was bossy, she was demure, she was effusive. I didn't like her. I didn't get her. Her acting chops and alleged va-va-voom hit me flat.

I peeped her trailer three days running. I observed the Marilyn Quadrafecta: pop pills/booze/barf/pass out. Robbie and Nat reported on-set consternation. Marilyn was "pulling a Liz." *Something's Got to Give* was dubbed *Cleopatra West*. Marilyn mimicked Liz Taylor's Euro antics, because she could.

Cleopatra put Fox on the Shitsville Express. Studio machers and wage slaves waxed apocalyptic. *Got to Give* was *Cleo* writ downscale. Marilyn was out to out-Liz Liz. Nat and Robbie pipelined the bad news and gloated. I pipelined it to Jimmy Hoffa.

Day #4 defined the Quadrafecta. Marilyn passed out for six hours straight. A gofer kicked her trailer door down. An ambulance hauled Marilyn back to Fifth Helena.

Her wilted waif act postponed the shoot indefinitely. Marilyn malingers at home. Nat and Robbie monitor her phone calls. Phil Irwin holds down eyeball surveillance. The golf course listening post gets crackling good reception.

Marilyn calls out. She whines to Shrink Man Greenson and chats up a pizza delivery boy she calls "Big Dick Dave." She eats anchovy pizza for breakfast, lunch, and dinner.

I habituated the *Got to Give* set and kept my snout down. The second-unit director shot scenes "around" Monroe. Cast and crew excoriated her jive film-goddess ways. *I* excoriated her. The Hoffa job was running on-course—but I was running a fever.

We had to hot-wire the Lawford spread. It was the hot-spot nexus of the Jack/Bobby/Marilyn cluster fuck. The house was crammed full of Lawfords, Lawford kids, and Lawford slaves at all times. My PC Bell contact kicked loose vital information. There were no secondary phone lines ascribed to the house. I thought Jack might have his own tête-à-tête and nuke-the-Kremlin line. Nix that. There's one phone number and six extensions.

Robbie and Phil played PC Bell repairmen and canvassed Lawford's neighbors. They tweaked them per celeb misconduct at the Lawford spread. An old biddy called the house a "hotbed of libertine behavior." Three neighbors confirmed the high volume of Lawfords and Lawford factotums. Said volume impeded the operation and drove me batshit crazy. I wanted to get inside and mike-up that house. I wanted to explore the cluster fuck. I wanted to invade Pat Kennedy Lawford's private habitat.

The Hoffa job is now all rotation. My guys rotate between Fox, Fifth Helena, and the golf course listening post. I rotate between Fox, Fifth Helena, the Sip 'n' Surf and east bluffside posts. There's no bugs and taps installed at the Lawford house. I've got sight lines and no audial access. I sit in the dark and look down at the house. Pat walks through lighted rooms sometimes.

Marilyn malingers at home. Shrink Man Greenson and Big Dick Dave visit her. The living room bug records shrink-session pap. Marilyn justifies her *Got to Give* misconduct. She calls her work-shirking ailments "manifestations of existential malaise." Greenson tut-tuts and upbraids her. He's a scold. Marilyn works to shock him. She blew the prez in the luggage hold on *Air Force One*. Greenson tut-tuts. Marilyn details her bitter rivalry with Liz Taylor. *Cleopatra* is pompous froth. *Got to Give* is froth that knows it's froth. We're movie-actress women. We rebel against the authority of the moguls and Nazi auteurs who represent the uncles and foster daddies who poked us you know where when we were eight. Liz and I are pulling deliberate work stoppages disguised as sicknesses to exact our subconscious revenge. Film studios are the mystified fascist oligarchies that Sartre critiques.

The bedroom bugs pick up mattress squeaks in sync with Big Dick

Dave's visits. Plus moans and groans muzzled by pillows and thrashed sheets. Hallway bugs pick up the housekeeper's vacuum cleaner and staticked Marilyn/housekeeper chats. I boxed and marked those tape reels "Subject at home/bogus work absence/nonrevelatory." The golf course post piled up reels of Monroe in hibernation. She broke loose at 8:00 p.m. on 4/26.

I tailed her to an all-girl pillfest at Jeanne Carmen's apartment. Sheriff's Vice ran a green sheet on these wingdings. Phil Irwin laid out the gestalt. He was ex-Sheriff's and knew his shit.

"They gab, they pop pills, they watch TV and pass out. They may or may not indulge in some muff diving. Jeanne used to snitch to the guys on the West Hollywood squad, and she spared no details when it came to the girl action."

That was Pillfest #1. Pillfest #2 ran 4/30 to 5/2. Robbie Molette snapped sneak pix through a bedroom-window gap. He caught Marilyn, Lila Leeds, and a butch golf pro in a nude pillow fight. Robbie's a smut man. His sister Chrissy's a shadow figure in the fuck film underground. He's developing duplicate photos. He'll peddle them at the Bearded Clam and Linda's Little Log Cabin.

Pillfest #2 fizzled out. Marilyn returned to work. I spot-tailed her, on and off the set. Robbie and Nat worked their grip gigs and got up eyeball-tight. Marilyn blew take after take. Director Cukor rebuked her. Marilyn pitched woe-is-me and sulked in her trailer. She boozed, she napped, she split Fox in a huff and shut down the shoot. I tailed her back to Fifth Helena. She put me through operational drudge work. We replayed the routine, six days straight.

Bugs, taps, spot tails, sit-still and mobile surveillance. Full-time listening post with A-level reception. We've got Doc Greenson and Pizza Man Dave. We've got nude pillow fights. Jack and Bobby K don't call. What's with Marilyn's coin stash and zaftig threads? Where's that forty grand she stashed under her bed? It wasn't there the night we hot-wired her. Where's all the dishy phone chats with Hollywood insiders?

I worked my sit-still shifts in a tree trimmer's truck. That girl in the '60 Corvair kept bopping by to peek over the hedge. I wrote down her plate number and buzzed my DMV contact. He supplied full license stats.

The sled:

Registered to Willard D. Farr/WMA/age 44. Swank Pacific Palisades address. Husband of Dorothy Denton Lowell, thirty-nine. The blond girl: Georgia Lowell Farr/DOB 3/22/45/Palisades High School junior. Snap call: she's a rich-kid Marilyn obsessive.

Like Jimmy Hoffa. Like me. Like my guys—we're all fan-club fools run amok.

The job proceeded. The rotations rotated. I triangulated. The Fox lot, the post, Fifth Helena. My lot prowls felt intrusive now. I was one-time notorious. Film studios are gossip pits. People must have made me. Jimmy Hoffa pulled strings and got my guys in. Fox was mobbed up from way back. Ben Siegel, Willie Bioff, the Aadland brothers. Mobbed-up unions ran the rank-and-file workforce. Fox felt like a snitch hive. LAPD Intel infiltrated the studio craft unions. Ditto SHIT—the Sheriff's geeks. The lot exposed me. I sensed it. I was ex-LAPD and tenuously tight with Bill Parker.

El Jefe and I went back. I owed him. He extricated me from dire shit on numerous occasions. The Chief was treading shit now. His boys blew up two Black Muslims outside a southside mosque. Nat Denkins' kid brother got embroiled. Nat spritzed outrage on his radio show. I issued a gag order. It stopped just short of a muzzle. Nat said he'd tone it down.

Fox was a gossip pit. I sensed informational seepage. Phil and Robbie sensed it, likewise. I curtailed my golf-cart prowls and stuck to the posts and Fifth Helena. Monroe abetted me. She blew off the *Got to Give* shoot and moped home in early May. I sensed long-term hibernation.

Nasty Nat developed a source on the main Fox switchboard. She placed the long-distance calls for the *Got to Give* cast and crew. She was married. Nat, likewise. They got a thing going and trysted at no-tell motels. Nat called her his fox at Fox. She eavesdropped on Monroe's calls from her trailer. They ran to type. Monroe called pharmacies and issued dope directives. Monroe placed twenty-one calls to the White House and Justice Department switchboards. She asked to be put through to the prez and AG. Line garble cut the calls off then. I knew why. The interior lines were security-scrambled.

Seepage. Boring repetition. Outcompensated by *this:*

Indications. Disparate working on coherent. Marilyn's bonking Jack and possibly Bobby. It's occasional. It's casual to them. It's urgent to her. She's desperate. She's unhinged. She's delusional. She's DEROGATORY PROFILE–defined.

I work the Hoffa gig. I keep the Eddie Fisher gig back-burnered. Art

Aragon's bodyguarding Eddie. I swoop by the Losers Club and gas on Mr. Cornuto. He's belting show tunes and spritzing raw.

He features Liz and Dick. They're fucking and sucking *here*. They're 69'ing *there*. He's got Roman geography *down*. Turn-away crowds wail and gorge on Eddie's self-abasement.

Art feeds me the up-close. Froufrou actor Roddy McDowall costars in *Cleo*. He calls Eddie from Roma and delivers the daily dish. Fox is now known as 20th Century–*LOX*. Rumors accumulate and mutate. It's biblical prophecy. Fox will implode by this, that, or this date. Fox execs and rank and filers are shit-your-pants shook. They're devising scams to build bankrolls for the Fox Apocalypse. Fake bearer bonds. Unload them in Mexico—it's a sure thing. Wife-swap clubs, pill-popper clubs, key parties. Dope smuggled in and out of T.J. And, now: Monroe's sabotaging *Got to Give* in the Lizesque *Cleo* style.

Monroe malingered. I stuck close. My tap feeds picked up her calls. She yelped to Doc Greenson. Jack and Bobby use me and pass me around like men always have. She called Jeanne Carmen. They planned future pill trysts. She swung with Pizza Dave and snarfed pizza three times daily. She walked out in plus-size dresses and big slouchy hats. I foot-tailed her to Barrington and Beverly Glen parks.

She's on a spy-mistress kick. She carries a drawstring purse stuffed with coins. She makes five and six phone booth calls and slinks back to Fifth Helena.

She employs enclosed phone booths. She hunkers down and crowds the coin boxes. I don't know who she's calling or what she's saying. PC Bell does not tally individual pay-phone calls. I can't track her callouts.

My phone taps remain undetected. I know that. She calls out on all three extensions. She's got a closet stuffed with nickels, dimes, and quarters. I sense design here. It plays inimical to her whole *vida loca*.

Monday, 5/14. Marilyn returns to the *Got to Give* set. Cast and crew applaud. The lovefest lasts three hours. A big row with George Cukor flatlines it. Robbie observed the fracus. Marilyn sulked back to her trailer and got smashed.

Tuesday, 5/15. Nasty Nat's switchboard plant reports two Marilyn calls. Call #1: to Doc Greenson. Shrink Man tells Marilyn he's taking a month's vacation. Marilyn moans. Greenson soothes her. The gist: he's got a backup shrink she'll love. Call Milt Wexler. We're office mates. You'll love Dr. Milt. He's a mensch. Call #2: to Dr. Milt's office. "Hi. This is Marilyn Monroe speaking." The receptionist goes *eeeek*. Wednesday, 5/16. It's payday and my summary-report-due day. Jimmy H. rigged a safe-deposit-box drop. There's two B of A's off of Wilshire and Western. I had two box keys. I snared the payroll at Box #1. I placed my report, tape reels, and transcription logs in Box #2. Jimmy left me a note:

"Breakfast. 8:00 Saturday. The Statler."

Thursday, 5/17. I was kicked back in my golf cart. I was bored and scratching my balls. Soundstage #14 was straight across a breezeway. The *Got to Give* shoot droned on.

A helicopter hovered and touched down in the parking lot. Peter Lawford opened the hatch. Marilyn ran out and passed him a garment bag. He blew her a kiss and slammed the hatch. The chopper took off. Marilyn waved bye-bye.

It hit me. Jack's birthday bash. Madison Square Garden. It's this Saturday night. Be there or be square.

I rolled to a pay phone and called L.A. International. I impersonated a Sheriff's lieutenant and demanded a passenger brief. A cowed clerk delivered.

L.A. to Idlewild. The Pan Am noon flight. Peter and Pat Lawford. Plus four kids and three servants. A Miss Monroe on a Saturday-noon charter flight.

There's Pat's private habitat. There's your big empty house.

8

Jimmy Hoffa said, "She won't last much longer on that movie she's in. Everybody's losing patience."

The same hotel suite. The same breakfast fare. The same chairs pulled up tight. Hoffa wore a tight gray suit and spit-shined shoes. A plastic seafood bib covered his chest.

"That's right. The studio's losing money on her, at a time when they can't afford to."

Hoffa sipped coffee. "The wall bugs don't give up much, do they? Mostly it's just boring conversation."

I shrugged. "House bugs are always an iffy proposition. The sound disperses, and you only score when the principals sit close together and talk pertinent shit."

"No calls or visits from Jack and Bobby, huh?"

I said, "She calls the White House and Justice from her trailer on the lot. It's in my summary. The internal phone lines are scrambled, so there's no chance to hear any actual conversations she might have."

Hoffa cracked his knuckles. "Forty thou in a lockbox, under the bed. That's interesting."

I went *Nix*. "It was gone the night Bernie and I laid in the wires."

Hoffa slurped coffee. His bib featured snarling lobsters and crabs.

"Greenson's skeeved on her, right? He comes to her house, and she comes to his place for cocktails. He coddles her, she confides in him, and some night when the moon's all full, he'll get up his nerve to pounce."

I laughed. "Greenson's going out of town for a month. He set Marilyn up with his office mate, Milt Wexler. I doubt if he'll accommodate her the way Greenson does."

Hoffa harumphed and squared his bib. He was short. His throne chair dwarfed him. His feet grazed the carpet.

"I blame Jack for all this permissive shit poisoning our culture. He's put the whole country in some fucked-up state of enchantment, with his Jew Frontier shit and civil rights and all this other high-minded shit, while he's meanwhile ramming this nutty nympho when he's supposed to be a good family man, like me."

I went *Whoa, now.* "You saw my evidence photos. Something's going on here. Why would Monroe have the main number for the L.A. Sheriff's Office listed on an odd sheet of paper?"

Hoffa cracked his thumbs. "I've been scrounging tips on that girl for years, ever since I learned she put out for Jack and Bobby and half the stray cock in this town. One, she hates the LAPD—going back to the late '40s, when she was supposedly a freelance call girl. Also, she hates them on political grounds, like that Black Muslim hoo-haw a few weeks ago. She loves the Sheriff's, because old Sheriff Biscailuz doted on her and always had her ride with him at the county rodeo, whereas the LAPD Intel Division has got surveillance film of her at about eight million pro-Commie rallies. The SHIT unit has more or less left her alone, probably because she's been known to blow Pete Pitchess on occasion. Confucius say, 'It not who you know but who you blow.' Pete's okay. He's a lawyer and an ex-FBI man, and he's Gay Edgar Hoover's choice to replace him if the Kennedys let him go."

I lit a cigarette. "I see where this is going. You've got no beef with old man Hoover. Bobby K's the thorn in your side, and the old man hates him. SHIT's tight with the Feds, because of the Hoover-Pitchess connection. The old poof loves Hollywood gossip—and SHIT feeds him the shit."

Hoffa twirled his coffee cup. "You're right on all that. That's why I'm a Pitchess guy, and that's why he's my choice to succeed the old man. He'll never take grief from Bobby K, and he'll leave labor and so-called organized crime alone."

I checked a wall clock. My Fifth Helena shift started *now.* Monroe's charter flight left at noon. The Lawford B and E job crunched me. Equipment checks would run—

Hoffa tossed his bib and jiggled his nuts. Hoffa stood up and stretched.

"Okay, so Greenson and this Wexler guy share an office. That simplifies things. I want you to break in, mimeograph any Monroe files you come across, and see if you can grab or make tape copies of any of those nutty little chats our girl and Greenson might have recorded. I'm kicking this thing into high gear."

The day turned hot. The tree-service truck trapped dead air. I zoom-lensed Monroe's front gate and cogitated.

Equipment checks. Tonight's the night.

Walkie-talkies. Police-band scanner. Power drills. Wire rolls and phone jacks. Flashlights, penlights, oscilloscope. Dust vacuums, Spackle paste and spreaders. Two inside men. That's Bernie and me. Phil stands lookout on PCH. He's ex-Sheriff's. The house straddles the city-county line. Phil's a Sheriff's reserve. He carries a badge. He could hold off nosy fuzz.

Robbie plays watchdog. He's couched in the bluffside post. He's got the down-slant overview. Nat lurks outside. He's our runner. He's in and out of the house. He pipelines Bernie and me. He shags emergency gear.

I cogitated. I popped two dexies and sipped Old Crow. I replayed breakfast with Jimmy H.

Jimmy played not quite askew. He's financing a sex-squeeze/cease-and-desist operation. He's eight-balling the prez and AG. Jimmy's a known prude and tightwad. Jimmy's funding a big party that may yield zilch. Jimmy's a money man. There's no fallback money angle should the plan go *pffft*. There's cease and desist and no correlative payoff. That's very *un*-Jimmy.

That maroon Corvair pulled up in front of me. Georgia Lowell Farr got out. She wore a Pali High cheerleader sweater and khakis. She walked across the street and straight through the gate.

I lens-tracked her. Marilyn Monroe entered the frame.

I pulled back and recentered the shot. There they are. The dissolute screen queen and swoony high school girl hug. Marilyn kicks the gate shut.

The front door slammed. They're inside now. Sit down and talk, kids. The room bugs will eavesdrop.

Time slogged. Time stuttered and stalled. My brain trip outran it. I fantasy-perved on Lois and Pat. The front door creaked open. I got out and stood on my back bumper. My lens world expanded. Monroe and the Farr girl walked toward the gate.

They were dirt-smeared and disheveled. They kept brushing off their hands. I snapped three photographs. They hugged good-bye. Georgia Farr was five-ten. She loomed over Monroe.

The gate popped open. Georgia stepped out. Monroe cut back across her front lawn. She moved diagonal. That meant the garage.

She had a noon flight east. I jumped back in the truck and cranked a quick U-turn. I punched it down to Carmelina, cut north, and parked. I perched for ten minutes. Finally—there's that dumb Buick. It's drifting down Sixth Helena. Monroe's driving weavy today.

She turned north on Carmelina. Away from the airport. She fishtailed into a two-lane drift.

I tailed her. My surveillance truck had no pop. Monroe swerved east on Sunset. I goosed the gas and barely kept up.

We breezed through Westwood and Holmby Hills. We entered Beverly Hills. Monroe straddled traffic lanes. Horn honks bombarded her. She drove oblivious. She left-turned on Benedict Canyon. I blew a red light and hung in.

We went north. It was a climb. The road went twisty and one-laned. Monroe scuffed her whitewalls and caromed off of curbs. We crossed Mulholland and two-laned downhill. The steep grade jerked me forward and ratcheted up my speed. Monroe tap-tapped her brakes. I rode her back bumper. Fuck her. She'd never notice me. She drove zombified.

It's a Valley run. I rode the clutch and slid between first and second. The terrain went Valley-flat. Marilyn made goofy right and left turns. Ventura, Moorpark, north on Woodman. An alley and a dead end at Saticoy. She veered left. I stalled out at an unmarked retaining wall and slammed the truck in reverse. I veered left on Saticoy and sped up. The Buick was flat gone.

I slow-cruised three blocks and scanned intersections. I scoped parked vehicles. I saw the dumb Buick jammed between an Olds coupe and cholo Impala. A quick blip blipped me. That's her. She's waltzing down an alley, ten o'clock–left.

Shit—

I'm moving away from her. The curbs and driveways are car-blocked. There's no place to park.

It's Blown Tail #2. I'm somewhere in dogdick Encino. There's high-end ranch homes behind me. It's jumped-up apartment blocks here.

It's atypical Monroe turf. The locale torqued me. It vibed dope buy or sex tryst. It's 9:40. She's got a noon flight. Why's that lunatic here now?

I found a parking spot. It was three blocks and a half mile east. I *re*-vibed it.

She's meeting someone. She's doing something wrong. It's a new money/flash money neighborhood. Pool-cabana apartment blocks. Stewardess hives, fag pads, kept-woman domiciles. The Aloha Gardens, the Hawaiian Lanais, the Tiki-Torch Village.

A notion buzz-bombed me. It was shitwork and drudge work combined. I didn't know where she was or who she was with. Parked cars engulfed me. I could jot down plate numbers and call my DMV guy. Plate stats might reveal hinky names and addresses. Underground garages engulfed me. They were gate-locked and remote-controlled. It restricted my access. It was all shitwork under the sun.

I worked it. I walked a three-block/car-to-car radius. Monroe's car was gone. She'd make her flight. I scrawled plate numbers for 143 vehicles. It took four hours. It was Valley hot. I sweated and soiled myself up. My tree-trimmer outfit oozed wet.

She's got something going. I'm the Derogatory Profile man. I want to know what it is.

It's Saturday night. We've got warm spring weather. There's bumper-locked cars crammed on PCH. It's party night. That means sound cover. It drifts house-to-house and muzzles entry sounds. It's 11:52 p.m. We're going in.

We'd stashed our cars at the bluffside post. Nat stashed our gear under a Lawford garage tarp. He did it brazen. In full daylight. He drove the tree-trim truck up on the curb and jammed the remote-control signal on the garage door. He cranked the door and dumped our gear. He trimmed two palm trees on the south walkway. The ruse took sixteen seconds, all told.

We lounged against parked cars. We wore party clothes and smoked cigarettes. Hula shirts, slacks, light windbreakers. That's Nat, Phil, Bernie, and me. We're four guys grabbing some air. We'll go back inside and *re*-party in a second. Robbie's our spotter. He's up in the bluffside post. He'll flash a red light to cue the intrusion.

Phil's got a police-band scanner. He'll lurk outside. Nat's the equipment runner. There's six phones on the premises. Three upstairs, three down. Bernie will wire up the wall bugs and tap the downstairs phones.

I'll do the upstairs. Nat packed our shit in duffel bags. He'll backstop the cleanup. We're covered every which way.

Robbie flashed the red light. It blipped clear from four hundred yards and high up. Nat cranked the garage door and let himself in. Phil lurked by a '61 Lincoln. Bernie and I hustled down the north pathway and braced the kitchen-side door.

Bernie penlight-flashed the lock. I jammed a #4 pick in the keyhole and poked around. The door popped open. We stepped inside and shut the door behind us. A penlight beam strafed the floor. It was Nat. He entered through the garage. He gave us the A-OK sign and hauled our duffel bags up.

I tapped my Man Camera switch. I'd memorized the interior floor plan and phone-installation spots. I grabbed my duffel bag. I bit down on my penlight and followed the beam.

The front stairway took me up. The second floor was plain big. Front and rear stairways. Four squared-off hallways. Two kid-size bedrooms on the south side. Built-in bathrooms, en suite.

Wide hallways. Long hallways.

The absence of common space vexed me. It militated against conversation. People did not gather to talk here.

The walls were flat-walnut paneled. Pricey plein air originals lined all four. The entire landing was recessed bulb/overhead lit. There were no standing lamps to plant bugs on. The thin Persian carpets would betray the bug mounts jammed underneath.

I nixed upstairs bugs. Bernie would bug the downstairs up the ying-yang. People talked there.

I clocked the north hallway. Three closed doors meant three large bedroom suites. It hit me, belated.

Separate bedrooms for Peter and Pat. Separate phone extensions, dressing rooms, bathrooms. I snap-judged the arrangement. It was Pat's call. Pat censured Peter. She exiled him. She worked within the bounds of the Kennedys-stay-married-but-ignore-their-vows dictum.

I went weavy. I grabbed a stair rail and steadied myself. I scanned the north hallway and walked the hall, east to west. I jiggled the first doorknob. The door was unlocked. I cracked it, just for scent. The air reeked of cleaning solvent and stale maryjane.

I walked to the middle door. It was snagged on a throw rug and open a hairsbreadth. The scent of Tweed drifted out.

She wore Tweed on a summer night in 1945. She wears Tweed today.

I walked to the west-end door. I saw it and stifled a laugh.

The door had been customized. The U.S. presidential seal was eye-level affixed. It was gold leaf and light blue enamel. Gold-leafed below the seal: *Jack's Shack.*

I opened the door and walked right in. *Hey, Jack—what's shakin', baby?*

The bedroom dittoed the hallways. Pricey plein airs and walnut panels. Two nightstands flanked a big Craftsman bed. Note the flanking telephones—red and black.

I examined the phones and tracked attached cords to wall outlets. The black phone was your standard PC Bell job. The red phone was rigged with buttons and custom volume controls. The cord was heavy-duty brass and attached to a separate feeder plug. It was a Secret Service tech installation.

Jack, you cocksucker. It's your hotline to launch the Big One. Remember me? We shared a few grins way back when.

I got out my tools and unscrewed the black phone's receiver. I inserted spacers and twisted wires and planted the taps. It took 2.4 seconds. I hauled my gear down to Peter Lawford's room. The stale reefer smoke made me sneeze. I tapped his phone in 2.0 seconds flat.

I heard TV noise and voices downstairs. Bernie and Nat haw-hawed and watched the news. A commentator recapped Jack's big birthday bash. Bernie said, "I heard he gets more ass than a toilet seat."

Nat said, "Freddy used to score for him. He's a one-a-day man."

Peter Lawford said something. The TV volume swooped. Marilyn Monroe sang "Happy Birthday." I'm a bug-and-tap pro. I know her voice now. She was zorched out of her gourd.

I walked into Pat's room. I smelled Tweed and felt trapped room heat. I tapped her bedside phone and dumped that task quick. A step-through closet hooked back to the bathroom. I flash-lit crewneck sweaters and navy blazers with the girls-school emblems excised. She owned one cocktail gown and fourteen pairs of saddle shoes. She owned one tailored suit and eleven plaid Pendleton shirts.

The closet enclosed a merged fragrance: Tweed and sandalwood blocks. I ran my hands through her sweaters. I felt the blocks and stirred the fragrance up. I touched something off-kilter—slick-surfaced metal and glass.

Keepsake, artifact, hidden treas—

I pulled it out. There we are/there we were. The black frame offsets us, we're soft within chaos, Pat's tortoiseshell beret gleams.

9

I'm a West L.A. locksmith. It's a B and E shuck. My Key King jumpsuit and tool kit ooze verisimo. I'm casing 408 Bedford Drive, Beverly Hills. Ralph Greenson and Milt Wexler shrink heads here.

My old Chevy hogged two curb slots. I chain-smoked and stalled the approach. Jimmy H. wants a file and/or tape grab. I pioneered head-shrinker B and E's in my *Confidential* prime. Juicy exposés resulted.

"Jittery Johnnie Ray. The Boys call him 'Nervous Nellie.' " "Nympho Call Girl Ring—June Allyson, J'accuse!!!" "Bibulous Bob Mitchum—this bad boy's head won't shrink!!!"

Jimmy Hoffa says, "Jump." I say, "How high?" My prime ran from '54 to '56. Shrinks got hip to late-night 459's. They code and vault their celeb dirt now. Jimmy's side gig vibed dud.

I stalled the walk-through. I popped two dexies to suppress ennui. I replayed my moments in Pat's bedroom and merged scents and sounds.

The wire job launched. The phone taps work swell. The Lawfords are back from New York and Jack's birthday binge. The downstairs wall mikes are shit. They spew garbles and fractured conversation. Yelping kids. Maids running vacuum cleaners. Peter Lawford watching TV. Barking dogs and no hints of Pat.

Monroe's back from New York. We've got her lockstepped, tapped, and bugged. She's at the Fox lot today. Nat called me two hours back. He relayed secondhand dish. His switchboard operator girlfriend reports:

Marilyn was tanked and holed up in her trailer. She called the White House and Justice Department main numbers. Nat's girlfriend put the calls through. She eavesdropped on the upshot. Both operators said, "We've been told not to take your calls, Miss Monroe." Nat's girlfriend was sure they worked off prepared scripts.

My three posts are now full operational. The two beach posts log Lawford-house calls, in and out. We're double-focused on the house. It's Jack's L.A. wet spot. The twin-post concept gets results. Two locations, two frequencies. It levels out wave crash and car boom. It brings Pat's voice alive.

I habituate the bluffside post. I've seen Pat four times in five days. She walks her ridgeback dog twice a day. She rotates the crewneck sweaters in her closet. She ties her hair back in the mornings and wears it down in the afternoons.

Marilyn's purportedly tight with the Lawfords. We haven't logged a single house-to-house call yet. Marilyn works the Fox day shift and the homebody night shift. She did a quasi-nude photo shoot on the *Got to Give* set. Gofers shooed off peepers and instilled decorum. Robbie Molette circumvented it. He shot some palm-camera pix and consigned them to his sister Chrissy. They now pervade the fuck film underground.

I worked the golf course post last night. I caught a hilarious phone schmooze. Marilyn Monroe and Georgia Lowell Farr joust culture and moral trend. Marilyn calls Miss Farr "Lowell." Lowell calls Miss Monroe "Marilyn." It's half sock hop, half perv slumber party.

Marilyn: "Save the woof-woof for your wedding night, sweetie. Listen to the voice of experience here, and don't get embroiled with politicians."

Lowell: "Don't you think President Kennedy's a dreamboat?"

Marilyn: "He's a dipshit. He screwed Anita Ekberg and gave Jackie the clap."

Lowell squealed and went kid gleeful. I heard cut-in clicks. Lowell's mom picked up an extension. Lowell said, "*Mom*—I'm on the horn with Marilyn Monroe." Mom sighed—*you and your crazy fibs.*

I got antsy. Jimmy Hoffa says "Jump." I say, "How—"

Giant ants got me itchy and crawled up my ass. I grabbed my tool kit and rolled.

The building was tinted-glass/brushed-steel sterile. I entered and elevatored up to floor 4. Greenson and Wexler shared Suite 419. I walked over and walked in.

Shrink suites run identical. Receptionist's cubicle, separate entrance for shrinkees. Offices and file room behind the cubicle. Short inner hallways and connecting doors. By and large unlocked.

I knelt by the hallway door. I fiddled with the lock spring and waved to the receptionist. She rolled her eyes and waved back. I slid two spacers up against the spring mounts.

Jungle Juice.

I brewed a batch and worked three days straight. I rotated listening post shifts, three per day. My guys caught a breather. I monitored calls and reviewed the tape and transcription logs for calls already received. I kept a scratch-pad list of calls that explicate my specific Monroe Bifecta: Monroe and the K boys/Monroe's Grade-A Crazy Shit.

Jeanne Carmen calls Marilyn. 6:09 p.m., 5/24/62. Here's the Marilyn-to-Jeanne extract:

"... and I've got to be very careful when I call out. I make my really high-priority calls from pay phones, because this really heavyweight and dreamy guy told me to. His name's José, and I met him on a mission to Mexico, which I am not at liberty to discuss."

Pat Lawford calls her sister Jean in New York. 2:42 p.m., 5/25/62. Here's the Pat-to-Jean lead-in:

"Jack and Bobby have dropped Marilyn." Jean responds: "Can you blame them? She's nutty as a fruitcake. I think she's a candidate for the rubber room. She was good in *River of No Return,* though."

Un-ID'd woman calls Pat. 9:17 a.m., 5/26/62. Here's the Pat-to-woman extract:

"Marilyn's been acting up. 'Acting' says it all. She's always acting. She's been sounding terrified, because she says she's been getting breather calls, and someone broke into her house and moved things around, and she got a nasty letter in the mail."

Jungle juice. Listening-post rotations. The posts had upsides and downsides. The bluffside post had proximity to Pat and threadbare décor. The Sip 'n' Surf post had surfer girls and no kitchen. The golf course post adjoined the practice tee at Brentwood CC. Stray balls popped off the roof and made me go for my piece. Jungle juice spawns cabin fever. I decreed a breather and logged work time outside.

Monroe's Valley jaunt. My blown tail. They perplexed me and wrenched me. I went by the Hollywood DMV and braced my contact there. I gave him my plate list. It ran to 143 numbers. He said he'd run them and get full license stats. We settled on five bucks per name and address.

Monroe's fan mail and personal correspondence. It vexed me and wrenched me. Where was it? It's not in her house. It might be safe-deposit-boxed. That notion crunched me. It entailed legwork. I cruised twenty-seven westside banks and savings and loans. I impersonated a Federal bank examiner and showed fake ID. I got twenty-seven "No, sir" responses.

My pending shrink's office break-in. It vexed me and wrenched me. It mandated cool-head circumspection.

Beverly Hills PD ran two graveyard-watch felony cars. They targeted residential and business-address burglars. Greenson and Wexler kept a narcotics safe. It was headshrinker SOP. Bedford Drive was Headshrinker Central. I called up cool-head caution and resolve. I logged two late-night surveillance shifts.

I lurked in an alleyway and eyeballed 408 Bedford. BHPD felony cars rolled by once an hour. The break-in mandated cool-head restraint and an eye for obfuscation. The narcotics safe and junkie burglars. BHPD would buy that.

I developed a plan and secured the appropriate props. They included a nitro spritz for the safe. I could peddle the shootable dope and refortify my pill stash.

Jungle juice. It wears you thin. The flight decrees the crash.

My three-day run ran down. I went light-headed. I saw sunspots and things that weren't there. I ate three candy bars for sustenance and gobbled three red devils. I crapped out at the golf course post. My sleep was all noise and dank colors.

Phone buzz stirred me. It was light outside. I'd slept sixteen-plus hours. I dove for my headphones and crashed into the chair by the console.

The voice activator kicked on. Tape spun. A man greeted Marilyn. I popped two dexies and called up alertness. I made the voice. Roddy McDowall. We had a circa '54 run-in. Drag ball hijinx. Roddy in a ritzy gown. Freddy O. peeps and exposes all.

I yawned and guzzled cold coffee. Marilyn said, "What time is it in Rome? Come *on*, baby. You know what I'm angling for."

Roddy said, "This will have to be a teaser reel, because it's late-late here, and I've got a friend coming over."

Marilyn: "'Friend.' Ho, ho."

Roddy: "Pietro something. Really, love. I deliver the transatlantic dish on a daily basis—to you, Sid Skolsky, and Eddie Fisher, and I never reverse the charges. Eddie's the only one with a vested interest, given Queen Elizabeth's misadventures, but you remain the most dish-crazed of the lot."

Marilyn: "I'll make it up to you. I'll buy you a pizza when you're back in town."

Roddy: "I know all about your penchant for pizza, and for the boy who delivers it to you. If you're not getting it for free by now, you never will be."

I laughed and lit a cigarette. Roddy gave good phone.

Marilyn: "Sweetie . . ."

Roddy: "All right. The highly abbreviated dish is that *Cleopatra* is the loser of all time, and I'll never get an Oscar nod, because this dog is both dramatically overbudget and drearily overlong, and once it's been cut, cut, cut, I'll be down to a bit part. But I'll get my revenge on Fox, though."

Marilyn: "Tell me how."

Roddy: "I happen to know of a certain storage room on the Fox lot where a great many Roman soldier costumes earmarked for the Lox of All Time are being stored. When I'm back in L.A., I'm going to enlist a crew and a dozen cute boys and make a fuck film that will demean, denigrate, and brilliantly satirize the overblown *Cleo*. As the uncredited director of *Whipout Man, Fat Girl Love, Miscegenation Generation,* and *The Sexistentialists,* you know what I'm capable of."

Marilyn: "I know you're jonesing for Pietro, but can't you—"

Roddy: "Liz is hopping mad at Eddie. His cheesy shtick at the Losers Club has pushed her over the edge. She's told her lawyer to take him to the cleaners. Now, love—"

Marilyn: "Don't you want to hear the latest on Jack and Bobby?"

Roddy: "Your latest dispatch from fantasyland? Darling, you shtupped Jack a half dozen times, and you told me he was hung like a cashew, and I doubt if you've ever shtupped Bobby, so—"

The call fritzed and dead-aired. Transatlantic feed lines ran temperamental. I took a piss and chained cigarettes. The dexies hit. Marilyn's phone re-rang. I jumped on the headphones.

The green console light blinked. It signified a Lawford house/Monroe house call.

Marilyn picked up. She said, "Hello?" Peter Lawford said, "Listen, and appreciate the fact that I'm not enjoying this task. You are not to call or in any way contact Jack or Bobby again, and that's straight from the president himself."

Marilyn gasped. Lawford hung up. The green light blinked off. Marilyn sobbed into her telephone. The voice activator kept tape running. I timed the crying jag at four minutes straight.

10

Shrink job. I'm up on the fourth floor. I jiggled the hallway door and got clicks. The spacers worked. The door popped open. I stepped inside.

I stood in the reception room. I'd crowbarred an alleyway door and breached the building there. That door *looks* locked. If the F-car cops shake alleyway doors, I'm fucked.

I'd parked my sled at Linny's deli. My squarejohn attaché is a tool kit. I'm dressed squarejohn. The building rates Z-grade secure. I excel at security breaches. I know how to break, enter, steal, and/or perv and get out.

Man Camera flashback. I reprised my first glimpse.

There's the waiting room. There's the receptionist's cubicle. That's the connecting door to the right. I bit down on my penlight. That door should be unlocked.

I walked to the door and turned the knob. There's the click. I'm in the shrink-prototype side hallway.

I penlight-flashed the walls. I noted two closed doorways left, two closed doorways right. Unmarked doorways, right. Marked doorways, left. I know this floor plan. I pulled six shrink jobs for *Confidential*.

Shrink-session rooms, right. Shrink's offices, left. Tasteful name plaques anoint them. Dr. Greenson's toward the front, Dr. Wexler's toward the back. The last door's the file room. Where's the narcotics safe?

Eyes right, eyes left.

The floor plan confirmed my prior jobs. I jiggled the right-side door-knobs. The doors popped wide. I flashed the interiors and confirmed details.

Shrinkee couches and chairs. Shrinker chairs. Shrinkee entry/exit doors. Shrinkees were skulkers and back-door habitués. They feared exposure and ducked reception rooms.

I jiggled the left-side doorknobs. Greenson's door was open. Wexler's door was locked. The probable file-room door was locked.

My first thought: The probable file room's a shrinkee pissoir. The receptionist has her own pissoir. Greenson and Wexler have en suite pissoirs. Where's the file room/where's the dope safe/your alleyway entry marks a 459 PC. Don't fuck with locked doors and leave tool marks. Don't individuate *this* office for 459 PC.

Let's imprint details. Here's the office of Ralph R. Greenson, M.D.

A big Danish Modern desk. Crazy tubular chairs. Picasso wall prints. Greenson's hep, Daddy-O. Hep plus smart. Dig his glass-encased shelves.

Floor-to-ceiling shelves. Crammed with patient files, stored spine out. Code numbers on the spines. No names revealed. Heavy glass. Eight hinged panes for reach-in access. Triple key-locked, eight times across. Burglar alarm tape seals all perimeters. I confront stymie, stalemate, defeat. This gig is *fucked*.

I peeped the room. I peeped the john. I sniffed Greenson's high-end toiletries. I peeped the receptionist's cubicle. Where's the dope safe? Maybe Wexler's got the dope safe. His door's locked. If I breach that door, I individuate this location. If there's no dope safe, there's no junkie-burglar ruse. Big Freddy O. takes it up the shit chute.

I walked back to Greenson's office and crashed in his desk chair. I yanked the right- and left-side drawer pulls and got no give. I tried the shallow middle drawer. It slid open, easy.

Peep it, numbnuts. It's your métier. It's all you're going to get.

I saw postage stamps, pens, pencils, erasers. I saw a brochure for the L.A. Civic Light Opera. There's a Richfield gas station receipt. Note the circa '50 Monroe publicity still. There's no visible ejaculate on it. *But*—there's a tape-spool box marked "Home Session, 2:40 p.m., 5/29/62."

It tweaked me. I closed my eyes and conjured. I smelled typewriter whiteout and heard typewriter keys tap.

Robbie Molette. His rolling stakeout report, three days back. Marilyn leaves her house at 2:26. She arrives at Greenson's house at 2:38.

I'm a toss pro. The drawer was still virgin. I know not to touch. I popped my attaché and grabbed my camera. It was prerigged with flashbulb attached.

The drawer was full extended. I framed the clutter and popped off a shot. I saw spots and smelled Marilyn's bedroom. I counted off sixty seconds and pulled out the print.

I overpacked for this gig. Gunpowder wicks and drills for the dope-safe ruse. My portable tape rig. The off chance I'd need to record on the spot.

The rig paid off. I felt like a taste now. I cracked the alleyway door at 1:59. It was 2:46 now. I could duplicate the tape on the premises. I could random skim and groove the gist now.

I slid the tape out of the box and spooled it on my rig. I kept the volume soft-murmur low. Marilyn said, "You make such good martinis." Greenson said, "It's not a skill I possess. My housekeeper whips them up." I goosed the volume. I pushed FORWARD/STOP/FORWARD and skimmed ahead on whim.

I caught Monroe in free-form monologue. It was all stale film-biz tattle. The reel spooled halfway through. I caught eleven "Jack betrayed me" prompts. #11 ran straight into a Greenson tut-tut.

Marilyn giggled. Marilyn said, "Hey, he speaks."

Greenson went *tut-tut*. Marilyn brought her voice butch-baritone low.

"I've got ugly, slimy dirt on Jack. I was just getting to it when you cut me off. I go back fourteen years with Jack. I'll use that dirt if he goes back on his promises to me, and if you keep cutting in on me just when I get to the punch line, I'll find myself a shrink who'll cosign all my crazy and not very nice ideas, and I'll leave you in the lurch like I leave everyone who stands in my way or starts to bore me."

The tape clicked off. Monroe's Jackalogue jazzed me. Baby, you closed strong.

11

"The job," "the gig," "the deal." We're right at two months in. It's late-spring hot in L.A. Long-term surveillance jobs are wear items. This one's started to fray.

I bailed on the Fox lot. Roving personnel ID'd me and my guys, for sure. Ex-deputy Phil Irwin ran into ex–Sheriff's lieutenant Del Kinney. It was smack upside Soundstage #14.

Kinney left the Sheriff's and gigged the State Beverage Control. He's now the Fox security boss. He shares spit with Jimmy H., the Aadland brothers, and kindred craft-union creeps. Kinney and Phil shot the breeze. Kinney might have detected our on-the-lot presence from the gate. Hoffa might have told him and bought us an impunity waiver. Kinney vibed breach. I pulled my boys off the lot.

It was prescient. Fox sacked Marilyn from *Got to Give*, 6/4/62. Studio flacks cited her "spectacular absenteeism" and "willful violation of contract." Zanuck and his high-command corps were browned off. They wanted to release *Got to Give* at Christmas and plug their *Cleopatra* cash drain. *"Marilyn Fired!"* scorched the tabloid news. TV camera trucks bottlenecked Fifth Helena. They derailed my static surveillance shifts. I suspended them. I forfeited all eyeball access. The job was down to bugs and taps, over and out.

Marilyn was a wear item. She'd worn out Jack and Bobby K. They blew her off. Jimmy Hoffa's goal of a tittle-tattle squeeze played like a wilted wet dream. Marilyn played Marilyn, all day every day. Her exotic eccentricities held me and hinted at a secret life within her life of sloth and minor misalliance. Her obese-girl wardrobe. Her pay-phone calls. The forty grand under her bed. That non sequitur jaunt to the Valley, 5/19/62. My DMV guy and his plate check on 143 sleds. That tape I played at Ralph Greenson's office. Marilyn's purported dirt on Jack the K and their alleged late-'40s convergence. Her annotated Paul de River book. She threatens Greenson. "I'll find a shrink who'll cosign all my crazy and not very nice ideas."

We're down to wiretaps and monitor-shift overlaps. My three posts still run twenty-four hours. I cruise the Brentwood and Sip 'n' Surf posts once a day and read through the tap-log transcriptions. They reveal zilch per the exiled Marilyn and exilers Jack and Bobby. I *live* at the bluffside post. It gives me candid home movies of Pat.

She walks her dog. She drives her kids to school. She rotates the crew-neck sweaters and saddle shoes I saw in her closet. I saw her wash her Bonneville ragtop. Her ridgeback capered in sudsy water.

I savored her phone calls. I caught them live and replayed them. I memorized her inflections. She never talked about me. That was no surprise. I wondered who she told about us. She wouldn't tell her dipshit hubby or Jack. She might tell Bobby. She wouldn't tell her sisters. She certainly told God and sought out means of atonement.

She coffee-klatched with sisters Jean and Eunice, long-distance. She excoriated Peter and critiqued his compulsive infidelities. Peter, the sloppy drunk. Peter's temper tantrums and fawning allegiance to Jack. "He married my family. He didn't marry me. He bought himself a second-hand bloodline. He'll always be a second-class citizen."

Lawford's calls out and calls in ran innocuous. He called agents and studio geeks. They called him. The Lawford house was bedlam. Kids ran through and grabbed phone extensions. They eavesdropped and tee-heed. Lawford indulgently rebuffed them. He yanked his bedside-phone cord while he slept. He made clandestine calls from the 76 station on PCH.

I foot-tailed him three times. He kept the phone booth door cracked for air. He consulted an address book and deployed his *"ooooh, baby"* voice. His pay-phone stints played obvious. Monroe's pay-phone stints played devious.

The summer loomed hot. Monroe holed up at Fifth Helena. It deterred newshounds out to exploit her Fox-lot antics and expulsion from *Got to Give.* The housekeeper came and went. Pizza Dave failed to show. Nat, Phil, and Robbie spot-cruised by on whim and took note. News vehicles crammed the street, straight down to Carmelina. I pulled my static surveillance, right on cue.

Robbie spot-cruised Jeanne Carmen's place. The pill-party cars never showed. Monroe hid out at home. The press hounded her. I sensed her life contracting. I worked the golf course post and tracked her calls out. She called Doc Greenson, Roddy McDowall, and Lowell Farr.

Greenson withstood monologues and went *tut-tut*. Marilyn mewed discontent: Jackie's frigid. Jack's entrapping Playboy bunnies now. I've nixed threeways umpteen times. Her Jack-and-Bobby bile runs the full fifty minutes. Long pauses induce line blur. Greenson's too bored to talk. I hear Marilyn chew ice cubes and slurp liquid. She's slamming Smirnoff 100 from 10:00 a.m. on.

Roddy McDowall engaged her and got her cranked up past self-pity. He dispensed schadenfreude and tales of Fox in duress. *Cleo* drains Fox. Roddy exploits the drain and rewrites Fox as Smut City. It's his vengeance for cuts in his *Cleo* role and no Oscar bid. Marilyn listens. Roddy's smut spoof of *Cleo—oooh-la-la*.

"Heads will *turn*, love. Just you wait and see." Marilyn, in her shock-the-world guise:

"I'd love to be in a fuck flick, if only good-looking, high-class people saw it, and it wouldn't louse up my career. I'd *die* if some fat Shriner saw me screwing and yanked his crank while he watched."

Wiretaps. Heard live, replayed, transcribed. The bug-and-tap job of a lifetime. And I've got the Wiretap Blues.

The detail work numbed me. I boozed and popped pills to stay fortified. Monroe's particular weirdness hinted at *something*. Her day-to-day indolence subsumed it. I felt unraveled. I kept losing details. I woke up in listening posts and didn't know how I got there. I might have to take the cure and steam-clean myself soon.

Monroe's got a late-call thing going with Lowell Farr. She gets the kid all gaga most midnights. Monroe listens more than she talks. Lowell reveals the kooky customs of the Pali High class of '63.

The big new thing? It's the prearranged makeout date. They transpire during weekend double features at the Bay. They're prearranged but anonymous. You know the boys from school. It's a nice kid's version of going to a motel. Girls' names and boys' names are dropped in a hat. You never know who you get. The kids are preselected. All porkers, uglies, and zit-faced kids are verboten. Lowell's had three dates, so far. She sort of remembers *The World of Suzie Wong* and *Gidget Goes Hawaiian*. Her friend Marcy supplies her with crib sheets to con her mom and dad.

Night owl Marilyn. Night owl Lowell. Night owl Pat tends to stay up late-*late*. I'd split the golf course post and roll to the bluffside post. Pat makes her night-shift calls up to 2:00 a.m. She calls her women friends and cuts loose on her limp-dick husband.

His drunkenness. His dope and girl habits. The "Girl Book" he keeps for President Jack's perusal. Nude shots of "wild and woolly" stewardesses. Samples of their wool taped to the pages.

"We're having a catered party on the fifteenth. Peter will be all over the waitresses. It's his well-established MO."

It's been almost seventeen years. Why not? That beach party sounds like a gas.

12

High-style Freddy makes the scene. Dig my dupioni silk blazer and pink linen shirt. Note the white buck shoes. Note my Facel Vega rent-a-car at the valet stand. Peter Lawford owns one just like it. Fuck him sideways.

It was balmy working on crisp. Six college boys shagged cars off the PCH embankment. Guests lingered outside. I made studio types and Mayor Sam Yorty's chief deputy. Nobody made me.

Peter and Pat were inside somewhere. Pat and party crasher Freddy. She'll register shock. She'll sigh or boot my ass out on the street.

I scoped arrivals. Neighbors walked up. Big-ticket sedans disgorged westside swells. Monroe might show. I'd make book on it. A green VDub pulled up. Jeanne Carmen got out. She wore a summer shift and sandals. The driver got out. She had a butch-girl haircut and wore a hula shirt and twill slacks. I saw golf clubs crammed in the backseat.

I recalled *this:*

Something Phil Irwin said. Jeanne as current or ex–Sheriff's snitch. Plus her pill-party chum—a lezzie golf pro.

They waltzed inside. They vibed item. Ex-deputy Phil. He's working the Sip 'n' Surf post tonight. He might have the fill-in.

Party crasher Freddy. Don't be a chickenshit. You've got a right to be—

I walked in. The foyer and living room were half packed. I knew the floor plan. Come *on*—I hot-wired the place!

It helped me maneuver. I dodged eye contact. Pat would magnetize me. I didn't want that.

The downstairs den. It's off the north-side beachfront. It's dusty and underutilized. I'd tapped the phone there.

I hugged the north-side wall and dodged cater waitresses schlepping canapés and drinks. I kept my head low and made the door. I cranked the knob and let myself in.

The room was lights-off dark. A window overlooked the beach. Hawaiian torches lit clumps of people. I got out my penlight and flashed the phone extension. I risked a five-minute call.

I locked myself in and dialed the Sip 'n' Surf post. I said, "Phil, it's me."

Phil picked up. "Yeah, and at the party no less. Monroe might be there. Nat worked the golf course post this morning. She told Doc Greenson she might drop by."

I said, "Jeanne Carmen's here. Her date's a young lez with a green VDub. There were golf clubs in the backseat. You told me—"

Phil cut in. "Deedee Grenier. It's got to be—"

I cut back in. "Is Jeanne still snitching for the Sher—"

"Whoa, Freddy. Slow down. She's strictly ex. She used to rat pill pushers to Narco, to buy out of her own busts. But she paid off her debt to her handler, so she's out of the whole snitch deal. But, Deedee's snitching to the Sheriff's now, for money, because there's no real bread on the women's golf tour. And she's always at Jeanne's pill parties—so she has to know Monroe, and Deedee is *nothing* but dirty."

I said, "Dirty, how?"

Phil said, "She runs badger games on small-time businessmen. She works out of Norm's Nest, which is a bumfuck cocktail lounge up in bumfuck Van Nuys. The owner's an ex-LAPD man named Norm Krause. He was on the PD from something like '46 to '59, and he was allegedly some sort of extortionist. Anyway, he quits the PD, gets a liquor license, and opens up the Nest. Now, you want the kicker? Deedee's enforcer in the badger-game deals, playing the role of the irate *husband*, is her real-life *brother*, Paul Mitchell Grenier. He's a bit actor at Fox, he did Chino time, and he's your classic mean-queen type."

I kicked it around. Phil held the line. Ambient pier noise garbled up his end. I said, "Dig up rap sheets and/or internal memoranda on Krause and the Greniers," and hung up.

Garbled party noise hit me. Samba music and voice overlap. I cracked the door and looked out. The bash rocked loud now. The hi-fi and chatter cliques sent up a roar. I looked through the kitchen and back hallway. A cater waitress lugged coats toward the rear storage-room door.

Makeshift cloakroom. It had to be. The dish starts *there*.

The waitress opened the door and dropped the coats on a ratty day-bed. Other coats and a pile of handbags had been dumped there. I had a clear shot through the kitchen. I stepped out and beelined straight in.

I tossed the bolt and propped a chair against the door. I exit-marked a beachside window and jammed up the sill. I worked by penlight. I inventoried nine women's coats and wraps and thirteen handbags.

Purse debris. Don't get distracted. Don't let female scents sidetrack you. Go for wallets and driver's license ID. Look for pocket address books.

I sat on the bed and rifled handbags. I clawed through cosmetics, cigarette packs, house keys, lucky charms. I smelled individual and aggregate women. I grabbed wallets and scanned photo sleeves. I orbed laminate licenses, pix of kids and hubbies, little books with innocuous names scrawled. I went through six handbags in fourteen minutes. I hit a black leather job with crossed-golf-club stitchwork—it had to be her.

Let's give it three minutes. Be thorough. Imprint what you see.

Chesterfields. A matchbook for Linda's Little Log Cabin. A Rancho Park scorecard, 12/4/58. Deedee shoots a 2-under-par 68. A Lanvin atomizer, half-full. I spritzed my pocket square and inhaled Deedee's musk.

A red leather wallet. Six transparent pocket sleeves. They contain *this:*

Deedee's driver's license. Pix of Jeanne Carmen, the Linda's Little Log Cabin softball team, a nudie pic of Lila Leeds.

A red leather address book. Pocket size. Let's savor this slow.

Deedee block-printed. She jotted phone numbers exclusive. She went alphabetical. The book ran "Annie" to "Zohra." Deedee's a sapphic sister. She's a grifter. She's circumspect. She gives nothing up. She lists only women's first names.

I recognized "Barbara's" number. As in Barbara Payton. She was an ex–film presence and part-time grifter. We went way back. "Jeanne's" number was Jeanne Carmen's number. I recognized "Lila's" number. Who else *but?*—Lila Leeds, the bait girl supreme.

I riffed to the *M*'s. They hopped "Margo" to "Melinda." They bypassed "Marilyn" and her Gladstone exchange.

My brain clock buzzed, my toss time elapsed, I smelled Deedee Grenier all over me. "Annie" to "Zohra"—that's it.

I repacked the handbag. I replaced the items in perfect order. I laid the wallet on top. I saw a paper scrap wadded into a photo sleeve.

I pulled it out. Deedee had block-printed four phone numbers. They seemed familiar. They were all GL prefix. My brain waves meshed and kicked out an imprint.

Pay phones. Barrington Park and Beverly Glen Park. The phones Marilyn Monroe used. In her big-girl disguises. On her Mata Hari kick.

I heard footsteps outside the cloakroom. I slid the chair aside and the dead bolt back and vaulted out the window. I tumbled onto hard-packed sand.

My pulse raced. I felt weavy and punchy. I brushed myself off and stumbled over to the south-side footpath. I lit a cigarette and ambled back to the valet-park stand. Neighbor guests walked up. I joined them and *re*-crashed the party.

The head count ran ninety plus. The living room overflow flowed up the two stairwells and packed the poolside deck. Three downstairs Portabars served up booze. I squeezed over to the bar by the north stairwell. The cater waiters did overflow biz. I scanned the room and didn't see Pat. I *re*-scanned the room and didn't see Marilyn. My wig felt loose. I scanned the room and tallied fourteen bug-mount locations. It resettled me. I pictured Phil at the Sip 'n' Surf. His bug-feed reception would play high-decibel loud.

Familiar faces bipped by. I matched their pedigrees. There's that TV actor. He threatened to sue *Confidential*. I kicked his ass outside Dale's Secret Harbor. A guy recognized me. He flipped me the bird and bipped off. I went *Huh?* I didn't know who he was or what I did to him.

The booze line inched forward. I looked around for Lois. My brain glitched and *un*glitched. Lois didn't know this crowd. Lois lived in New York.

A cater waiter smiled at me. I stuffed a fifty in his vest pocket and pointed to a highball glass and his sour-mash jug. He got the picture and filled the glass. He pointed to a wingback chair beside a wall credenza. I eased myself over and sat down.

Body heat and talk overlap. It fucking deluged me. I smelled Deedee Grenier's crazy life all around me. I guzzled half the glass and lulled the volume way down. I got an urge to take the Deedee lead and cut and run. I got a counterurge to hold on for Pat.

Peter Lawford saw me. I caught it, full-on. I watched him walk over. He was flush-faced and half in the bag. I stood up. Lawford stepped in, too close. He ran a cheap-shot number upside my face.

Who'd you steal that coat from, Freddy? Put the screws to any closet queens lately? Dope any racehorses while you were at it?

I went *boo!* Lawford turned tail. I sat back down and sipped my monster drink. I caught stray chatter. It was flatline consistent. *Marilyn was fired/oh, God—Cleopatra—can you BELIEVE?*

My pulse decelerated. The room temperature dropped. The high-volume talk leveled into a hum. Eddie Fisher and Bo Belinsky walked in. They didn't see me. The partygoers saw them.

They entered big. They constellated the crowd. Women swooned for Bo. They darted up and squeezed his left bicep. Their husbands ballyhooed his recent no-hitter. Party fools chanted, *"We hate Liz!"* Eddie yelled, *"Liz who?"* Fools whistled, cheered, and spilled drinks.

I sipped sour mash and made memory imprints. Peter Lawford hounds cater waitresses. Mayor Sam Yorty, coma-conked in a leprechaun hat. A starlet with a squirt gun filled with crème de menthe. She's telling people, "Open wide."

The party thinned out. I had a straight view of the pool deck. Here's an all-time imprint.

Deedee Grenier chips golf balls into the swimming pool. She aims at a floating Hula-Hoop and puts most of them inside. Three Lawford kids watch. They giggle and squeal.

"I can't believe you're still alive, and that you had the balls to show up here."

The madras shift, the saddle shoes, the too-big man's watch. Don't touch up that new gray hair—I won't let you.

We dragged deck chairs down to the wave line and kicked off our shoes. Pat brought a bottle of Pernod. We kept still more than we talked. I glanced back at the party and saw things.

Marilyn Monroe's late arrival. Bo Belinsky swarmed by horny wives. Peter Lawford as the big bad wolf. He's pie-eyed and stumbly. Cater waitresses elude his grasp.

Pat said, "My Christmas cards weren't enough. The brevity of the encounter failed to deter you. The services you provided my brother seem not to embarrass you. You display not one whiff of deference, given what the man has become."

I lit a cigarette. Pat lit up out of my pack. Propane torches flanked the pool deck. A breeze fanned orange light our way.

"I'm happy for you, for Jack, and for that other brother I met a few times, the one who always scowled at me. I was driving by, and I saw all the cars pulling up. I thought, Come on. The worst she can do is bounce you or call the cops."

"You're saying there's nothing more to it than that?"

I said, "That's right."

Pat said, "I don't believe you."

I said, "Don't put the skids to this too fast. It's late, and the party's boring you, and you'd have sent me home if you didn't have some half-assed urge to talk."

Pat tossed her cigarette. "I met a handsome young Marine, and what happened happened. The handsome young Marine became a police-man, and by all accounts a crooked detective. You're right. It's late, the party's a bore, and I have more than a 'half-assed' urge to talk—but I only have one question."

I sipped Pernod. It burned going down.

"I know the question. It's 'How can you do what you do?' The answer is 'I like poking around in people's shit and making money.'"

Pat laughed. "Have you kept my Christmas cards?"

I said, "Yeah, but I always x out your husband's picture, and I always spend a lot of time looking at you in your Christmas threads and won-dering what's kicking around in your head."

Pat nudged me, leg-to-leg. *"So?"*

I nudged her back. "So, you're bored, and vexed. There's all of it—your family, the world crawling up your ass because your brother's what he is, your shoddy marriage, the whole deal. I read people. It's what I do. The woman in the '58 and '59 cards is not the woman in the card I got last Christmas. You're kicking around inside your own head because it's the only place you can be alone and feel safe."

Pat tapped my knee. "You're right. It's all too much. Just don't pro-pose yourself as a solution, because that's a line I won't cross."

I said, "You'll leave Peter the moment Jack's reelected."

Pat said, "I told him that very thing, just last week."

13

Homework. Nightwork. Unamphetamized and boozed. It's late clerk duty. It's nothing more than that.

I typed a week's worth of tap transcripts and a 6/16 to 6/21 summary. I ripped off the cover of the current *Life* magazine and pinned it to my pictorial corkboard. There's the quasi-nude Monroe. She's got wet hair and one leg hooked on a swimming pool ledge. I pinned Robbie Molette's on-the-sly nude beside it. The *Life* pix were a worldwide sensation. Robbie's pic scorched the L.A. underground. It's a steal at fifty bucks per.

The pictorial corkboard oozed Monroe. It featured the Polaroids from my 4/11 break-in. The dissolute bathroom and bedroom. The forty grand stashed in the lockbox. The jumbo-girl clothes. The coin stash. The lists of lovers and dope-dispensing physicians. The name-scrawled sheets of paper. Monroe's nutty screed stuck inside Paul de River's nutty book.

The adjacent corkboard featured the week's random notes. I unpinned them and typed them into bullet-point briefs.

I started with Pat's emphatic assertion: Jack and Marilyn coupled a half dozen times, from '54 up to now. They were abbreviated assignations. Always conducted in neutral locations. Calvinist Bobby wouldn't poke Marilyn with a long stick. Marilyn attended last week's Lawford-house do. I feigned interest in the Jack/Marilyn rumors. Pat supplied the above tattle. I dissembled my way to Pat's punch line: Marilyn and the K boys were now kaput. Pat said she encountered Marilyn at the Palisades Gelson's. Marilyn spun a tale of recurrent break-ins at her new pad. The burglar moved around various objects and left her weird-o notes. The burglar besieged her with breather calls. Pat cited Marilyn's "mystery intruder" on a prior tapped call. I've got Marilyn dialed. The "mystery intruder" was Monroe fantasia.

I used Pat to get this information. The big reunion went down. I exploited Pat for dish to levy against her big brother. It felt ghastly. I did it anyway.

I bullet-pointed the week's legwork. That paper slip in Deedee Grenier's wallet supplied a solid lead. She'd jotted pay-phone numbers for Barrington and Beverly Glen parks. I spot-surveilled the two locations, all week. Monroe failed to show. The phones never rang. Nobody called out on them.

Legwork to brainwork. I contemplated another Monroe house B and E. The housekeeper's intermittent presence and Monroe's persistent presence deterred me. I contemplated rousting Paul de River. His sex-crime book. Monroe's florid note stuck inside it. She extolled heavy shit. Let's *contravene passive and reactive behavior with direct criminal action.* I nixed the roust. A de River approach was imprudent. De River was too volatile.

Brainwork to static surveillance. I put Norm's Nest under the spotlight. It was a dingy cheater bar in north Van Nuys. I installed Robbie there. He's the inside man. I'm too well known to work an ex-cop-owned joint.

I hovered outside. Robbie worked inside. Deedee Grenier and her brother Paul Mitchell no-showed. No badger games went down. No other badger-game women appeared.

Phil Irwin glommed Sheriff's green sheets on Deedee and Paul Mitchell. Here's the gist:

Deedee Montfort Grenier/WFA/DOB 8/8/29. Lezzie bar rousts: '56, '58, '61. Paul Mitchell Grenier/WMA/DOB 1/23/26. Six busts for possession of maryjane/no convictions. One stat-rape conviction, 6/54. Three years at Chino. Subsequent fruit roller busts/no convictions. Bit player at 20th Century–Fox, rumored smut-film artiste. 6:00 a.m. to 2:00 a.m. surveillance of Norm's Nest continues.

I bullet-pointed the above. I typed in a Monroe/Lowell Farr conversation.

Tuesday, 6/19/62. I boom-miked a backyard koffee klatch. Marilyn and Lowell dished the dish.

Lowell harped on her makeout dates at the Bay Theater. She said she had one penciled in for tomorrow night. I peeped said date. Lowell cuddled a tall boy with a jumbo pompadour. I sat through half of

The Man Who Shot Liberty Valance. The kids made out and eschewed conversation. No Monroe leads resulted. I split for the bluffside post. I caught Pat's midnight dog walk. Pat wore her pink crewneck sweater and scuffed saddle shoes.

I rolled in a fresh sheet of paper. Nat Denkins left me a tape spool marked *URGENT.* He recorded it live at 2:00 a.m. today. Nat speaks Spanish. A Baja operator put the call through. The caller's name was José Bolaños. Nat grabbed our Baja reverse directory and looked him up. Bolaños lived on Calle Hueracho in Ensenada.

I slipped the spool on my tape rig and pressed START. I put on my headphones and hunched over my typewriter. I transcribed as Monroe and this unknown cholo jive-talked.

JB: "I will not soon forget, darling. Winter Storm Lucita and Winter Storm Marilyn."

MM: "Yes, but I was traveling incognito."

They spoke languid. Monroe was half-lubed. I typed fast and kept up.

JB: "I've forgotten the name you employed. I intend to recall you always as 'Marilyn,' as many lesser men than I have."

MM: "I travel incognito when we work together. I'm a business-woman in disguise."

JB: "You have a capacity for business that I did not deem possible in a woman of your station."

MM: "Well, I'm Winter Storm Marilyn, so what did you expect?"

Winter Storm Lucita. It raked Baja in mid-February. I could buzz U.S. Customs. They could run visa checks.

JB: "What is that noise you are making? It sounds like slurping."

MM: "I buy cherry sno-cones at Wil Wright's and refreeze them. Then I douse them with vodka and green Chartreuse. It's kicks and grins, baby. Like you, and like moving freight for you."

"Freight." "Freight" as dope synonym. "Traveling incognito."

JB: "Speak discreetly, *mi corazón.* Our relationship is not all kicks and grins, and I am as much '*Señor* Bolaños' as I am 'baby.'"

MM: "Don't be a drag. It's two in the morning, and I'm slurping a sno-cone."

JB: "Phone taps, my darling. The L.A. police are known to tap the telephones of enlightened people in the film colony."

MM: "They're in Dutch now with the press, I have to say. They shot two Black Muslims, a couple of months ago. One guy was really cute, like Harry Belafonte. My cleaning lady said he played the bongo drums.

She's a Negro, so she's hep to what's happening with her people. And Chief Parker's a souse. That's a well-known fact."

JB: "You should invite him over for a relaxing sno-cone."

MM: "You're funny."

JB: "Not when it comes to fascistos like Parker."

MM: "Whoa, baby, whoa. Don't get so het up. I'm getting a nice drift off my sno-cone, and you're messing with it."

JB: "I am a businessman, as well as a Marxist-Leninist. Men such as I despise indecorous women."

MM: "'Businessman,' huh? I'll be generous and let it go as 'freight mover,' but that's just a euphemism."

JB: "Marilyn, you wound me."

MM: "The fascistos are a yawn. And I've tattled the LAPD to Jack and Bobby Kennedy, *mucho* times."

JB: "Marilyn, you are a fantasist and a name-dropper, nonpareil."

MM: "You'll change your tone when Jack divorces Jackie and marries me."

JB: "Marilyn, you are delusional."

MM: "Look who's talking. Look who'll be left holding the bag, if and when I put the screws to Jack Kennedy."

JB: "Jack and Bobby are genteel fascistos. Believe me, I know."

MM: "I like you when we plan our visits, and you do your Latin-lover routine. Otherwise, you wear me thin. Okay, José? That's just a word to the wise."

JB: "You are the world's number-one woman, and still you exasperate."

MM: "I'm just an overhyped movie star who wishes she was something else. You dig? I lick sno-cones and talk to strange men at two in the morning."

The long-distance feed severed. Loose tape flapped off the spindle. I hit the kill switch and doused the machine.

Phil Irwin knew a Customs guy. He could check travel visas and passenger lists. Winter Storms Lucita and Marilyn. Mid-February. It was a solid lead. We might score some good—

My work phone rang. I grabbed it and got "Yes?" out. Robbie Molette overrode me.

"I'm outside the Nest. Deedee Grenier's working a mark inside, and Paul Mitchell's in the tail car, down the block."

———

The North Valley. Shitkicker pads and juke joints. Machine shops and discount bottle stores. Vacant lots clumped with sagebrush and scrounging coyote packs.

Norm's Nest. A prefab Alamo, built to scale. Sandblasted adobe drilled with mock bullet holes and dribbled with mock blood. The façade was sign-plastered. FREEDOM ISN'T FREE, AMERICAN SPOKEN HERE, ORVAL FAUBUS FOR PRESIDENT. The Nest sat beside a disused Christmas-tree lot. It now thrived as a bomb-shelter lot.

Robbie and Phil stood outside. I parked down the block and walked up. Phil said, "Deedee's inside. She's got a mark, shit-faced and nothing but horny. Her brother's parked across the street, down near the corner. That blue Ford's the tail car. Deedee left her VDub in the lot."

I opened the door and peeped the room. Bar/Naugahyde booths/small dance floor. Remember the Alamo wall art.

TV show stills. Fess Parker as Davy Crockett. Raggedy-ass cowpokes and Mexicans piled dead. Three booths down: Deedee Grenier and a fat guy in a western-style suit.

I shut the door. Robbie said, "His Pontiac's parked next to Deedee's roadster. Deedee's been trying to move him out for a good half hour."

Phil passed his flask. We took triple pops. I said, "We'll jump them at the cars. Robbie, you run the mark off. I'll dump the brother."

The lot was dark-dark. We passed the flask and hunkered near the car slots. 1:00 a.m. came and went. Drunks straggled up. They snagged their sleds and peeled dirt. The lot thinned out. We're getting close. The Nest shuts down at 2:00.

We waited. We drained the flask. 2:00 a.m. came and went. We pawed the dirt. 2:01, 2:02, 2:04. That's *it*—the door *slams* shut.

I heard *oooh, baby* coos. Deedee drape-walked the mark toward the car slots. She held him up. He was far-gone blitzed. He hummed some Spade Cooley lament.

He fumbled his car keys. Deedee hovered close. Shadows covered us. I cued up the swoop.

One, two, three—

Phil and I ran up and grabbed Deedee. Robbie grabbed the mark and frog-marched him off. He went drunk-compliant. I hand-muzzled Deedee. I said, "We're friends of Jeanne's. It's a grand for an hour's talk."

Deedee kicked dirt and squirmed and made *yes* nods. Robbie and Phil rifled the mark's pockets and tossed his car keys into some weeds. He staggered off, zonko. He set out for the Alamo or the Planet Mars.

Deedee went *Shit* and *Shitfuck*. Robbie baby-talked her. I pulled my belt sap and ran straight at Paul Mitchell's old Ford.

Brother-hubby hit his high beams and lit me up bright. I blinked away the glare. He piled out and came straight at me.

He was big and lean. He threw haymakers. I got inside him and launched sap shots. I smashed his nose. He screeched. The sap stitches severed an earlobe and cut through his lips down to his teeth. I sapped his knees and put him prone in the gutter. He slithered under his car. I grabbed his legs and pulled him out and kicked his nards raw.

We two-car schlepped to Ollie Hammond's. Phil drove solo. I drove Deedee. She kept it zipped. She put out zero boo-hoo per her shit-kicked brother.

Ollie's was near dead. Robbie split to work the Sip 'n' Surf post. The maître d' set us up with a back room and after-hours liquor. Deedee was a Sheriff's informant. I crowned her Snitch Queen for a Day.

The queen and her court. Waiters brought refreshments. A pitcher of Old Crow highballs, steak skewers, fried shrimp. I laid ten C-notes on the table. Deedee lit a cigarette and snatched them up. I said, "It's about Marilyn Monroe. That's all you need to know."

Deedee blew smoke rings. "I know Marilyn. We share a history. Not much of one, but still."

I twirled my ashtray. "I'll get to her. We've got some lead-in questions first."

Phil sipped his highball. "Why do you and Paul Mitchell badger out of the Nest?"

Deedee laughed. "In a nutshell, Norm Krause. He's in The Life. He's tight with zillions of grifters and bent cops. He got fat off an ad-lib extortion deal, back in '49. Freddy here was Mr. *Confidential*. I'll bet he knows the story."

I said, "Try me."

"Norm was a motor cop then. He was working Wilshire Division, and he caught the state comptroller, Tom Kuchel, blowing a poof in a parked car off of 6th and Cloverdale. He arrested them, but Kuchel and the poof bailed out. Old Chief Worton hushed the deal up, but Norm *still* had the balls to extort Kuchel, and Kuchel *lacked* balls and paid big. That's it, in a nutshell. It's how Norm got the seed money for the Nest. He quit the PD around '59, and now he just lives off the Nest."

I downed half my drink. "Let's see if I've got this straight. It's a cheater bar. It caters to married folks looking for strange. They couple up there, they continue to socialize there. Krause refers them to hot-sheet motels and takes a cut. If the cheaters want pills, or maryjane, or weekends in Baja, Krause refers them."

Deedee said, "On the money."

I said, "The drift is that you snitch for the L.A. Sheriff's. If so, did Jeanne Carmen pass the gig on to you?"

Deedee sipped her highball. "Yes, I talk to the Sheriff's. Yes, Jeanne got me the gig. No, I will not reveal the name of my handler."

Phil speared a shrimp. "What specific division are you in touch with?"

"The West Hollywood squadroom guys, because those fools drool for gay dirt and dope tips. And I'm sure the squadroom guys share their dish with SHIT."

I popped two Dexedrine. "Does SHIT keep a dirt file on Marilyn Monroe?"

Deedee went *Gimme*. I tossed two dexies on her placemat. She chased them with highball dregs.

"No, SHIT does not keep a Marilyn file, because Marilyn has been known to lay her goodies on Pete Pitchess, once in a blue moon. LAPD Intel *does* keep files on Marilyn—and I got that from Marilyn herself."

I lit a cigarette. "Lay out the SHIT versus LAPD Intel deal. I sense a rivalry here."

Deedee blew concentric rings. "LAPD Intel is fully self-contained. SHIT is heavily in league with the FBI because Pitchess is an ex-agent, and he's rumored to be old man Hoover's choice to succeed him if the Kennedys give him his pink slip."

Deedee gives good dish. The Hoover/Pitchess dish confirmed persistent rumors.

"Keep going on that."

"LAPD Intel has got Marilyn files and surveillance footage up the ying-yang. Sometimes, Intel and SHIT have actual bidding wars and favor trades for documents and political rat-outs. A lieutenant named Daryl Gates represents the unit. Jim Hamilton's old and sick, and Gates is slated to take over when he retires or kicks off. A sergeant named Mike Bayless represents SHIT. He's called 'Motel Mike' because he torched some Mexicans at an eastside motel about six thousand years ago."

Motel Mike in a nutshell. Deedee was good. She rubbed her brush cut and cracked her thumbs. She was wired for sound and snitch-frenzied.

"Intel and SHIT have got half of freak-o, Commo, gay, and weird-o L.A. hot-wired and filmed. Bill Parker's got Sam Yorty in his pocket, because Mayor Sam digs threeways with lezzie girls, and Parker's got evidence. I've tricked with Mayor Sammy myself."

I brain-strained it. Dirt wars were my métier. I knew good dirt inside out.

"Why would Monroe have the main Sheriff's switchboard number written down on a scrap of paper, at her place?"

Deedee yocked. "Because she's got to schedule her next blow job with Pete Pitchess?"

Phil yocked. "Is Motel Mike your handler?"

"No, but he took my cherry a zillion years ago, and it pushed me toward girls in a very large way."

I yocked. "Current L.A. cops. Who does Norm Krause fraternize with?"

Deedee chained cigarettes. "Norm's a right-wing nut. He's tight with a West L.A. Division patrol sergeant named Jack Clemmons, and a nut pamphleteer named Frank Capell, who lives back east somewhere. They're all big pud yankers and boozehounds. They're members of some fringe group called the White Dog Bund, which probably has a total membership of three. Norm gave me a Bund armband. Marilyn tried it on once. It gave all the pill-party girls a laugh."

Phil laughed. I laughed. Phil went *Gimme*. I tossed two dexies on his place mat. He chugged them with coffee.

"You haven't asked Freddy or me who's behind all this. As in 'Who's the one with the money and the big curiosity about Marilyn and all her unhinged shit?'"

Deedee went *Nix*. "No, and I'm not going to. Freddy's a well-known bird dog for Bill Parker, but Freddy knows next to nothing about LAPD Intel and SHIT, so that rules Parker out. This is one of those deals where a girl is better off left in the dark."

I sipped my highball. "How did you meet Marilyn?"

"I met her through Paul Mitchell, way back when. They were in Holly-grove together. You know, that orphans' home, off of Waring and Vine. That was something like '35 to '38. I was a very little kid when they met, so I went to foster care when our parents ditched us, and Paul Mitchell went to the Grove, because he was Marilyn's age. She and Paul Mitchell still connect once in a while on the Fox lot, because Paul Mitchell gets bit parts and does grip work there. I got dumped in the Grove in '41, and I met Marilyn when she'd show up at alumnae meetings, during the war. And, for what it's worth, I used to run into Marilyn in the late '40s, when I played golf at Cal State and she was a quasi-starlet and call girl about town."

I said, "Why would Marilyn have forty grand in a lockbox stashed under her bed?"

Deedee made the jack-off sign. "Don't jerk my chain. Marilyn is *incapable* of hoarding that kind of money. She gets bank drafts through her agent and has a manager who writes all her checks and pays all her bills. She's in hock to half the quack doctors, shrinks, and pharmacies on the west side."

"A Mexican Communist named José Bolaños. Ring any bells?"

Deedee reprised the jack-off sign. She reprised it *two*-handed.

"Listen. Marilyn talks red and goes to Commie demonstrations, and she beats the drum for civil rights and all that jive—but she is nothing but a scene maker, as well as being *the* fantasist and premier bullshit artist of our time. That girl cannot stop lying. Who's José Bolaños? I don't know—but Marilyn *has* been making up fantastical Mexico stories for months, like she's been going in and out, disguised as a farmworker. If Marilyn ever set foot in Mexico, it's to score dope in the legal pharmacics in TJ. *Comprende, muchacho?*"

Sí, yo comprende. But—

The plus-size garb in Marilyn's closet. The disguises she wears to—

"I rifled your purse at the Lawford party. You had numbers for the pay phones in Barrington Park and Beverly Glen Park. Were you calling Marilyn there?"

Deedee flipped me off. "You're a pal, Freddy. You rifle my purse, then you kick the shit out of my brother."

"Deedee, come on."

"The answer is no. Marilyn force-fed me those numbers. It was all part of some fantastical intrigue number she was running on me. For the record, Marilyn almost never gives out her home number. Get it? Don't call me, I'll call you. Get it? She's the pathetic waif of all time, but she exerts total control over her gal pals, and she only *really* rolls over for celebs and pump jockeys and the guys who write her dope scripts."

I said, "A shrink named Paul de River?"

Deedee chained cigarettes. "Not a name I know."

"A shrink named Ralph Greenson?"

Deedee whooped. "Aka Marilyn's fool, slave, master, and psychiatrist in pursuit. Marilyn thinks he slams the ham while he listens to the tapes of their sessions. Marilyn likes Greenson—but she doesn't respect him—because he's not radical enough for her. He's a pill source and a soft shoulder to cry on, but there's no ethical boundaries in this deal. Would you belt martinis with your shrink?"

Headshrinkers. Conventional to radical. Marilyn studies and interprets Paul de River. Marilyn to Greenson: "I'll find myself a shrink who'll cosign all my crazy and not very nice ideas."

I brain-waved Deedee's shrink pitch. Greenson/de River/de River's specious criminalistics.

"Deedee, is Marilyn fixated on crime and criminals, and the whole criminal mind-set?"

Deedee went *Yup.* "She is. I mean, she and Jeanne worked call jobs after the war, and she must have known that type then, and she knows lots of people in The Life now, because half the grips and stuntmen and studio types are in The Life, in one form or another. Marilyn's been around Fox for years, and Fox and dickhead criminals go way back to the '30s. You've got Willie Bioff, Ben Siegel, Mickey Cohen's guys. Union guys like the Aadland brothers—smut peddlers, kidnap brokers, white slavers—fringe guys like that. It's Hollywood, baby. Everybody knows everybody—and they all brag about it."

I said, "Marilyn and the Kennedy brothers?"

Deedee said, "Unrequited love and delusion. Such despair. Jack pokes her at the Lawford place, when he's not running the world. She's got it just as bad for Bobby, but he considers her shopworn goods."

"Jack and other women?"

"Ask Peter Lawford. He keeps some so-called Girl Book that lays out potential stuff for the prez. Peter's Jack's chief pimp and dope supplier—which I heard you used to be."

I went *Ouch.* "Who told you that?"

"Pat Lawford. She also said you tripped the light fantastic together, back on V-J Day. She said she's never figured out if it was you or the historical moment."

Phil said, "You struck a nerve. Freddy's blushing."

Deedee said, "Maybe he's got a soul after all."

14

They're moving.

Wall wires, rug clamps, refitted phone jacks. They're changing colors and starting to fray. They're squirming. They're untangling out in plain view.

They wiggle. Bore holes leak Spackle. Discolored Spackle—alive with a glow. Tape drops from lamp bowls. Lamps topple and fall. Tap wires pop through handset perforations. Mike installations explode. They stain wallpaper metal-flake shades.

They're moving. They're pure combustion. They're out to set me aflame.

I opened my eyes. I recalibrated. The post was full dark now. I passed out in my work chair. Console blips are not tendrils. That's PCH out the window. That's Pat's beach spread just beyond.

I weaved to the bathroom and doused my face. I stepped on the scale. My weight clocked in at 174. My normal weight was 195. High-hoppers, booze, cigarettes. They caused the drop. Plus bad sleep or no sleep. Plus my all-candy-bar diet. My memory's in the shitter. My retention's in the tank. There's evidence threads I should remember—but don't.

It's the borderline DT's. I know the phenomenon and the solution. I should boil myself clean and jump-start the gig anew. L.A. featured luxe dry-out spots. Steam baths. Blood transfusions. Round-the-clock naps. Freddy O. takes the cure. I've done it twice before.

Let's resituate. Let's recalibrate. Pat's right across the street. Let's call up her glow.

I had a big fucking nightmare. Shrink your own head, dipshit. You just brain-screened a horror cartoon.

Here's the subtext:

You hot-wired Pat's home. Say she finds out. She'll hate you then. Fuck V-J Day. You're lower than snake shit. You blew your shot at some sort of reprise.

I crossed myself. I popped two dexies and gargled Old Crow. I lit a cigarette. Let's resituate and recalibrate. There's bum interior mounts at the Lawford house. They mandate quick attention. Line squelch spells that out plain. I need to get inside and rewire.

Post hoc ergo propter hoc. I show up at Pat's party. We rekindle or resizzle or re-something someplace good. The bum wires might buzz audible. That would tip Pat off. She detects the surveillance and knows that it's me.

The beach-view window stood open. I picked up my zoom-lens camera and scanned the house. The north-side door spilled light. Pat's ridgeback jumped out and pranced.

Pat followed. They turned toward the beach and cut off my sight line. Pat wore white tennis shorts and a pink polo shirt. I caught one half second—over and out.

Nightmares. Brain static. Booze-and-dope excess. Frayed neurons. Frayed wires at the Lawford digs. Long-term surveillance jobs are wear items. The gig was three months and six days in. It was running frayed into threadbare.

The K boys have abandoned Marilyn Monroe. There's no telephonic contact to or from. I've hopped gates and mailbox-skimmed Monroe's incoming and outgoing correspondence. There's no Kennedy mail or letters from Monroe's purported "burglar," "breather," and "dirty note writer." She gets studio mail, notes from Lowell Farr, and notes from ex-husbands DiMaggio and Miller. Monroe remains housebound. She only ventures out in big-girl disguise and only to make pay-phone calls. I braced a hinky PC Bell lineman. He told me pay phones cannot be tapped without judicial-district warrants. He added, "And don't think of trying to bribe me, because I'll call the cops."

I misplaced or lost the vehicle list I compiled on 5/19. It compounded my blown tail on Monroe. It scotched my shot to determine the purpose of her jaunt to the dogdick Valley. My DMV contact lost *his* copy of the list and his tally of the plate numbers he'd run thus far. Monroe's Valley run felt hinky then. It still feels hinky now.

I pulled the static surveillance on Fifth Helena. Justified paranoia dictated the move. Phil Irwin saw an old lady scrawl the plate number on his truck. Patrol cops cruised by and gave Phil the fish eye. That's it, we're gone, it's my unilateral call.

My access to Monroe has dramatically contracted. She visits shrink Greenson at his home now. I can't record their calls. José Bolaños hasn't called. Roddy McDowall calls less. Lowell Farr's off at Lake Arrowhead with her mom and dad. There's no phone in their cabin. I'm down to zero visual access and 80%-reduced telephonic. I put Deedee Grenier on the Hoffa-snitch payroll. She relays pill-party drift and lays out Monroe in banal extremis.

More pills. More booze. More liquor-drenched sno-cones. The girls watch the TV news and shoot squirt guns at images of Jack and Bobby. Marilyn consults a voodoo book and consigns Jackie's death to Baron Samedi. Marilyn sleeps with a Jackie voodoo doll.

The gig had full-scale contracted. My brain overrevved to compensate. I popped pills, boozed, and cogitated. I lived in dark listening posts. Quack shrink Freddy O. He puts Marilyn Monroe on the couch.

I recalled three early mobile tails. I blew two of them. Tail #1: Monroe cops pills in Beverly Hills and visits Ralph Greenson. She bangs her car over the San Vicente median strip and plows shrubs. She flips off random drivers and tongue-kisses a hotel doorman. Here's my retrospective interpretation:

It felt calculated. It vibed Actors Studio exercise. Monroe's acting out some newfound liberation.

Tail #2: Monroe drives to that Holmby Hills party. She drives just as erratic. Her right-hand wheels scrape the curb and send hubcaps spinning. *But*—she never came close to causing a wreck.

Tail #3: Monroe's non sequitur trip to the Valley. She drives just as erratic. *But*—she eludes a seasoned mobile-tail pro.

I pursued the theory. I paid an LAPD traffic cop to research Monroe's driving record. She secures her California license, 8/49. Her record stays clean up to 10/61. Since then? *She was stopped for reckless driving fourteen times and let off with warnings.*

I brain-strained it. The conclusion came easy. She vamped fourteen L.A. traffic cops. She flirted, she played coy, she planted playful kisses and dared them to cite her. Theories are theories. I braced three of the cops and got embarrassed confirmation. Two men said she shot them some tongue.

Marilyn Monroe's got a secret life within her overarching life of dissolution.

It affirms her resolve to plow a thoughtful and steady course as internal chaos subsumes her. I'm stitching evidential and theoretical links. They encompass her cash stash, her disguises, her surreptitious phone calls and her Valley jaunt. Add her wacked-out driving exploits and minor cop seductions. It all adds up to a revitalized bravado and a lunatic contempt for the gilded world she lives in and now seeks to violate by means of a startling and startlingly anonymous new portrayal. Add José Bolaños. He points to the fact that it's not all in her head.

Surveillance jobs are by nature reactive. This surveillance job is a smear-by-association effort geared to validate cease-and-desist extortion. The worse Monroe looks, the worse the K boys look. Monroe's public profile is bad marriages, pill OD's, nervous breakdowns and psychiatric clinics. Her shrouded life within may reveal itself as design or simple psychic incoherence. I'm forty-two grand ahead as of now. That's eight shy of the fifty the prez stiffed me for. I'll be up to a hundred grand by summer's end. Jimmy Hoffa wants the dirt. He knows I'll dig it up wherever it leads me. I love the work and want the money. The cease-and-desist aspect still seems naïve. Jimmy Hoffa plays strictly for money. He's a prim man without my need to know *WHY?* I want to milk this gig past summer's end. That means busywork *right now.*

Norm's Nest. It was 3.4 miles northeast of Blown Tail #3 and my license-plate tally. I knew a bent ex-cop named Harry Fremont. He retired out of Ad Vice four years ago. I slipped him five yards. He slipped me the Ad Vice package on the Nest.

Deedee Grenier was dead-on. Norm Krause was a right-wing nut. The Nest hosted boozefests for the National Renaissance Party, the National Indignation Party, and the Moose Lodge Anti-Communist League. The White Dog Bund? Total membership, three men. That's Krause, patrol sergeant Jack Clemmons, and pamphlet pounder Frank Capell—author of *A-Bomb Jew York City (A Modest Proposal)*. Krause, Clemmons, and Capell were lapsed Lutheran dog worshippers. The Nest served as an "underground railroad" for divorced dads ditching out on child-support payments and Cuban exiles who venerate *los perros blancos*. The convivial nitespot warmly welcomed wife swappers from the nearby Lockheed aircraft plant, and members of a "dirty shutterbug club." Norm's Nest catered to stone white trash and was in no way Marilyn Monroe's scene.

The dexies kicked in. I got that urgent stomp-the-world rush. I zoom-lensed the Lawford house. There's the ridgeback, trailing his leash. There's Pat. She's been wading. She's barefoot and soaked to the knees.

They ducked inside. I blew a kiss. The console lit up. Amber-light incoming—Peter Lawford's got a call.

I slid on my headphones. Two rings reverberated. Lawford picked up.

He said, "Hello? It's Peter, and it's getting late. Say something provocative, or I'll doze off on you."

A woman said, "Hi. It's Eleanora. Remember me, Peter? I was a cater waitress at your party last month. Remember? You told me I could call you."

The party. Cater waitresses galore. Tight black slacks/white shirts/red vests. All young, all fetching. Actress-manqué types.

Lawford said, "Elean*ooora*. I remember you. You said you were an actress, and your boyfriend doesn't approve, and I told you I knew how *that* scene went, because my wife hates what I do, but what *can* I do? My wife's an incipient zombie, but she's a *Kennedy,* so she provides a good deal more pizzazz than most society girls do. So, who am *I* to deny that aspect of the marriage?"

Eleanora: "I see what you mean."

Lawford: "Anyway, who am *I* to complain? I'm just a movie star and John F. Kennedy's secretary of Young Fox Procurement, which allows me cabinet-level status, and my very own Playboy Club key for the oval office. I'm serious. Hugh Hefner is the president's chief domestic adviser."

Eleanora: "It's nice to see a man with the world by the shorts who can still make fun of himself."

Lawford: "Oh, well. You come in on the up-and-up, and people still think you're working for laughs."

Line pause: 16.4 seconds. Eleanora: "Peter, it's not that I'm not enjoying our chat, but I'm trying to find a man who owes me money."

Lawford: "That's a drag, because I was just starting to grok this conversation."

Eleanora: "I was grokking it, too."

Lawford: "How much do you need? I'm a soft touch, and I'm not averse to being paid back in trade."

Eleanora: "That's not my scene."

Lawford: "Boy, you're erecting roadblocks."

Eleanora: "His name is Rick Dawes. He's a cater waiter. I thought you might have a line on him."

The name ditzed me. I'd heard it before. I've got booze-and-dope aphasia. This summer dislodged some brain cells.

Lawford: "I don't know any Rick Daweses, baby. Sorry, no sale."

Eleanora: "It was just a shot in the dark, and it was good of you to talk to me."

No-class Lawford tried to hustle Eleanora. Eleanora cut him slack and stayed on point. The dynamic surprised me. Eleanora worked Lawford from jump street.

Lawford: "I'll tell you one thing that might interest you. I heard a rumor about house burglaries in Beverly Hills, all in what you might call the wake of cater-waitered and -waitressed parties. How's that grab you? Jewels and furs were stolen, and cater waiters turned out to be the suspects the cops were looking for."

Eleanora: "Well, that *does* sort of sound like Rick's scene. He's also been known to fruit-hustle."

Lawford: "Sorry, luv, your pal Rick doesn't ring any bells with me."

Eleanora: "*Que será, será.* I thought I'd give it a shot."

Lawford: "I'm glad you called. No lie. You've got the Rick Daweses of the world who owe you bread, and the Peter Lawfords of the world who'd *loooove* to blow bread on you, as in trips to Vegas, Aspen, places where a girl like you could really swing—"

It hit me. The name Rick Dawes. Monroe's house. My 4/11 break-in and peremptory prowl. The plank bookshelf. Monroe's scrap-paper scribbles. Monroe wrote *this:*

"Rick Dawes. Mean—maybe a fag." Beside it: ballpoint-pen cross-outs. They were telephone-answering outfits. It was one big, illegible list.

15

Double duty. All fucked-up phone work.

Monitor the Sip 'n' Surf feed. Record Lawford-house calls. Skim Yellow Page directories. Cold-call caterers and phone-message outfits.

Double duty. With fucked-up distractions.

There were frayed wire mounts at the Lawford house. They induced sound belches past comprehension. It's okay for now. Nobody's calling in or out.

The Sip 'n' Surf *blasts* sound. It's "Bikini Twist Party" Wednesday. Beach babes gyrate ten feet from my console enclosure. An overamped hi-fi cranks the "Peppermint Twist."

My headphones itched. That distracted me. The cold-call volume daunted and vexed me.

Dig it:

There are 171 caterers in the L.A. Yellow Pages. There are 256 message outfits. It's epic dreckwork. I've been at it since 8:00 a.m.

That "Eleanora"/Monroe/"Rick Dawes" lead scorched me. I checked the paper-scrap Polaroid I shot and tacked to my board.

The "Rick Dawes" is full legible. The phone-service listings are *illeg*ible. The crosshatch marks beside them indicate phone numbers. The half-legible word *serv* indicates "service." Monroe scrawled four lines of words that end in "serv." The service *names* read as gobbledygook.

Peter Lawford hustles "Eleanora." He mentions Beverly Hills house burglaries. Cater waiters emerge as suspects. It's a good tangential lead. Tough shit. I can't solicit BHPD for their 459 files. I've got no police agency standing. I can't bribe my way in. It's too risky. I'm a well-known shitbird PI.

I've called twenty-one phone-service switchboards. Twenty-one operators refused to divulge their client lists. I've called twenty-four catering switchboards. I've impersonated an LAPD Burglary detective. I've stressed "Eleanora," "Rick Dawes," Beverly Hills 459's and cater waiter suspect pools. I've stated that I have no physical descriptions to work from. I've gotten "Huh?" "No," and "Beats me," twenty-three times. One major-domo type leveled with me.

He said, "Look, cater waiters and waitresses in L.A. are all so-called actors and actresses, and they use stage names, pseudonyms, and aliases routinely. In other words, they're invariably hustlers, prosties, call girls and boys, pill pushers, pot peddlers, and opportunists hustling the L.A. film folk for all they can get. Burglary or fingering burglary is in no way beneath the moral range of these kids."

I yawned and scratched my ears. The Lawford pad broadcast skreek and dead air. I was up late last night. I wrote Jimmy Hoffa a summary report. I ran my projector and screened Lois in *Alcoa Presents*. I thought about Lois to quash thoughts of Pat. I thought about Pat to quash thoughts of Lois. I reskimmed *The Sexual Criminal*. Paul de River crawled up my ass. *Hey, Marilyn—why are you so hipped on this guy?*

Fetish murder. Demonic delusion. Blank-eyed psychopaths. De River's got a monkey on his back.

I yawned and walked out to the beach deck. Hi-fi reverb twanged the boards and made my shoes vibrate. I looked in at the Bikini Twist Party. The "Percolator Twist" assailed me. Twist girls shimmied. Their bikini bottoms wriggled hairpie low.

The bar and tables were SRO packed. Summer twist shows drew pierside gawkers and a big lecher crowd. I orbed a front table. Four coeds in Pali High sweaters peeled shrimp and dunked clams. The man with them stood out.

I made him. I'd met him on the PD. Sid Leffler. A West L.A. squad-room dick. Curly-haired, glasses, a nebbish type. Mid-fifties. A going-nowhere guy working divisional detectives. His part-time PD gig was "Officer Sid." He toured westside high schools and inveighed against Commies and dope. Sid, the shtickmeister. Some kind of film-biz pedigree. Fuck him. He's feeding underaged girls zonk-your-ass mai tais.

I walked back to the post and locked myself in. It squelched the music and muted the roar in my head. The amber console light blinked, on-off.

Outgoing call/Peter Lawford's extension. I pulled on my headset. I caught Lawford mid-spiel.

". . . and, Diana, the man loved you. I mean, he called me from the oval office to say, 'Peter, I'm no fan of oaters, but something told me to tune in *Bonanza,* so you tell Miss Van der Vlis the next time I'm in town I'd enjoy—'"

Line warp cut him off. Bum wire mounts induce line warp. The line stuttered and spit background noise. Lawford said something, the actress said something, an off-line voice cut in.

Quit pimping for my brother, you fucking—

The actress screeched and hung up. The broadcast cleared exponential. Lawford said, *"You fucking bitch."* Pat said, *"You goddamned—"*

Then crash sounds. Then hurled-object sounds. Then *"Get your hands off me or I'll—"*

Then shattered-glass sounds, line blur, and blank air—

Line blur. Blank air. Pat on a stutter tape inside my head.

Get-your-goddamn-hands/Get-your-goddamn-hands/Get-your-goddamn-hands—

I bolted the Sip 'n' Surf and hauled to the bluffside post. I got dead air off the console. I zoom-lensed the house. I saw no window movement and no shadows and no movement on the grounds. Both garage doors stood open. Lawford's Rolls and Pat's Bonneville were tucked in. I gobbled dexies and guzzled Old Crow and worked my pulse up and down.

I eyeballed the house. I ran zoom-lens circuits. The calm status quo held. I called Nat and Phil and issued directives.

Grab your walkie-talkies. Drive to the 76 station on PCH and perch. Marital tiff. Red Alert. I know this shit. They'll pull a two-car driveaway. Nat, you tail Pat. Phil, you tail dipshit. I've got my handset here. Call in at one-hour intervals. Track your mileage away from the site.

I waited. I watched the house. Spots popped in front of my eyes. My arteries pinged. My feet went numb. I lost weight as I tried to sit still. My watch dangled slack on my wrist. I saw things that weren't there. I saw the Taft Building on August 15, 1945. Pat and I stood naked, in our room across the street. We watched the Miller High-Life sign blink.

5:19 p.m. Pat enters the garage. Three kids trail her. She dumps two suitcases in her Bonneville. She backs out and peels *northbound* on PCH. There's Nat's Ford wagon. He peels out of the gas station lot and bird-dogs her.

5:53 p.m. Lawford enters the garage. He hops in his Rolls and peels *southbound* on PCH. There's Phil's Valiant coupe. He peels out of the gas station lot and bird-dogs him.

I shut my eyes. I ran Man Camera clips. I replayed Freddy and Pat, start to finish. I recalled our opening dialogue, near verbatim. My handset squawked at 6:22 p.m.

Nat reported in. Pat's still heading northbound on PCH. She just passed Oxnard. Nat thinks she's headed to Santa Barbara.

My nerves decohered. I popped two yellow jackets to tamp them down and quash this schizzy limbo. My handset squawked at 6:56 p.m.

Phil reported in. Lawford was holed up on Ewing Street in Silver Lake. The place reeked of love crib. He checked his reverse directory. The crib was owned by one Lorelei Gudis. Phil ran her through Sheriff's R&I. She had twelve pandering priors. They went back to '55.

I crossed myself. I grabbed my tool belt, a ski mask, my beavertail sap.

I could do it. I knew that. I knew I had options. I could take it just so far and stop there. I could take it all the way and frost a homicide beef. I thought, *Restraint.* I thought, *Don't blow the gig. If you do it, you'll burn the gig and burn Jimmy Hoffa. He'll kill you, no questions asked.*

My head hurt. I saw spots. My numb feet put me up on my heels. I splintered a window ledge and vaulted my way in. It was sloppy work. It decreed a mock-459 ruse. I went straight to the kitchen. I filled two paper bags with sterling silver flatware and placed them by the front door. I left my pill stash back at the post. I verged on an overjolt and knew it.

The Lawfords stocked their liquor cabinet with the most and the best. I siphoned high-test juice from six bottles. My headache abated. The spots vanished. My tremors subsided. I troubleshot the six phone extensions and the downstairs bug mounts.

I replaced the handset wiring and the listen/speak microphones. I bunched the defective wires and mikes up in a tool belt pouch. The new wires and mike flanges were silicone-coated. They would not fray.

The booze jolt diminished. I prayed off an urge to fall out on Pat's bed. I restrung the downstairs bug mounts and spackled the mount holes.

I spray-painted the dried Spackle the perfect wall-color shade. Spackle dust billowed. I vacuumed it up and hand-plucked every stray fleck of grit. I squinted my way along baseboards and started seeing double and triple. I hand-plucked every stray fleck of grit. I'm sure I did. I quadruple-checked my work. They'd detect the burglary. They'd note the missing silver. They'd never detect the surveillance gear. That meant *Pat would never know.*

Dipshit was shacked in Silver Lake. Phil sat on the house. I fine-tuned my hearing and willed the key in the door lock. That meant *you do it.* Pat took luggage. She'd be gone several days. Lawford would odds-on roll home at noon. Phil would cue me. Two short phone bursts. *He's on his way.*

I passed out standing up. I woke up prone on the living room floor. I collapsed in a wingback chair and woke up in a kitchen chair. DT blobs grew faces and went for my eyes. I screamed and covered them. They ate their way through my hands and bored into my face. I muffled screams with a kitchen towel. I *heard* a key-in-lock sound or *willed* a key-in-lock sound so I'd do it. It sounded real. Peter Lawford coughed and made it real, for sure.

I slipped on my ski mask and pulled my sap and ran toward the sound. I slammed Lawford low and jammed a wad of acoustical baffling in his mouth. He thrashed and pissed his pants. He bleated. I sapped his legs, his feet, his back. I drop-kicked him in the balls. I pulled his gag so he wouldn't gorge on puke and suffocate. He twitched and made funny noises. I sapped him in the ribs and heard bones shear. I picked up the bags of silverware and ran.

16

Kwan's Chinese Pagoda. A C-town mainstay since 1928. Open-all-nite. After-hours booze for LAPD, Sheriff's, and DA's Bureau brass. Hop Sing Tong–allied. The basement opium den goes unmentioned. Chinese interns at Queen of Angels do research in underground suites. Six rooms house inebriates in need of deep rest.

I've dried out there before. As in '51 and '57. I split the Lawford house and drove straight to Kwan's. I dumped the stolen silverware down a sewer hole en route. I called Phil and told him to boss the gig for a week. Work the posts, run the taps, surveil the Lawford spread. Sniff out the presence of fuzz. Determine if Lawford reported the beating and 459. Determine if the repaired wires are back at 100%. Track Pat's whereabouts. Tell me when she crawls back home.

I doused the lights and went *Adieu*. The interns hooked me to an intravenous sleep drip. I woke up and smoked opium. The interns fed me pork fried rice and lobster à la Kwan and put me back to sleep. My room was windowless and air-conditioned. There was no wall clock. They hid my wristwatch and smothered all my notions of time. I slept through a head-to-toe blood rotation. My putrified blood was replaced with the hormone- and herb-packed blood of some new Asian master race. I slept twenty-plus hours a day. I purged in steam baths and ice-water plunges. I floated in space-age decompression chambers, buoyed by saline-infused water and fragrant oils. I slept. I did not dream. My brain wires reconnected. I brain-screened real and imagined moments with Pat. I recited long Bible passages, verbatim. I first memorized them as a kid in bumfuck, Massachusetts.

The freight weighed in at fifteen grand. I paid out in Jimmy Hoffa's

C-notes and tipped the interns a grand apiece. Phil picked me up and drove me home. He reported in full.

The Lawford house taps now worked 100%. Fuckhead visited a doctor and limped for a week. He did not report the thumping or the burglary. Pat crawled home, three days later. The restored tap lines now hum. Presidential pimp Lawford cranks calls. He's been buzzing actresses King Jack has seen on TV. Jack digs the Method type. Shirley Knight, Joan Hackett, Whitney Blake. If Lawford perv-calls Lois Nettleton, I'll kill him.

Phil said the gig felt tapped out. Monroe hides at home. She's poised to go back to work on *Got to Give*. She calls Roddy McDowall in Rome and Lowell Farr at mom and dad's place. She gets late-breaking dish from the *Cleopatra* set and ripe accounts of Palisades High intrigue. Monroe alternates shrink-session modes with Doc Greenson. It's backyard cocktails at his place or her calls to him. Her anti-Jack-and-Bobby rage ascends, call to call. Phil said her most repeated phrase is "I've got the goods on them."

Phil said he's getting paranoic. He's seen private security guys down the street from the golf course post. I said, Let's get inside and pull the Monroe mounts. Phil agreed. He said, Monroe might not cooperate. She's turned recluse. She doesn't don disguise and make pay-phone calls. She eschews Jeanne Carmen's pill parties. Deedee Grenier hasn't phoned in dirt briefs. José Bolaños hadn't called. Phil summarized his update. "Freddy, the gig feels atrophied."

But I felt good. And I looked good. Who's that handsome camel fucker in the mirror?

Transfused, reborn—it's your call. I regained my lost weight. I felt quietly revitalized and determined to push forth on the gig. I X-marked my wall calendar. Days off booze and dope. Seven, eight, nine, ten, and counting.

I took a weeklong breather. I schemed gig strategy and considered Pat and the risk I took to avenge her. She's a dilettante sunk by astounding privilege and my inimically idealized better half. I considered Lois. She's as ill-born and hardscrabble as I am. I'm her slum reclamation project. I fulfill her penchant for the outré. I considered Marilyn Monroe and her secret life and made the three women a troika.

I sheet-draped my living room corkboards. I covered my evidence photos and pinned-on notes and crafted a No-Monroe Zone. I banned visual stimulus and went at her through straight reflection.

She craved the authentic. Material success had failed her. She had the world by the shorts. Affluence offended her. She embraced the pervy Weimar Berlin aesthetic. "Authentic" connoted dark photographic art. Her wall frieze. Bull dykes shooting dope. Defective kids in Mickey Mouse beanies. De River's *Sexual Criminal*. Traumatic case histories. Banal brutality as the fount of true human horror and thus great art.

And the incubating force behind her own vastly overpraised gifts.

De River has replaced Lee Strasberg and the Actors Studio. He can render her authentic in a way that no New York stage guru ever could. Monroe is now attempting to achieve authenticity. Her new mode? A sustained and most likely criminally defined portraiture that film moguls and her trillions of idiot fans will never see.

I ran sight tails off of Carmelina and Fifth Helena. It was her one car lane to L.A. at large. I staked it out three full days. Day #3/2:12 p.m. There's Marilyn's Buick. The housekeeper's with her. Nail it: she's going to the store.

I tailed them to the Brentwood Market. I figured it gave me ninety minutes, tops. I drove back to Fifth Helena and impromptu B and E'd it. The day was hot-hot. I stepped through a gauze-curtained window and worked dervish quick.

I pulled all my bugs and tap mounts. I yanked all attendant wires. I put myself in a bind with Jimmy Hoffa. It forced me to scheme some all-new method of approach.

I went out the back door and pored through her trash cans. I found twelve empty TV dinner containers and sixteen empty cans of Metrecal. I found four empty Nembutal vials. Marilyn had crossed her name off the labels. She wrote in their place: "Not my name anymore."

17

It was hot. My window units rattled. I sat in the living room and brooded the day up.

I stared at my evidence boards. Thumbtacks stretched the sheet drapes taut. They cloaked photographs/tap transcripts/report carbons/ bug logs/jotted notes/photo close-ups of odd scraps of paper. They detailed the gig from 4/10 to now. They shut down my visual memory and forced me to extrapolate with reduced stimuli.

Marilyn Monroe in extremis. What's going on here?

Brain loops had me light-headed. I smoked myself hoarse. I levitated in my favorite chair.

Door knocks blitzed my concentration. It pissed me off. I got up and opened the door.

She wore a pink linen dress. No stockings and scuffed white bucks. She wore her hair down and parted left.

She was still gawky, working on regal. She ran gaunt now. There were no soft planes to her face.

She said, "Your scent lingers."

It felt rehearsed. It fell flat. Her arms were too thin. Her man's wrist-watch dangled. I must have stared.

She said, "My party in June. You wore that cheap lime cologne in 1945, and you're still wearing it today. My kids told me they smelled it for a week."

Everything went *TILT.* I got *"This can't be"* out. Pat jiggled my hands and pushed me inside. I kicked the door shut.

———

Reprise.

The bedroom-window unit rattled. Cold air merged with trapped air and the wet we'd stirred up. Pat pulled a sheet over us. She shivered, I trembled. I know she caught the distinction.

We stretched out under the sheet. We were tall and spanned the whole bed. We reached up and laced hands and laid them on the headboard.

Her too-big wristwatch slid off. I grabbed it and stuck it under a pillow. Pat laughed. I said, "You'll start thinking you've got a husband and kids out at the beach, and you'll be gone before I can blink."

Pat squeezed my hands. "That's your injunction. Here's mine, and it has just as much to do with time. Don't mention a certain moment and place and tell me what you recall, because I remember it a certain way, and to me it's sacrosanct."

Our eyes were dialed tight. Hers were red-flecked hazel. I'd just noticed it.

"That's the best thing anyone's ever said to me."

"You mean a woman's ever said to you."

"Men tell me 'Fetch, Freddy, fetch' or 'Shake down this guy, will you?' So, you're right. There's a distinction."

Pat said, "I noticed two things in your living room."

I gulped. "Yeah. My covered-up boards and what else?"

"A framed theater Playbill from October '56. Somebody circled a notice. 'Lois Nettleton replaces Barbara Bel Geddes in the role of,' and then some folderol about the play itself."

I laughed. "Lois is a friend of mine. We see each other intermittently, but compared to you and me, we've been shacked up from the gate."

Pat roared. Some tears squeezed out. I kissed them away.

"Let's not talk about Lois, or Jack, or your pressing engagements out at the beach."

Pat said, "Freddy's a party crasher."

I said, "'Freddy loves Pat.' I carved it on a tree at the LAPD Academy, three weeks after I met you."

Pat shut her eyes. I did the same. We squeezed our linked hands into fists and tapped the headboard. I saw things and heard things. Pat's kids trip on bug wires. Pat picks up her bedside phone and hears telltale clicks.

I said, "You honor me."

Pat said, "Oh, dear. I have made such a hash of it."

I said, "We're running neck and neck there."

Reprise.

Man Camera meets stopwatch. It lasted two hours and fourteen minutes. Pressing engagements, superseding commitments. She almost ran out the door.

I paced my living room and bumped into furniture, dead sober. I was all *Tilt* and *Swirl.*

The phone rang. I grabbed for it and capsized an end table. I caught the receiver two rings in.

"Yes? Who is this?"

There's that prairie twang. "It's Bill Parker, Freddy."

I said, "Yes, sir."

Parker said, "I need you. It's a kidnap, and a film-mogul acquaintance of mine needs a favor. Open your front door and look out."

I put the phone down and did it. Bill Parker excels at presentation. He outdid himself here.

Four big men stood beside an unmarked prowl car. I saw five pump shotguns propped up in the backseat. The men wore pearl-gray suits and straw fedoras. Max Herman, Red Stromwall, Harry Crowder, Eddie Benson. Who else *but* for kidnap grief?

I blinked.

The men waved.

I crossed myself.

Oh shit. I'm jungled up with the Hat Squad, once more.

PART 3
TRUTH JUICE

(AUGUST 4–20, 1962)

18

Okay—she's dead. It's some all-new cluster fuck now. Bill Parker has designs. Robert Kennedy was en route. The press would grab the dead bait girl and not let go.

I parked across the street and watched the house. I called Phil first thing. He rolled out and parked three car lengths behind me. The street was otherwise dead. Midnight passed. It's Sunday morning now. Phil and I eye-strafed the house. We walkie-talkie gabbed to kill time.

Bill Parker has designs. He told me to meet the Hats at PC Bell. The Chief seized opportunities. Like yesterday. *Hey, Freddy—I've got a kidnap play. Dump this guy, will you?*

My thoughts tumbled. I killed a man and caressed a dead woman. Heat left her body. My hand went cold. I saw Motel Mike Bayless rescue Gwen Perloff and logged anomalies. Monroe scrawled the main Sheriff's number on a paper scrap. Deedee Grenier goes back with Motel Mike.

Headlights bounced east, off Carmelina. The left light glared defective. That meant the housekeeper. She pulled up beside the front hedgerow and walked through the gate. I heard key-lock sounds. Okay—she's inside. There—that's her bedroom light.

I'd locked Monroe's bedroom door. I knew the house routine. Moms won't check the door before noon. I've got time to work angles. Bill Parker's got time to fine-tune his play.

The housekeeper's light blipped off. I smoked and ran the car radio. A 1:00 a.m. news flash blared. *Bold kidnap job! LAPD detectives and celeb PI kill one suspect! One suspect arrested, three suspects at large!*

I smoked myself hoarse. I was still half-cranked on jungle juice. The housekeeper's room light blinked on. I clocked it at 2:42.

I heard *thunk, thunk, thunk*. She's knocking on Monroe's door. She's the petulant and persistent type.

Phil buzzed me. I hit the RECEIVE switch. Phil said, "She'll know something's wrong in about two seconds."

I hit the SPEAK switch. "She'll call Greenson. It'll take him twenty minutes to get dressed and drive out here."

Phil rogered out. I clicked off my handset and squelched shortwave skreek. I counted minutes off the dashboard clock. Greenson drove a road-hog Lincoln. It cut up Carmelina at 16:32.

He parked behind the housekeeper's car and went through the gate. Moms stood in the doorway. Greenson trudged the front lawn. They left the door ajar and veered toward Monroe's bedroom. I heard *thump-thumps*. I *knew* that sound. Pops throws elbows at the doorjamb and yelps each time.

I got out and peeped over the hedgerow. Greenson ran outside. He held an andiron. He ran around to Monroe's French windows and smashed the glass in. I heard him kick away shards and stomp through the bedroom. He opened the door and let moms in. The old lady screeched.

Okay—she's dead. Can the boo-hoo, let's get on with—

I heard phone-dial sounds. Greenson's calling a doctor colleague or the local fuzz. I perched in the car and gauged response time. It's twenty minutes for the doctor, fifteen for the fuzz.

I was antsy. Time schizzed on me. A late-model Cadillac pulled up to the house. A slender man got out.

Phil buzzed me. "That's Dr. Engleberg. I tailed Monroe to his office in June."

Engleberg entered the house. The door stood wide open. It was 3:09 a.m. Brentwood was dark-dark and hushed-quiet. The Monroe spread glowed bright-*bright*.

An LAPD black-and-white skidded up. It nudged Engleberg's back bumper and scraped his BAN THE BOMB sticker off. It looked deliberate.

The driver got out. I made him. Robbie Molette shot surveillance pix at Norm's Nest. It's Sergeant Jack Clemmons. He's Norm Krause's tight pal and White Dog Bund *Kamerad*.

He grabbed a clipboard and walked up the lawn. He wore Bill Parker's scowly subdue-the-masses look. I got out and stood on my back bumper. The crowd ran to four now. Housekeeper, Clemmons, Greenson, Engleberg. No deputy coroner. No squadroom detectives, no lab crew, no photo car. It's a dead celeb. They'll send a mortuary sled and rig a temporary freeze. The coroner would take it from there.

I heard voices. Greenson and Clemmons groused. A K-car jammed up behind the black-and-white. Bob Byron got out. He was Parker's man at West L.A. station. He'll call the shots now.

My walkie-talkie buzzed. I jumped in the car and hit the sound switch. Phil said, "It's on the civilian radio. KHJ has it. Somebody at the station must have spilled."

I hit the kill switch. The sound gap juked voices up on the lawn. Byron gave Clemmons what for. Call the mortuary. Get some bluesuits. There's news bulletins. That means crowds. Chop, chop. You know the drill.

Clemmons trudged back inside. Byron huffed off and drove off. Greenson slammed the front door and shut out looky-loos. My day loomed long.

Meet the Hats at PC Bell. Spot-check the Lawford spread. The Chief would issue directives. The Hoffa job had me backlogged. Some sort of new job would swamp me. I popped two dexies and *re*-revved.

Dawn broke. The day vibed scorcher. Clemmons walked out and peeled out. He left the doctors to deal with the mortuary guys. Cars turned off Carmelina and beelined right here.

Reporters and camera dinks piled out. They parked haphazard and blocked doorways. They climbed the gate and swarmed the front lawn. They went from zero to forty-odd, fast. They passed around wake-up jugs and dropped film wrappers and cigarette butts on the grass.

They talked loud. They raised a ruckus. Neighboring houses lit up. Doors popped open. Yokels plopped into porch chairs and grooved on the show.

Fan types drove up and walked up. Triple-parked cars tight-packed the whole street. Fans climbed up on car roofs and hoods. They got wide-angle views. Fans piled out of cars and trampled front yards to get close. Fifth Helena went claustrophobic. Parked cars blocked Carmelina. Lowell Farr crawled over a high-backed old Dodge. She cut her hands on a window ledge and wiped blood on her sweater. She was weeping.

It got crazy bad. The crowd quadrupled. Daddy types waltzed kids around on their shoulders. The kids futzed with portable radios. KHJ broadcast the Fifth Helena Show. KNX broadcast an all-Marilyn retrospective. An ice-cream truck hawked Popsicles down near Carmelina.

Parked cars and raucous mourners boxed me in. The mortuary van no-showed. I lost sight of Lowell. Patrol cops shooed souvenir hunters off of Monroe's lawn. They were ripping out clumps of grass and stuffing their pockets.

I had to move. The van would probably traverse Sixth Helena and off-load the stiff through the garage. TV truck broadcasts blitzed my walkie-talkie frequencies. Phil was boxed in thirty yards behind me. This shit would build and burst. Desist! warnings would fizzle. Tear gas might work. LAPD would eat police-brutality shit and further besmirch their image.

I backed my sled up on some squarejohn's lawn. I brodied on wet grass and popped the clutch in first gear. I slid-skid west. Mourner-revelers dodged me. I plowed lawns, toppled water fountains, cracked driveway paving. I knocked over mailboxes and caromed off parked cars. Kids in Davy Crockett hats waved. I made Carmelina and punched it. I fishtailed and swung right on Sixth Helena. I shot clear up to Monroe's garage.

It was 7:10 a.m. I timed it on the dot.

The death van was parked snout out. The loading hatch was wide open. Monroe's dippy Buick was jammed upside a pepper tree. Scavengers pored through it. They snipped upholstery swatches with pruning shears.

Four male nurse types wheeled a gurney up. Monroe's sheet-draped and buckled-in. Six cops ran interference. Grass snippers and upholstery slashers stopped to pitch boo-hoo. The cops and nurses tossed the gurney up and in. A cop slammed the hatch. A nurse took the wheel and laid tracks.

They shot down Sixth Helena. I stuck right behind. The hearse was a '59 Caddy. The exhaust pipes spewed grit. We turned south on Carmelina and west on San Vicente. We cut south on Moreno Drive and back east on the San Vicente one-way. They drove slow. I drove slow. Two-car funeral cortege.

We passed through Brentwood Village and curved south on Barrington. We caught the light at Wilshire and curved east. We cut by the VA hospital and cemetery. The van jockey veered right and turned right at Wilshire and Westwood Boulevard. A pocket funeral home was tucked behind Truman's Drive-In. The van pulled straight up to it. An intake crew stood by.

They knew the protocol. So did I. Hold the stiff. The coroner's men would grab it and schlep it to the morgue. Doc Curphey would order the autopsy. Scalpels and organ scales at 2:00 or 3:00 p.m.

I thought about Pat. PC Bell was out at the beach. I had time to swing by the Lawford house and still make my meet with the Hats.

Wilshire was Sunday-morning lulled. I caught next to no traffic and a long string of green lights. I breezed through Santa Monica and caught the California Incline down to PCH. The run north took ten seconds. I parked on the landside curb and eyed the Lawford spread.

Pat and dipshit Peter stood out on the sand. They wore hokey presidential-seal robes and sipped coffee. Pat looked haggard, dipshit looked hot to fawn. They stared up at the sky. I heard rotor thumps and saw a chopper approach.

It throttled down and hovered low. It landed twenty feet from them. A cockpit door popped open. Robert Kennedy hopped out.

PC Bell was on Wilshire, due east of the beach bluffs. I got there early. I parked curbside and built lies, full blast.

The Hats would snatch Monroe's phone records. We'd scan them. Names, dates, phone numbers, and call times would jump out. I'd memorized and imprinted the gist of most of the calls. The Chief had no clue. I told him I'd worked a recent Monroe gig. He expected full disclosure. He knew my bug-and-tap expertise. He didn't know who hired me. He would interrogate me himself. I could prevaricate, dissemble, fabricate, concoct, and play off his vanity. I could not lie away the breadth of the Hoffa gig.

I brain-segued. I jumped from Bill Parker to Pat. Bucktooth Bobby was huddled with the Lawfords now. Peter would tell him he found Marilyn dead and suborned me. I'd told him I was Bill Parker's man per this deal. Bobby has a file on me. He knows what I do. He'll think bug job tout-fucking-sweet. He'll tell Pat. She'll confront me. I'll falter. She'll see straight through me.

I glanced up Wilshire. A PD prowl sled was parked outside Biff's Char-Broil. Max Herman stood in the doorway. He saw my car and waved a manila folder. I got out and walked over.

We shook hands. Max said, "It's been too long, son."

I lit a cigarette. "As in last night. It's all coming back to me. We tossed a man off a cliff."

"We saved the girl, though. The Chief chilled us, and it's the Sheriff's headache from here on out."

I tapped the folder. "Monroe's phone records?"

Max eased me inside. "That's right. And toll tickets, up through Thursday night. The Chief has a hunch you're up-to-date on the conversations, but he'll discuss that with you himself."

I gulped. Max steered me to a back booth. Red, Harry, and Eddie wolfed steak and eggs.

Red said, "There's Freddy."

Harry said, "Freddy the O. Twice in twenty-four hours. Just when you think you've seen the last of him."

Eddie sniffed the air. "Freddy's in the shit. He just can't seem to avoid it."

I sat down. Harry poured me coffee. Max passed me the folder. I skimmed names, phone numbers, dates.

Jeanne Carmen. Ralph Greenson. Temp shrink Milt Wexler. Familiar times, dates, chitchat. Calls to the White House and Justice Department switchboards. The house-to-D.C. calls peaked and decreased. Monroe utilized the Fox switchboard toward the end. Calls to Roddy McDowall in Rome. Pharmacy calls. Calls to La Barbara's Pizza. Pizza Dave worked the delivery route. Calls to Fox, the Lawfords, studio flacks and gofers. The call tallies flatlined in May and June. Monroe was on a pay-phone kick. No Monroe-to-Lowell Farr calls were listed. Brentwood to the Palisades was a toll-free zone. Monroe did not call Ensenada. José Bolaños called her.

I passed the folder back to Max. The Hats skunk-eyed me.

Red said, "Well?"

Max said, "Marilyn called the pizza delivery boy 'Big Dick Dave.'"

Harry said, "I'll bet you're wondering how we know that."

Eddie said, "Here's a hint. You didn't mention it during your perfunctory phone chat with the Chief last night. You told him you worked a recent Monroe gig, and left it at that."

Red said, "Nobody can say that you weren't forthcoming. The Chief requested a forensic, and you complied."

Max sighed. "Freddy's waiting for the punch line."

Harry sighed. "Freddy deserves the punch line."

Eddie sighed. "Freddy's trustworthy. We trusted him to toss a kidnap freak off a cliff, so we can sure as shit trust him with the punch line."

I sighed. I rolled my eyes. I'm too bored to live. I'm shitstorm-prone. Here comes Shitstorm #389—

Red lit a cigar. "2:00 a.m., this morning. Wilshire Vice nailed Robbie Molette on fourteen counts of pandering, peddling goofballs, stat rape, and receiving stolen goods. The Vice dicks knew we shared a history with Robbie, so they brought him to us. We leaned on him, and took him to Georgia Street Receiving for a little cleanup. Robbie said, 'Okay, I'll give,' so we bought him breakfast at Kwan's. He had three double Bloody Marys. They got him all loosey-goosey. He gave up your Monroe gig in minute detail, and bought himself an immunity waiver off of Miller Leavy. *He's* in the clear, but your boys Irwin and Denkins are *not*. Your fate appears to be ambiguous, but you are not without friends."

Max lit a cigar. "Turn around and look out the window."

I did it. I saw two black sedans parked on Wilshire. They were cop sedans. They had smoked windows and fringed antenna flags. A sea breeze pulled them taut. The LAPD crest and the Justice Department seal fluttered.

Red and Max grabbed my elbows and pulled me up. They nudged chairs aside and frog-marched me to the sidewalk. Robert Kennedy stepped out of the PD sedan and stepped into the Fed car. He left the back door ajar. Max went *After you*. I slid in beside Bill Parker.

He wore civvies and a Jesuit lapel pin. He winked and slapped his knees.

"You've held up well, given the hoops I've put you through. The kidnap job and Monroe in one go is a stretch."

I lit a cigarette. "I said I'd brief you the next time we talked. I was planning to, and I didn't intend to withhold. It looks like Robbie Molette and the Hats got there first."

The backseat featured a Portabar. Parker poured two short ones. Early Mass and a face-off with the AG. He deserved a jolt.

"I've just cut a deal with the attorney general. In consideration of a 'certain favor,' I will be appointed director of the FBI, after President Kennedy has been reelected. The 'certain favor' is you, Freddy. You are to work a variant of your recent operation for a crooked labor leader. You are to create a scandal sheet—wholly defamatory, but factually verifiable—on the late Marilyn Monroe. It will posthumously serve to damn Miss Monroe and discredit, refute, or at least mitigate any public awareness of her possible misconduct with *Les Frères* Kennedy. Accordingly, the sheet will also defame John and Robert Kennedy. You will stiff the AG with a second, entirely disingenuous set of reports and general memoranda, which will purport to be the 'real skinny,' but which will be pablum when compared to the dirt you report to me. This 'smear sheet within a smear sheet' will provide me with an extortion wedge should that feral cocksucker Bobby renege on our FBI-boss deal. Your other job is to quell newspaper, radio, and TV speculation per Miss Monroe's death. No unseemly hints of homicide, conspiracy, or any sense of unseemly alliance with the Kennedys may see print or appear on the airwaves."

I bolted my drink. Parker bolted his. He quick-built two refills.

"You will be issued valid credentials for the L.A. District Attorney's Bureau of Investigations. You will be sworn in as a lieutenant. This appointment has been vouched by DA McKesson and his chief criminal prosecutor, J. Miller Leavy—who, quite frankly, despises you. That's of no import, because Mayor Sam Yorty likes the cut of your jib. You will have a carry permit, a badge, and the power to issue subpoenas and search warrants written by Miller Leavy and run by a 'rubber stamp' Superior Court judge. You will work out of the LAPD's Intelligence Division, under Lieutenant Daryl Gates."

I popped sweat and weaved. I blinked and saw double. Two Parkers harangued me.

"Your three listening posts will be raided, late next week. All your evidence will be seized and held by the Justice Department, with all tape and written documents duplicated and held at LAPD Intel. The seizure of Lawford-house evidence will put you in the shit with Robert Kennedy, but you've been in the shit with the Kennedys before, and I want you in the shit now—it will put Bob Kennedy on the edge. The Kennedys must fear debilitating exposure, *now,* and your shitbird reputation is a surefire means to make this occur."

I guzzled my refill and crossed myself. *Dear Lord, Pat will know.*

Parker tapped his wristwatch. "We're due at St. John's. I trust you to be forthcoming, but I don't trust your memory."

———

Coerced performance. Interrogation. Brain scrub.

The room spooked me. Straitjackets and bite restraints were piled on wood-plank shelves. The metal table was bolted to the floor. I was strapped tight. An anesthetist mixed the jolt.

Scopolamine, Amytal, Pentothal. Some space-age compound. Parker called it the "KGB Cocktail."

He stood by the table. Ditto the Intel exec, Daryl Gates. Robbie Molette sat by the door. He'd feed Parker and Gates prompts and cues. Max said the hump revealed the full Hoffa op. I believed it. I had three goals here. Gauge the questions and determine what they knew. Restore my booze-and-dope-maimed recollections. Rebuff all queries per Pat.

The doctor fed a spike and swabbed my arm. He hit a fat blue vein. The rush hit head-to-toe ecstatic.

It was a warm-water plunge. I swam in bright colors. I saw Pat and Lois naked. It shamed me. I asserted brain control and screened bland settings. Parker jumped on my 4/11 break-in. I fed him fluff on Monroe's bedroom sloth. Gates jumped on the money in the lockbox. I lost Pat and Lois. They swam off into a waterfall. I described the forty grand and the Polaroids I took. I blabbed wiretap outtakes. Eleanora and dipshit Lawford discussed some cat named Rick Dawes.

Gates mentioned José Bolaños. I gave up the Monroe-Bolaños tap call. Parker brought up my blown tail to the Valley. My brain glitched. I saw myself with the Hats. It was just last night. We're chasing Sheriff's prowl cars. We're hot to rescue Gwen Perloff.

Parker asked questions. Gates asked questions. Robbie fed them cues. I ran mental-solvency tests and answered questions hit or miss. Parker and Gates looked perplexed. The doctor looked bored. Robbie looked apprehensive. I saw that morgue shot from last night. It's Carole Landis, it's '48, she's on a gurney just like mine. Monroe's in the morgue now. Why did *she* have *that* photo? Why am I seeing *that* photo at *this* time?

The doctor said, "He's a lousy subject. He only submits so far. I think this summer's a blur to him, and that's why you're getting these frag-mentary responses."

Monroe Gig #2. Day one was all mortification. #2 supplants #1. The first job was all money, peeper kicks, and sunshine. #2 connotes legal jeopardy and high-stakes censure.

The truth juice wore off at St. John's. I snoozed on the gurney. Parker and Gates took off. Robbie *slunk* off. I walked back to PC Bell and got my car. I drove straight to the wheelman lot at Beverly and Hayworth.

I steered herky-jerky. I wore palm-and-finger-weighted sap gloves. Steel weights were stitched in.

My thoughts tumbled.

The evidence raid was slated for late next week. I had four days to hide my office stash and listening-post documents. That meant four all-day workdays.

I pulled up to the lot. Punk wheelmen loitered by the pay phone. Divorce lawyers called in and hired surveillance guys. They tailed cheating spouses to hot-sheet flops and kicked doors in. Flashbulbs and divorce decrees popped. I'd done the work myself.

Robbie stood by the Coke machine. I hit him at a full sprint. He cartwheeled. I pinned him prone and stuffed a handkerchief in his mouth. I threw right and left uppercuts. Robbie gagged on the hankie and spit teeth and gum flaps in my face.

I heard his jaw break. My knees snapped his collarbone. I went downstairs and slammed his ribs. Sheared bones poked out at odd angles. Nat Denkins ran up and bear-hugged me. Phil Irwin said, *"Whoa, Freddy, whoa."*

19

I was dead asleep. The truth juice fucked with my system. I *thought* I heard things and heard things, straight up.

I woke up. Metal scrapes roused me. I heard lock-pick sounds out on my porch.

Little pokes, digs, and prods. There's a *twist*. There's male whispers. It sounds like three men. There's the *snap*.

They can't get in. I'm wise to lock picks and stealth. I installed blocker strips.

I grabbed my bedside piece. I screwed on the suppressor. I heard mutters and shuffles. The front door came down.

It crashed. It hit the floor, flush. It cracked floorboards and made *very big noise*.

I heard footsteps. Three penlight beams strafed the bedroom. I saw three men. I saw dark suits and wide bulletproof vests.

They sensed me, they smelled me. They saw me and charged me in bed.

I shot them flush and hit them. Muzzle flash lit the room. They caught two vest shots each. Big-bore shots knocked them flat on the floor.

I jumped out of bed and tripped on top of them. They cursed and screeched. They got up and dogpiled me.

They threw elbows and rabbit punches. They wrestled me and grabbed at me. I kneed them in the balls and went for their throats. They pinned me down. They had dinky Fed badges pinned to their belts.

A Mex type drop-kicked me and smothered me with a pillow. Two paddy Feds kicked me in the head.

Ratfuck Bobby fucked us. He staged the evidence raid four days early. I got sandbagged. I had no time to prepare.

They got everything. My corkboards, my bug-and-tap logs, my boxed tapes. They got my photo sprays, my scrawled notes, my pictures of Pat. They dressed me, they cuffed me, they hauled me outside.

Three Fed sleds lined the curb. They packed the trunks with my evidence. They bagged all my paper scraps and operational minutiae. They strongarmed me into the lead car. Their vests were bullet-pocked and dented. They groaned and rubbed the welts on their chests. They limped from my nut shots.

Three Feds, three Fed sleds. The Mex type took the lead car. I rode in the backseat. The two paddy Feds followed close. My neighbors stood on their porches and gassed on the show.

We caravanned west on Sunset. I was concussed. I saw quadruple everything. The Mex type motormouthed. He said he wasn't Mex. He was proudly *Cubano.* As in vintage '59 Cuban exile.

He was a Justice Department lawyer/investigator. His name was Edgar Chacõn. *Señor* Bob Kennedy was his personal *jefe. Señor* Bob put him through Georgetown Law School and helped him pass the D.C. bar exam. He has a swell garage apartment at *Señor* Bob's Hickory Hill estate. He's *Señor* Bob's bodyguard and dirty trickster. He drives *Señor* Bob's kids to school and walks *Señor* Bob's dogs. He's killed lots of Castroite militiamen. He scalped them and cut their dicks off. He drinks with *Señor* Bob and *Señor* Jack at the White House. He has *personally* fucked fourteen thousand women and is widely known as the "Lizard of Love."

The caravan veered south on Barrington and west on San Vicente. That bodes a golf course raid. We hooked around the median strip and hit the side street by Brentwood CC. An LAPD unmarked car beat us there. Phil Irwin and Nat Denkins were cuffed in the backseat. Two plainclothes cops loaded Monroe-pad gear in the trunk.

Eddie Chacõn idled up to the LAPD car. I recognized a West L.A. squadroom guy.

Sid Leffler. A nosebleed cop from way back. "Officer Sid." Mr. High School Toastmaster. I saw him at the Sip 'n' Surf, midsummer. He was feeding underaged girls booze.

The other cop was square-jawed and fit. Eddie Chacõn pointed to him and hissed.

"J. T. Meadows. In my informed opinion, a *maricón*. In my view, all handsome men are suspect."

I yocked. "What about me? I'm handsome as shit."

"You are ugly as shit, *pendejo*. However, on occasion ugly men supersede handsomeness. As proof of this, I point to the fact that Vice President Johnson gets more ass than *Señor* Jack."

I *re*-yocked. Leffler and Meadows dumped my transceiver and headphone sets in their trunk. The Fed follow cars peeled out, northwest. My guess: a run to the bluffside post. It's one big evidence stash.

Eddie Chacōn hung a U-turn. Leffler and Meadows piled in their car and pulled up behind us. I craned my neck and scoped Phil and Nat. They looked glum. I knew why. They saw this deal as indictment/trial/conviction.

The deal was half shuck. They didn't know that the LAPD would extend their employment. The raids were a crack-the-whip ploy. Ratfuck Bobby and Bill Parker colluded. They wanted us cowed.

We cut north to Sunset and west to PCH. Chacōn tapped his red lights and siren. Next stop: the Sip 'n' Surf lounge.

Eddie played it bravura. He sluiced through oncoming traffic and brodied all the way up on the pier. Salt-racked boards creaked and partially snapped. Leffler and Meadows fishtailed up behind us. Bait-shop crews and surfer riffraff goggle-eyed the scene.

Eddie got out and brandished a pump shotgun. Ditto, Leffler and Meadows. They hit the Sip 'n' Surf at port arms. The joint evacuated. Barflies, kitchen help, bikini girls. It was one big exit sprint.

I heard door-crash noise inside. I heard kicked-over chairs and consoles and phone mounts ripped out of walls. I heard file cabinets dumped and high-line bug gear slammed into boxes. Chacōn and Meadows ran out with their arms full.

They filled their trunks. They got back in their cars and spun U-turns. They gained, lost, and gained tread. Cracked boards sheared and dropped in the surf.

We made PCH southbound. Pier geeks shot us fuck-you fingers. I trembled. I knew our next stop.

I shut my eyes and prayed it off. Eddie zoomed there. He pulled right and grazed the beachside embankment. He cut the ignition. I opened my eyes.

The two paddy Feds dumped bug mounts on the north footpath.

Peter Lawford examined a yanked-out telephone. Pat stood close by. My window was rolled up. She stared straight at me.

I stared straight at her. She walked over and spit on the window. She did it a dozen or two dozen times. She spit-covered the whole window glass. Nobody backed down. We held dead-on stares.

20

Monroe Job #2. I eased into it.

The Feds whomped me good. A doc at Georgia Street fixed me up and shot me some righteous pain dope. Ratdog Bobby made nicenice. He sent a crew out to refit my kicked-down door and trashed floorboards. Jurgensen's Market dropped off a bottle of Dom Perignon. Bobby included a note: *"Freddy—all the best."* He signed it *"RFK."*

I called Jimmy Hoffa and shoveled up a snow job. Boss, I'm *sorry.* The LAPD lab turned up my prints at the Monroe post. They leaned on my guys and took it from there. Hoffa seemed to buy it. He took the pricey blown op nonchalant. He said he'd pay out the pledged bonus bread.

I mollified Jimmy. I expressed confidence. The Feds and LAPD won't jump you for suborning the op. Jimmy said, "Fuck them if they do. I've already burned the tapes, logs, and all your paperwork."

He's paying out unearned wages. He's dispensing unearned bonus bread. He destroyed essential evidence for no good reason. He's got to have a *money* motive. I thought so at the gate.

I've penciled in a week's transition. I drive by the Monroe pad twice a day. Nutty fans congregate. They bring guitars and throw hootenannies. They revise old labor ditties and blame Monroe's death on "The Man." Candlelight vigils extend to 2:00 a.m. High-school kids plug phonographs into car dashboard lighters and play swami music. I've seen Lowell Farr three times.

My Monroe World is high-stakes extortion. The world's Monroe World is disingenuous schmaltz. Gene Kelly was "deeply shocked." He "just didn't understand it." Anita Ekberg was "shocked, and so sad." Yeah—but Marilyn told Lowell Farr that you gave the prez the clap and he passed it on to Jackie. Liz Taylor was "very sad, and deeply shocked."

Yeah—and Marilyn and Roddy McDowall ragged on your fat ass on a near-daily basis.

The Fourth Estate weighed in. *The New York Times,* the *L.A. Times, Klansman* magazine, *L'Osservatore Roma.* They blamed Marilyn's childhood privation, the film biz, her orphanage stint, Father Coughlin's Rosary Crusade, and the Learned Elders of Zion. Local disk jockeys played "Image of a Girl" twenty thousand times a day. Noted clerics inveighed. Marilyn exemplified "America's permissive new malaise." Jive genius Dizzy Gillespie told an unknown police source, "That's too bad. She was a fine muthafuckah." Local newshounds played up the death of almost-star Carole Landis. She was another "busty bombshell." Curvy Carole "pounded pills and sadly succumbed to suicide." Yeah— and I found a Landis morgue pic in Monroe's pad.

Coroner Curphey called me. He laid out the autopsy call: barbiturate OD or suicide. It was strictly routine. Monroe was a long-term dope fiend. Here's two non sequitur tweaks:

Tweak #1: minute puncture marks on Monroe's left earlobe. Traces of liquid collagen pooled at the spot. Curphey said, "It might have bloated her face somewhat. Maybe it was for a role she was playing."

My first thought:

José Bolaños calls Marilyn. They discuss her Mexican travels. She rolls "incognito." She might be "moving freight." Marilyn tells Deedee Grenier that she hits Mexico in disguise. She's done up as a migrant farmworker. Collagen injections? Deliberate facial bloating? I'll buy that.

Tweak #2: a healed and faded human bite mark. It's "some years old." It's smack on Monroe's left bicep. Curphey said, "It looks like a sicko sex wound."

My first thought:

The fuckee-suckee pix I saw on my 8/4 break-in. They were '58 or '59 vintage. Marilyn and a cruel-looking stud enact the Kama Sutra. I saw no such bite mark or bite mark scarring. Curphey's noted bite mark was most likely late '59 or early '60 vintage.

Crazy Marilyn. Collagen injections. Bite marks. Her forty-grand stash. Her plus-size threads. Her nutty pay-phone calls.

It's one big cluster fuck. She OD'd or pulled the plug. I attended the funeral. It was a sanctified cluster fuck. LAPD Intel shot surveillance film. Thirty-five friends and Dust Bowl–esque "family" showed up. Eight hundred fans mobbed Wilshire and Westwood Boulevards.

Lowell Farr stood among them. She pitched muted boo-hoo by teenage-girl standards.

Monroe's ex–acting coach eulogized her in the *Herald*. Natasha Lytess was tight with Monroe, '49 to '56. Miss Lytess nailed a noxious gestalt.

"She projected a shopworn enchantment. It entrapped only those susceptible and most willing to succumb. She wore most people out in the end."

Amen, sister. You've got the last word so far.

Daryl Gates called me. It was noon on 8/10. He relayed urgent bad news.

Ratfuck Bobby filed a superseding-evidence writ. He filed it with a Ninth Circuit Court judge. The judge signed the writ. Four Justice Department investigators served the warrant and enacted the provisions. It went down at 10:00 last night.

They seized the LAPD's cache of all my tapes, transcript logs, and mimeographed reports to Jimmy Hoffa. They seized LAPD's copies of my corkboard evidence, bootjacked by the Feds on 8/6. I now have no access to the photographic evidence I compiled during my 4/11 and 8/4 break-ins.

Ratfuck Bobby orchestrated a two-prong attack. His goons kicked down my door and tossed my pad-office. His goons usurped the LAPD's copied, logged, and filed evidence. I would have utilized said evidence in my new gig for Bill Parker. The grab resoundingly states that Robert F. Kennedy does not trust Bill Parker, Daryl Gates, and Big Freddy O. It suggests that Kennedy may take the evidence to a Federal grand jury and seek suborning and criminal-conspiracy indictments against Jimmy Hoffa, me, and my men. Said indictments would render me a bit player in the Hoffa/Kennedy war. They would most likely net me big Federal time.

I brooded it up to a fucking fare-thee-well. I plotted remedies, countermeasures, solutions. It came down to replication.

Nat, Phil, and I could confer and replicate the pertinent tap calls. Only I could replicate what I saw and imprinted on 4/11 and 8/4. Hans Maslick inspired me. Maslick developed the techniques of photographic memorization that I employ today. He was a Berlin homicide cop, part-time Brownshirt, and full-time dope fiend. He worked overlapping murder jobs and lost his synaptic grip on priority cases in the overall glut of his *werk*load. My 4/11 and 8/4 prowls served up Marilyn Monroe. I sensed it then and know it now. My snapshots provide a verifiable record of my first impressions. I'm sober now. I was zorched to the gills on 4/11 and 8/4. I need to replicate the enhanced acuity of B and E under the influence. I need to replicate the sex thrill of a strange woman's dwelling. I need to merge recollection and imagination and yoke them to my eideteker's mental discipline and voyeur's need to know.

I got out a notebook and pen. I cooked up a batch of jungle juice and took three good jolts. I took two more jolts. I got my first replicative buzz. I *smelled* the wet towels in Monroe's bathroom.

Mental pictures enhanced the smell. I relived camera clicks and flashbulb glare. It's all transposition—recalled sights become words on paper.

Monroe's bathroom and living room. Evidence Pix #1 to 7: pill vials, hashish cubes, bathtub grime.

Into the bedroom. I smell *her*. Stale sweat/presumptive sexual exertion. Pic #8: soiled bedsheets. Pix #9 and 10: the lockbox and the forty grand spread out on the bed. Pix #11 to 23: Monroe's crazy handwritten lists.

I smelled the paper. I replicated shutter clicks and bulb glare. Pharmacy lists/dope-refill lists/"nice Drs." lists. Replication, immersion, transposition—I got all the names and dates right. Not so fast—there's the random-lover list and dick-size drawings. Shit—I can't recall the men's names.

Replication, immersion, transposition. Separate Sheet of Paper Pic #1: "Rick Dawes. Mean—maybe a fag." Illegibly crossed-out names of phone-answering outfits. Separate Sheet of Paper Pic #2: the main number for the L.A. County Sheriff's Office.

Camera glitch/aphasic lesion/fuckup. I *know* I shot a list of first-name-only men. They were tagged "studio grip," "makeup man," "studio flack." Then was then, now is now. I can't recall their names or any listed phone numbers.

Replication, transposition. Scrawled Bookmark Pic #1: "Jack at White House," plus switchboard number. "Bobby at Justice," plus switchboard number.

A headache tapped in. I saw flashbulb glare and caught break-in blips out of sequence.

The pillowcase stuffed with coins.

The closet stuffed with big-girl threads.

Monroe's quote in Paul de River's book:

"When all other forms of applied therapy have failed, it may be possible to contravene absent, passive, and self-destructively reactive behavior with the imposition of direct criminal action."

The headache abated. I saw Monroe dead. I didn't conjure her. She just appeared. I jumped to 8/4/62, unbidden. I felt the hot air of nine nights ago.

I saw the print-wiped clock radio. I saw the footprints on deep-pile carpet. I saw the left-behind bug mounts. I saw Monroe's head on the pillow. I touched her leg. It was still warm. I slid my hand up and pulled it back. I lost track of what was *then*, what was *now*, what I *wish* I'd done then.

I took two more jolts. The juice electrified me. Replication, transposition. I'm back in sync.

Underwear Drawer Pic #1: Marilyn's underwear. Underwear Drawer Pic #2: morgue photo of Carole Landis. Underwear Drawer Pic #3: note composed in cutout/glued-on magazine letters.

"I loved her before I loved you. She was nicer. You're more desperate and pretentious. I had to learn to love you. She made it easy."

Underwear Drawer Pix #4 to 11: pornographic snapshots.

Who's the cruel-looking stud? He looks familiar.

It's '58 or '59. There's no bite mark on Monroe's left bicep.

Note the crusted semen. I scraped a sample off and froze it. It's in my icebox. The Fed goons never checked. Talk to Daryl Gates. He'll order lab comparison tests.

Replication, transcription. I retrieved and described eleven pages of Polaroid snapshots. It stands as 85% recall.

She was dead. I felt her and smelled her all over me.

The foot.
Max Herman says, "Sink him, Freddy."
The foot.
Daryl Gates said something about a foot.

I yawned myself awake. It was full daylight. I crapped out on the couch. Notebook pages covered the floor.

I gathered them up. I recalled the retrieval. That's right—eleven full pages. That mug on the floor—it's cold coffee.

I was out for fourteen hours. The jungle juice revved me up high and laid me out flat.

I weaved to the can and took a leak. The foot dream resurrected. Gates said a motor cop found Richie Danforth's left foot. It was three miles north of the dump site. Vultures ate the meat and Richie's left sock.

I weaved back to the couch and scrawled a task list:

1) —Take frozen jizz to lab.
2) —Find missing report on blown MM tail job to the Valley.
    2-A)—Why did Valley locale look familiar? (It's a recent memory, I'm sure.)
    2-B)—Per tail job itself: I compiled list of 143 parked-car plate #s, on adjoining blocks. MM rendezvous? With whom? Locale non sequitur for MM. List now missing/ DMV list missing/Do Justice cops have my list?
3) —Per Separate Piece of Paper Pic #1: "Rick Dawes. Mean— maybe a fag." Work off subsequent tap call: "Eleanora" to Peter Lawford. "Eleanora" pumps Lawford for info on cater waiter "Rick Dawes," possible Beverly Hills 459 suspect. Contact BHPD per Dawes. Continue canvass of (200-odd) cater biz's & (131) phone-answering services.
4) —Check with U.S. Customs. Did MM fly to Mexico, 2/62, in disguise as migrant worker?
    4-A)—Run paper on José Bolaños: Local PD's, state & fed HUAC (Bolaños is Commie). Also check LAPD & LASO Narco.

I walked out to the porch and snagged the *Mirror*. Monroe hoo-haw smeared the front page. She was a vixen, a sexpot, a bombshell and beyond. She was a tigress, a coiled serpent, an enchantress, a rebuker of the stodgy and unhip. Again, Natasha Lytess logs the last word:

"The world had yet to become exhausted with her. She was taxing the world's patience, however."

I went back inside and skimmed the paper. I hit *"Kidnap of Starlet"*/

"Sheriff's Detectives Bemoan Dearth of Clues." I speed-skimmed the lead paragraph. It was the *Mirror*'s standard crime blah-blah.

Sergeant Michael J. Bayless/blah-blah/three suspects at large/two suspects now regretfully dead.

That set me back. *Two* dead? Richie Danforth and who else?

I flipped six pages forward. There's the lead: *"Kidnap Suspect a Suicide/ Grisly Death at Highland Park Station."*

I speed-skimmed the gist:

August 4 kidnap/starlet Gwen Perloff/suspect Hershel "Buzzy" Stein— suicide in his cell/suspect Richard Danforth—killed by Hat Squad stalwarts and celeb PI Freddy Otash, specially deputized by—

I heard door knocks. I tossed the *Mirror* and opened the door.

Pat came at me. She hit my face, gouged my neck, kicked me, and kneed me in the groin. I grabbed her wrists. She sobbed. She pushed me half off my feet. I looked past her and tried to hold her still.

A Fed sled was parked at the curb. Eddie Chacón leaned against it. Who's that beady-eyed putz in the backseat? It's Ratfuck Bobby the K.

21

I bopped through the DA's Bureau squadroom. Twenty-four cops worked at partner desks. I wore a drip-dry summer suit and starched white shirt. My Marine Corps service pin echoed the Big War. I packed a belt piece and a beavertail sap. I felt ring-a-ding good.

The cops checked me out. Shitbird Freddy's back. He walks among us, he's one of us, he outranks us all.

Such pissy outrage.

Miller Leavy's office adjoined the squadroom. He prosecuted high-ticket homicides and put sex slashers and cop killers in the Green Room. He burned Caryl Chessman and the Santo/Perkins/Barbara Graham mob. He built his Airedale a mock-gas-chamber doghouse.

His door stood open. I breezed in like King Shit. I dragged a slat-back chair up to his desk and perched.

He saw me. I dangled my arms off the chair back. He said, "I was opposed to the idea of a ceremony. I would have handed you your credentials in a back alley somewhere, but the DA and Bill Parker overrode me. Don't extend your hand to me. I won't shake it."

I lit a cigarette and grabbed an ashtray off the desk. Mr. Green Room flinched.

"How's the count, Mr. Leavy? You've burned eleven, haven't you? By the way, you owe me for Fred Stroebel. I traced the little girl's underwear back to his garage, and I kicked the shit out of him at the Wilshire DB."

Leavy smirked. He was short. Three seat cushions scooched him up to eye level.

"I can hardly blame you and the Hats for dumping Richard Danforth, and Buzzy Stein's suicide is between him and God. The three actual kidnappers remain at large, though. I would appreciate it if you would attempt to identify and apprehend them."

Nuisance. Minor irritant. The kidnap deal low-simmered. Only putzo legal types cared.

"I'll poke around, if I get the chance. Kidnap's a gas-chamber bounce. You could make hay there."

Leavy beamed. Daryl Gates and Mayor Sam Yorty walked in. Gates was Bill Parker's hand-picked successor. He watchdogged Mayor Sam for the Chief. Mayor Sam ran fascist-police-force riffs during the '61 campaign. Ad Vice cops set him up with two call girls and shot peep-hole film. Mayor Sam got apostatized. He recanted his fasco spiel and embraced the Chief. They booze at Ollie Hammond's most Tuesday nights.

I stood up. Miller Leavy stood up. We huddled by Leavy's desk and dispensed backslaps and Freddy's-the-Man pap. Gates tossed me my badge and credential folder. Mayor Sam told me to raise my right hand.

I complied. Mayor Sam invoked a jive oath of service. I whooped. I'm back on the fuzz, citizens. It's a license to steal and a ticket to ride.

Mayor Sam produced a flask. He took two pops. I took two pops. Gates and Leavy declined. The boys checked a wall clock. *Macht schnell*—let's move this along.

Mayor Sam said, "Governor Brown told me a good one. A lion is fucking a zebra. The zebra looks over his shoulder and says, 'Oh shit, baby! I see my husband! Quick—pretend that you're killing me!'"

Gates and I laughed on cue. Leavy said, "I don't get it." Mayor Sam scoped the wedding-stone cut on my cheek.

I said, "A woman who used to love me. I was overmatched."

We walked to the PAB. Gates reserved me a wall cubicle at Intel. I could work there, nest there, make phone calls. His secretary would shag my message slips.

The division fielded forty-eight detectives. They deployed in round-the-clock shifts. Intel was down from Robbery and Bunco. It ate up twice the floor space. Forty-eight partner desks—that's de rigueur. Ditto the wall offices and conference rooms. Equipment rooms goosed the extra space.

They stored movie cameras/still cameras/strobe lights/electric power packs/bug-and-tap mikes/installation tools/refrigerated film-

can vaults/partitioned-off darkrooms and extensive film and tape librar-
ies. Plus boom mikes, radio transceivers, and detachable prowl-car
two-ways with individual-frequency reception. A wallboard held keys
for fifty-six surveillance rides. A photo room was plastered with racy
pix from a current political entrapment.

Identify, scrutinize, surveil. That's Intel's ethos. Eyeball and collect
data on:

Commies/Commie front groups/left-leaning dimwits/rowdy civil
rights groups/jerkoff right-wing groups/politicians and Third World
potentates out to get bombed and get laid. Plus film-biz stupes known to
fraternize with the above. Plus anybody who fucked with Chief William
H. Parker and the LAPD.

We talked in Gates' office. I tossed him a changeup straight off.

"Early a.m. Sunday, the fifth. Phil Irwin and I have Monroe's house
staked. The housekeeper calls Doc Greenson, who calls Doc Engleberg.
They call the West L.A. desk. A patrol sergeant responds. His name's
Jack Clemmons. He's a tall blond guy, about thirty-eight. An informant
told me he's a right-wing nut. He's in the White Dog Bund, whatever
that is. He's tight with an ex-PD motor cop named Norm Krause. This
dink owns a juice joint out in the Valley, and he allegedly extorted the
then state comptroller, Tom Kuchel, for public fellatio, back in '49. He's
in the Bund, too. Does any of this ring any bells?"

Gates said, "None. I don't know or know of Clemmons and Krause,
the Kuchel deal, or the Dog Bund. Who cares? It's got nothing to do with
our Monroe business at hand."

I lit a cigarette. Gates slid his desk ashtray over and hit the AC switch.

"First, the Chief and I know you'll dissemble and omit—but don't
overdo it. Second, let me restate the parameters. Our deal with Bob
Kennedy entails the demonizing of Marilyn Monroe, to discredit her
if talk of her alleged romantic attachment to the Kennedys surfaces to
the world at large. Our *side* deal entails that you develop a concurrent
derogatory profile on John and Robert Kennedy, to utilize if Bob renegs
on his pledge to shoot the Chief the FBI job. And, of course, facilitate
my ascent to Chief."

I grinned. "I understand. And, parenthetically, an informant told me
that old man Hoover wants Pete Pitchess to get the job if the Kennedys
can him. Pete's a lawyer, and he's ex-FBI. Maybe SHIT has some ops
going to juke Pete's shot at the job."

Gates shrugged. "It's possible."

I said, "Okay, Justice sandbagged us. They've got all the copies of all my evidence from the Hoffa gig, which leaves us holding our dicks. Do you think that little hump Bobby will convene a grand jury and deploy the evidence against Hoffa, which would sure as shit bring collateral indictments down on me and my boys?"

Gates said, "It's possible. We should also consider the fact that you killed a man while on temporary assignment from the Chief, and that you've been publically identified in the press."

"It's a 'put-up job,' Daryl. Danforth was saying that as he waltzed off the cliff."

Gates squared his necktie and shot his cuffs. He was fastidious. He wore a gold-coin wristwatch.

"'Put-up job' wouldn't surprise me. Buzzy Stein drinking lye in our custody troubles me, though. A jailer at Highland Park told me he was terrified of something or somebody. He refused to talk to our guys, after he witnessed the dump job and revealed Gwen Perloff's location. Why mince words? This bullshit caper—whatever it is—could bite us on the ass six million ways."

I crushed my cigarette. "Did the Sheriff's come by Highland Park and brace Stein? Mike Bayless is the lead IO. He's working it for the West Hollywood squad."

Gates said, "Oddly, they did not drop by. Not so oddly, you see where all this is heading. The Chief and I would like you to look into the kidnap deal, and stand ready to squelch any anti-PD rumors that might arise."

I said, "I'm on it."

Gates smiled. "You're susceptible to guilt, Freddy. It's one of your more humanizing aspects. Do you feel bad about Danforth?"

I flinched. "I need to brace Paul de River. Monroe was fixated on him. She annotated a copy of one of his books. She told Greenson she was in the market for a 'more radical' shrink."

Gates yawned. "Brace him. Stay aware of the fact that he hates us. Bill Parker sacked him, and he's never gotten over it. He'll rat us to the *L.A. Times* in a heartbeat."

I nodded. The office went hot to cold. Gates futzed with a jade paperweight.

"Talk to your man Nat Denkins. Have him put out some counterintel on his radio show. All rumors about Monroe and powerful politicians are bunk. I'm offering two concessions here. I'll allow the weekly crap game in the KKXZ basement to continue, and I'll cut his brother Kareem loose. We've got him for CCW in that Muslim snafu, and I'll get the charge dropped."

I stood up. Gates stood up. He fidgeted and quashed the urge to primp.

"One last thing. We've been informed that Morty Bendish at the *Mirror* has a tattle piece on Monroe and the Kennedys in the works. Put the squelch to it. Morty's peddling beaver pix of Monroe in the morgue. You might squelch that, as well."

22

The *Herald* morgue. L.A. in mid-August. Four rooms crammed with chairs and file shelves.

News clips glued to cardboard sheets. Big boxes crammed full. News clips culled worldwide. Monroe kicked eleven days back. Her clip glut totaled seven thousand–plus obits and puff pieces.

I was fourteen hours in. I locked the outside hallway door and worked in my skivvies. I aimed a porta fan at my balls and stirred up a breeze. I scanned clip-to-clip. I trolled for tidbits on Monroe and the K boys. I got Jack's New York birthday bash and no derogatory dish or inuendo. Moldy newspaper induced sneeze attacks. It was shitwork, par excellence.

I was seven clip boxes in. I had one box to go. Beside my chair: one thin-ass *L.A. Mirror* file.

The Gwen Perloff kidnap job. *So what?* The crime-king *Mirror* gave it short shrift.

I saved the file for kicks and grins. It goosed me to speed-read the Monroe shit. The clips played soporific.

Jean-Paul Sartre said, "Marilyn was devoured by the psychic nothingness of American values." This sentiment pervaded the Euro press. The U.S. dailies and news glossies spritzed celeb kudos and kvetchy grief. On to the UCLA *Daily Bruin*, the USC *Daily Trojan*, the Cal Berkeley *Golden Bear*. More kudos and kvetch from a college-kid perspective. *The New York Times, New York Herald Tribune, New York Journal-American*. "What killed Marilyn?" Hollywood and the too-cruel world—*J'accuse!!!* Here's a mitigating laugh. Trumpet boss Miles Davis tells a *DownBeat* scribe: "She was déclassé, baby. I always thought of her as Dorothy Dandridge for the poor."

The clip cutters went all out. They glommed clips from the daily rags of L.A. high schools in summer session. Lowell Farr wrote "Bop Requiem for Marilyn" in the Palisades High *Daily Dolphin*. Dig the text:

We lost sacred Bix and Bird back in paleolithic times;
Now Marilyn splits this jive earth and rings our mourning chimes;
She follows cool Carole Landis to the Pill Parthenon;
The sick and the sentient wonder where she went wrong.

Lowell published her dirge in the 8/9 *Dolphin*. Fan letters followed. The "Bop Requiem" drew some critical flak. "Big Bob" Berglund slammed it in the 8/12 *Dolphin*. "Lowell Farr's Monroe poem was a pretentious shuck. Let's admit it, Lowell is a pseud."

Lowell fires back on 8/14. "Big (Ha!) Bob Berglund is a nosebleed, a nimrod, a ho-daddy and a pseudosurfer. He's not a natural blond. He bleaches his hair, and he's never been to the beach. Let's admit *that*. Moreover, the Dolphin intelligentsia scoffs at him."

I cogitated. Lowell's dirge buzzed me past the laugh stage. As in the Carole Landis reference.

There's the Landis morgue pic. There's the crazy note, beside it. "I loved her before I loved you." The note was spelled out in excised/glued-on magazine letters. It's a classic sex-fiend missive.

I found a letter scrap and a glue daub on my living room floor. They were right below my pictorial corkboard. The Fed raid missed them. The LAPD crime lab keeps a cut-letter exemplar set. I ran my letter scrap through it, yesterday. I studied glue-sample charts/paper-stock notations/named-magazine lists. I got no matches and no evidential tweaks.

Lowell Farr tweaked me. Monroe spilled Jack-and-Bobby dish to her. On at least two dozen tap calls. I don't want Lowell to regurgitate it. She's seventeen. I'll need mom and dad's consent to debrief her. Miller Leavy can set it up.

I quick-skimmed the last Monroe box and lit a cigarette. I replayed a long skull session with Phil Irwin. We crashed in my new Intel office. We brainstormed and re-created a tally of Lawford and Monroe house tap calls. The total hit 281—to, from, and between. The preponderant tap topic was the grave vibe at 20th Century–Fox.

Giant lox *Cleopatra*. Fox veers toward bankruptcy. Celebrity sex skank in Roma. Roddy McDowall's pornographic *Cleo* spoof. Fox execs and rank and filers hatching money schemes. They're fail-safes should *Cleo* tank the studio. There's endemic frayed nerves and bad behavior on the lot.

Monroe's antics tanked *Got to Give*. Monroe worked for Fox. Ditto, Gwen Perloff. Fox deserved a look-see. An unknown caller tipped Darryl Zanuck to the kidnap play. Zanuck tipped LAPD. Hence "Sink him, Freddy" and big potential grief.

I skimmed the Perloff file. It was threadbare local news. Perloff, thirty-six, is an "aging starlet." The three snatch men wore Fidel Castro masks. Short sleeves reveal two white males and one Latin-type male. The snatch car descriptions vary. '57 Imperial, Chevy Nomad, '51 Ford coupe. Vehicle checks go *pffft*. The Sheriff's triple-canvass Miller Drive and the cross streets above the Strip. It goes *pffft*. Perloff has a boss crib in a boss modern building. She's jumped outside. Switchboard glitches stall the eyewit calls to West Hollywood station. The patrol desk sounds a belated alarm. The LAPD's "famous" Hat Squad and "celeb" PI Freddy O. are tipped to the hideout pad of suspects Stein and Danforth. The Hats plus Freddy O. bust them. Danforth is killed during a "pitched battle" with Max Herman, Red Stromwall, and Freddy O. Stein reveals the San Fernando Valley location where Perloff is currently stashed. Sheriff's Sergeant Michael J. Bayless leads a daring rescue raid. The stash pad was rented by a "heavyset" older woman. She paid cash in advance and employed an obvious alias. Sergeant Bayless called the case "one big baffler."

Two sidebar columns laid out Gwen Perloff. She's an L.A. native and "plucky hard-luck girl." She lost her parents in a car wreck and grew up in foster homes and an orphan facility. Her eight-year-old sister, Mitzi, disappeared off a Hollywood street on 2/17/37. Gwen was not quite eleven then. The riddle of her vanishing and probable death has remained unexplained.

Gwen studied at the Pasadena Playhouse and worked as a runway model for Jantzen swimwear. She secured Universal and Fox contracts. She appears in dance-craze flicks and horror movies. She was notable in Universal's *The Tattered Dress* and Fox's *Sons and Lovers*. Columnist Hy Gardner said, "Yum-yum—she's the American Anna Magnani, minus all those pasta pounds." Now, Miss Perloff essays strictly B-film roles. She plays the "sexy older woman" in dance-craze and monster flicks geared for a teenage market.

A *Mirror* clip featured a swimsuit ad. It's 6/18/54. There's *La* Gwen in a floral-print bikini. She's ever the schoolmarm knockout. She's sporting her trademark tortoiseshell specs.

I went home and showered off the morgue. I put on a drip-dry blazer and poplin slacks. It was a ranking cop's ensemble. Let's flash the new credential and see who scoffs and who quakes.

West Hollywood station was close by. I waltzed through. The squad boss told me Motel Mike just rotated back to SHIT. I asked to see the Perloff file. The squad boss nixed it. My DA's buzzer hit him nonplussed.

Squadroom cops fish-eyed me. A kid deputy was working a tip-line phone on the job. I scoped his call-log sheet. The tipsters were logged as "bored anonymous women." That's your standard L.A. kidnap drill.

Beverly Hills station was close by. I waltzed through. I braced the squad boss per the 459 series with cater waiter suspects. I stressed "Rick Dawes" and "Eleanora's" tap call to Peter Lawford. The squad boss addressed me as "Lieutenant" and dropped the gate.

I will not share information. You cannot see the file. You may not interview the IO's. Submit a formal DA's Office request.

I broomed back downtown. I adjusted my rearview mirror and admired the wedding-stone scar on my face.

Pat landed flush. I stepped into the punch. She roughhoused with her candy-ass brothers and knew how to grapple a bit. She was the tall and strong sister. Drawn and gaunt worked for her. I knew I'd never see her again. Not with this new gig, not on Ratfuck Bobby's dime.

I conjured up Lois. She'd be thirty-five tomorrow. I'd send her red roses and mark the card *"I Remember You."* We met in '55. Lois was a telephone trickster. She met her husband that way. He had a radio call-in show in New York. Lois dug him and kept calling him. That's how she met me. She called *Nasty Nat's Soul Patrol* and dropped my name. That's how I met Nat. I shook down a film-biz geek, fall '57. It force-fed me the blues and the guilts. I bought KKXZ and tossed Nat the deed. You get what you pay for. Nat got a radio station. I got sporadic stints with Lois Nettleton.

The day went hot and smog-choked. The 101 was backed up to Normandie. I took surface streets downtown. The Hall of Justice lot was swamped. I boxed in two steno-pool cars and stuck an OFFICIAL VEHICLE ON CALL card under my wiper blades. The Sheriff's DB was up on Floor #12.

I elevatored up. SHIT was wedged between Homicide and Auto Theft. The squadroom was half the size of LAPD Intel. The equipment rooms were laid out identical. Deputies got partner desks. Sergeants got wall cubicles. Lieutenants and up got offices. The wall pix lionized Pete Pitchess.

Sheriff Pete with Duke Wayne, Kirk Douglas, Joan Fontaine. Sheriff Pete with Miss America finalists. Sheriff Pete outside the Green Room. Thrill killer Stephen Nash sucks gas.

Mike Bayless had a neat corner cubicle. His view featured Lincoln Heights and smog. He sat at his desk and flipped paper clips. He wore a mid-gray suit. Sheriff Pete espoused the Fed automaton look.

I grabbed his desk chair. Motel Mike flipped a paper clip in my lap. I flashed my credential. Motel Mike lip-synched *Eat me.*

"Woo-woo. Mr. Shakedown's working for the DA, and I'm guessing he's a bird dog for Bill Parker, who's got justified concerns that Mr. Shakedown and the Hats dusted one of my kidnap suspects, and now my case is dead stalled. Does that sound accurate to you?"

I made the jack-off sign. "Woo-woo. Motel Mike toasts four beaners back in the ice age, and it goes to his head. Motel Mike's so far up Pete Pitchess' ass that he buys his suits at Oviatt's, clothier to Gerald L. K. Smith and Gay Edgar Hoover."

Motel Mike sighed. "Tell me what you want."

I said, "A two-minute Perloff case summary and access to the file."

"Yes to the summary, no to the file. Here's your overview. The case is dead stalled. Gwen Perloff was banging Darryl F. Zanuck. Mr. Mogul got a tip call from a woman, who gave up Richie Danforth and Buzzy Stein and spilled where to find them. Then Zanuck called in Bill Parker, because the LAPD has got more marquee value than my department. Enter Mr. Shakedown and the overzealous Hat Squad. Now, Danforth and Stein are dead, and Parker and Daryl Gates have sent you out to see what I've got, because Parker and the PD took it in the shorts on that Black Muslim deal, and you're out to squelch potential bad press on Danforth, vis-à-vis that dive he took."

I whistled and clapped. Motel Mike bowed. I went *Don't stop now.* Motel Mike complied.

"We've worked this job into the ground. We triple-canvassed a half-mile radius and hit the not-at-homes twice. There was not one credible description of the snatch car, so we couldn't run vehicle checks. We ran full forensics on both stash-pad locations and got nothing. Our informant queries turned up zero. Our tip line, likewise. Richie Danforth's a cipher. He's got no extant print cards within the Continental U.S.—state, Federal, or U.S. Armed Forces. He's got no state crime bureau record extant—and that's for all fifty states. Your dump job scotched our shot to roll his prints. Truck tires pulped his hands and feet. We're eleven days in, and we've got nothing worth a shit to work off."

I lit a cigarette. "Give me Perloff's account."

"What's to give? She was chloroformed, blindfolded, and gagged. She came to in the closet of that Tiki-Torch dive. The snatch guys hooked a hose from the air-conditioner inside the closet, so she could breathe and stay cool. They fed her water and two hamburgers. They walked her to the can, twice, and there was no pervy stuff. She did not recognize their voices. You see what I'm up against—"

I cut in. "I watched you waltz her outside. She didn't look like a kidnap victim dumped in a closet."

Motel Mike flipped paper clips. "I gave her ten minutes to get herself together. She's an actress. She's got that 'show must go on' mentality."

I said, "Known associates. Criminal types at Fox. Lovers, ex-boyfriends, powerful guys she's shtupping, besides old man Zanuck. Shithead film-biz guys who know guys who know guys. You see where I'm going here."

Motel Mike lit a cigarette. "The Sheriff would like to see this job vaporize. He's kowtowing to old man Zanuck on this. You know Del Kinney, right? He's the Fox security chief, and he used to be on the Sheriff's and the ABC."

Kinney. Monroe Gig #1. The full Otash crew roams the Fox lot in plain view. Kinney might have known or suspected.

"Yeah, I know Kinney."

"Well, old man Zanuck told him to keep cops away from Gwen. He's got the Sheriff's backing in that regard. This means my investigation is hamstrung. Zanuck's got X number of young talent on his string at all times, and he's determined to keep them all anonymous."

I crushed my cigarette. "Parker and Gates want me to shake some doors on this deal. Regardless of what the Sheriff and Darryl Zanuck want."

"So, do it. Watch out for Del Kinney, though. He goes way back with Gwen Perloff. It's a big brother–kid sister thing they've got going. It's powerful, and when you see them together you can sense it."

I said, "What are you telling me?"

"I'm telling you that Gwen's kid sister got abducted and sure as shit snuffed. It was up in Hollywood, maybe '37 or '38. Mitzi was eight, and Gwen was something like eleven. Kinney ran the Sheriff's mounted posse part of the job. They were digging up dead kids in Griffith Park, but they never found Mitzi's remains."

I crossed myself. Motel Mike crossed himself. He flipped paper clips at me. I tossed a changeup.

"Does SHIT have surveillance film on Marilyn Monroe?"

Motel Mike shrugged. "We have some. She was a pinko and a ban-the-bomber, so she mandated our attention. Why do you care? LAPD has ten times the footage, so ask Daryl Gates for a peek. LAPD's the font of show-biz dirt in this town, not the Sheriff's."

I stood up. "It was good seeing you, Mike."

"Mr. Shakedown. Destined for the Shit Magnet Hall of Fame."

Motel Mike's spiel percolated. He worked the case pro forma. Studio politics intervened. He was borderline credible—with one red flag up.

Richie Danforth cartwheels. He shrieks *"It's a put-up job"* as he spins.

I drove north on PCH. I decided to recanvass the Lawford house and Monroe house turf. Nat and Phil would launch a full-on canvass within forty-eight hours. Daryl Gates was working up bogus credentials. Nat would be Customs, Phil would be Treasury. They'd concoct cover stories. They'd press for Monroe/K boys dirt. They'd be out to disprove and defame, simultaneous.

My credentials were legitimate. I devised a Big-"H"-hits-the-beach cover and walked a beat north of the Lawford spread. Pat and Peter's neighbors were show-biz and real-estate stiffs. I deployed scare tactics and stressed the proximity of our squeaky-clean prez and AG. The neighbors knew that Jack and Bobby partied at the Lawford digs. I dropped Monroe in, oblique. Oh, yes—they'd seen Marilyn at cocktail dos. So tragic—and to die so terribly young!

Yawn, snore, the Secobarbital Express. One geez said the Lawfords threw "degenerate-type parties." His wife said, "You're just chagrined that they didn't invite you."

Yawn. Snore. Nobody tattled sex shit. I fed them cues. Nobody did a big double take and spooned out the dish. I shagged my sled and cut east to Brentwood.

8:00 p.m. traffic snagged and crawled. I passed Pali High. I thought of

Lowell Farr. I passed the Bay Theater. Now playing: *The Notorious Land-lady* and *The Devil at Four O'Clock*. I thought of Lowell's anonymous make-out dates. "It's a nice kid's version of going to a motel."

Traffic unsnared at Mandeville Canyon. I made good time to Fifth Helena Drive. I caught a beach party five miles inland.

A dozen kids sunned themselves on Monroe's front lawn. A boy cooked hot dogs on a hibachi. Kids twisted and danced the wah watusi. Transistor radios wafted "Marilyn's Song," "Image of a Girl." Teen queens preened in Marilyn drag.

I parked across the street. I recanvassed Fourth Helena and Falkirk Lane. I laid out my pitch and logged deadpan looks—*Huh?* and *What?* predominant.

A pissy guy said Robert F. Kennedy was Monroe's drop-in lover. His pissy wife contradicted him. No, he was a UPS driver. He just looked like Robert F. Kennedy.

The recanvass slogged. I got *Huh?* and *No.* I got *The Kennedys?* and *Her life was such a tragedy.* I hit Dunoon Lane and scored three houses in.

A man was outside, pulling weeds. I badged him and reran my spiel. I got to "Marilyn Monroe's house." He cut me off and bored straight in.

"Well, here's something that might interest you. An older, sickly looking woman rented a house on Dunoon, right after Miss Monroe bought her place. And I have to tell you, this sickly woman bought the dumpiest house in all of Brentwood. She used to skulk around Miss Monroe's house late at night. I even saw her up on her roof, peeking through binoculars at the house."

23

Nat said, "Jimmy Hoffa sent me a bank draft for ten grand. He's paying bonus bread for a job the Justice cops fucked up to a fare-thee-well. I should be jubilant, but I'm nothing but scared."

KKXZ, 56th and Figueroa. Nat's broadcast room/command post. Album covers pinned wall-to-wall. Gone sides from Diz, Bird, Miles, and Nat's house band—the Synagogue Sid Trio.

It was blast-oven hot. Three floor fans stirred wet air. We lounged in scuffed Eames chairs. We shared one ottoman. We kicked each other's feet to make points.

I said, "You're scared because it's un-Jimmy. I feel the same way. It has something to do with Monroe and the Kennedys, and I intend to suss it all out."

Nat kicked my feet. "Money. Let's remain on the topic. What's your pal Gates paying us? I know it won't be Hoffa-type bread, but he's got to match your daily rate, or Phil and I will go on strike."

I said, "He'll match it. Intel's got a big expense fund. There'll be bonus money, and he's already done you two solids."

Nat went *Huh?* Nat hummed "Money, honey."

"He needs a favor, so he's fed you two in advance. One, your weekly card game is now LAPD-sanctioned. Two, Gates got Miller Leavy to drop the CCW charge on Kareem. He's out, and he's sleeping it off at my place as we speak. In consideration of this, you will abstain from theorizing per Monroe and the Kennedys on your show, and put out some counterintel. I brainstormed a semicomprehensive list of calls Monroe made to the White House and Justice switchboards. We've got the times, dates, and the length of the calls. Cite them, and lay out some jive on Monroe calling up to gab civil rights. Brace your main switchboard squeeze at Fox, and slide her two g's to alter her callout log, and to erase all documentation on Monroe's calls to the two switchboards."

Nat tapped my shoes. "All right. That's fair enough."

I lit a cigarette. "What else are you afraid of?"

Nat ticked points. "The upscut of that raid on your pad. Federal indictments. Open-court testimony on a guy who snuffs guys routinely. They raided my place and scared my wife half to death. I hit that Cuban guy with a fungo bat, which is ADW on a Federal agent. I know you vest-shot the three guys, which is worse, but then you're braver and stupider than me. The list goes on and on. If you don't perform for Parker and Bobby, life for us fools is preemptively over."

I popped my briefcase. I grabbed a U.S. Customs/special agent's badge and ID holder. Plus a small white calling card.

On the front: "Bill Parker." Plus his home phone number. In cursive, on the back: "This man is a close personal friend. Please extend him every courtesy."

Nat snatched the swag and perused it. He wore a loud Hawaiian shirt. Goose bumps popped up his arms.

I tapped his feet. "You're Customs, Phil's Treasury. I want an extensive canvass. Up PCH a mile north and south of the Lawford house, and a half mile out from the Monroe house. Concoct jive cover stories. Buzz every house you talk to on Monroe and the Kennedys. Work for defamation *and* exoneration. At the same time, go for times and dates that might prove verifiable. Keep detailed logs, and hit the not-at-homes until they *are* home. I want certifiably depraved shit on Monroe—because that's one level of our assignment. The second level is safeguarding the Chief's FBI-boss deal with dipshit Bobby. Blackmail's our only protection there. Get me Jack and sex, Jack and dope, Jack and jailbait, Jack and all those TV actresses Peter Lawford sets him up with. It's a heavy-duty skank deal. And skank's the only thing that will stop Bobby from waltzing us in front of a Federal grand jury."

Nat whistled. "That's a two-week canvass. What will you be doing all that time?"

"Trying to decode Monroe's last four months on earth, based on what we've got so far."

Nat stood up and stretched. "We should find work for Kareem."

"Gates needs a man inside the mosque at Slauson and Broadway. It's a hundred and fifty a week and expenses. And tell Kareem no liquor

stores. There's stakeout squads all over the southside, and they're looking to take scalps."

Nat smiled. "Lois called me. She's in town, and she wants you to
know she's been thinking about you."

Lois ran nocturnal. Her métier was the late-night phone call. She snared
her husband that way. She snared me with calls to KKXZ.

She always made me wait. I perched by my phone, up to 1:30. Waiting
implodes me. I shook loose and drove to Brentwood. The dumpy house.
Dunoon Lane. The "sickly old lady" with binoculars. It was a lead. It
was a peep-the-peeper task.

I found the place. It was a stand-alone eyesore. Faded peach stucco.
Weed-clumped grass. Add-on top floor, built askew. It's two hundred
yards northeast of the Monroe spread. There's a flat roof and downward
eyeball path. A '49 Ford stood in the driveway. It accessorized the dump.

I parked and walked up the driveway. The Ford reeked of sickbed
balm and stale sweat. The windows were down. I penlight-flashed the
steering column and checked the registration strap. Natasha Lytess
owned the heap. I made the name, fast.

Monroe's ex-acting coach. Mordant per Monroe. A standout eulo-
gizer. Monroe and her shopworn enchantment.

I flashed the front seat and strafed a Vicente Pharmacy bag. I
reached in and pulled out a vial of four-grain Dilaudid. *There's* some
enchantment.

I unscrewed the vial and popped two Big "D" 's. I walked back to my
sled and grabbed my binoculars. The house had thick window ledges
and raised cement ornamentation. I circled the perimeter and gauged
hand- and footholds. The north-side neighbor's fence would cloak me.

I hung the binoculars around my neck and climbed a drainpipe. The
cement strips held my weight. Two footholds, two handholds. I vaulted
up on the roof.

The Monroe house was south-southwest. I walked to the edge of the
roof and dialed my distance gauge tight. I saw blue-green grass, night-
muted stucco, and yellow window light.

It's the east-facing living room window. I *know* that room. I've peeped
it and worked it and smelled it. The colors were off, the shadows were
wrong, a candle light flickered, left to right.

I dialed in, dialed out, stepped back and reframed. The dope hit me. It cocooned me, warm and safe. It resituated the shadows and magnified the candlelight.

Lowell Farr walked across the room. She wore a Pali High sweater and a red beret and carried a paintbrush. She stood by the north wall and painted a woman perched on a bedside.

She worked in bold red. The dope let me mute and enhance shades at will. Lowell switched brushes for the detail work. Black paint for definition, flesh tones, blue-gray for the eyes. Blond hair, then gray, then chalk white. It's Monroe twice her age. Lowell sees her inside out.

She switched brushes. She blacked out the bedside perch and recolored Monroe's hair. She x-ed out the old Monroe's face and gave her a tall and ungainly girl's body. She painted an arrow. It extended from the X mark to a clean white swatch of wall.

She painted a close-up there. It was her own face in extremis. She got the kid good looks, the bumpy nose, the not quite buck teeth. She borrowed Marilyn's eyes and something from her smile. *She's* the enchantress. *She* achieves transmogrification.

24

Silver Lake. Due east of Hollywood. High hills above the smog line. I climbed in low gear. Morty Bendish had a stilt house off the reservoir. Silver Lake was mudslides and collapsed foundations. It was a beatnik/film-slave enclave. Wags called it the "Swish Alps."

I afterglowed on the filched dope and Lowell Farr's art show. I slept in the Intel cot room. I rolled out early and worked.

Lab work first. I dropped off the frozen jizz caked on the Monroe/Cruel Stud fuck pix and buzzed Ray Pinker for quick results. Ray cited his *829* preserved jizz vials. It would take at least three weeks to log comparison tests.

Phone work next. I got out my cater-biz list and called seventeen outfits. I got zero, zilch, nein, and nyet. Nobody knew a cater waiter named Rick Dawes. Nobody knew a cater waitress named Eleanora. Cater waiters were by nature dicey. They were all fly-by-nights.

I ran "Rick Dawes" and "Richard Dawes" through LAPD and Sheriff's R&I. I got hits on twenty-four Negroes and two old white guys. A phone book check fizzled. There were no Dick Daweses or Richard Daweses in the L.A. area white pages.

Dawes to José Bolaños. I stiffed formal file-request calls to state and Fed HUAC and the Mexican State Police. They pledged results "within one month." I called Miller Leavy and begged favors. He refused to brace BHPD for their 459-string files. "No, Freddy—not off a slip of paper and one illegal wiretap call." I told Miller to contact Mr. and Mrs. Willard D. Farr and request an interview with seventeen-year-old Lowell. Miller balked. "He's a *big* Republican fat cat! Mayor Yorty would kill me!"

Scratch Lowell for now. I called my casting director contact at Warner's and dunned him for dish on Natasha Lytess. He checked his files and dished good.

Born in Russia, 5/16/11. Studied under the "revisionist" Vsevolod Meyerhold. Immigrates to the United States. Tanks as a second-lead actress. Gets a drama coach gig at Metro. Meets Monroe on *The Asphalt Jungle*. Becomes infatuated with her. Follows her. They work studio to studio and film to film. Bunks with Monroe briefly. It's now 2/56. Monroe's shooting *Bus Stop* at Fox. Lytess has become clingy and overbearing. Lezbo rumors circulate. Monroe and Fox dump Lytess cold. Lytess plagues Monroe with calls and weepy letters. Monroe's lawyer makes her desist. '56 to '62: some sort of torrid torch burns—

There's Morty's hut. It's all space-age prefab. Aluminum panels and tinted Plexiglas. A crushed-rock carport. Stilt-anchored terraces and three dark rooms. *L.A. Mirror* foto art throughout. Morty on dead-body calls, Morty on the gas-chamber beat up at Quentin.

I parked and walked right in. I heard Morty cough and beelined for the rear terrace. A breeze stirred, the stilts swayed, a striped awning flapped.

Morty worked at a stand-up draftsman's table. The surface was crammed with foto proofs, news clips, pencils, pens, and pocket-size pamphlets. Morty hunkered low and proofread. He saw me and rolled his eyes.

"Hi, Freddy. It's been a while."

I said, "Can the piece on Marilyn Monroe and the Kennedys. Bill Parker finds that sort of thing offensive."

Morty scratched his balls. He wore a soiled T-shirt and plaid boxer shorts.

"I covered the interfaith prayer breakfast at Temple Beth Shalom. Bill was half in the bag. He told Cardinal McIntyre and Rabbi Magnin the story of Come-san-Chin, the Chinese cocksucker. He shouldn't drink in public."

I yocked. "Give up your source on the Monroe piece."

Morty tossed me a pamphlet. The title: *Weird-O Death of a Sex Siren*, by Mr. Fearless Fuzz. The cover art: Monroe in a Milady brassiere ad, circa '46.

I quick-skimmed the text. Fearless Fuzz "scandalously scoped" the sleek Marilyn, dead in her bed. Her "boss bod" was dotted with leprous puncture marks. Fearless Fuzz "determinedly deduced" that the

Kennedy mob decreed her death. Their motive? To quash "rampant rumors" of her liaisons with John and Robert and their plans to establish a "Mormon ménage" at the president's Camp David retreat. A civil wrongs gang performed the snuff. Marilyn's collection of Harry Belafonte records underscored her "race-mixer tendencies."

Fearless Fuzz predicted the collapse of the Kennedy mob and mass suicides within the Kennedy family—once the *whole* story is laid out in this groundbreaking pamphlet series.

I lit a cigarette. "How far out in the ozone does this Monroe/Kennedy rumor fly?"

Morty bummed a cigarette. "It's afloat in hip circles, where everyone spritzes. What *true* insiders—like you and me—know is that Jack's a two-minute man, and that he allows an hour for his assignations, which includes the martini, the club sandwich, and the conversation. And before you ask, Bobby don't stray. Take that to the bank."

I said, "Who's Fearless Fuzz?"

Morty dredged his ears with a paper clip. "A nutty West L.A. Division patrol cop named Jack Clemmons, who got the call to view the dead Marilyn. You know me, Freddy. I go for verisimilitude, and even then, my standards are low. If I dig it, I figure it's true, and I publish it. Corroboration is strictly for Communists and fags."

Clemmons. Deedee Grenier snitched him off. He was tight with ex-cop/lounge lizard Norm Krause. Big Norm worked Wilshire Motors, circa '49. He extorted now–U.S. senator Tom Kuchel on a fruit beef. Clemmons and Krause: right-wing nuts and pals of pamphlet putz Frank Capell.

I sifted it. I drained it and strained it dry. I pointed to a stack of tabloid foldouts. They were ultralurid and green-inked.

Morty pooh-poohed me. "It's a private skank sheet that I sell to subscribers. Don't worry—mum's the word on Marilyn and the K boys."

I peeled off five C-notes and dropped them on the table. Morty went *Oooh-la-la.*

"In consideration of your squelching the Monroe piece and burning all the beaver shots, along with the negatives."

Morty went wistful. *Oh bird thou never—*

"Somebody snitched off your piece to Daryl Gates at Intel. Who do you think?"

Morty picked his nose. "My guess is Motel Mike Bayless, at SHIT.

Gates and Motel Mike trade dirt tips on a regular basis. It's like baseball cards. I'll trade you dirt on the Muslims if you trade me dirt on some *faigelah* deputy browning guys in Ferndell Park. Motel Mike's a *ganef*. Maybe he's got his own hustle going."

I tossed a slider. "That kidnap babe, Gwen Perloff. She vibes bait girl to me. What have you heard?"

Morty tee-heed. "I heard you and the Hats dusted one of the kidnap guys, and now Parker and Gates fear repercussions."

"*Perloff*, Morty. What have you heard?"

"I heard she's been around. I heard she couriers sketchy notes and bearer bonds for mogul types like Darryl Zanuck, Jack Warner, and Lew Wasserman. I'd call that a bait girl–adjunct thing to do."

Bearer bonds. It confirmed rumors. Like the *Cleopatra* cash drain and Fox in deep shit.

The Pico gate guards waved me in. My new credential flummoxed them. I didn't slide them cash or wink. They went *You're seeing who?* I went *Don't fuck with me—I'm with the DA now.*

I cut over to the casting office. I parked outside and barged in brusque. The waiting room was packed with teenage girls in bikinis. They mulled around and practiced dance steps. They wore signboards marked with the name of the audition flick: *Twist Party Stakeout.*

They twisted and mash-potatoed all around me. I badged a stooge dispensing signboards and demanded a full credits sheet for Gwen Perloff. He dug through cubbyholes and passed me a glossy leaflet. I walked out to my car and went through it.

La Gwen. Her Fox credits dated back to 1951. They ran intermittent. Frequent Jantzen swimwear gigs diverted the flow. *Big* Gwen—5'10"/140. She always wore glasses. She part-time modeled for Eyeking Opticians. She played third leads in expose-the-wetback-problem screeds. She played soon-to-die sexpots in monster films. She played somebody's nympho mom in four recent exploit-the-surf-craze jobs.

It was snoresville. Darryl Zanuck's office was close by. I strolled over and stood by his private side door. I primped and pulled my coat back to display my belt shit. The door stood ajar. I ambled right in.

He saw me. He made me. He quashed a scowl. He scrolled my pedigree and barrage of crimes against Fox in two seconds.

My exposés. My smear jobs. My gay film folk exploited and Fox stars vilified. My bugged bathhouses and contract studs entrapped at the Manhole and the Cockpit.

Say something, Pops. Pretend you're not scared. Hide behind your big desk. Pace your office and act bluff.

Zanuck said, "All right. I know who you are. The gate guards buzzed me. You're on the lot, and you want something you think I—"

I pulled a leather wing chair up to the desk. I snagged a big cigar from a big humidor. I lit up and blew smoke rings. Zanuck went sclerotic red.

"It's about Gwen Perloff. I represent Bill Parker and the DA's Office. I thought I'd spare you the ignominy of a trip downtown."

Zanuck lit a cigar. The room fumed up. He popped two pills, on the sly. My bet: digitalis.

"I already spoke to a Sheriff's sergeant named Bayless. I was extremely forthcoming, and he seemed to be satisfied."

I went *Nix*. "Did you receive a blackmail demand?"

"No. You know the chain of events, because you were a participant. A wheezy old lady called me and informed me that Miss Perloff had been kidnapped. She gave me the names of two of the men holding Miss Perloff hostage, and the address where she was being held. The old lady didn't know the names of the men who actually grabbed Gwen. I called Bill Parker and explained the situation. He sent you and the Hat Squad in. You know the rest, because you were there."

I said, "Did you recognize the old lady's voice?"

"No."

"Did she call you through the Fox switchboard?"

"No. She called my direct office line."

"How'd she get the number?"

"I don't know."

"Could she have been an ex–Fox employee?"

"That thought occurred to me."

I plopped my feet on Daddy-O's desk. A family portrait capsized.

"Are you shtupping Gwen Perloff, Pops? Is *that* the lit fuse behind this whole deal? Is *that* how the old lady knew to call you?"

Zanuck gnawed his cigar. He bit through the end and severed it. He grabbed the burning part and snuffed out the ash. Wet tobacco popped off his lips.

"Miss Perloff and I have a mentor-protégée relationship."

I made the jack-off sign. "Give me the drift on her private life. Who else is poking her? Does she swing both ways? Do you put her out as bait to rope in big investors?"

Zanuck sputtered. He gagged on tobacco mulch and spit in his handkerchief.

I said, "How'd you meet her? Who introduced you? It was 'Some Enchanted Evening,' right?"

Zanuck wiped his face. His flush subsided. His eyes stayed red. He went albino white.

"I was walking through the accounting office. Someone—I can't recall who—said, 'Boss, this is Gwen.'"

A side bar adjoined Daddy-O's desk. I poured a double brandy and guzzled it.

"Rumors abound, Pops. They all pertain to your lox, *Cleopatra*. There's lots of talk that your execs and rank and filers are scuffling for bread, should the whole studio tank. Some of the shit's legal, some of it's not. I got a tip that Gwen Perloff was running bearer bonds. For you and some other big studio guys."

Albino white back to red. The "bearer bonds" did it. I grabbed a fistful of cigars and waltzed.

Fox ran a twenty-man guard force. They were more than ornamental and less than full-sworn. Del Kinney ran the show. Mike Bayless said Kinney went back with Gwen Perloff. Kinney was pedigreed up the ying-yang. He was an ex–Sheriff's lieutenant and ex–ABC agent. He ran the Sheriff's mounted posse, '37–'38. He led the search for Mitzi Perloff's remains. The Fox cops were ex-LAPD and Sheriff's war hires. That means undraftable. That means low-rent by L.A.-cop standards. The PD and Sheriff's bounced them in '46. Get out—we've got our real guys back now. Kinney hit Fox in '53. He hired up a new kop korps. Kinney purportedly sold ABC vault liquor to the Aadland brothers. They were Foxed up the ying-yang. So was Del K.

The cop hut was locked tight. Nobody saw me. I grabbed a tethered golf cart and cruised the accounting building. It was soundstage-size. Somebody set Pops Zanuck up with Gwen P. "Boss, this is Gwen."

Accounting had its own parking lot. I counted fifty-four slots, full up. I cruised the rows and scrawled plate numbers in my notebook. It was one big DMV/R&I job. Hot names might jump out. Hey, look at *me*. *I'll* tell you about Gwen.

The plate job took two hours. I felt unraveled. I had Lois and Pat on the brain. I planned to buzz-bomb Lois tonight. I might buzz-bomb Pat tomorrow. Hit the Lawford spread. Hard-nose Peter. Coerce a look at Jack's top secret Girl Book. Pat might swoon. She loves to see Peter emasculated.

I split Fox. *Fox* felt unraveled. Zanuck lied per Gwen Perloff. Zanuck might fink my intrusion to Bill Parker. The Chief would dig it. The Parker-Kennedy deal observed laws and ignored laws and condoned shit-magnet intrusions. The intruders spawned fear and demanded information. The intrudees complied in the end.

Monroe Job #2 unraveled me. One evidential omission *glared*. Monroe, the pack rat. Her notes inked on paper scraps. Break-in #2. The Carole Landis morgue pic, 7/48. The magazine-letter notes. How many other perv notes and/or pix did Monroe receive? If any, where are they now?

Her known bank accounts have been examined. Her will has gone through probate. Where are her fan letters and pervy keepsakes? Nobody has turned an address book. Not me, not the West L.A. cops. Did she rent safe-deposit boxes under a fake name? I ran some quickie West L.A. bank checks and got zilch.

I drove downtown. I stopped at Andrews Hardware and purchased a shitload of office supplies. I drove to the PAB and hauled my gear up to Intel. I redid my cubicle, wall to wall.

I replicated my home corkboard motif. I marked Corkboard #1 *"Monroe"* and Corkboard #2 *"Kidnap."* I tacked note slips below the headings. Red slips for *"Monroe,"* green slips for *"Kidnap."* I pinned my eleven-page list of jungle-juiced recollections to Corkboard #1. I jotted red-slip observations and pinned them right below.

(Jack Clemmons views body. Early a.m., 8/5. Significant?) (JC tight with Norm Krause, ex–shakedown man.) (Deedee Grenier: Monroe KA. Attends Jeanne Carmen's pill parties. DG's brother: Paul Mitchell Grenier/ex-con, fruit hustler, runs badger games with DG.)

Plus: *Lowell Farr, Pat & Peter Lawford, Roddy McDowall, Natasha Lytess. (Lytess moved into house near Monroe & was seen peeping her.)*

I jotted green-slip observations and stuck them to Board #2:

("It's a put-up job": Richard Danforth, 8/4/62.) (Mike Bayless: borderline credible per kidnap chronology and Sheriff's response.) (Darryl F. Zanuck: decep-

tive on all Perloff queries. Denies that Perloff couriers bearer bonds. Rebrace &
further intimidate DFZ.) (Brace Del Kinney, per Perloff.) (Amass data before
Perloff approach.)

My cubicle featured a pneumatic tube gizmo. It shot message slugs
straight to R&I. I stuck my Fox accounting list into a slug and added a
cover note: all plate numbers/all vehicle stats/all personal stats/all rap
sheets. I stuck the slug in the chute and heard it go *whoosh.*

I segued to phone work. I called Nat and Phil and told them to
take over the cold calls to catering and phone-message outfits. Yeah,
now—fuckers. On *top* of your Lawford house/Monroe house canvasses.
I grabbed a Yellow Pages and cold-called mid-Wilshire banks myself.

I talked to thirty-two branch managers. I logged thirty-two straight
noes. It took four-plus hours. No, Lieutenant—Miss Monroe did *not*
rent safe-deposit boxes from us.

She could have employed a pseudonym. She could have utilized
forged credentials. She could have worn a bulked-up disguise.

Shit.

She'd prepare. She'd expect me to bring flowers. She'd expect a late arrival. She'd orchestrate the moment. She was a wait-by-the-phone type,
just like me.

The Chapman Park Hotel and Bungalows. *Her* bungalow. The canopied swing on the terrace. It summoned rainstorms. I already felt a
breeze and wet air. There were no visible stars at 10:20 p.m. Lois Nettleton wrote the book on enchantment.

I parked in the rear lot and walked over. She sniffed the air and
laughed before she saw me. I overdid the flowers, like I always do.

There she is—my midnight caller.

In a twill skirt and blue oxford shirt. Note her brown penny loafers
and white ankle socks. Add a new shag hairdo. She's back to her natural
mid-brown.

I set the flowers in a room-service pitcher. The white wine and
chilled lobster salad were laid out. Lois patted the swing and rocked it
back. I sat down beside her. We put our heads together and looked up.
Lois said, "Your cheap lime cologne." Pat always mentioned it.

I held a hand out. Three raindrops hit home. The Ambassador and
Cocoanut Grove were just across Wilshire. Dick Haymes was headlin-
ing. I caught strains of "How Are Things in Glocca Morra?"

Lois smiled. She loved the song. I said, "So, how are they?"

Lois said, "Routine. I live there and work there. I'm married there. When I've had enough, I concoct an excuse to come find you."

I smiled. "I hope Nat didn't tell you what we've been doing."

Lois sipped wine. "He did. He told me I should tell you, because he would regret withholding from you, and you mustn't think he dissembled. He said he can't believe the sheer scope of it, and how many ways it could go wrong."

I said, "He's right about that. There's no certain way to get through it. That's the troubling thing."

Lois slipped off her wedding band and tossed it in the salad. A lightning flash backlit Wilshire.

"I thought you'd open with 'I've got some money. Let's go someplace and fall down together.' Nat said you were flush."

I went *Nix*. "Enough of that. You're here, and I'm here, and you're here for reasons that have nothing to do with me. You know I'll always be here, and I'll always be receptive."

Lois lit a cigarette. "I got a costar gig at Metro. It's a stewardess-in-love flick, and it shoots early next year. I'm in for early rehearsals, and I'm testing for two B films at Fox. One's a teenage dance turkey, and the other's about a ghetto rat who eats nuclear waste and grows ten feet tall. Fox is hitting the B flicks hard—they're losing a fortune on *Cleopatra*."

Rain doused our dinner. Lois put out her cigarette and shivered. She smiled as a segue. I caught the cue and carried her inside.

We undressed in the bedroom. I threw the south-facing curtains wide. We got lightning and high-tide Wilshire Boulevard. Lois killed the room lights.

We got in bed and played hide-and-seek under the sheets. We didn't do it because we've never done it and we probably never will.

Hide-and-seek diminuendoed. We kissed and touched and entwined ourselves in new ways. We fell asleep. It rained all night. I saw Marilyn Monroe and Lowell Farr in a dream.

I recalled a certain day. Marilyn and Lowell walked to the front gate. They were visibly dirty. I figured they were rooting in the garden. That wasn't right. They were too dirty. It had to be something else.

25

I parked on PCH. The curb slot was Lawford property. It put me in Federal breach. Doofus Peter had issued a restraining order against me.

I had Fed shit and Kennedy shit on the brain. Eddie Chacón called me. He addressed me as *Señor* Freddy. He said *Señor* Bob requested my presence tomorrow. 9:00 a.m./the U.S. Attorney's Office. I brain-waved a jazzy evidence prop. *Señor* Ratfuck would *shit*.

I bopped down the north footpath. I wore last night's clothes with Lois and drove to Villa Pat. Scent-hound Pat. Maybe she'll be here, maybe she'll sniff last night's rendezvous.

The gate stood open. I hit the back terrace. Lawford lounged in a deck chair. He wore tennis whites. He sipped a Bloody Mary and bounced a volleyball.

He saw me. He sighed. He said, "You've got a nerve."

I looked left. A sliding glass door thumped and creaked. Pat looked out. I winked at her. She deadpanned it.

Lawford stood up. I pushed him back down and kicked the volleyball into the surf.

"I want the Girl Book you keep for Jack. We're going inside. You're going to hand it over."

Lawford said, "In a pig's eye."

I grabbed him by the hair and pulled him upright. He yelped. I bitch-slapped him and shoved him into the door glass. He hit nose-first. He yelped. He shouldered the door aside and tripped into the kitchen.

I followed him. He dripped blood on the floor and veered toward a side hallway. I crashed in the breakfast nook and poured myself a Bloody Mary. A Nikon camera was hooked on a wall peg. I checked the exposure slot. A full film roll was tucked in.

Lawford weaved back to the kitchen. He pressed a towel to his nose and lugged a leatherette notebook. I snatched it. The cover was presidential seal–embossed.

I yocked. Lawford said, "You're a cheeky fucker."

I said, "I'm on a top secret mission for the attorney general. Attorney General Kennedy would not condone the president's access to this book."

Pat chuckled. I pegged her location.

She's in the back alcove. She's out of sight and within eavesdrop range.

I flipped pages. The book featured overlit snapshots. Lesser-known actresses displayed their oooga-boooga. Full beaveroo, attached pubic hair. Names, phone numbers, measurements, and TV credits. Rubber-stamped once per page: "Ask not what your country can do for *YOU*—ask what *YOU* can do for your president!!!!!"

I adjusted the camera lens and shot the first eight pages. Lawford hovered and weaved. The nose-blot towel seeped and dripped blood.

"Where did you get it, and who put it together?"

Dipshit hijacked my Bloody Mary and siphoned it. He wiped blood and tomato residue off his lips.

"A cater waitress peddled it to me, maybe three months ago. I don't recall her name, but she was a queen-bee type. She'd heard whispers about Jack and figured he'd gas on the book. Jack said he'd peruse it the next time he blew through."

I tap-tapped the book. "Midsummer. A cater waitress named Eleanora called. You leched on her, and she pumped you on a cater waiter named Rick Dawes—who's a possible fruit hustler and burglary suspect. Do you recall this conversation? Is Eleanora the 'queen-bee type' who sold you the Girl Book? Do you recall *any* aspect of this conversation?"

Lawford blubbered. "I don't know, lots of chicks call me. I'm a well-known swinger and sugar daddy. . . . shit, my nose hurts."

I shot the last eight pages. I nailed more overlit snapshots. Stewardesses displayed their woof-woof. Full beaveroo, attached pubic hair. Names, phone numbers, measurements, and airline affiliations. The stews wore their pillbox airplane hats.

Lawford tittered. "Every cloud has a silver lining. I know a doctor who makes house calls. He'll give me a shot and put me in the Twilight Zone."

I hauled the Girl Book to the kitchen sink. I hit the garbage disposal switch. Lawford bitch-shrieked. I ripped out pages and shoved them down the drain. Gears shredded and whined. Paper pulp and taped-hair strips blew back out. Orange rinds and coffee grounds spritzed my Sy Devore coat.

I grabbed the camera and split. Sink-rotor skreek and bitch shrieks trailed me. Somebody'd stuck a note under my wiper blades. I pulled it out.

Well, then.

"I like you again. P."

26

Ratfuck Bob sweat-boxed me.

Eddie Chacõn picked me up and drove me downtown. We smoked Darryl Zanuck's Cuban cigars en route. Eddie kvetched. *Aaaay, caramba*— your Magnum loads tore up the vests of three Federal agents and severely bruised our chests. I yuk-yukked it off.

Traffic snarled, the heat index spiked, the smog layer rose. Eddie double-parked his Fed sled and ushered me inside. I expected an office confab. Eddie dumped me in a twelve-by-twelve box.

One table, two chairs, three blank walls, one mirror wall. Hot-wired for sure.

Bobby was late. I'd brought my briefcase. I duplicated the Girl Book pix at Intel and tagged them "Exhibit A." Bobby despised Peter Lawford. The pix should fan that flame.

The door popped wide. I stood up. Bobby lugged a leather evidence case. I said, "Sir." He said, "Lieutenant." Our ensembles matched. We wore white shirts, blue ties, gray Dacron suits. It was off-the-rack cop couture.

Bobby unlatched the case and flashed the contents. My Hoffa gig evidence was crammed in. He pulled out a manila envelope and slid the case under the table. I sat down. He sat down across from me. Okay— it's on.

I suppressed a grin. Bobby emptied the envelope on the table. Three photo stacks tumbled. He snapped off the rubber bands and formed photo sprays.

Man Camera redux. We're back at my 8/4/62 break-in.

"Snapshots number five to twenty-seven. All living room. The left-behind electric wall mounts and telephone-mike spacers. Who do you think installed them?"

"Initially, I thought the prior owners of the house were being surveilled. I checked them out through the Realtors who sold the house to Monroe. They were complete squares, who in no way played as surveillance targets. The mounts look like FBI or L.A. Sheriff's issue, and SHIT does a lot of wire work for the Bureau's L.A. office. My best guess is that it was an amateur operation, which employed professional equipment. I'm thinking it's either hoods or rogue cops working independent."

Bobby said, "Okay. Marilyn's underwear drawer. Snapshots number four to eleven, the pornographic ones. Tell me the status of the crusted-on semen. Do you have a possible make on the man in the pictures?"

I said, "The semen is being comparison-tested at the LAPD lab. That entails going through hundreds of already logged samples. Phil Irwin and Nat Denkins have gone through a total of forty-three LAPD and Sheriff's mug books for leads on potential westside perverts. We came up 100% empty."

"Okay. Marilyn's undie drawer, again. The Carole Landis morgue photograph and the crazy note composed in magazine letters. What *is* this?"

I said, "It's most likely nutty fan bullshit. Those Landis morgue shots have been all over town since the late '40s. A morgue jockey duplicated them and made a million copies, and I used to peddle them myself. Some nut sent one to Monroe, and she ended up going out behind yellow jackets, just like Landis. *So what?* Likewise the letter—which brings up a request I want to make. It pertains to the issue of hidden fan mail."

The AG drummed the table. "I'm listening."

I drummed the table. The AG, RFK, Lord Fauntleroy incarnate. I mimicked his impatience.

"This occurred on May 19. I was surveilling the house and saw Monroe and Lowell Farr walk out the front door, very dirty. At first, I thought they were gardening in the backyard, but then I came to believe they were doing some digging under the house. I want a search-and-seizure warrant."

Bobby sighed. "I'll get you one. While you're begging favors, is there anything else?"

Scrawny lace-curtain Irish cocksuck—

"I misplaced a sheet of paper with one hundred and forty-three license-plate numbers on it. I'd tailed Monroe out to the Valley, but I lost her. I ran a radius check to run through the DMV. The locale played weird for Monroe. Also, I've got a memory of that location that I can't quite pull up. It's messing with me, and it seems to be a memory from *after* I tailed Monroe that day."

"You're thinking that the sheet of paper might be in with the ones that Eddie and his boys removed from your apartment? All right, I'll look for it."

I rocked my chair back and stretched. Baby Bobby tapped his coat pockets. He smoked cigars, like Big Baby Jack. I tossed him a hijacked Cuban. It bounced off his necktie and hit the table.

He scowled. I flicked my lighter and leaned close. He took the light.

"Let's move on to 'Eleanora's' call to Peter Lawford. What are you doing about following up on the 'Rick Dawes' burglary lead?"

I ticked points. "I've got Phil and Nat cold-calling every cater-waiter service and telephone-answering outfit in L.A. They've been stonewalled so far. Miller Leavy refuses to dun the Beverly Hills PD for their burglary files."

Bobby smoked his cigar. "As well he should. I wouldn't mess with municipal police departments, either."

I popped my briefcase. I'd prepped my own photo sprays. Two cardboard sheets and Scotch tape. Twenty-four TV actress and stewardess pix. Girl Book de-luxe. All nude/full beaver.

I laid them on the table. Up close and offensive. Bobby examined them.

"I took these off Peter Lawford yesterday. They were displayed in a binder embossed with the presidential seal. Lawford told me that a 'queen-bee type' cater waitress passed the pictures to him. Lawford intended to give the so-called Girl Book to the president the next time he passed through L.A., but he does not recall his telephone chat with 'Eleanora.'"

Bobby stubbed his cigar on the floor. His killer gaze decohered. He full-on *blushed*.

"I owe you a thank-you for taking the book away from Peter. I owe Mr. Denkins a thank-you for his reinterpreting quite a few of Marilyn's calls to the White House and Justice. I owe you a warning as to your blunt and overly familiar references to members of my family, and I would caution you never to mention my sister Pat."

I leaned in. "Fuck your thank-yous, warnings, and cautions, Mr. Kennedy. In lieu of them, you might assure me that you will not take the evidence that I accrued while in Jimmy Hoffa's employ and call me up before a Federal grand jury to testify against him, which may well get me two slugs in the head in the long run."

Bobby leaned in. His killer gaze *re*-cohered.

"Under no circumstances. Because I know that Bill Parker has charged you to build a subsidiary dirt file on my brother and me, to supplant the derogatory profile on Marilyn that the Chief and I have agreed on. It's his hole card to assure that my brother and I won't renege on our promise to can Hoover and give Parker the big spot. Can you candidly tell me that that is not Parker's design?"

I said, "No. I can't tell you that."

"All right. What have you dug up on us so far?"

I cracked my knuckles. "A right-wing-nut cop wrote a crazy tract about the two of you and Monroe. I put the skids to it. I confirmed that there's no mention of you and Jack—I mean, the president—in the twelve million press clips I've read. The president's inclinations are well known in film-biz circles—but not outside of them—and my canvasses have confirmed that a dozen times over. So far, nobody's inclined to talk. Jack—I mean the president—is safe there."

Bobby said, "Call him Jack. Do you think I'm so pious and chickenshit that I'd object to that?"

I cracked my thumbs. "Hoffa concerns me. It's not so much you slamming him in court, and me getting subpoenaed. It's his attitude in regards to you busting up his Monroe gig. He's *nonchalant*. He's paying me and my boys our bonus bread, unsolicited. He's got to be playing a money angle somewhere, or this whole blackmail-the-prez-and-the-AG-over-movie-star-pussy deal makes no damn sense."

Bobby dug through his evidence case. He snagged a sheaf of tap-call transcripts and quick-skimmed them.

"This is Marilyn and my sister. Marilyn tells Pat that her house has been burgled, things have been moved around, she's received nasty letters and breather calls. How do you interpret it? Is this the jerk who sent the Carole Landis picture and the magazine-letter note, or is it just more of the humdrum crazy-fan ilk?"

I shrugged. "I don't know, but my guess is that she's performing for Pat. Boo-hoo, 'I'm scared, look at me.' Pat's all empathy. She's Monroe's perfect audience."

"Yes, she is. And she's your perfect audience, as well. Don't go all red-faced, Lieutenant. I'm the brother Pat confides in, and her confidences err on the candid side."

I grabbed my briefcase and stood up. My legs fluttered. Bobby skunk-eyed me.

"Take care, son. You toss a kidnap suspect off a cliff, and it can come back and haunt you."

27

Three-man dig. That's Nat, Phil, and me. We stood outside Fifth Helena. We brought shovels, pry bars, and entrenching tools. Bobby K got our warrant. Miller Leavy ran it by a Superior Court judge. It sanctioned us to bust down the door at 9:30.

We lounged by said door. We chain-smoked. Fifth Helena was flat quiet. West L.A. patrol cops ran the party kids off last night. They popped six kids for vag and possession of maryjane. I read the arrest sheets. Lowell Farr dodged the rousts.

I was glad. Lowell was a witchy kid. She B and E'd the pad and communed with Monroe on her own stick. I peeped her from Natasha Lytess' roof. I couldn't shake her wall art. Monroe as herself/herself as Monroe. The imagery shook me.

I fidgeted. I had fan-letter caches, private-mail caches, and psycho-fan caches on the brain. Monroe's will went through probate. Daryl Gates wrangled an inventory. "Routine correspondence" went to her lawyer. Small sums of money, books, and furniture went to her white-trash kin. The will took me nowhere.

Lab tests and records checks, likewise.

The jizz-stained photos—still being checked. The file runs on José Bolaños—no kickbacks yet. No R&I kickbacks on the cars parked outside Fox Accounting. I called Fox Personnel and requested a list of all Accounting Department employees. A supervisor blew me off. *Who introduced Gwen Perloff to Darryl F. Zanuck?* I compiled a list of names from Peter Lawford's Girl Book. I added physical descriptions and airline affiliations for the stews. I submitted the list to the file-room cops at Intel and R&I. I logged no results yet.

Phil tapped his watch. *It's 9:30—let's go.*

I had Intel's master key. One turn got us in. The living room was swamp hot. Nat and Phil opened windows. A cross breeze circulated. I walked straight to the south-facing wall. Lowell Farr's portrait had been obliterated.

Kid vandals sprayed it with kandy apple paint. Kid pundits scrawled it up. *"Fuck Apartheid," "Surf Nazis Rule," "We Shall Overcome," "Goldwater in '64."*

We fanned through the house. We looked for wall, floor, and closet-space inconsistencies. Marilyn and Lowell were dirty that day. They weren't digging *outside*. I scoped the exterior twenty times since that day. They were digging *inside*. It had to be.

The walls sat flush. They felt solid. The closet floors were void of trapdoor cracks and hinges. We studied the floors. The house was '20s vintage. All the rugs were gone. Bedrooms, hallways, living room. The floors were down to scuffed hardwood planes.

The bedroom floors were pristine. No mismatched planks, no hinge-crack indicators. The hallways dittoed the bedrooms. We walked back to the living room. The walls were solid white stucco. I eyeballed the floorboards, Man Camera tight.

Back and forth, up and down, sideways. North, south, east, and west. One time, two times, three. What's that by the south-facing wall? That's the kid-artwork wall. What's that right—*there*.

Anomalous floor planks. Extending off the artwork wall, five planks across. Unscuffed new wood. Extending out six feet. Planed and sanded. Enjoined to old wood planks. Rugs covered the new planks before. I caught the inconsistency now.

Nat and Phil hovered. I pointed down. Bright lads—their brain bulbs popped bright.

I saw a quarter-inch crack at the wall juncture. It extended across all five planks. I stuck my pry bar in at a midpoint and pulled up.

A hinge mechanism kicked in. All five planks creaked and sprang up at a forty-five-degree angle. Nat and Phil gasped. I looked straight down.

It's a hideaway/stash hole/big secret compartment. Rough wood foundation walls and a packed-dirt floor. The walls run identical to the living room walls. There's a wall-mounted ladder right below me.

Nat whistled. Phil handed me a flashlight. I went down the stairs. The temperature dropped. The dirt stink made me sneeze.

I flashed the wall right beside me. My beam hit a light switch. I flipped it. An overhead bulb lit the stash hole. I saw *this:*

The floor, the walls. A basement built on the living room floor plan. Empty, except for *this:*

A big steamer trunk. Old and weather-beaten. A clasp-affixed top pushed up at a right angle. Two sets of footprints from the trunk to the ladder. Coming and going prints. Easily ID'd.

Marilyn had small feet. Lowell had big feet. I saw drag marks from the south wall to the middle of the hole. The girls dragged the trunk over. The big foot/small foot prints spelled it plain. They opened the trunk under the overhead bulb. They wanted maximum light.

I walked over to the trunk. Nat and Phil tumbled down the ladder. They coughed and sneezed and walked up. I knelt down and framed close-ups. Nat and Phil lit the trunk. I went through it, item by item. I inventoried *this:*

A crayon sketch. Red crayon on old sketch paper. The sketch depicts a late '40s moderne house. The sketch is dated 6/22/48. The sketch is signed NJB. The initials *must* designate Norma Jean Baker. It was Monroe's kosher name then.

A gummed stack of physician's prescription pads. Also old and weathered. Embossed with "Sheldon Mandel/M.D., Practice in Psychiatry." Plus a Bedford Drive/Beverly Hills address. Plus a four-digit Crestview phone number. The four digits denote the 1940s.

A rotted paper bag. Spilled maryjane buds and leaves. Fat buds and leaves. It's good maryjane.

Empty pill vials. Legibly labeled. Scripts filled at the Beverly Wilshire Hotel pharmacy. Scripts for phenobarbital and sodium secobarbital. Prescribed to Norma Jean Baker. Prescribed by Dr. Sheldon Mandel.

The "Norma Jean Baker" had a black ink line running through it. Monroe printed "Not my name anymore" beneath it. Man Camera reprise. I went through Monroe's trash, one month back. I found an empty Nembutal vial. She'd crossed out the "Marilyn Monroe." She wrote "Not my name anymore" beneath it.

Man Camera reprise. I B and E'd Ralph Greenson and Milt Wexler's office. I played a Greenson-Monroe tape. Monroe told Greenson she had Jack-and-Bobby dirt going back fourteen years. That meant 1948.

Here's the final item. It looks brand-new. It's a laminated business card.

The card advertises "Foxtone Services." It features a leering-fox logo. The furry fucker is panting. He's got a big forked tongue. He wears a fetishistic spiked collar and sports a jumbo two-headed *schvantz*. The card reads:

"Foxtone Services/PO box 6969/L.A., Calif/Your Wife Or Mine?/ Investment Opportunities"

*FOX*tone. 20th Century–*FOX*. *Cleopatra* as cash drain, *FOX* in the shit, *Cleo* bleeding *FOX* dry.

I broomed west on Fountain. The Foxtone fox hovered behind me. He was the hellhound on my trail. We were three hours into the chase.

He chased me downtown. I went by Intel, Ad Vice, and the Postal Inspection Service. I got the lowdown on PO box 6969. The 69 box block was assigned to "Bev's Switchboard." It was off of Fountain and Crescent Heights. The proprietress was one Bev Shoftel.

It's a legitimate storefront mail drop. The clients possess front-door keys. The keys permit them to enter and grab their mail, twenty-four hours. Bev caters to low-life Hollywood. Lunatic actors and actresses, call girls and boys, smut-film purveyors, hipster artistes.

I went by the DA's Office and jacked Miller Leavy. *Get me a search warrant, boss.* Miller said, "The U.S. mail is *Federal.* You'll need a *Federal* warrant." I zipped over to the U.S. Attorney's Office and hit up a second-rung guy. I dropped Bobby the K's name and laid out my rationale for the paper. The dink said he'd think about it.

I pulled up to the storefront and parked. I sized the place up. It had triple-thick window glass. Plus a steel-plate door and roll-up window mesh. It looked impregnable.

The door was propped open. I walked in. The dump was small post office size. It was box-shaped. Pull-out mail slots covered the side and back walls. They ran floor to ceiling. Bev Shoftel sat in a lawn chair and sipped a Lucky Lager. A transistor radio belched a Dodgers game. Bev wore pedal pushers and a Dodgers scoop neck.

She saw me and went *Show me.* I walked up and flipped my credential case. She shook her head. I got out my billfold. She crooked a finger. I dropped three C-notes in her lap.

She said, "I don't reveal my clients' names. I don't snitch off the specifics of what they do. Your three yards entitles you to an overview and no more."

I said, "Box 6969."

Bev said, "Aaahhh, the much-coveted *soixante-neuf* series of boxes. I will guardedly state that the whole series is rented by so-called entrepreneurs employed at 20th Century–Fox. They're out to capitalize on the *Cleopatra* fiasco. My fool renters are hawking Fox Savings Bonds, along with whatever other fool scams they can think up."

The same bungalow. The same terrace. The same canopied swing. The same white wine and cold lobster salad.

I said, "Eddie Fisher's back at the Losers. I'm working the gigs. They just fell back in my lap. Three nights only. You should check it out."

Lois checked the sky. There were no clouds at dusk. That meant no rain.

"What's wrong with you? All this intrigue you've got going isn't enough?"

"Come on. It's three nights at a nightclub."

"You work yourself frazzled, you work your men frazzled. Nat and I gab on the phone, as you well know. He said he and Phil are putting in twelve-hour days on the canvass."

I laughed. "Nat's indiscreet, but he's got limits. He's not going to give up the inside dirt on the deal, which I know you've been angling for."

Lois lit a cigarette. "He told me you've got a thing going with Pat Lawford."

"He's not quite up-to-date."

"I saw her with her sisters at the Peppermint Lounge. She's too tall and too thin. I know her type. Coffee, cigarettes, and two salads a day, tops."

I jiggled her hands. "Pat saw you on *Alcoa Presents*. She said you're short, and your eyes are too close together. She said you look like a Siamese cat."

Lois howled. "I do look like a Siamese cat."

I laced up our fingers and stretched our arms full length. Full dusk hit. The temperature dipped.

"The canvass is a bust. It had to be done, so we did it, and I'll hit some of the places Nat and Phil marked as questionable. The Hollywood people have heard stories, but not the rich squarejohn folks. Here's the bottom line. Jack and Marilyn. It's out in the ether, and the ether's running thin."

Lois twirled her ashtray. "The story's inevitable. Jack and Marilyn.

Bobby and Marilyn, when the wind drifts a certain way. People pick up glimmers or bits of stories, and they embellish like mad."

I feigned a yawn. Jack and Marilyn/Bobby and Marilyn. Nat and Lois talk. Pat confides in Bobby. It's all extraneous yak-yak.

"Let's change the subject. You've got the stewardess-in-love flick, and you're reading for this schlock guy at Fox, Maury Dexter. I heard he's a pillhead in the Freddy O. mode. What else? Oh, yeah—he's got a giant-rat job and a twist flick, and you'll have to settle for scale."

Lois dropped an ice cube in her wineglass and kicked off her shoes. She rechecked the sky. No summer storm tonight.

"I'll get both jobs, and I'll get more than scale. I'm a name in New York, and Maury knows it. I'll play second fiddle to a large rodent and a bevy of stacked high school girls. They twist all night, while a psychopath stalks them, and a daring cop lays in wait. Can you believe it?"

I said, "*Twist Party Stakeout*, right? I was passing through Fox and caught some auditions."

Lois rolled her eyes. "That's it. And the truly funny thing is that some working L.A. cop wrote the screenplay."

I hooked a chair over. We put our feet up and slouched on the swing. Lois laid her head on my shoulder. I smelled her green-tea shampoo.

"Here's a curveball. Have you ever been headshrunk? It's not a critique. All actresses go that route, don't they?"

Lois tickled me. "No, not all actresses. I've never been headshrunk, let alone headshrunk by Ralph R. Greenson, currently well known to readers of the *L.A. Herald-Express.*"

I sighed. "You're right. I've got this job on the brain. Monroe's on the couch with Greenson, but she's looking for a more radical shrink who'll cosign her criminal tendencies, and Nat and Phil and I found a pill vial prescribed by—"

Lois squeezed my arm. "A shrink named Shelley Mandel, right? I talked to Nat a few hours ago, and he told me. Well, Doc Shelley never shrunk me, but he cruised all the pageant girls back when I was Miss Chicago."

I whistled. "'48, right? '48 into '49?"

"Right. I was a Miss America runner-up, and the show junketed through L.A. The big postwar VD epidemic was at its height, and our chaperones had Doc Shelley lecture us. He also passed out prophylactic kits, but that was strictly on the sly. I read him as harmless. He leched on the girls and wrote pep-pill scripts, which shocked a few of us, but not me. He purportedly knew all sorts of call girls and bottom-line starlets, which is hardly startling news, given the time and place."

Confluence, showbiz, postwar hijinx. I grabbed it and filed it.

Lois rubbed her chin on my shoulder. Her shag hairstyle worked. Miss Chicago, '48—despite her weird eyes.

I said, "Do you love me?"

Lois said, "I'll think about it."

PART 4
SHRINK WRAP

(AUGUST 21–28, 1962)

28

Doc Greenson served coffee and cakes. He'd served Monroe martinis. I peeped their sessions at this selfsame spot.

Miller Leavy set up the confab. He furnished my cover. I was adjunct fuzz on coroner Curphey's "Blue Ribbon Panel." The panel's goal: to analyze the glut of suicides and inadvertent OD's for creative types. It was a full-fledged phenomenon. I cited Monroe and Carole Landis. I thought bloviator Greenson would bloviate on Monroe and Landis. He'd groove them as sicko sisters under the skin. He didn't bloviate on them. He bloviated self-justification.

"It's these radio call-in shows hosted by women with undergrad psych degrees. The callers are 99% women. They despise male psychiatrists and attribute the basest of pathologies to those who treat female celebrities. I'll concede that I might have been overly available, but to assert that I was at Marilyn's 'beck and call,' as some of those women have, is preposterous."

I witnessed it. Deedee Grenier embellished it. Greenson was Marilyn's slave and faux daddy. He pulled his pud while he spun tapes of their sessions. Marilyn tweaked him with lurid sex jive.

"There *have* been shrinks who've violated their psychiatric briefs by performing gynecological exams right there in their offices, so these accusations do have a basis in fact. I could name you—"

I cut in. "Dr. Shelley Mandel. An informant told me that he gave starlets and call girls prescription pads as stocking stuffers. Of course, that was back in the swinging postwar era."

Greenson sipped coffee. His hands shook. The cup and saucer rattled.

"Shelley was a gifted immunologist. He specialized in sulfa drugs and dabbled in psychiatry. He liked racy young women to an untoward degree, rather like the late Marilyn and powerful politicians."

I said, "I was at a party, shortly after Miss Monroe's death. People were discussing Miss Monroe's liaisons with John and Robert Kennedy, as if they were established facts."

Greenson buffed his glasses on his necktie. He spotted cake crumbs on his shirt and brushed them off.

"You're straying rather far from the panel's mandate, Lieutenant. But I'll humor you, because Marilyn's fantasy apparatus intensely interests me."

I said, "I'm listening, sir."

Greenson smirked. "Well, there's no smut here, so I'm afraid you'll have to indulge my abstractions. Simply put, Marilyn was a congenital liar and a ham-handed fantasist, with a very weak grasp on verisimilitude. Her initial perceptions of John F. Kennedy were quite lucid, and I believed them because she portrayed the president as feckless, shallow, usurious, and even more self-involved than she was. She did not inflate the sexual value of their first coupling, but she gradually, session by session, escalated her own importance to the point where the president of the United States was no more than her sexual submissive, while his brother Robert feared for his mental solvency and took over the role of Marilyn's lover as an 'issue of national security.' From there, Marilyn's romantic fantasies grew to include the banishment of Jacqueline and Ethel Kennedy, mass divorce, and Marilyn installed as First Lady. Concurrently, her alcoholism and drug addiction spiraled, apace with her fantasy life."

She knew you dug the stories. You fed the cues/you said, "Jump"/Marilyn said, "How high?"

My office break-in. That tape I played. Marilyn says she's got filth on Jack and Bobby. It was fourteen-year-old filth. That meant '48. Carole Landis suicided in '48. Monroe knew Shelley Mandel in '48. 1948 triggered jackpots.

I said, "I'm fishing here, Doctor. Did Miss Monroe come to the realization that her relationship with the brothers was entirely fantastical, and at that point did her fantasies turn vindictive?"

Greenson checked his watch. My questions vexed him. Some Blue Ribbon panelist. I wore him thin.

"Yes. Her narrative arc described her sexual dominance, her instigation of domestic chaos, and her intention to 'get' Jack and Bobby for the 'degradation and debasement' they inflicted upon her fourteen years ago, although she never stated just what that degradation and debasement was. Once they were revealed, it would strip them of their power, and she'd beneficently help them to rebuild their lives."

I said, "That was white of her."

Greenson said, "Touché."

I twirled my coffee cup. "Miss Monroe claimed to have received breather calls and perverted letters during the last days of her life, and she told friends that her home had been burgled. Did she tell you this, and did you believe her?"

Greenson said, "No. She told me the same thing. It was patent fantasia."

"I understand that she was in the market for a 'more radical psychiatrist.' One who would encourage her more aggressive fantasies."

Greenson flinched. "I don't recall her pursuing that line of chat with me."

You lying sack of shit.

Paul de River. Real name Paul Joseph Israel. Reconstructive surgeon and ophthalmologist. A psychiatric dabbler, à la Shelley Mandel.

I parked outside his office. He had a top-floor duplex spot off of Oakwood and La Brea. It was lower-Hollywood residential. He must keep criminal-patient files and psycho-treatment narcotics. Top-floor spots were rough entries. You had downstairs neighbors. You had exposed landings. De River knew from security. The door frames and window casings were steel-reinforced. That meant interior bolt mounts. Note the "Brinks-patrolled" decal on the front door.

My thoughts ping-ponged. I stalled the door knock. I did law library and Intel file research last night. I exhumed Carole Landis and Mitzi Perloff. I put Del Kinney and Doc de River under the lens.

The Hearst rags gave Landis big play. She was twenty-nine. She lost at love. She was a yelp-for-help suicide attempter. Her career was skidsville. She breezed through husbands. She was now on #4. She had a big spread in the Palisades. Boo-hoo. Nobody loves me. She had a torrid tilt with Brit heartthrob Rex Harrison. "Sexy Rexy" refused to dump waifly wife, Lili Palmer. Carole pulled the plug—7/5/48.

It was straight-up suicide. It was investigated and adjudicated as such. It's fourteen years later. Sexy Rexy's playing Julius Caesar in *Cleopatra*.

Call it boo-hoo redux. Marilyn Monroe offs herself. Some nut sent her a Landis morgue shot and a note.

"I loved her before I loved you."

It was fourteen years ago. The nut had to be at least an adolescent then. '48 to '62. Who'd the nut perv on during that interval? Did the nut send the pic and note and leave it at that? Is the nut the burglar-breather that Monroe beefed to Pat and others? Did the nut pull similar shit with Landis way back when? I checked the Landis DB file at Homicide. Souvenir-hunter cops had picked it clean. All Landis-to-Monroe throughlines had been snipped.

Landis to Monroe. On to Mitzi Perloff. The law library kept a full run of *Vivid Detective* magazines. The rag wrote up the Mitzi snatch in the May '37 issue. Mitzi vanished on 2/17/37. She was eight. Sister Gwen turned eleven in March. The girls were Hollywood born-and-bred. They lived in a foster home on De Longpre and Wilton. Mitzi was a roamer. She picked flowers in the gardens of Immaculate Heart High School and Ferndell Park. The LAPD's Hollywood squad and the Sheriff's mounted posse worked the job. Local pervs were *hard*-braced. No leads surfaced. Pervy IH boys and ped-o priests were *hard*-braced. No leads surfaced. The mounted posse scoured Ferndell and Griffith Park. They dug up three skeletized little girls. Tests were performed. They were ID'd as circa '28 sex-fiend victims. Sergeant Delbert W. Kinney, Jr., led the posse. The search extended to the Pasadena-Monrovia foothills. Two more skeletized little girls were found. Tests were performed.

They were circa '26 sex-fiend victims. Sex-fiend files were reviewed. No leads surfaced.

Intel kept blue sheets on ranking L.A. cops. I found one on Del Kinney.

Delbert Welbourne Kinney, Jr. DOB 9/13/09/Sparta, Wisconsin. Joins LASO, 1/18/31. Works custody at the Mira Loma and Wayside honor ranchos. Promoted to sergeant, 4/36. Runs the Sheriff's mounted posse, '36–'39. Runs the Sheriff's Alien Squad and supervises the round-ups of Japanese nationals and native-born Japanese in the wake of Pearl Harbor. Promoted to lieutenant, 11/44. Lateral transfer to the state Alcoholic Beverage Control Board, 7/46. Directs undercover operations. Investigates liquor hijacks out of three ABC field offices. The focused subject of an internal investigation, 9/49.

Two trucks packed with un-tax-stamped liquor are jacked at a rest stop off the 101 southbound. The ABC agents driving and guarding the shipments are gagged, hog-tied, and left in a secluded shack nearby. The robbery was accomplished in a brusque and professional manner. The stolen liquor was brand-name/top-shelf/high-retail-per-pour stock. The shipment was tagged "Level-one security."

Four ranking ABC men knew the what and where. Del Kinney was one of them. The internal investigators called him their top suspect. They had no proof. They filed no charges. They worked off of rumored affiliations and surmise.

Del Kinney was "cordial" with film-studio humps/white slavers/labor agitators/pornographic-film distributors Hershel Aadland (1904–)/Meyer Aadland (1906–)/and Ira Aadland (1907–). The Aadland brothers purportedly trafficked in counterfeit tax stamps and owned a chain of bar and grills that served contraband liquor. Lieutenant Kinney weathered three grueling interrogations and cleaved to his innocence. The investigators pressed him on the two prevalent rumors that came to their attention.

One: that Kinney owed significant gambling debts to Hersh Aadland, and fingered the booze shipment to pay off the debts. Two: that Kinney interceded on the behalf of a young woman who had embezzled large sums from two Aadland-owned roadhouses in Monterey County. He fingered the booze shipment. It repaid all outstanding debts.

Kinney remained on the ABC. The Aadland brothers hid behind their lawyers. The hijack case remains unsolved. The young woman was not identified. Kinney retired from the ABC, 4/53. He got the security-boss gig at Fox a month later. The Aadland brothers are big machers at Fox. It is widely held that they got Del K. the job.

What's the lowdown here?

Who's the young woman?

Kinney to Paul Joseph Israel/aka Paul de River.

Eye doctor, sawbones, psychiatric hobbyist. Sex-fiend afficionado. He studies them, interviews them, writes about them. He gets Marilyn Monroe hopped up on them. He ran his "Sex Offense Bureau" out of LAPD. He held sex fiend coffee klatches and group therapy sessions. Sex fiends test-piloted Dr. Paul's gourmet dope compounds. Dr. Paul watched sex fiends masturbate while hooked up to respirators and blood-pressure cuffs. Dr. Paul arranged blind dates for male and female sex fiends and chaperoned them to Walt Disney flicks and burgers and malts at Bob's Big Boy. Ex-chief Worton admired de River. Bill Parker hated him. He canned him and dissolved the Sex Offense Bureau. Thus, de River hates the LAPD.

2/28/51. The State Board of Medical Examiners censures him. The beef? The "indiscriminate prescribing of narcotics." His medical license is nearly revoked. He gets a chump admin job with the VA. His wife dies in '61. He sells their Orange County home and moves back to L.A. He's sixty-nine now. He still consults and sees patients. He's got that steel-buffed/unbustable office, right across the street. L.A. breeds swinging sex fiends. I can't fault his return.

Hey, dad—remember me?

Dads was wisp-thin. He spoke raspy. His New Orleans drawl was a shuck. He skimped on his office. The rugs ran threadbare. His analysand chair gored my ass. He splurged on his file-tape room.

Steel-reinforced doors. Blinking sensor lights. Alarm-rigged file compartments—make book on it.

No receptionist. He answered my door knock. My credentials rubbed him wrong. He hated and feared cops. He tried to door-slam me. I eased him back inside. He flopped in a ratty Barcalounger and glared impotent.

I shot my cuffs. " 'When all other forms of applied therapy have failed, it may be possible to contravene absent, passive, or self-destructively reactive behavior with the imposition of direct criminal reaction.' Why would Marilyn Monroe have written that in your loopy book *The Sexual Criminal?*"

De River said, "I have not the slightest notion. I never met the late Miss Monroe."

Liar. Prevaricator. Dissembler. Here's the tell. His hands spazzed up at "Marilyn."

"She took her home-decorating cues from you. She collected photographs in that pervert-modernist style you seem to favor. She posed for pornographic snapshots with a rough-trade boy who disguised his identity with whiteout eye strips. They were just like the ones you put on Otto Stephen Wilson."

De River said, "Steve was a horrible boy, but I rather liked him."

I said, "I beat him half dead at Lincoln Heights. Just for kicks and grins."

De River coughed. His lungs were shot. He was frail. His life span loomed as next week.

"For a DA's Bureau investigator, you're rather coarse. And I can't see you as a member of coroner Curphey's Blue Ribbon Panel. You seem to lack compassion for Miss Monroe."

"Miss Monroe told her shrink Ralph Greenson that she was in the market for a more radical analyst. I thought of you right off the bat. Miss Monroe goes back with headshrinkers, by the way. Dr. Sheldon Mandel was feeding her dope back when she went by the name Norma Jean Baker. I'll bet you crossed paths with Shelley. You're both physicians with an amateur psychiatrist bent."

Doc Shelley buzzed him. Here's the tell. His stick legs spazzed.

"Did you headshrink Monroe, boss? Did she play to your vanity? Did you hear out her twisted fantasies and get your rocks off? Did you soothe her and baby-talk her and tell her that her puerile fixation on fuckhead criminals and freaks was avant-garde, and that she was the most misunderstood and underestimated artist of our era?"

De River scoped me, half gaga. He gnashed up his hands. His out-sized veins pulsed.

"Why would Marilyn Monroe make a great many pay-phone calls and dress up in fat-girl disguise to do so?"

De River went *deep* gaga. His eyes went dope floaty. He levitated somewhere off Planet Earth.

"Why would Marilyn Monroe keep forty grand in a lockbox under her bed? Why would she fly to and from Mexico, under a false name, in disguise, vouched by false documents?"

De River rocked his Barcalounger. His legs twitched.

"Does the name José Bolaños sound familiar to you? He's a Mexican Commie, and a probable dope pusher. Does he ring any bells?"

De River sighed. His dentures protruded. They were nicotine-hued.

"Did you inject her with collagen, to alter her appearance? Did she explain the bite scar on her upper left bicep? You must have known quite a few psycho biters. Did you introduce her to criminal manqués you thought she might find engaging? Did you set her up with a sweet guy who mails out morgue photos of movie stars and sends glued-on-letter notes along with them?"

De River plotzed. He covered his mouth with a seat cushion and stifled a whimper or screech.

Dads was infirm. He verified zilch. He reacted to digs. He lived and breathed the criminal demimonde. His reactions might indicate fore-knowledge. His reactions might be plain neural response. I ridiculed his expertise. I humbled him. I learned one thing. He fucked with Monroe on some level. I *know* that. I had to get at his files. That meant a kami-kaze play.

I stopped at a pay phone and stiffed update calls. My DMV man was backlogged. He hadn't run the plate checks on my Fox accounting cars. R&I was backlogged. They hadn't run the name checks on Peter Law-ford's Girl Book.

Backlogs. That means loose ends. Loose ends in West Hollywood. Here's a tweaker—Jeanne Carmen lives just off the Strip.

I swooped over and parked out front. The gate opened up on a court-yard pool and lounge pit. Out-of-work actresses splashed and chugged mimosas. Jeanne's pad overlooked the pool. The door was wide open.

I walked up. I caught a pill-party hangover, full stop.

Deedee Grenier was passed out on the couch. Babs Payton snoozed in a chair. Lila Leeds dozed in a sleeping bag on the floor. An old-fashioned glass was propped up against her. Jeanne putted golf balls in and around it.

"Freddy O.'s here. Let's hope he brought money. There's a horror festival on Channel 9 tonight. Pizza and booze would be nice, but we're flat."

I passed her two yards. She air-kissed me and sank a long putt.

"Marilyn Monroe's old drama coach, Natasha Lytess. Unload her for me."

Jeanne said, "She's dying. She's got the Big C, and she's cutting out fast. She's known in the biz as the 'Bride of Dracula,' when she'd rather be known as the 'Bride of Marilyn,' but Marilyn don't fly that way, except for brief moments. She's been goony for Marilyn ever since *The Asphalt Jungle*. She's very pushy, and Russian. Marilyn got sick of her, and Darryl Z. banished her from the Fox lot. She's an acquired taste that not many people acquire."

I lit a cigarette. "Would it surprise you to know that Miss Lytess moved into a house within peeping distance of Marilyn's place on Fifth Helena?"

Jeanne blew a short putt. It hit Lila's head and ricocheted. Lila dozed on.

"There's your intro right there. You're fellow peepers."

I yocked. "Dr. Shelley Mandel. You landed here after the war, so you must have known him, or heard of him. Why would Marilyn have a prescription pad of his from '48?"

Jeanne lit a cigarette. "All the girls in The Life knew Shelley. He gave away script pads as goodwill gestures, like the Marshall Plan for young chicks. There were lots of pervs afoot in L.A. after the war, because the war messed with their heads. Shelley's big thing was getting call girls to double-date when they went out on jobs, because there's safety in numbers. That's how I met Lila, back in '47. We used to shtup in adjoining rooms at the Roosevelt. Marilyn was working call jobs then, and I know she had a girl she doubled up with, but I don't know who."

I said, "What happened to Shelley Mandel?"

"The last I heard, he was still around. He was moving black-market penicillin during and after the war, and the BNDD has been halfheartedly looking into him ever since V-J Day. He's mobbed up, in a very minor way. He's related to the Aadland brothers by marriage."

The Aadlands. Fox. Del Kinney. Shelley Mandel. The Aadlands. That name spool-threading through—

"Come back for the fun tonight, Freddy. We're painting a wall tribute to Marilyn."

Flowers and champagne. Amends for the dope I filched. She might be testy. It couldn't hurt.

Her old Ford was parked in the driveway. It torqued my memory and sent me eidetek. I leaned on the doorbell and got no response. I walked around to the back.

There's Miss Lytess.

She reclined on a lawn lounger. A date palm half shaded her. She wore an old cardigan and a mauve slip. It was 96 and humid. She shivered. She clamped down on the lounge slats and stanched tremors.

She looked bad. "Cutting out fast" said it. She coughed into a handkerchief. The fabric was bloodstained.

I coughed. She noticed me. She said, "Don't you start doing it."

I dragged a matching chair up. Miss Lytess studied me. I passed her the champagne and flowers. She popped the cork and spritzed up her slip. It clung to her rib bones. She was tall. She weighed in at ninety pounds, tops.

She said, "I've seen you before."

Her old car. It retweaked me. I snagged the full memory.

"November '54. You were sitting in your Ford, parked on Waring and Kilkea. You were staring at an apartment house window, because you thought Marilyn Monroe was engaged in an assignation there. It turned out that she wasn't. Miss Monroe was married to Joe DiMaggio then. I was there, and Frank Sinatra was there. DiMaggio was jealous. We kicked in the wrong door."

Miss Lytess chugged champagne. She grasped the jug two-handed. The effort taxed her. Her arms fluttered.

"Yes. The notorious 'Wrong-Door Raid.' Yes, you kicked in the wrong door, but Marilyn was next door, in an adjoining apartment. She was with her silly lover, Timmy Berlin. He was a film editor on *Bus Stop* and *River of No Return*."

"It sounds as if you disapproved of him."

Miss Lytess went *ha!* "I disapprove of all men who do not acknowledge me as the creator of Marilyn Monroe. Additionally, I disapprove of policemen who ply me with cheap domestic champagne before they introduce themselves, and share the purpose of their impromptu visits."

I stifled a grin. "My name's Otash. I'm with the DA's Office, and we're conducting an inquiry into Miss Monroe's suicide. Rumors have surfaced, and we're obliged to verify or dispel them. You were seen observing Miss Monroe—repeatedly and acutely—during the last months of her life. You were close to Miss Monroe at one time, so I'm quite anxious to get your perceptions."

Miss Lytess coughed blood in her handkerchief. She dug a pump inhaler and a pill vial from her pockets and dosed herself. She wheezed and expelled green shit. She chased two Dilaudid with my champagne.

She smiled and winked at me. *Oh, you kid.*

"The liquid tastes like fennel and wintergreen. The pills induce a certain enchantment."

I smiled and winked—*Oh, you kid.*

"All right. You're spying on Miss Monroe, and—"

"I have spent a goodly part of my life spying on Marilyn Monroe, and the last fallow months of her life were no exception."

"Why 'fallow'?"

"Fallow, because I sensed her moving toward her tether's end in a prosaic, entirely predictable, and boring fashion."

"For instance?"

"For instance, her sexual antics with a pizza delivery boy and a United Parcel Service driver who rather resembled Robert F. Kennedy. Her waddling out her front gate in ensembles designed for three-hundred-pound women, lugging pillowcases stuffed with God knows what. Her boon companionship with a very tall teenage girl who lavished adulation on her and would have continued to do so for another few months, until Marilyn dropped her flat. Her self-destructive behavior on her last film, widely reported in the press and on television. Her obscene performance at our sexy young president's birthday do in New York, and her—"

"When did Miss Monroe meet the president? Can you narrow it down?"

Miss Lytess unclenched. Her dope load hit. Her eyeballs pinned.

"I witnessed the fatuous moment of their convergence. Charlie Feldman threw a party. It was summertime in '54. They were there. They played themselves superbly that day. Marilyn dumped me in '56, you know. But for the last two years that I knew her, she harped on young Senator Jack to no end. She predicted his election, lived for their very infrequent quickies, and blathered on and on about herself as our 'shoo-in' First Lady. I blew up at her one evening and demanded that she say something real about the young man. Marilyn giggled and said, 'He has a small penis.'"

I strained it. I sifted and shifted it. It confirmed my foreknowledge.

"Did Miss Monroe ever indicate that she knew Jack Kennedy before she met him at that party?"

"Yes, but she was in her cups, because young Jack had stood her up on the occasion of their latest quickie. She said she had met him 'years before' Charlie Feldman's party, and she had 'impeachment-level' dirt on him, which she would 'go public with,' should he fail to divorce Jackie and marry her. I pressed Marilyn for more details, but Marilyn said, 'My lips are sealed.'"

I said, "Did Miss Monroe know the late Carole Landis? Do you recall her discussing Miss Landis' suicide?"

"No. I met Marilyn late in '49. Miss Landis was already dead. She wasn't a current topic of conversation."

"I know that Miss Monroe broke off with you sometime in '56. I would assume you haven't seen her since then. I'm trying to determine the genesis of a bite scar on her left bicep."

Miss Lytess made a face. "I have reviewed many magazine photographs of Marilyn. I recall no such scar."

"Did you actually converse with Miss Monroe during the time you were living here and observing her?"

"No."

"She told friends that her house had been burgled, that articles had been moved, and that she had received nasty letters. Did you observe men prowling in the vicinity of her house, and placing objects in her mailbox?"

"No. And I am not the type to burgle houses and peek in mailboxes myself."

I leaned in close. "I think Miss Monroe fell in with some people, near the end of her life. I think she indulged in a great deal of risky and perhaps dangerous behavior. I sense this very strongly. Are you privy to what might have occurred? Did you witness any incidents? How accurate do you consider my speculations to be?"

Miss Lytess sipped champagne. "Marilyn overestimated her sway over people. She played her cards too quickly and desperately, in her efforts to impress and seduce them. She gave herself up cheaply, in all ways. If these people you posit were canny and properly reserved, and if she wanted to imitate their self-sufficiency and general hauteur, she would have set out to prove herself to them in most dangerous ways."

29

I tracked the scar. Sex biters were rare turds. My "psycho biter" crack buzzed Doc de River. I worked in the Intel screening room. I studied late-'50s magazine clips with a photo loupe.

The jizz-crusted Polaroids. Four in all. I sensed the Cruel Blond Stud as the biter. They were '58 or '59 vintage. Monroe was younger. The Feds seized my photos and bootjacked the PD's copies by court decree. I'd memorized every detail. I compared the thirty-two or thirty-three-year-old Monroe to a glut of news mag pix. I saw no close-up/bare-arm shots. I got no indications of healed and faded scarring.

I set up a projector and raided the surveillance-film vault. I selected four no-sound reels. They covered 5/59 up to this summer. The boxes were marked: time/date/location/gist of surveillance. Monroe gambols at ban-the-bomb/civil rights/bash-the-fuzz demonstrations. They were marked "daytime-exterior." They were shot outside City Hall and the PAB.

I doused the lights and spooled in a 5/59 reel. Black-and-white footage hit the screen. The specific date is 5/16. We're facing north. We're slow-panning east to west along the 1st Street sidewalk. The City Hall lawn provides a backdrop. Sixty-odd pinkos agitate.

They schmooze and pop placards. Beatniks, college kids, suffragette spinsters. They don't dig the A-bomb. Their lips move, no sound emits, their faces contort. Their placards read:

BAN THE BOMB. I DON'T WANT MY CHILD GROWING UP WITH STRONTIUM 90 IN HIS BONES. THE BOMB IS NOT GOOD FOR CHILDREN AND OTHER LIVING THINGS.

Establishing shots, a slash cut, close-ups and slow pans. There's Monroe. She's waving a strontium 90 sign. Protest punks point to her. *Hey, look who's here!*

The camera zooms close. The cameraman's gassed on Monroe. She's sporting a dark skirt and a head scarf. She's wearing a bare-arm blouse. The cameraman zooms ultraclose. He gets Monroe and bongo king Preston Epps in one shot. *Tilt*—there's no scar on her upper left bicep.

There are no new scar or healed-scar fade marks. Monroe had soft-toned arms on 5/16/59. My instinct solidified. The bitedown occurred during the let's-shoot-fuck-pix assignation. My '58–'59 shoot date was pure conjecture. It could have been later than that.

A memory tugged me. *Why does the Cruel Blond Stud look familiar?* This protest Monroe is the same Monroe as the fuck-pix Monroe. Her facial set and age lines run identical.

I yawned. I slept bad last night. Natasha Lytess got to me in some weird way. I traded Teletypes with Bill Parker. The Chief was pissed. Old man Zanuck beefed my smackdown. I Teletyped Parker back. I told him I had to juke my shit-magnet antics at Fox. I wanted to *re*-brace Zanuck. I wanted to hardnose Del Kinney before moving on Gwen Perloff. Parker Teletyped me back. He said he'd call Zanuck and tell him to grin and bear it. He'd lay in a threat: accommodate Lieutenant Otash or endure a search-warrant barrage.

I changed reels. It's 3/8/61 now. We're back outside City Hall. We're beefing segregated lunch counters. It's the same north-facing/east-to-west-track motif.

And there's Monroe. She's performing today. She's signing auto-graphs. Fuck social protest—let's party! She signs a butch nun's WE SHALL OVERCOME! placard. Harry Belafonte walks into the frame. They perform for the fans. Marilyn grabs Harry. They break into the dirty dog twist.

Monroe's wearing a skirt and bare-arm blouse. The voyeur cam goes close. *Re-tilt*—there's the faded scar and skin-tone contrast. It's vivid in crisp black and white.

I'm convinced:

Cruel Stud bit Marilyn. I've revised my date range. The fuck-pic shoot and bitedown occurred between 5/16/59 and 3/8/61.

Slash cut. The camera pans the Broadway sidewalk. We're west-facing. Beatniks and disaffected squares mingle. Slash cut and perspec-tive shift. The camera pans curbside spectators and parked cars. There's a 1960 Valiant sedan. The L.A. Sheriff's drive Valiants, exclusive. Two men stand by the car and gas on the show. It's Sheriff Pete Pitchess and Motel Mike Bayless.

Deedee Grenier dished Marilyn and Pete. They had an intermittent thing going.

The spool fluttered and slipped off the spindle. I slipped on a 5/4/62 spool.

We're outside the PAB. It's a Bash the PD bash. The Black Muslim shoot-out was hot news. Biracial protestors mingle. The camera spotlights the west sidewalk. Marilyn's wearing a black mourning dress. She's jabbing a sign. It reads CHIEF PAR*KKK*ER MUST GO!!!

I laughed. The camera cut off of Marilyn and focused on the jumped-up hoi polloi.

A time code ticked off. The lower left screen flashed a display. Sixteen minutes elapsed. Protestors bopped down Los Angeles Street, north to south. It bored me. I yawned. Then I saw something.

A dress. A dress I saw in Monroe's bedroom closet. A Large Marge is wearing that selfsame dress. She's jabbing a CHIEF PARKKKER MUST GO!!! sign.

I squinted. The camera swung low. I saw legs and feet but no faces. I caught the hemline on the dress. I caught thin ankles and the black pumps Monroe wore as herself sixteen minutes back.

She went somewhere. She changed clothes. Why did she do it?

The camera arced up and panned faces. It caught Monroe as Large Marge. Her face looks puffy now. She shot herself up with collagen—or someone else did. She switched identities in the middle of a roiling protest gig. She's got the "dreamy eyes" Doc de River attributes to sex psychopaths. Schizo Marilyn. The '48 pill vial I saw. The '62 pill vial I saw. Marilyn crossed out "Norma Jean Baker" on the '48 vial and wrote "Not my name anymore" beside it. Marilyn crossed out the "Marilyn Monroe" on the '62 vial and wrote "Not my name anymore" beside it.

The room went claustrophobe hot. I turned off the lights and walked back to my cubicle. An R&I green sheet was squared off on my desk.

Per "Girl Book" photograph #6. Be advised that subject has been identified as: Ingrid Norma Irmgard/WFA/DOB 12/8/33. Mexicali Airlines stewardess. Felony possession of marijuana/12/14/60/International Airport PD/Dismissed at arraignment. Crnt address: 1750 N. Lucretia Ave, Echo Park/NO-32859.

Scando Fox, Vivid Valkyrie. I reprised the Girl Book snapshot. Mexicali pillbox hat and full beaver. Saunas. Frozen vodka. Call Ingrid for the "Norway Doorway."

Ad Vice had an updated address card. 1750 Lucretia—a stewardess rotation flop behind El Mundo Bestbuy Market. Suspected hot-sheet hut. *Se habla español* at El Mundo and Casa Ingrid. Mexicali and Aeroméxico stews rule the roost.

I drove over. I parked in a curb slot and walked back. Four Mexicali pilots squeezed by me. They wore snazzy blue uniforms. They smiled and went *Buenos días.* I smiled back. They were airport-bound. They sipped Bloody Marys in plastic cups.

The hut was sandblasted stucco. Old paint jobs peeled off pink and lime green. Ingrid sat on a tin-roof porch. She wore a crocheted bikini top and tight jeans. She saw me and gulped.

I hopped the steps and leaned on a porch rail. Ingrid scooched her chair back. She turned and plugged in a porta fan. I caught her right-shoulder tattoo: "El Manny" and crossed boxing gloves.

"It's nothing you should worry about. It's just a few questions, and I don't intend to toss the place."

Ingrid lit a cigarette. "You wouldn't find anything in my space, but I can't vouch for my roommates or their visitors."

I smiled. "It's about Peter Lawford, and some photographs you posed for. I'm interested in how you met Lawford, how you came to be photographed, Lawford's so-called Girl Book, what resulted from the photos, and how things stand with you and Lawford now."

Ingrid blew smoke rings. "You want to know a lot, don't you?"

"Not a lot. A few candid answers, and I'll leave you alone."

"You could stick around. My roommates on the Mazatlán layovers are whipping up margaritas."

I rubbed my back on a porch post. My coat gapped. Ingrid caught my belt shit.

"Okay, Peter Lawford and yours truly in a hundred words or less, even though it's really embarrassing."

I twirled a finger. Let's move this along.

Ingrid said, "Okay, I part-time gig as a cater waitress. It's what you might describe as a semireputable line of work, and I've worked for some semisketchy people—and before you ask, I won't give up the places I've worked, because my Manny hates snitches, and I subscribe to his code."

I tingled. "Cater waitress" did it.

"That's all right. Just keep going."

"Okay. As you may know, most cater waiters and waitresses are in The Life. They hustle, they hawk their booties, they do favors for movie people so maybe they can catch a break. Okay, so I met Peter that way. I dated him, and I posed for some pictures, and all that was fine, but when Peter tried to set me up with his wife's brother, the president, I said, 'No, sir. That's just too creepy.' My Manny keeps me on a long leash, but I'm not a call girl or a concubine for that swishy John F. Kennedy. My Manny's a Nixon man. He says Kennedy's a *puto communisto*, and his daddy bought him the presidency."

I said, "Lawford told me that a 'queen-bee-type' cater waitress conceived the Girl Book deal, but he didn't know the woman's name. Queen-bee cater waitresses. Give me your first response."

Ingrid shrugged. "What response? All the cater girls I know are wage slaves and would-be actresses. Peter took some semisketchy pictures of me, but it was a single-o kind of deal, and I don't know any other cater waitresses who stew, or stews who cater-waitress. Stews and cater girls are all big blabbermouths, but nobody's ever told me they posed for beaver shots for a queen-bee type *or* for Peter Lawford. And, before you ask, I will *not* ask around, because my Manny would kill me."

I went *Whoa*. "Two names. Eleanora and Rick Dawes. Eleanora's a cater waitress, and she's a candidate for the queen bee. Rick Dawes is a cater waiter, and a possible fruit hustler, and a possible suspect in a string of Beverly Hills house burglaries."

Ingrid crushed her cigarette. "No to Eleanora, no to Rick Dawes. My Manny got popped for 459 once, but it was a humbug rap, because he's a straight-arrow guy. He was twenty-four and sixteen as a welterweight, but he wasn't that good. He took a night-school course to be a TV repairman, and he got a job at a repair shop in Brentwood. I brought my TV in to be fixed, and that's how we clicked."

Two Aeroméxico pilots weaved outside. They sipped Bloody Marys and noshed celery sticks.

"One last name. José Bolaños. He's a jack-of-all-trades. Communist, dope pusher, Hollywood suck-up."

Ingrid mock-spit. She supplied sound effects. It was vivid. *She* was vivid. I dug on her.

"No. I know lots of Josés, but no Bolaños."

I zinged her. "Ingrid, are you running dope to Mexico, for El Manny?"

"Not in this lifetime. It's not his bag, and it's not mine."

———

Stage-door Freddy. I fit the role. I'm built to yearn, watch, and wait.

Fox. Soundstage #11. Lois reads for schlockman Maury Dexter. The audition room was polar-AC'd. Bikini girls huddled in anoraks. A stooge scrounged them off a sex lark called *Baby, It's Cold Outside*.

Bill Parker came through. He called Darryl Zanuck and told him I had on-the-lot carte blanche. It sanctioned me to work raw. The Chief was up Ratfuck Bobby's ass on the FBI-boss deal. Monroe/Kidnap. I was two-front sanctioned to intimidate at will.

Lois read for schlock king Dexter. She's a divorced mom and chaperone for a twist party–cum–nightmare. It was a B quickie. Zanuck planned to flood the B market at Christmas. It was a *Cleo*-loss ploy.

Lois would be miscast. She's thirty-five and childless. She's no man's full-time woman and nobody's mom.

I was bughouse. I called Daryl Gates and told him to run the moniker file for thirtyish cholos named "El Manny." I gave him the soundstage call number and went *Chop, chop*. I told him to glom me a copy of the IO's task list on the kidnap job. He said it might be problematic. I told him to set it up as an Intel/SHIT trade. Offer up pap on the mosque at Slauson and Broadway. Pete Pitchess might succumb.

I paced the soundstage, front to back. I saw a pile of *Cleo*-esque debris in a corner. Swords, scabbards, breastplates. Spiked helmets and steel-cup jockstraps. Roddy McDowall popped through a side door and poked through them.

He's back from Rome and the dizzy debacle. I logged a hundred Rome-to-Brentwood tap calls. Roddy regales Marilyn. He's going to craft a gay smut film. It will utilize *Cleo* detritus and reframe *Cleo* as epic farce. It will be a work of stunning revisionism and "sound the prophetic tonal chord for a whole new era of revolutionary filmmaking."

I yocked. Roddy caught it and saw me. He flipped me off and scrammed out the door. *Confidential* skewered the Saints and Sinners drag ball, eons back. Roddy's date was Miss Drag America, 1953. He was six-eight and shot hoops for the St. Louis Hawks.

I bopped back to the audition room and watched Lois read. I snagged a copy of the *Twist Party Stakeout* script.

The title page ditzed me. Doofus Sid Leffler wrote it. Sid, the nebbish squadroom cop. "Officer Sid," high school toastmaster. Sid feeds Pali girls booze at the Sip 'n' Surf. I saw it myself.

Lois read with a gum-popping coed. *Gee, mom—a psycho killer is loose in the Palisades! Does that mean I can't go to the beach? Do I have to cancel my party tonight? Well, Sally, we'll just have to see about that!*

The wall phone rang. I grabbed it.

Daryl Gates said, "We got one hit on El Manny. Your guy has to be Juan Manuel Salas, DOB 11/4/26, L.A. One Chino bounce for stat rape, August '54. One dismissed house burglary charge, May '57."

Lois winked and flashed a thumbs-up. She aced the audition and got the job.

30

My tube gizmo rattled. I heard a telltale *whoosh*. The feeder lid retracted. I reached over and pulled out the tube.

Daryl Gates delivered. I spread the task list out on my desk. Motel Mike Bayless block-printed. It was a thought-through memorandum. It laid out straight-ahead detective work.

Motel Mike bossed a five-man crew. West Hollywood station ran a twenty-four-hour tip line. They ran nationwide paper on the late Richie Danforth, the late Buzzy Stein, and Gwen Perloff. Gwen came up clean. Buzzy Stein's sex priors were noted. Danforth came up *nationwide* clean. It confounded Motel Mike. No print cards, no NCIC numbers, no fifty-state arrest records. Danforth's hands were pulped, Danforth's feet were severed and mashed. It scotched state, local, and Federal print runs and a shot at baby footprints in hospital archives. There were 284 Richard Danforths culled in the 1960 census. All were contacted. All were accounted for. None was him. Nobody knew shit about him. Buzzy Stein's wife and three kids were braced. They revealed jackshit and hid behind Buzzy's lawyer brother.

The Hats and I popped Danforth and Stein at a back house off of 6th and Dunsmuir. A "heavyset older woman" rented it. The same woman rented the Tiki-Torch pad where the Sheriff's rescued Gwen. The heavyset woman paid cash in advance and stiffed the managers with a phony name and unverifiable references. Both locations had been print-wiped and solvent-scrubbed. Sheriff's techs snagged zero latents. Fiber collections went *pffft*. The three go-throughs snagged innocuous grit. Door-to-door canvasses revealed zilch. Six eyewits viewed the snatch. They described six dissimilar vehicles. That scotched DMV checks. Gwen Perloff was chloroformed and remained unconscious for the city-to-Valley haul. She was blood-checked at Queen of Angels. Tests revealed the chloroform and six grains of sodium secobarbital. The kidnap guys fed her heavily spiked burgers and induced a long snooze. Perloff was unconscious for most of her confinement.

She was interviewed three times. She repeatedly stated that she had no enemies and did not know who snatched her. Motel Mike ran checks on the casts and crews of the last six films Perloff appeared in. Numerous drunk-driving and spousal-battery beefs were revealed and dismissed as irrelevant. The men were interviewed and cleared. Perloff refused to discuss her romantic life. She denied a wingding with Darryl F. Zanuck. Motel Mike interviewed Zanuck. DFZ denied the wingding.

Motel Mike asserted that the Hat Squad and Freddy O. blew the case. The Danforth toss was a "vigilante action." He urged Sheriff Pete Pitchess to seek legal redress. Pitchess refused.

We shouldn't have tossed him. I know that now. So do the Hats. We also know *this:*

Danforth's exit line: "It's a put-up job."

Gwen Perloff was in on the snatch.

I staked out her building. I parked across the street and just sat there. It was a two-story/hipster-moderne job. She lived in the upstairs front. Her living room window looked out on me. Gwen, this is Freddy. Freddy, this is Gwen.

She was home. I preprowled the underground garage and tossed her sled. She owned a '59 Triumph. I master-keyed the driver's door. I found a copy of yesterday's *Hollywood Reporter* on the seat. I leafed through it and caught a back-page squib. It was inked in trade paper–ese:

"Kidnap vict Gwen Perloff to star in saucy self-scripted biopic. It's on tap as 'Hard Luck Girl.' Fox to produce. DFZ himself 'to provide personal input.' Pic details kid sister's baffling disappearance and probable lust murder. Talent hunt for nifty child actress to play Miss Perloff as a 'busty preadolescent.' Fox's 'Baron of the B's,' Maury Dexter, to direct."

In the glove box:

A staghorn-grip .38 Smith automatic. Six in the clip, one in the chamber.

I disassembled the piece. The serial number had been acid-dipped. It was a no-provenance cold piece. It confirmed rumors of Gwen in The Life.

Behind the seat:

A triple-reinforced pillowcase. Filled with nickels, dimes, quarters. I got ice chills. I got whiplash. *Perloff/Monroe/Perloff/Monroe.* I could not think beyond the two names.

That was three hours back. My mind spooled that stutter loop, non-stop. I heard the names and stared down Perloff's front door.

I was shot to shit. I spent half the day at the County Plans Office. I studied postwar file photos of recently built houses. I tried to match pix to Monroe's sketch of 6/22/48. Nothing came close. Why should it? I found the sketch in a hidey-hole. It footnoted Monroe's crazy life.

Perloff/Monroe/Perloff/Monroe. I couldn't think past it.

She walked out her door. She wore sun-bleached jeans and a man's white shirt.

She eyed the street. She made me. She knew I was perched there. She looked away. I hit the horn. She heard it and ignored it and walked back inside.

Del Kinney checked my badge kit. It was disingenuous. The Pico gate guard called and prewarned him. Pops Zanuck must have warned him. We're hamstrung, Del. Bill Parker wants this. He'll nuisance-warrant us if we don't comply.

The security hut was scrunched behind a Gay Nineties set. It featured a muster room/guard's lounge/golf-cart repair shed. Kinney's office was air-cooled and knotty pine–paneled. His desk was half Zanuck size. He's got a comfy wing chair. My chair wobbled on uneven legs.

He tossed the kit back. It dropped in my lap.

"You've come up in the world, based on what I know about you. I'll talk to you, within discreet limits."

I snickered. "Clarify something for me. Were you tipped that I was running a crew on the lot from April through June?"

Kinney lit a cigarette. "Hersh Aadland called me, at Jimmy Hoffa's behest. You, Denkins, Molette, and Irwin had already been seen habituating the *Got to Give* set, and Mr. Hoffa's message was to leave Mr. Otash and his boys alone. I figured you were jobbing Marilyn Monroe for Mr. Hoffa, and given that you're you, the deal was extortion."

I flushed. Kinney opened strong. I dug my legs in. My chair wobbled—*Whoa, now.*

Kinney said, "Okay, so Marilyn's dead, and you're credentialed up.

Here's my guess and Pete Pitchess' guess. You've switched sides, and you're doing mop-up work for Bill Parker and the Kennedys. Let's put Freddy O. out as a dirt sieve and see what he collects. You're dirty on the Hoffa job, and you and the Hats are dirty on the Perloff snatch. Really, Freddy. Did you have to waste that Danforth guy? Couldn't you and the Hats have just thumped him until he gave up Gwen's location?"

"Gwen, huh? I dig the intimate tone."

It fell flat. I fizzled. Kinney evil-eyed me.

"I met Gwen when she was ten years old. I ran the mounted posse when her sister disappeared. She's the kid sister I never had, and I'm the big brother she never had. Watch what you say about Gwen."

I bore down. "All well and good. But she's dirty, and the kidnap caper's dirty, and that trumps all your brother-sister jive."

Kinney splayed his hands. They covered half his desk. He had strongarm-goon mitts.

"I'll concede the point, and I'll toss you a bone that will permit you to walk out of here with your balls intact."

I gulped. My Adam's apple popped. Kinney saw it and smirked.

"Bill Parker and Pete Pitchess have a handshake deal to let the kidnap job go. Pete knows it's dirty, and he doesn't want to sully his department. Parker wants you to work it for the sole purpose of covering LAPD on the Danforth deal. Miller Leavy sees the job from an entirely different perspective. He's waxing fifty-fifty right about now. Half of him wants to can the job. Half of him wants to burn you and the Hats for Danforth."

I coughed. It was camouflage. It hid my borderline shakes.

"Gwen Perloff. She couriers bearer bonds for Zanuck and some other studio hotshots."

Kinney said, "No comment."

"Gwen Perloff. She's banging old man Zanuck, and he set her up in that vanity *Hard Luck Girl* production."

Kinney said, "No comment."

"Fox is in the shitter. People here are scared. Bonds, dope, wife-swap clubs, you're taking calls from the Aadland brothers, and they're as bad as they get."

Kinney said, "No comment."

I bore down. "Let's keep both our sets of balls intact. Give up Gwen's known associates that you just cannot tolerate because you've got this big fraternal thing going with her."

Kinney resplayed his hands. "Or you'll do what?"

I said, "I'll do you a solid going in. LAPD Intel has a blue sheet on you. It pertains to you laying off hijacked booze on Hersh Aadland, and it suggests a *cherchez la femme* angle. I'm betting Gwen's the *femme,* but I'm too much of a gent to ask you. I shred the blue sheet, you give up Gwen's shitbird KAs."

Kinney futzed with a toothpick. His hands shook.

"Paul Mitchell Grenier. He's a real piece of shit. He works as a grip here, and he acts in fuck flicks and runs badger games with his sister, Deedee. He did time at Chino for stat rape. Something like '54 to '57. I've seen him talking with Gwen, here on the lot. He swings both ways. He gets in brawls at leather bars and bites guys. Is that unsavory enough for you?"

Deedee Grenier. Her snitch aria, early summer. Paul Mitchell and Monroe/Hollygrove/1930 something. Paul Mitchell's a biter. The bite mark on Monroe's arm.

"SHIT. Motel Mike Bayless. Toss me some crumbs."

Kinney rolled his eyes. "Bayless is Pete Pitchess' muscle guy at SHIT. There's this crazy LAPD hump, Jack Clemmons. He filed for the Sheriff's election race, early in March. Bayless extorted him out of the race, and Pete ran unopposed."

The Bonneville ragtop clued me. The red stood out. I knew the plate number. The hood was warm. She parked two curb slots north of the Strip.

I parked under my building. I knew her MO. My MO diverged. She lurked. I yearned and peeped.

Okay—I'll play.

I hooked around and up the front pathway. She stood on my porch. She lit a cigarette and worked at ennui. I noticed new things. Her loose wristwatch drooped too loose. She wore new white bucks.

I ambled over. She pulled off her barrette and shook her hair loose. Her hemline rode high. Knock-kneed women jazz me.

"I'm starting to see where this is going. Every time I do something bold and stupid, you reward me."

"I'm calling a time-out on my marriage. Can you blame me?"

"I'll get us a motel room on PCH next time. It'll save you the commute."

Pat touched the wedding-stone scar on my cheek. I ducked my head and nuzzled her hand.

The bedroom broiled. Late August L.A. Swamp heat and smog drifts. Lois willed thunderstorms. Pat lacked the gift.

We stretched out full length. Our feet drooped off the sheets. We laced our hands up and tapped the headboard. Pat orbed her watch. I grabbed it and slid it under the mattress.

"Your duties back at the beach bore me. Get your slaves to feed the kids and walk the dog. Tell Jack you've got something going, and you're neglecting your family for the foreseeable future. Tell Bobby I'm on the job, so leave me alone."

Pat dug through her handbag. She pulled out today's *Variety* and held it open. I saw "Luscious kidnap victim," *Hard Luck Girl*, and a swimwear pic of Gwen Perloff. Big Gwen—always the glasses.

Pat jabbed the photo. "I saw Peter and this woman on the beach, late this spring. I couldn't hear their conversation. Peter passed her some money, and she passed him a large manila envelope. It was months before she was kidnapped and you were called into the whole thing. I thought you'd want to know."

It was the Girl Book. Lawford lied to me. He said a "queen-bee" cater waitress sold it to him. He claimed not to know her name. Ingrid Irmgard lied to me. She was a cater waitress. She said Lawford shot her Girl Book pix. She claimed not to know any queen bees. Gwen Perloff defined the queen-bee prototype.

Pat watched me cogitate. She caught a tremor and pressed my hand to the bed. I skimmed *Variety*. The gist mimicked the *Reporter*.

Gwen Perloff. "Busty Bawd of the B's." *Hard Luck Girl*/foster-home kid/who grabbed Gwen's little sister?

Variety mimics the *Reporter*. It diverges right here:

She's a foster-home kid. Plus an orphanage kid. She was dumped in Hollygrove, '37–'39. It's conclusive. *She was in Hollygrove with Marilyn Monroe and Paul Mitchell Grenier.*

The room spun. *Monroe/Kidnap/Monroe/Kidnap Monroe/Kidnap.* The two case lines of 8/4/62 intersect.

Pat said, "There's something else you should know. Peter and I attended a reception two nights ago. It was mostly city government people.

Peter buttonholed a DA's man named Miller Leavy and cut into you. He told Mr. Leavy that you killed that kidnap man in cold blood, and Mr. Leavy's face lit up."

I said, "Oh shit."

The Losers Club. Eddie Fisher's three-night stand launches. He's back. He's here to croon his corny repertoire and spritz his self-loathing. The Liz/*Cleo* mess drags on. He's here to reair it. He's got a packed house.

Eddie and Bo Belinsky were holed up in the greenroom. Nat and Phil worked the rope line. I stood near the bar and gassed Eddie's opening act.

Milt Chargin and "Junkie Monkey."

Milt's a low-rent ventriloquist. Junkie Monkey's a stuffed chimpanzee. He's got a hinged jaw and mouth. He wears a porkpie hat. There's a dope spike glued to his left arm. Their patter runs phantasmagoric.

Milt said, "I heard you've been doing some traveling, baby."

Junkie Monkey said, "Yeah, dad. I hopped a spaceship out of Cape Canaveral. Five Martians were at the controls. We headed for the Belgian Congo. We wanted to catch all the political upscut, live and up close."

Milt said, "Was it a nonstop flight?"

Junkie Monkey said, "Naw. We had to stop in Cuba to refuel."

The crowd tittered. Milt said, "That sounds dangerous. That putz Castro's the big bossman down there."

Junkie Monkey said, "He's a swell cat. He loaded me up with goodies, just for Eddie's debut gig here at the Losers."

Milt reached in his pockets and pulled out two fistfuls of five-cent cigars. He threw them out at the crowd. Dipshits reached, grabbed, spilled drinks and toppled tables. The room roared. A hi-fi kicked on and blared Afro-Cuban riffs. Drink girls sambaed and mamboed. The hi-fi clicked off. The crowd stomped and cheered.

Milt said, "Calm down, you *schnorrers*." The *schnorrers* calmed down. Junkie Monkey said, "We picked up some hitchhikers in Havana. They wanted to groove on the Martians, and beat feet to the Congo and catch the scene."

Milt said, "Who *were* the hitchhikers? Did you catch anybody of note?"

Junkie Monkey said, "Count Basie and his Atomic Band, twenty-four Playboy Playmates, Governor Orval Faubus, Lenny Bernstein and thirty-two sailors he picked up at Lavender Leo's Lovenest, the Mormon Tabernacle Choir, four Klan geeks from Moosefart, Mississippi, Miss Mahalia Jackson, that dink who plays Captain Kangaroo, and forty-one Hollywood High cheerleaders."

The crowd yock-yocked. Milt went *Whew!*

"Wow! It must have been packed in that spaceship!"

Junkie Monkey said, "No, but it was *stacked*—that's for sure!"

The crowd *re*-yocked. The drink girls did bumps and grinds.

Milt said, "Did you ever get the chance to refuel?"

Junkie Monkey said, "We didn't need to. Dr. Feelgood broomed down from the Apple and geezed the gang up with joy juice. We got there on our own head of steam."

The crowd re-*re*-yocked. They were lubed. The Losers served triple shots.

Milt said, "So, you arrive in the Congo. What happened then?"

Junkie Monkey said, "The head Martian split the spaceship and walked up to the nearest native. He said, 'Hey, man—take me to your leader.' The native said, 'Lumumba, Tshombe, Mobutu, or Kasa-Vubu?' The Martian said, 'Hey, man—we'll dance later. Right now, take me to your leader!!!'"

The crowd stood and cheered. They knew from punch lines. Women chanted "Edd-ie, Edd-ie, Edd-ie!"

Enough.

I ducked into the greenroom. Eddie was backstage, yakking up his combo. Bo Belinsky plucked pills from the goofball and high-hopper bowls.

He said, "This can't be legal."

I said, "It's not."

"The pink ones and green ones look good."

"Don't plan on driving home tonight."

Bo popped a pink one and a green one. He stretched out on the couch to await results.

"Eddie's miffed at me. Liz told a paparazzi guy in Rome she wants to shtup me. I keep ribbing Eddie about it. I keep saying I'll shtup her if she gives him an alimony reduction. The joke went stale after a while."

"Jokes tend to do that."

Bo said, "You're downbeat tonight, Freddy. The world's crawling up your ass, and you can't take much more of it."

Monroe/Kidnap/Monroe/Kidnap/Monroe/Kidnap. It kept spooling. The tape ran on, unspliced.

I camped out in a lounge chair. Bo drifted off. I almost popped a pink one and a green one. Sam Yorty walked in. Two bodyguards backstopped him.

They about-faced and shut the door. Mayor Sam said, "I tracked you down through your service. They said you'd be here."

I got up and poured him a scotch. He said, "Forewarned is forearmed," and chugged it.

I said, "Tell me."

Mayor Sam kicked the couch. "Bo Belinksy, down for the count. A no-hitter in May, and he owns my town. Now, he's a stooge for a pussy-whipped crooner."

I winked. "It's Bill Parker's town. You're just the mayor of it."

"Ain't it the truth."

"'Forewarned is forearmed,' Mayor Sam. I'm here to listen."

He poured a refill. He chugged it and cut loose.

"I ran into Miller Leavy at the Jonathan Club. He was beet red about you and the Hats. You're Nazi thugs. You're Bill Parker's Brownshirts, you killed that kidnap chump for kicks, you're a DA's Bureau lieutenant now, and isn't it disgraceful? He wants to burn you and the Hats for Murder One. He wants to singe Bill Parker while he's at it. He said he's already talked to Bob Kennedy. Mr. AG expressed intense interest. Miller thinks he can wrangle a Federal judgeship out of that numbnuts, because he'll be the man who took down you and the Hats, and blew up the overhyped LAPD in one go."

The club closed at 3:00 a.m. Eddie did turn-away biz. Ring-a-ding—he took two drink girls home with him.

Bo snored it up in the greenroom. He'd be coma-conked at least fourteen hours. Nat and Phil faded back to their canvassing gigs. Milt Chargin and Junkie Monkey bopped home to their tract pad in Pacoima. Pat was home with her kids and presidential-pimp hubby. Lois was back at the Chapman Park Hotel. She was probably calling up strange men.

Monroe/Kidnap/Monroe/Kidnap/Monroe/Kidnap.

I leaned toward straight convergence. Monroe kept coin stashes. Perloff kept a coin stash in her car. *Monroe/Perloff/Paul Mitchell Grenier.* Late '30s Hollygrove alums.

Bar-brawl biter Paul Mitchell. Marilyn's bite mark. Fuck-film actor Paul Mitchell. The jizzed-on fuck pix in Marilyn's drawer. A dozen record checks, lab tests, and shit tasks unfulfilled. *Monroe/Kidnap.* Don't stamp it strict convergence—*quite yet.*

Gwen Perloff sold Peter Lawford the Girl Book. Ingrid Irmgard might play out dirty. What's with Juan Manuel Salas? Lawford blows me off to Miller Leavy. Mayor Sam gets more specific. Leavy wants to burn me and the Hats.

I sat in my car. The Losers lot was eerie still. I ran options. I tagged conclusions. The Hats wouldn't crack. I wouldn't crack. Perloff wouldn't crack. It boiled down to hearsay witnesses and Leavy's courtroom flair. I had to stop it short of indictments. I had to ID the kidnappers and kill them.

31

Three days. Psychic limbo. I'm paranoid-schizo. The world's out to get me. Shrink-wrap me, baby. Call Doc Greenson and Doc de River. Rack me out on the couch.

The world's out to get me. Plus the Hats. Bobby K. and Miller Leavy suck the world's poison dick and enact the world's poison mandates. I huddled up Max Herman and Red Stromwall. They cosigned my plan. Let's kill the kidnappers and squelch Murder One, preemptive. Harry Crowder and Eddie Benson concurred. Freddy O. and the Hats ride again.

Shrink-wrap me. I'm paranoid. I see wisps and hear voices where there might be none.

What's Jimmy Hoffa's play? He told Hersh Aadland to call Del Kinney. Hersh A. complied. Freddy O.'s on the lot. His men, ditto. Jimmy told Del to ignore us.

Shrink-wrap me. The world's pulled a work slowdown on me. My lab checks and record checks slog as I hit overdrive.

The lab can't match the jizzed-on pix. They've checked 621 samples. They've got two hundred plus to go. I buzzed the personnel boss at Mexicali Airlines. He cited Ingrid Irmgard's squeaky-clean work record. I checked Ingrid's work sheets back to January and scanned passenger manifests. The name José Bolaños did not appear. Customs supplied inbound and outbound U.S.-to-Mexico passport pix. I scanned ten dozen. I trolled for Mexican fat women who might be Monroe in disguise. I got *todos nada* there. State and Fed HUAC shot me suspect sheets on José. They were 85% redacted and thus meaningless. The redactions meant Bolaños was a snitch. He ratted Commie motherfuckers and skated on his own misdeeds. Customs won't cough up their Bolaños files. The Mex State Police have flat refused.

I drove Hollywood and West L.A. streets for ten straight hours. It was futile. I could not tag the house that Monroe sketched in '48. The search warrant for Bev's Switchboard is still "in the works." I need to *re*-brace Darryl Zanuck. He said a "wheezy-voiced" old lady called in the tip on the Danforth/Stein/Perloff location. I took Natasha Lytess a bottle of scotch and some flowers. I wanted to jolly her and set up a shot at a second interview. She had a wheezy voice. She might have called in the tip. *Her* tip would push *Monroe/Kidnap* to full-stop convergence.

The old Monroe-pad bug mounts still tweak me. I found a carpet displacement pic I shot during the 8/4 break-in. I took it to the lab. Ray Pinker did a walking portrait. He called the cat six-one/190/size 11 feet/slight left-leg limp. That narrowed it down to ten million men.

Nat and Phil concluded their Lawford house/Monroe house canvass. Here's their final assessment:

The Monroe/Jack liaison was an open secret in showbiz circles. Basic rumors circulated. They were repeatedly embellished. They devolved into fantasia. Bobby did not pour Marilyn the pork. UPS men and pizza-delivery boys poured her the pork. Nat and Phil agreed: it's banal for a derogatory profile.

I ID'd the other stews in the Girl Book photos. I chopped the head-shot portions off the beaver shots and flashed personnel honchos at four airlines. I got names and glowing work reports on the young women. I ran them through R&I and got zilch. I nixed hard-brace interviews.

Nat and Phil worked the "Rick Dawes"/"Eleanora"/cater waiter front. They made cold calls. They repeatedly caught the same drift:

Who's Rick Dawes? Who's Eleanora? Come *on*. These cater kids are all hustlers and hopheads.

I itched to study my own master file. I had to reconnect with the bug-tap transcripts and photo evidence. Justice hoarded the file. I Teletyped Bobby K. I besieged his ass. Let me view the file. It won't leave the U.S. Attorney's Office. The little prick relented. I read the file, dawn to dusk. Eddie Chacōn watched and kibitzed. The file was rife with penciled-in check marks. They denoted felony infractions. Said infractions were attributable to:

F. Otash, J. Hoffa, Nat D., and Phil I. It justified my paranoia. Bobby's out to slam us all.

I studied the file. I took notes. I Man Camera'd the four-month mis-adventure. It refitted my memory. I found a long-gone wad of papers crammed down a file-box seam.

There it is. My report on events of 5/19/62. I tailed Monroe out to the Valley. She blew the tail. I compiled a plate list of 143 cars parked near the location.

I rescribbled the numbers and Telefaxed them to Daryl Gates. He put in a superrush order with the DMV and R&I. I got the results, nine hours on:

One hundred and forty-three cars. Full stats per the registered own-ers. Thirty-four misdemeanor busts between them. My eidetek memory unscrambled. I retrieved that post-5/19 brain glitch:

I thought, *I've been here before. Why does this West Valley turf seem familiar?* Here's why:

I tailed Monroe to the locale on 5/19. I was back at the locale on 8/4. I saw Mike Bayless and a Sheriff's crew rescue Gwen Perloff at the Tiki-Torch Village apartments.

Here's the punch line:

Gwen Perloff parked her '59 Triumph a half block from the spot where she was rescued. She parked there seventy-odd days BEFORE she was kidnapped. It was one block from the spot where Monroe blew my tail.

Monroe/Kidnap. Monroe/Perloff. Spell it out. It's officially coincidence into convergence.

Cut to *Monroe/Perloff/Paul Mitchell Grenier.* They're Hollygrove kids, way back when.

Hollygrove. The "Grove." The orphan's home just north of Melrose and Vine. Film-biz largesse built the place. The kids got TLC, good chow, local public school classes and outings. I charted the overall con-vergence. I craved intimate details. I planned a low-key approach.

It backfired.

I dropped in and dropped on the headmistress. I badged her. I told her I had a tangential interest in Marilyn Monroe. It shut her down. She railed at Monroe sycophants, hagiographers, and obsessives. I requested the files on all the kids from '36 to '38. She said, "No." She said, "Get a court order." She said, "Our lawyers will attempt to block it every step of the way."

I slunk off. I replowed old forensic ground. I went by the county morgue and viewed Richie Danforth's pulverized remains.

He was footless. His hands were too pulped to pull prints from. His teeth were cracked and ground to dust. I couldn't issue a fifty-state dental alert. This stone criminal went unprinted and was fifty-state clean? He had to be deploying fake ID. He had to be ID-able somewhere.

Forensic shitwork. Clue-chaser shitwork. I had to interview Lowell Farr. I placed a request with the PD's juvie division. I wanted to *re*-brace Natasha Lytess. She held back last time. I sensed it loud and clear. I goosed R&I and my DMV man per my plate list for the cars outside Fox Accounting. The goose job worked. I got ownership stats on the fifty-four vehicles—and a paucity of rap sheets on the owners. But— one name stood out.

Albert Morris Aadland/WMA/DOB 7/12/24. No criminal record. One illustrious surname.

I called Del Kinney and ran the name by him. "Is this guy related to the Aadland brothers? Distantly related to Dr. Shelley Mandel?"

Del confirmed me. "Yeah, that's Albie. He's a nebbish and a Fox wage slave. His mom and dad had a late-in-life baby. He ain't like his badass brothers at all."

Albie Aadland. It was a weak lead. It was a probable dud. Shelley Mandel hawked barbs to the pre-Monroe Norma Jean Baker. He's a probable dud lead himself. It lays out as a film-biz/Foxed-up confluence. L.A. is one big confluence its own self.

The Fox confluence. It *re*-tweaked me. Paul Mitchell Grenier triple-tweaked me, resultant. Grenier. He's a leather-bar biter. He was at Hollygrove with M. Monroe and G. Perloff. He's an ex-con. He's a Chino grad. He's a Fox bit player. He's a switch-hitter/fuck-film actor. Let's revisit this shitbird.

I prowled regional Vice Squad files and read old occurrence reports. I hit Central Division, Wilshire Division, Highland Park and Hollywood Divisions. I got gay bar/bar-brawl notations at Central. I got a gay bar/*bite*-brawl notation at Highland Park. I scored on a male prosty sheet.

Hollywood Division, 1/14/58. Parked-car assignation, Selma and Las Palmas, 2:20 a.m. Paul Mitchell Grenier attacks a trick with his teeth. The trick rats Grenier to the fuzz and later declines to press charges. Two mug shots are attached to the sheet.

I studied the shots. I saw Grenier earlier this summer. Phil Irwin and I busted up the Deedee Grenier/Paul Mitchell badger game at Norm's Nest. I sapped Paul Mitchell's punk ass. I saw him on a dark street. We were under duress. He's much thinner now. These early '58 mugs slap on twenty pounds plus. Cut to 8/4/62. I view the Monroe/Cruel Stud fuck pix. I thought Cruel Stud looked familiar. Here's why:

Cruel Stud was Paul Mitchell Grenier. The white strips over his eyes concealed the fact then. He weighed twenty-plus pounds more then. The fuck-suck pix are '58–'59 vintage. There's no bite mark on Marilyn's bicep. I saw 5/16/59 shots of Marilyn at a ban-the-bomb rally. There was no raw bite mark or bite-mark scar on her bicep.

Let's track Marilyn's age backward. Let's track Paul Mitchell Grenier's appearance. The pix are surely '58–'59 vintage. Marilyn is unmarked on 5/16/59. Cut forward. Go to 3/8/61. Marilyn's surveilled at a civil rights wingding. We see the faded bite mark now. We mark her sustained relationship with Paul Mitchell Grenier. Sex biters are very rare. Marilyn knew only one in her lifetime. Grenier mauled Marilyn sometime between May '59 and March '61. He's a sex psycho. Dangerous people converged with Monroe in the months preceding her death. I'm sure of it. I'm double sure this piece of shit Grenier was one of them.

32

Zanuck mandated Round Two. I Teletyped a case update to Parker and Gates late last night. Gates wrote back. His brief: the whole deal is Fox-derived. Make more noise on the lot. Parker wrote back. His brief: be a shit magnet. It's what you do best.

I strolled the lot. I unplugged a golf cart outside Soundstage #6 and zipped up to Zanuck's side door. I had carte blanche now. I'd lubed Del Kinney. The nuisance-warrant threat vouched me. I barged right in.

Pops was alone. He saw me and moved slow. He went for his desk phone. I yanked the wall cord. He went for his intercom. I kicked out a floor plug. He yanked drawer pulls. I saw a Minnie Mouse purse gun and beat him to it.

Zanuck said, "You won't always be a policeman, and Bill Parker won't always enjoy the kind of pull he has now. I won't always run this studio, and I'll deal with you at my leisure then."

I ejected the chamber round and popped out the clip.

"What's the latest on the *Cleo* drain?"

No response.

"How deep in the shit are you?"

No response.

"Somebody at Accounting introduced you to Gwen Perloff. Was it Albie Aadland?"

No response.

"Did you green-light *Hard Luck Girl* so Gwen would keep it zipped on the kidnap?"

No response.

"Did you ever run into a psycho bit player named Paul Mitchell Grenier?"

No response.

"Was the wheezy-voiced woman who called you and ratted off the kidnap deal Natasha Lytess?"

No response.

Gear shift. Let's shaft this geek.

I pulled out a Foxtone Services business card. As seen in Marilyn Monroe's basement. I mimeographed three hundred duplicates last night. Nat and Phil were combing the lot now. They were tagging parked cars. One card per left wiper blade. Let the word spread.

Zanuck fumed and mush-mouthed his cigar. I dropped the card on his desk. Note the leering-fox logo.

"Your wife or mine?"

"Business opportunities"

"Contact PO box 6969"

Zanuck examined the card. His eyes clicked off-kilter. He flushed and pulled down his necktie. He gasped and expelled his cigar.

"I heard you're a wife swapper from way back, so I thought you'd want to see what some colleagues of yours have got going. And check the *schvantz* on that fox. It's got two heads. You think *he* gets laid?"

Pops dry-popped digitalis. His veins throbbed, purple-blue.

"Organized prostitution, postal-code infractions, felony financial malfeasance implied. I'm thinking there'll be Federal and municipal grand juries, and you'll be called to testify. Not to mention this. Surrender all your personnel files to me, or I'll lay everything I suspect on Morty Bendish, and he'll slam your ass in a groundbreaking *Mirror-News* series."

Zanuck palsied and jittered. He's Jello-O in an earthquake. I poured him a nice glass of scotch.

The casting hut overflowed. *Twist Party Stakeout* and giant-rat-flick hopefuls spilled into the prop barn. The coordinator said Lois and Maury Dexter were checking out the set house. It was somewhere in the Palisades. Pali High girls kibitzed and swooned for the *Stakeout*/rat bifecta. Maury needed sixty dance kids and run-from-the-rodent kids. He said it was a big motivational stretch.

I walked into the barn. I saw Roddy McDowall pawing *Cleopatra* discards. He fondled leather breastplates and red velour capes. A lanky man separated scabbards and steel jockstraps.

Confluence. Film-biz scavengers. Dipshit cop Sid Leffler wrote *Stakeout*. Roddy culled costumes for *Cleo Goes Greek*.

He looked up and saw me. He did an arch-queen double take. The lanky man looked up. Roddy said, "Timmy Berlin, Fred Otash. You two share a history, which you may or may not want to acknowledge."

The name ditzed me. Natasha Lytess mentioned this guy. Click—the Wrong-Door Raid. Berlin was Monroe's backstreet lover.

We shook hands. Berlin grooved Roddy's aside. The raid, the star-lit cast, the event lingers.

I said, "I talked to Natasha Lytess recently, Mr. Berlin. Please accept my condolences for the loss of Miss Monroe."

Berlin went somber. Boo-hoo. He studied his shoes. *Nobody knows de trouble Ise—*

Roddy stage-tittered. "Freddy's on his best behavior, but he never just drops by to chat. *Soooo*, Freddy—*who* or *what* is it this time? And don't tell me this isn't you with questions, and me with answers, and that you're not obliged to provide compensation."

Berlin slapped his knees. I slapped my wallet. Roddy struck a hands-on-hips pose.

I said, "It's about Gwen Perloff, and a Fox bit player and alleged smut-film performer named Paul Mitchell Grenier."

Berlin reacted. He deadpanned the "Perloff." The "Grenier" slammed him. He unzipped his windbreaker. I saw a hip-holstered .38 snubnose.

"He's a very disturbed man. He was in Hollygrove with Marilyn, you know—and he was capable of talking her into almost anything."

Roddy jiggled the gun grip. He lived for the dish. Don't stop *nooooow*.

Berlin slapped Roddy's hand and zipped up his jacket. He studied his shoes and sucked in his breath.

"I kept in touch with Marilyn after we fizzled, and—several months ago, I'd say—she told me she wanted to make a smut film, just for grins—and she wanted me to edit it. She said she was on a consorting-with-hoodlums kick, and she wanted to see how far she could take it."

I got goose bumps. I scalp-bristled and twitched.

"Where does Grenier fit in?"

"He was Marilyn's proposed costar, but Roddy told me about his reputation. I tried to warn Marilyn off, but she ignored me. Grenier approached me, independently, and said he wanted me to cut the film, but I said, 'Never.' He left me alone then, but I carry this gun in case he ever comes back."

I said, "Do you know if the film was made?"

Berlin said, "No, it wasn't. Marilyn assured me of that."

"Be careful, sir. Grenier's nobody to mess with."

Berlin skulked off. He played the wounded boyfriend with Method aplomb. Boo-hoo. Marilyn loved me and left me. He ducked his head and kicked prop boxes out of his way.

Roddy said, "Freddy, you spawn bad juju wherever you go."

I said, "Give me your perspective on Grenier."

Roddy rubbed his thumbs and forefingers. I slid him three yards. Roddy mimed a pitching ace winding up.

"You may or may not know that I've directed smut reels, and you probably do not know that I know Paul Mitchell from the Tradesman, the Jaguar, and the Falcon's Lair, or that he appeared in my films *Whipout Man* and *Fat Girl Love*. You *do* know that I collect rumors, and if I *trust* the rumors, I pass them along—in your case, for money."

I lit a cigarette. "I'm with you so far."

Roddy bummed a cigarette. I lit it. Roddy reprised his windup. Here's the pitch:

"Some Marilyn rumors I buy, some I distrust and decline to repeat. I buy the rumor that she and Paul Mitchell posed for a fuck deck—that is, a run of fifty-two pornographic playing cards, which were produced in a limited edition and sold, on an exclusive basis, to wealthy perverts who wanted to possess the decks as a collector's item and investment. Other name and would-be-name actresses had gone the fuck-deck route before—because the decks went for ten g's per, and the performers got a substantial cash cut. Plus, the pervs traded the decks among themselves, just like baseball cards. As in, 'I'll trade you one Ann Savage for one Barbara Payton or Lila Leeds.' But *of course* a Marilyn Monroe fuck deck would be a much more valuable commodity."

Monroe. Grenier. The Polaroid pix. '58–'59 vintage. Possible fuck deck outtakes?

"When were fuck decks a big deal? I've seen black-and-white shots of Monroe and Grenier, but they were from '58 or '59."

Roddy nixed me. "Fuck decks were full color, beautifully produced, and the craze peaked in the late '40s. This is not dreck we're talking about."

"What about a Carole Landis fuck deck?"

"Not to my knowledge. Poor Carole pulled the plug at the onset of the craze. Carole Landis morgue shots, however, are as common as dirt. You sold me mine on the set of *Midnight Lace*."

I said, "Gwen Perloff. Tell me something I don't know."

Roddy went wistful. "She may be one for the ages. She's everywhere you concurrently want and don't want to be. If you *must* view the goods, there's a horror double bill at the Wiltern tonight."

Spawn of the A-Bomb. Universal, '56. Gwen Perloff at twenty-nine. Plus, *The Red Ant People.* Universal, '58. Gwen two years on.

Cheesecake posters lined the lobby. Beach shots. Bikini chicks flee large insects and mutant reptiles.

Spawn rolled first. Summer-vacation kids hogged the orchestra and balcony. They sent up a ruckus. The cartoon and newsreel drew jeers. They booed John F. Kennedy and civil rights stalwarts. They craved monsters and sex.

I took an aisle seat, close in. I was bleary. I'd played hunches and run checks all afternoon.

The downtown library. Local newspaper coverage. 2/17/37. Mitzi Perloff disappears. Let's confirm Gwen's Hollygrove arrival. Let's buttress the Monroe/Perloff/Grenier meet and greet.

Mitzi goes *poof!* Gwen remains in the foster home at De Longpre and Wilton. The *Herald* and *Times* supplied that detail and no more. *Variety* ran another puff job on *Hard Luck Girl*. Script scribe/star Gwen P. was "raised primarily in Hollywood-area foster homes and orphan facilities." I called the L.A. child-protective service and chased Gwen's orphanage stint. A nice old lady combed files and told me *this:*

Gwen went wild after Mitzi vanished. The foster home canned her. She hit Hollygrove in mid-March '37. This confirms the convergence. Monroe and Grenier were already there.

How did Gwen go wild?

She boosted ensembles out of Hollywood shops and sold them to kids at Le Conte Junior High.

She was a grifter then. She was not quite eleven. It was back in '37. I was fifteen then. I was peeping windows in Dogdick, Massachusetts.

Kid grifters and peepers. Fuck decks. Psycho biters and movie stars embroiled in felony smut. Here's some good late-breaking news:

Bobby K. delivered the search warrant. We raid Bev's Switchboard at 10:00 a.m. tomorrow. The Hats plus Freddy O., Daryl Gates, and two postal inspectors. Pump shotguns and legal sanction to trash the place.

The newsreel ended. The kids booed. *Spawn of the A-Bomb* rolled. The kids cheered. It was black and white. The kids razzed it. Credits beamed over a static shot of Malibu Beach.

Cut to the gist. Two young women slink at the water's edge. They wear low-cut bikinis. It's big, rangy Gwen and a skinny blonde. Gwen's wearing her tortoiseshell specs.

High-school boys woof-woofed and wolf-howled. Their dates shushed them. Gwen delivered her first lines:

"Marge, I don't want to sound like a Commie—but the atom bomb gives me the creeps."

I knew that voice. It was "Eleanora's" tap-call voice. She called Peter Lawford, midsummer. She worked him for dirt on cater waiter "Rick Dawes." Monroe wrote "Rick Dawes. Mean—maybe a fag" on a pack-rat scrap of paper.

33

We're on. It's classic cop overkill. We're convoyed up on the south side of Fountain. Bev's is straight across the street.

Eight cops in three prowl sleds. Two matrons in civilian cars. I perched with Daryl Gates. The Hats had their own ride. Two postal cops rolled in a Fedmobile.

Walkie-talkies cinched us up. We jump at 10:05. The boss fed would cue the move. Shotguns and crowbars. The mail slots were hard-fixed to the walls. Bev might hide her master keys.

It's a sweep-through. We hit en masse. Customers will be grabbed and held on the premises. The matrons will toss female patrons' handbags and skin-search them in the can. The postal cops will slam Bev Shoftel with the warrant and demand her master keys. Gates and I will hit box 6969. Foxtone, here we come.

I chain-smoked. My nerves were shot to shit. Convergence plus no sleep and an overamped agenda. I was up all night. I typed out a detailed Monroe/Kidnap brief. It was soundly reasoned and up-to-date. I mimeographed copies for Bill Parker, Gates, the Hats, and Ratfuck Bobby. I dropped copies off at the PAB and the U.S. Attorney's Office. I went out to find Paul Mitchell Grenier and hard-roust him.

He had no fixed address. My DMV contact informed me. He forfeited his driver's license in 1/58. He got popped for that bite assault plus unpaid traffic citations. He had no busts or citations from that point on. I went by the Falcon's Lair, the Jaguar, the Tradesman, the Klondike. The boys said Paul Mitchell slept around with one-night guys. I went by Arthur J.'s and the Gold Cup. Fruit hustlers hobknobbed there. Their consensus: Paul Mitchell was out in the ozone. He's pushing amyl nitrite poppers. He's got a "base of operations" somewhere. He's a skin dog. He digs the donkey show in T.J. Try the Planet Mars.

My walkie-talkie crackled. The boss said, "We go *now*."

Gates and I piled out. We lugged shotguns and pry bars. The Hats and postal cops piled out. They held 12-gauge pumps at port arms. The matrons piled out. They packed handcuffs and come-along chains.

We caught a break in the traffic and ran across Fountain. Max Herman and Red Stromwall kicked the door off its pins.

It crashed inward. It hit the floor. The glass door panes shattered. Overkill meant Big Noise and Riveted Attention. We got it here. Crash noise/shattered-glass noise/overlapped shrieks.

Bev Shoftel screeched. Three male patrons evinced tremors. Two female patrons screamed. The matrons quick-marched the women into the can. The postal cops dropped the warrant on Bev and dumped her purse out on her desk. They grabbed a ring of PO box keys and lobbed them at Gates. Bev squawked and beat her fists on her legs. The postal cops cuffed her hands behind her back and shoved her down in a chair.

The Hats headlocked the three men and hauled them out to the alley. Gates and I beelined for box 6969. I fumbled the key in the lock. My hand shook *that* bad. The key clicked, the door popped, I looked inside. The box was stone empty.

I said, "Shit."

Gates said, "Shit."

I unlocked box 6970. It was stone empty. I unlocked box 6971. It was stone empty. I heard wood-crack noise and screeches. The postal cops pry-barred crazy Bev's desk drawers. Bev screeched police-brutality shit.

I unlocked boxes 6972, 6973, 6974 to 6981. They were all stone empty. I unlocked box 6982 and saw *this:*

Four tabloid-foldout pamphlets. Green-inked covers. Identical to rags I saw at Morty Bendish's pad. Morty published a "private circulation" dirt sheet. *This* had to be *that.*

I scanned the four covers. Morty titled his rag the *L.A. Lowdown.* The cover line promised a "priapic preview" of a new Mr. Fearless Fuzz exposé. *"Pssst—Whiskey Bill Parker cut a deal with ball-busting Bob Kennedy. It's Fearless Fuzz's sex-soiled sequel to Weird-O Death of a Sex Siren, Part 1."*

I squelched the Part 1 pamphlet. *This* pamphlet was mailed prior to my warning. Morty B. would not knowingly fuck me. And, Morty told me *this:*

Fearless Fuzz was West L.A. patrol sergeant Jack Clemmons. And Del Kinney told me *this:*

Clemmons filed to enter the spring '62 race for L.A. County Sheriff. *But*—Motel Mike Bayless coerced him out and Pete Pitchess ran unopposed.

I stuck the pamphlet down my waistband. I unlocked boxes 6983 to 6988 and got zilch. I unlocked box 6989 and pulled out *this:*

A printed flyer. An announcement. There's an upcoming key party and wife-swap bash. "Write to box 6969 for details."/"Couples only"/"$200 at the door"/"Other fees apply."

I removed the flyer. I looked at Bev Shoftel. She said, "Fuck you and the camel you rode in on." I scanned the empty boxes. They'd been cleaned out. Someone passed the word. I got lucky on boxes 6982 and 6989. Bev's perv contingent rented the 69-series boxes and deployed them as in-house mail drops. Bev's patrons had front-door keys and twenty-four-hour access. Their system was foolproof.

Then it hit me:

I passed the word. I sabotaged the raid. Nat and Phil plastered Foxtone cards to cars in the Fox lot. I told them to tap three hundred sleds.

I weaved on my feet. Crazy Bev cackled at me. I heard Daryl Gates and the Hats hard-nose the pervdogs back in the alley. The matrons waltzed the female pervs out of the can. They were handcuffed. I dug in and went back to work.

I unlocked box 6990, box 6991, box 6992, and box 6993. All four were empty. I unlocked box 6994. A single sheet of paper was tucked in.

It's a typed receipt. It acknowledges two hundred dollars received. That's the key-party fee. It's a box-to-box communiqué. There's the time and date of the bash. Somebody sketched Foxtone's leering-fox logo. Foxtone's throwing the bash.

10:00 p.m. Sunday, September 2. 1464 North Havenhurst, West Hollywood.

PART 5

WIFE SWAP

(AUGUST 28–30, 1962)

34

I print-dusted PO boxes. It was penance shitwork. My Fox antics blew the raid. It was in-close detail work. I dusted hinge flaps and interior surfaces. I worked solo. A patrol cop blocked the kicked-down door.

I'd elimination-rolled the cops, the customers, Bev Shoftel, and myself. I tape-transferred the prints to a cardboard sheet and photographed them. The box grab was low-yield. The print grab was all smudges and smears.

The Hats warrant-checked the male customers. All three came up clean. The matrons warrant-checked the two women. They had traffic warrants extant. The Hats grabbed the address books in their handbags. I photographed all the pages. We'll run the names, addresses, and phone numbers through R&I. Criminal names and/or locations might pop up.

The male pervs waltzed. The female pervs went to jail. Bev Shoftel was popped for smut-through-the-mail violations. She'll bail out sure as shit.

Max Herman called me with an update. Red and Harry grabbed Jack Clemmons at his Mar Vista crib. They took him to the downtown DB. A hard smackdown bodes. Max and Eddie picked up Morty Bendish and ran him downtown. Bill Parker might can Clemmons. His "Fearless Fuzz" shit plays psycho. I think we should suborn Morty B. His brief? Newspaper propagandist and paid lapdog. Fetch, Morty, fetch!

I dusted box 6969. I turned up a rubber-glove partial. Glove prints scream criminal design. A torn fingertip revealed partial loops, tents, and whorls. I tape-transferred the partial to a glossy-backed card and photographed it in tight. It looked like a male right index finger.

The print job loomed as all day/all night. I dropped the card in my briefcase and lit a cigarette. I grabbed a copy of the *L.A. Lowdown* and skimmed the "priapic preview":

Mr. Fearless Fuzz. He's Sergeant Jack Clemmons. He's a White Dog Bund *Reichsführer* and Norm's Nest habitué. The preview enhanced the cover line. Whiskey Bill Parker and Bobby the K. Their doomonic devil deal. Parker covers up the Monroe snuff and whitewashes Monroe's ties to the K boys. Jack and Bobby dump Gay Edgar Hoover. Lawyer/cop Parker's the new FBI boss.

It wasn't a snuff. Bobby did not poke Monroe. The cover-up part was all true. Somebody fed Clemmons the rumor. I've got a hunch who.

The *L.A. Lowdown. This* issue was mailed before I told Morty to cease and desist. "Weird-O Death of a Sex Siren, Part 1" was already out in the smog. I skimmed the text at Morty's pad. It was fanciful shit. Morty pandered to pervert-lunatic subscribers. The *L.A. Lowdown* posed no threat to the K boys.

I skimmed past the priapic preview. I hit *"Sicko Psycho in Furtive 459 Prowls!!! Passive Putz or Fitful Fiend Soon to Explode???"*

The author? Detective Slithering Sleuth.

The piece ran four pages. Slithering Sleuth mimicked *Confidential*'s jive prose style. The piece laid out six soft-prowl/nobody's home B and E's in Brentwood and Pacific Palisades. The "Sicko Psycho" targeted the "swank" houses of single women. "*Sex*-clusive! How many posh pads did he hit altogether? Six women *reported* the pad break-ins. There may be more!!!"

The crimes ran from 11/18/61 to 3/12/62. Slithering Sleuth described the crime scenes. He merged jive prose and copese here. He dropped words like *victimology* and phrases like "white female American." Sicko Psycho did not loot the posh pads. He dumped furniture and wall artwork. He dumped medicine chests. He jacked off and shot his load into underwear drawers. He left notes. They were composed in glue-fixed magazine letters. The LAPD crime lab examined them.

The letters and paper stock were "markedly archaic." The Sicko Psycho's MO escalated. He destroyed property and jizzed twice at the sixth victim's pad. All semen scrapings went to the lab. Sicko Psycho was poised to further escalate. His final break-in occurred on 3/12/62.

The ceiling dropped. The floor dipped. The room contracted. My blood pressure red-lined.

Marilyn Monroe moved to Brentwood in March.

35

Sweatbox #3. It's twelve-by-twelve and mirror-walled. There's one table and four chairs. Hallway speakers supply sound. Note the phone book on the table.

At the table: Max Herman, Red Stromwall, Jack Clemmons.

I stood under the speaker. Max and Red drummed the table. Clemmons hemmed and hawed. I grokked him, up close. The blond crew cut. The black-frame glasses. The chinos and windbreaker. No brown shirt and no White Dog Bund armband.

The party lulled on. I came in late. I concluded my print work at Bev's Switchboard and hauled downtown. Plain watching gored my goat. I got antsy and went through the door.

Clemmons stirred. Max said, "Hi, Freddy." Red said, "Lieutenant Otash is here. Jack, tell the lieutenant what you finally told us. What it took you four hours to reveal."

I straddled a chair and lit a cigarette. Clemmons scratched his neck and adjusted his basket. He was scared.

"Well . . . okay. I'll concede that I made up *Weird-O Death of a Sex Siren*, but you've got to admit it could have happened that way. You don't get to see high-quality stuff like Marilyn Monroe dead and naked, not just any old day. Maybe my imagination got the better of me."

Max said, "You made up Part 1, maybe. You succumbed to the moment, because you're a wishy-washy guy."

Clemmons huff-huffed. Me, wishy-washy? Address me as *mein Führer* or I'll put you on report.

"What's with the Part 1? I made the whole thing up. Morty encourages his contributors to go for the pizzazz. He learned under William Randolph Hearst."

Red said, "Here's what Sergeant Herman's trying to tell you. Some-body leaked you the drift on Chief Parker and the AG."

I said, "Give it up, shitbird."

"Give *what* up? Nobody leaked shit to me. *You're* the only shitbird in this—"

I grabbed the phone book and head-smacked him. His glasses flew off. He rubbed his left ear. Phone-book shots induce reverb.

Max passed him his flask. Clemmons took two nips. Red made nice and passed him his glasses. They fit crooked now.

I patted the phone book. I *Sieg heil*'d Clemmons. He's the beat-on Bundsman. Red stifled a yock.

Clemmons sniveled and wiped his nose. He wore a cheesy signet ring. Dig the snarling mastiff. He's got green rhinestone eyes.

"Motel Mike Bayless. That Sheriff's sergeant at SHIT. He told me about the Chief and Bob Kennedy. What LAPD Intel don't know, SHIT does. Them two units are always trading intelligence, because cops are the world's worst gossips."

I said, "Why would Bayless even know you exist?"

Clemmons shrugged. Max waved the phone book. Clemmons wrung his hankie—white flag for defeat.

"Bayless turned me out as an informant. I filed to run in the Sheriff's race, last spring. I figured my pals in John Birch, the Minutemen, and Pastor Smith's crusade would turn out, and I'd have a shot to unseat Pete Pitchess. Well . . . right about then . . . I met a woman. She was a real looker, and she called herself Gail Penrose. She just shows up at Norm's Nest one night, and one thing leads to another."

Red said, "We're linking the dots, Jack. Don't stop now."

Max said, "We know where you're taking us, but we need to hear it from you."

Clemmons sucked the flask. "It was a tank job. We were asleep at a motel in Van Nuys, and I woke up and checked her purse while she was sleeping. Her real handle was Gwen Perloff, and if it sounds familiar, that's because she was the kidnap victim on that job where you guys dropped that guy on the freeway and got him creamed. I'm married, and guess what? Some SHIT guys shot infrared film of me and the Gwen chick going at it. Then I get a phone call telling me to withdraw from the Sheriff's race, which I sure as shit did. Then Motel Mike makes it his business to find me and tell me he might request some information now and then."

Monroe/Kidnap/Perloff. Case lines intersect. Max and Red winked at me.

I said, "Is the dump job common cop knowledge now?"

Clemmons said, "Yep. And it's getting to be common knowledge that Miller Leavy wants to burn you for it."

Max said, "And you just happened to get the Marilyn Monroe dead-body call? You were on your way to a Klan bash, and the call just happened to hit the desk?"

Clemmons grinned. "Sometimes you just get lucky—and movie-star OD's are the cream de la cream."

Red lit a cigarette. "Do you honestly believe that the Kennedys ordered the snuff on Monroe?"

"No, I made it up. But I pulled that rumor on the Chief and Bob Kennedy off the cop grapevine. Morty Bendish liked it, so there we are."

I said, "How do you know Morty? Did somebody introduce you to him?"

Clemmons rubbed his ear. I phone-booked him good. The reverb lingered on.

"Sid Leffler introduced me. He's Morty's brother-in-law, and he's worked the West L.A. DB a dog's age. You guys know Sid, right? We call him 'The Author' and 'The Professor.' He wrote a sensational piece for the *L.A. Lowdown.* Morty says it's a masterpiece of the docudrama style. Sid and his partner, J. T. Meadows—who's a nice kid, but a bit of a nosebleed—worked this twisted 459 string, which ran to six jobs total. It went on for a while, then just stopped. Sid wrote it all out, and Morty loved the piece, but they didn't catch the guy in the end."

I blinked. I flashed Man Camera outtakes. I caught bulb glare. A crazy notion formed in that blink.

We moved Jack out and moved Morty in. Morty spooked easy. The phone book scared him.

"It looks bad for you, Morty. Don't shit a shitter, right? You're facing a battery of Federal charges. You sent subversive materials through the U.S. mail, and you aided and abetted Bev Shoftel in violation of six statutes on the dissemination of felony pornography. You've suborned prostitution, and you're looking at lewd and lascivious conduct raps up the ying-yang. You're just lucky I talked the postal cops into placing you in LAPD custody."

Morty went *Oy*. Morty fretted his mezuzah.

"That a sterling champion of free speech should come to such an end."

We yakked in Sweatbox #3. An audience grooved Morty. The hallway was full-packed. Bill Parker, Daryl Gates, and the Hats. They watched and caught the speaker feed.

I slid Morty my flask. Morty glug-glugged. I said, "The Chief and I don't want to see you take it in the shorts. We venerate free speech as much as you do. I'm cooking up something that could get you a skate. I'm finalizing it in my head right now."

Morty said, "Anything, Freddy. I've got no beef with the LAPD. I soft-pedaled all that Muslim shit, and I pooh-poohed those cops who drilled that retarded kid."

I lit a cigarette. "Fill me in on Sid Leffler and that 'Sicko Psycho' piece he wrote for the *Lowdown*. The case interests me, and I'm thinking I could work it into this deal I'm cooking up."

Morty said, "Sid's a genius. He's the smartest guy I know. He exudes talent. He's got a flick in preproduction at Fox, and he wrote every word of it. He's educated, and he knows the criminal mind—which is why this 'Sicko Psycho' piece is so pithy. He studied under that shrink—what's his name—the guy who analyzed all those sex dinks up at Quentin."

I said, "Oh, you mean Paul de River?"

36

Predawn Wilshire. Green lights straight through Beverly Hills. Pat told me the AG was shacked at the Lawford house. I planned to intrude.

I'd been up two full days. I succumbed to fried-brain syndrome and popped two Dexedrine. We cut Jack Clemmons and Morty Bendish loose. I huddled up Parker and Gates. A late skull session ensued.

They'd read my case updates. Mimeo copies went to the Hats and Ratfuck Bobby. I updated the Bev's Switchboard misadventure and took the blame for blowing the raid. I laid out "author" Sid Leffler and his "Sicko Psycho" piece in Morty B.'s dirt rag. I laid out my specific plans for Morty and my plan to craft a big diversion. It would quash all potential Monroe/Kennedy rumors and secure the Chief the FBI-boss gig. Said plan would force the AG to desist on the get-Otash front. It would squelch Miller Leavy's plans to burn the Hats and me for Richie Danforth.

Parker clapped. Gates went *Woo-woo*. Parker said he'd lean on the BHPD. We need the names of their cater waiter suspects. Gates praised Morty Bendish. He's a born propagandist.

Parker stressed Gwen Perloff. Work her. Deploy your reputation. She's jungled up in bad-money schemes. Make like you want in. Gates stressed Sid Leffler and partner J. T. Meadows. Work them. Be a shit magnet. They may play out unclean.

I cut down the California Incline and cut north on PCH. I U-turned and parked outside the Lawford spread. It was predawn dark. I leaned on the doorbell. *Brrrr* noise drilled the house. I stood by the door-front peephole. I heard foot scuffs inside.

Eddie Chacõn opened the door. He wore a "Free Cuba" T-shirt and plaid boxer shorts. He held a .45 automatic.

He said, "*Señor* Freddy. And at such an hour."

I said, "Mr. Kennedy, now."

Eddie loomed. I eased his gun hand off to the side. He about-faced and quick-marched upstairs. I timed the wait.

The AG coughed to announce himself. He rolled out in six-plus minutes. Bobby, you shouldn't have.

America's Top Cop dressed for me. Polo shirt/madras shorts/deck shoes. Very Hyannis. It upstaged my wilted suit. He walked up. He rolled an unlit cigar.

"The kitchen. You know where it is. Eddie pulled a bug mount off a lamp bowl."

I followed him in. He grabbed a coffeepot off a warmer and poured two cups. I perched in the breakfast nook. Cups, saucers, cream spout— the AG served me.

"Justify your intrusion. Make it good. Don't tell me you came to beat up my sister's husband again."

I smirked. "Have you read my most recent summary reports?"

"Yes. They were persuasive, but there's no hard evidence to prove that Marilyn's death and the kidnapping case are anything but coinci- dental occurrences within a movie-business sphere. You portray Mari- lyn in a well-documented and defamatory light, which shows her to be drug-addicted and psychically impaired. That's nothing but good. You posit her as a consort of criminals who traffic in pornography, which I especially like. That said, you have not given me a salutary throughline, one which will serve to dash all specious public discourse on Mari- lyn's alleged involvement with my brother and me. Also, the issue of public exposure concerns me, especially as it pertains to the people whose names you stated in your summary. Public exposure means pub- lic inquiry. Public inquiry means scandal. Two things trouble me here. One, assuming the public silence of the people you name in your sum- mary. Two, supplying the public with a factually valid alternative solu- tion for the death of Marilyn Monroe, one that will invalidate Marilyn's fantastical rantings about my brother and me, and one that will seduce and entertain Joe and Jane American and scrub their dirty minds free of filthy thoughts regarding the brothers Kennedy."

I sipped coffee. Depth charge. It spiked the juiced blood in my veins.

"I've got the alternative solution. I'm working on it now. It's factually valid, and I'm working up a newspaper source to put it out there."

Bobby rolled his cigar. "You must control the public exposure of your named suspects and expurgate their attributed statements."

I said, "Convene a sub-rosa Federal grand jury. Handpick Democratic Party–stooge jurors. Subpoena the key people mentioned in my summary, promise them immunity, let them read prepared statements, and hold those statements in abeyance as a wedge to keep them from going forward. The grand jury proceeding will serve as an extortion move to ensure their permanent silence."

Bobby lit his cigar. "What do you want for yourself?"

"Your promise not to prosecute me, or my men, for the Hoffa operation. Your pledge to steer Miller Leavy off of attempting to nail the Hats and me for the Danforth job."

Bobby said, "As of this moment—no."

I sipped coffee. I jiggled the cup and burned my hands.

"I need a Justice man to help me black-bag a doctor's office."

Ratfuck Bobby. Smug little shit. He blew perfect smoke rings.

"Eddie's good at that sort of thing."

I heard footsteps behind me. A man cleared his throat. I knew it was dipshit. I smelled Pat's Breck shampoo.

I turned around. They wore White House souvenir robes. Robert F. Kennedy brayed.

"Pat, your boyfriend's here. Peter, don't grovel or explode. The noted camel fucker is joining us for breakfast."

37

Babs Payton and Lila Leeds car-hopped. They hopped Stan's Drive-In at Sunset and Highland. It was a front. They peddled goofballs to Hollywood High kids. They supplied local night crawlers and raked in their real bread. Chef Fritzie whipped up biphetamine-laced malts. I craved one. I was work-slammed and running on fumes.

Breakfast with RFK and the gang. It was too tense to be funny and veered to depraved. The beach to the PAB. Phone work with the Hats. We photographed the address-book pages glommed off our Bev's detainees. Miller Leavy got us quickie phone-bill subpoenas for all five. Plus Gwen Perloff, Paul Mitchell Grenier, and Ingrid Irmgard.

We scanned bills. We looked for Fox-specific names in the calls-to columns and general names to run through R&I. We hit Grenier, Perloff, and Irmgard first. Fly-by-night Grenier had no fixed address and got no phone bills. Perloff made innocuous calls to Fox B-flick personnel. No calls-to names mandated attention. Irmgard called her Mexicali work boss and her boyfriend Juan Manuel Salas. Her calls seemed innocuous. El Manny might be innocuous. I should roust him on GP and find out.

We worked. We eyeball-hopped. We went from case-file scans to detainee scans. We scorched our eyeballs. The detainees called lots of people. No hot names scorched us. Our consensus so far:

The detainees are new-breed swingers. They swing within set guidelines and steer clear of the fuzz. *That* meant *this:*

More shitwork loomed.

I pulled into Stan's. I'd called ahead. Babs and Lila saw my sled and skated over. Babs schlepped a car-door tray. On it: three pineapple malts.

She hooked it to the driver's door. I pushed the seat back. Babs and

Lila piled in. They dumped their skates. We snuggled in, three across. I passed out Chef Fritzie's specials. Babs said, *"L'chaim."*

Prom date or pervathon? It's your call.

We lit cigarettes. We sipped our malts. I caught that good dope aftertaste.

Lila said, "This is a bait gig, right? You're not here because you love us and you can't live without us."

I caught a bloodstream jolt. My scalp prickled. I got *re*-vivified.

"We're attending a wife-swap party, next Sunday night. Babs, you're my date. Lila, your date is a cop named Harry Crowder. You get five hundred apiece. We're there to look for hinky shit, which might well pertain to hinky shit at Fox. I'll probably be recognized from my so-called heyday, which is okay. The job's complex. I'm looking to bait some bent motherfuckers and see how they react."

Babs sipped her malt. "Okay, but Harry Crowder's a cop, so what's the point of it all?"

"It's about squelching some Marilyn Monroe rumors, plus a tangent angle on that kidnap deal from three weeks ago."

Babs hooted. "'Kidnap deal'? You and the Hat Squad guys dusted a man, and a motor cop I know told me it put your dicks in the wringer."

I mock-groaned. Lila said, "The kidnap's got 'publicity stunt' written all over it. And I know Gwen Perloff, going back eons. She and the late Marilyn worked call jobs together, back in the late '40s, when I was teamed up with Jeanne Carmen."

Confluence/convergence. More back-page lives connect.

Babs sipped her malt. "Listen to the voice of experience here. I know from wife-swap and key parties, and they are strictly moneymaking propositions. There's always a strict ratio of men to women, and lots of fees and extras you've got to pay if you're looking to swing. And there's no built-in random factor to spice things up. Pictures have been pre-screened, to make sure no uglies and fatsos get in, and the whole drop-your-keys-in-a-bowl-and-go-home-with-somebody aspect is nothing but a shuck. People just pair off—and nobody gets stuck without a date. Motel rooms and hotel suites—all that's arranged in advance, and that's another extra you've got to pay for."

It made sense. "Moneymaking propositions." It jibed with Foxtone Services and Fox in duress.

I said, "Fuck decks. Roddy McDowall enlightened me, a few days ago. Raise your hands if you're familiar with the phenomenon."

Babs raised her hand. Lila said, "Ancient history, but I remember the craze."

I went *So?* Lila said, "I would have, but I never got the chance." Babs said, "We should have been so lucky."

I laughed. "The possibility that Marilyn posed for a fuck deck with Deedee Grenier's brother, Paul Mitchell."

Babs shuddered. "I'd call it remote."

Lila said, "No, but Marilyn mentioned something along those lines. We were at a pill party a few months ago, and she said she wanted to do a smut film based on the 'Wrong-Door Raid'—which, of course, *you* were involved in, Freddy."

That's a scalp crawler. I said, "Don't stop there."

"Who's stopping? She said she wanted her ex, Timmy Berlin, to play himself, while she played herself. Smut pros would play Sinatra, DiMaggio, Phil Irwin, and you. She wanted an old lady with smut experience to play the old lady whose door got kicked in, and she wanted to shoot the film on the real-life locations."

Babs lit a cigarette. "Fuck decks, key parties. You're taking me back."

I said, "Don't stop there."

Babs said, "The deck craze started with these aspiring actresses working the call-girl circuit after the war. These investor types would come around and try to suss out which girls had a shot to become real movie stars. They paid the aspirant stars to perform in the decks, with these stud-type costars. Then they supposedly held back distribution of the decks, so the aspirant types had a chance to become real stars."

Calculated. Perverted. In equal measure. Hot kicks in the moment. Profits down the line.

Babs crushed her cigarette. "Then the decks would be auctioned off in some sort of rich perv circle, for big bread. Nobody I know has ever seen a fuck deck, but these rumors persist. I heard things like Barbara Bates, Joan Camden, and Ella Raines in a lezzie deck. The only thing that's for sure is that the biggest deck investor was this bent headshrinker named Shelley Mandel. I think he might have invented the decks, and I know for a fact that he tapped beauty pageants, where all the girls were aspirant stars, and he told them that for one hour in a motel room, the money they made would put them through the Pasadena Playhouse."

More shitwork.

More cross-checks. More paper glut. More phone bills and R&I sheets to study and more names to anoint. We worked in the Intel squad-room. We worked at five jammed-tight desks. Intel cops worked around us. They fish-eyed us and judged us. *Oh, those clowns. They pushed a guy off a cliff. It's on the cop-talk Teletype.*

We worked. Daryl Gates told his secretary to comb Ad Vice and divisional Vice files. She indexed a list of organized-vice offenders. We worked off photographed address-book pages, the detainees' phone bills, rap sheets, and the index. We hopped page stack to page stack and scanned columns. We stalked names, names, and names. We crossed out names and X-marked them. The Hats worked diligent. I worked, unraveled and schizzed.

Babs Payton's riff. Shelley Mandel in all guises. Penicillin peddler/call-girl hound/scrutinized by BNDD. He conceives the "fuck deck." He might have sideswiped Lois. Doc Shelley habituates beauty pageants and slides the girls rubbers and pills. He snuggles up to pageant girls and proclaims the fuck deck gospel. It fucked with my wig and threatened to quash my love for Lois. She meets him, she talks to him, she face-to-faces him and provokes his lust.

She was Miss Chicago, '48. She pageant-toured L.A. Doc Shelley was out to corrupt young women. He would have buzz-bombed Lois. He would have touched her. He would have contaminated her and poisoned her freewheeling heart. Aspirant actresses are susceptible to charm and easily bamboozled. I saw Lois and cheap studs in fuck-deck poses. I was still full-up wired. I couldn't punch STOP and squelch the brain reel. I saw Lois in poses we had never and would never assume. I saw it and saw it. I tried to pray it away and faltered. I wanted to see it because I'd never see it for real. It was all Man Camera/bulb glare/shutter click verisimo. The obscene brain reel spun on and on.

It poisoned my imagination. It devoured brain cells. I prayer-hexed it to a stasis and willed my mind pure and white-screened.

I blew off the desk work an hour back. The Hats went *Huh?* I holed up in my cubicle and called Eddie Chacón. I told him to expedite a check on Dr. Sheldon Mandel. I ran down the particulars. Eddie said he knew agents at BNDD. "Give me a half hour. I'll call you back."

I waited at my desk. The juice jolt wore down. I maintained my blank brain screen. The effort drained me and left me limp. Eddie called me back. He said he had information. He told me *this:*

Doc Shelley was a longtime BNDD informant. He ratted overpre-scribing headshrinks. He didn't sell black-market penicillin. He donated it to Zionist groups during the '48 war. So did other Jewish physicians. So did Mickey Cohen, Neddie Herbert, the Aadland brothers. Jewish mobsters ponied up big. The BNDD investigated Shelley. They desisted in '49. They succumbed to political pressure. The Truman gang backed emergent Israel. The word filtered down to BNDD. Leave this guy alone. He's borderline harmless. He's giving the medicine away. BNDD worked out of Treasury. An agent turned Shelley as his snitch. Shelley knew low-rent Hollywood and the shrink netherworld. He snitched overprescribing shrinks, wholesale. He *still* does. He's tight pals with the agent. They play golf once a month. Shelley lives in seclusion some-where. He's very weird. Treasury loves him. Are you satisfied, *Señor* Freddy? If so, leave this *pendejo* alone.

Okay, *mi amigo*—for now.

I went back to work. Max Herman said, "Hey, the lieutenant returns."

Red Stromwall said, "He outranks us now. I still can't believe it."

Harry Crowder said, "Freddy got me a date for the wife-swap party. Lila Leeds. She had some kind of movie career, and she's still a dish."

Eddie Benson said, "The jury's out on Freddy. If he gets Miller Leavy off our ass, I'll grant him real-cop status."

The chitchat vaporized. The Hats resumed work. I scanned phone bills and cross-checked them. Time vaporized. I crafted a work void. It kept my mind off Lois and what she did/might have done/would never do.

I stifled yawns. I imposed a no-dope vow. Phone bills, R&I sheets, the Vice index. I scanned columns and got bupkes. Red said, "I've got a match. One of our female detainees called a hairdresser at Fox."

I stifled more yawns. You've got five full-time cops. A full day's work nets one match. This deal's a probable wash.

Time *re*-vaporized. A uniformed policewoman walked through the squadroom. I registered her as Lois and blinked. Phone-bill columns and green-sheet type blurred. I shut my eyes and went out.

Max said, "I've got a match. A male detainee called a woman in the index. She was running a housewife prostitution ring in Burbank."

I opened my eyes. Harry said, "The lieutenant awakes."

A secretary walked up. I stood up. My legs held. She passed me a thick folder.

"For you, sir. It's that BHPD burglary file the Chief requested."

I cleared space and dumped the contents on my desk. Five flapped envelopes/five 459's/an early '62 time string/five north-of-Sunset cribs, de-luxe. The envelopes were date- and address-marked. The contents were listed below:

Crime-scene reports/victims' statements/stolen-item inventories/canvass reports.

I spread the folder wide and looked for loose sheets. An envelope dropped out.

It was clasp-sealed. It was hand-marked: "Cater waiters questioned & released."

The Hats oohed and aahed. I hefted the envelope. It felt like a photo stack. I dumped it out on my desk.

It was photographs. They were six-by-eight mug shots, all black and white. The subjects ran to a type. They oozed actors with no pot to piss in. They ran from twenty-three to thirty-five. They oozed insolvency and rage and *I'll be a movie star by next Tuesday*. There were fourteen pix in all. The Hats moved up to my desk and scanned them, left to right. I trawled at their speed. Max tapped Photo #14. All five of us gasped.

We knew this guy. He's not listed as "Rick Dawes" or "Richard Danforth." He's listed as "Ronald Dewhurst." We knew this guy. We killed this guy. This guy put us in a whole world of shit.

Max said, "Gwen Perloff was calling around, looking for him, months before the kidnap job."

Red said, "Yeah—she called Peter Lawford."

Eddie said, "That cinches up the kidnap as a humbug deal."

I crossed myself. I saw Dewhurst/Dawes/Danforth sail off that cliff.

We bypassed the white wine and cold lobster salad. Lois saw me stretched and weak on my feet. We blew off the swing and the nightclub music across Wilshire. We went into the bedroom and doused the lights.

We undressed in the dark. Lois pulled the curtains wide. The radio reported rain about 10:00 p.m. I crashed on the bed. I jammed my face in the sheets. Lois stretched out on my back. She threw her full weight down on me. She pushed down on me and opened me up and made me breathe past spurts.

Her knees raked my back. It felt good. I sucked air in and got words out. I got out Shelley Mandel/pageant girls/dirty pictures. *Shutter click/resultant bulb glare*. I saw the pictures/Lois and cheap studs/fifty-two-card decks. Lois pulled me up and laid me out sideways. She got our eyes close and slapped me. She said, "I wouldn't do that."

She slapped me. She said, "No one could make me do that." She slapped me. She said, "I wouldn't do something so ugly." She slapped me. She said, "I would never do something so shameful and hurt the people I love."

She bloodied my face and blotted it dry with a pillow. She tucked a bunched-up sheet under my head and made me breathe deep. The room swirled. I smelled my blood and her Chanel No. 5. She slapped me, hard. She said, "I knew I'd love someone like you one day. That's why I didn't do it. I had every chance to do it, but I sent up prayers and walked away."

38

Shit Magnet.

It's your definitive pose. Reprise it now. You've got an all-cop audience. Bill Parker sanctions you. Fetch, Freddy, fetch.

Lois banged me up last night. Her welts looked like razor burns. She slapped. Pat used her fists. She left that wedding-stone cut. My two women marked me. It enhanced my shit-magnet panache.

West L.A. station. Santa Monica and Purdue. I parked across the street and got my wig tight. The BHPD folder induced aftershocks. It cinched the case for Danforth/Dawes/Dewhurst as one man. Monroe knew him, Perloff knew him, he was a probable 459 man. I ran beaucoup record checks. R&I/FBI/NCIC/fifty-state queries. All their Ronald Dewhursts were old, fat, colored, imprisoned, or dead.

Daryl Gates told the Hats to work the Dewhurst/459 angle. That meant file study and phone calls. Nat Denkins and Phil Irwin were frog-tailing Deedee Grenier. Big brother Paul Mitchell traveled underground. A rolling Deedee stakeout might flush him. I called the California Adult Authority an hour ago. I talked to Juan Manuel Salas's ex–parole officer. He shot me a glowing report. El Manny went straight. *Es la verdad.* He took a TV-repair course during his Chino bounce and did follow-up work at Cal State L.A. His '57 house-break bust? Humbug from the gate. The DA refused to file. El Manny was a canvasback welterweight—but, man, can he fix TV sets!!!

I orbed the upstairs squadroom window. Sid Leffler and J. T. Meadows walked through my frame. I read their personnel files yesterday. Bill Parker and Daryl Gates had them memorized. I'm here to bootjack their "Sicko Psycho" investigation. I'm here to revise the facts to fit Monroe/

Kidnap and squelch Monroe/Kennedy rumors. "Shit magnet, Freddy. You live to offend." Daryl Gates does not speak with forked tongue.

I grabbed my briefcase and locked the car. It was hot. The station doors were propped wide. I walked in, bold and bad. Desk cops moped and glugged soft drinks. They made me. *Oh, shit—it's Freddy O.*

They saw me, they sniffed me. *Is he still around? Yeah, that's Freddy. His camel's double-parked outside.*

I walked upstairs. The squad bay featured partner desks and a CO's cubicle. I tagged fourteen men. That's seven roll-out teams. I sniffed thick cigarette smoke and heard typewriter clack.

Eyeballs clicked my way. *Hey, isn't that? Yeah, it is. What's with the briefcase? I heard he's credentialed up. That kidnap deal, remember? He stepped on his dick there.*

Leffler and Meadows sat upside the far wall. I beelined and dragged a stray chair. It thunked on the floorboards and sent up a racket. Dirty looks drilled me.

I propped the chair up against a wall post. I faced Leffler, head-on. He wore aviator glasses. He wore a cheap pinstripe suit and fruit boots with elastic side gores. Meadows vibed afterthought. He was tall and too handsome. He wore a hopsack blazer and gray slacks. He worked the vice traps in Will Rogers Park and entrapped crotch honkers wholesale. His personnel file glowed.

I flashed my credentials. Leffler and Meadows took long looks. Meadows went *What's this?* Leffler rolled his eyes. He knew from harrassment. I slow-orbed the room. No typewriters clacked. It's all eyes on me. My shitbird rep precedes.

I turned back to Leffler. I went stentorian. I pitched the whole room, loud and clear.

"Intelligence Division is assuming command of your 'Sicko Psycho' investigation. That's direct from Chief Parker. The CO is Lieutenant Daryl Gates. I'm the lead field man. The DA's Office liaison is Miller Leavy. The Hat Squad will be working with me. You and Officer Meadows have just been rendered redundant, but I'll shoot you some clue-clown work, so you can save face with all your colleagues who now know that I've got your balls in my pocket. I won't need to interview Officer Meadows. He's clean in my book. But, Leffler—you're borderline sketchy. You've got dubious ties to Morty Bendish, illegal smear-sheet journalists, and nut cops like Jack Clemmons. That piece you wrote for the *L.A. Lowdown* violates fourteen Federal postal codes per the illegal passage of unregistered mail, and the Postal Inspection Service is building a case against you and Bendish. We also have the matter of your Officer Sid gigs at high schools within this division. I'm wondering if it's nothing but a smoke screen for you to exercise your penchant for underage cooze. I personally observed you plying a group of Pali girls with booze at the Sip 'n' Surf."

Leffler trembled. He popped sweat. His glasses slid down his nose. He pushed them back up. Meadows stood up. I grabbed his waistband and pulled him back down. I scanned the room, I *owned* the room, all eyes on *me*.

I said, "Stand up."

Leffler stood up. He went weavy and futzed with his glasses.

I said, "Walk to the front hallway, turn right, step into the second interrogation box on the left side."

Leffler complied. He grabbed chair backs to steady himself. He walked pigeon-toed. He kept his head down and plumb-lined off the floor. He cut right and almost toppled. I stepped ahead of him and got the door.

He stepped inside. The box was prerigged. Bolted-down table/two bolted-down chairs. Two-way mirror wall. Phone book on the table. Full-sound hookup. Outside-hallway feed.

I spread Leffler up against the wall. I frisked him. I pulled off his holstered .38 and placed it on the table. I plucked his wallet and went through it. I pulled him upright and shoved him into a chair.

I sat down across from him. He said, "You've ruined me."

I lit a cigarette. "You're dirty. The Chief thinks so, Lieutenant Gates thinks so, I think so."

Leffler waved off my smoke. "Here's what I'm thinking. I'm thinking this is some kind of buyback deal you've got going. I was part of that PD-Justice raid on your listening posts. You were working bug jobs on Marilyn Monroe's house and the Lawford place. A Justice cop told me the raids were strictly cosmetic. The Palisades and Brentwood. Get it? The Monroe house is right there. The 'Sicko Psycho' pulled his jobs not that far west of there. Parker's afraid the kidnap deal and the number you and the Hats pulled with that Danforth guy will blow wide, and he's looking to buy some good press for the Department, because the Department sure needs some good PR."

I clap-clapped. I slid my flask across the table. Leffler took two pops.

"My Hoffa op. How far is it blown?"

"It's strictly cop gossip. It's not out in the world with the squares."

"Who spilled on the Hoffa op? That Justice cop and who else?"

Leffler said, "Jack Clemmons."

I made the jerk-off sign. "Who's in with you and Morty B. in your little pamphlet venture?"

Leffler went *harumph*. "Clemmons is batshit crazy. I'm a serious writer and student of human psychology, who also happens to be a veteran police officer. I'm Morty's highbrow guy, and Clemmons pitches to Morty's lowbrow readership."

I blew smoke rings. "You don't fraternize with Clemmons or an ex–motor cop named Norm Krause, who owns a dive bar named Norm's Nest?"

Leffler went *harumph*. "No. Certainly not."

I said, "Okay, you did strikebreaker work at Fox, back in the early '30s. Fox interests me, so I'll toss you a compliment before we go any further. You weren't far off when you called Monroe and the kidnap job a buyback deal. That said, let me throw some Fox-associated names at you."

Leffler smirked and sucked flask juice. He's getting cocky. He mandates a smackdown.

I said, "Gwen Perloff. Have you ever met her?"

"No—but I know she was the victim in that kidnap job you and the Hats botched so bad."

"Paul Mitchell Grenier?"

"No. I've never heard of him."

"Del Kinney, Jr.?"

"Everybody in L.A. law enforcement knows Del. I don't know him from Fox, but I knew him from the Sheriff's and the ABC."

I said, "Albie Aadland?"

Leffler said, "Well, he's an Aadland. I'm a Jewish kid from L.A., and all us landsmen know the Aadlands, and we've all got the good common sense to be afraid of them, and I'm not ashamed to admit that I benefited from their largesse, back when I was a kid, starting out."

I tapped the table. "Explain that."

Leffler shrugged. "What's to explain? Hersh, Ira, Meyer—they lent money to Jewish families in trouble, and they'd hire kids to run errands and cause a little *tsuris*. I threw a few stink bombs and broke a few windows for them, and then I graduated to more suitable adult work."

I said, "Such as?"

Leffler flushed. I hit a nerve. The Aadlands rattled his cage.

"Well, it's the '30s into the '40s, up to and after the war. It's not that I'm proud of it, but the brothers ran a string of fuck pads. You know the concept. Hot-sheet joints, sin pits. You've got sex shows, smut films, illegal pharmaceuticals, interracial fraternization, jam sessions, all that avant-garde stuff. It was all right, I guess. At least by prevailing standards then. The Depression, the war—people needed to unwind. You had quiet little places in quiet little neighborhoods, and a high-class clientele. I worked those places as a doorman and something of a security guard. You read my personnel file, right? I spilled all that at my background interview. It was the Depression and the war. The background cops made allowances."

Yes and no. Leffler hired on in '42. He was a temporary war hire. War-hire standards ran low. He went on the regulars in '47. His war-hire record was good. He wasn't re-background-checked.

I said, "Let's get back to Albie Aadland."

Leffler said, "Why? He was much younger than Hersh, Meyer, and Ira. He was underfoot when I broke up some picket lines at Fox, which are probably the only times that I ever saw him."

I cogitated. Leffler sucked flask juice. He gassed on the Q and A. He rolled with the flow.

"Fox, today. A general sense of panic. *Cleopatra*'s headed for the shitter. Criminal conspiracies are popping up. Dope, bearer bonds, vice shit. You're an old Fox hand. What have you heard?"

Leffler drummed the table. "*Cleopatra*'s common knowledge. As for the rest of it, I've heard bupkes."

I drummed the table. I dead-eyed him. He was bent. He craved young stuff. He knew I had his shit dialed.

"Okay, I'm starting to get it now. Monroe was shooting her last picture at Fox. The kidnap girl was working at Fox, so somehow it's the focus of your buyback deal."

I twirled my ashtray. Three full circuits. Leffler's nerves stretched.

"You're a ham. You're a movie buff. You did crowd-extra work, you met people and made connections. You've got the writing bug, you wrote detective magazine pieces under a pseudonym, you've got a master's degree, you took some of Paul de River's classes, you went on LAPD as a war hire in '42, and a regular in '47. Is that about right?"

Leffler sneered. "Hey, the man knows how to read a personnel file."

I said, "Don't take that tone with me. I'll kick the shit out of you the next time."

Leffler put his hands up. Okay, okay, okay.

"Did you have a close personal relationship with Doc de River?"

"No, the old dink gave me no personal attention."

I mock-sighed. "You're a talented cat, Sid. I've got a source on *Twist Party Stakeout,* and I heard you wrote the script. I'm wondering if you exploited your 'Officer Sid' assignment and recruited the underage girls who will appear underclad in the dance scenes."

Leffler said, "Yes, I did recruit them. And they're not underclad by any and all enlightened standards."

I cracked my knuckles. The phone book vibrated. I packed brass knucks and a beavertail sap.

"Do not *ever* feed underaged girls liquor. I'm out to nail you for contributing and put you in the fruit tank at Mira Loma."

The Sidster laughed. "Who's your source on my picture? Tell me, so I'll know who to avoid."

I said, "Lois Nettleton."

Leffler laughed. "That Method actress drip? I hope you're not poking her, bec—"

I went with the phone book. I threw a sidearm shot to the head. It ripped the leg bolts out of the floor. The chair toppled. Leffler hit the wall face-first.

PART 6

SEX CREEP

(AUGUST 31–SEPTEMBER 8, 1962)

39

The PD kept a suite at the Ambassador. Two bedrooms/living room/ office/kitchenette. It housed out-of-town jurists and high rollers. Ranking cops entertained illicit girlfriends. Boozefest conclaves ran twenty-four hours.

Parker, Gates, and I hogged the office. A room-service waiter laid out a plush spread. We noshed eggs and smoked lox and gulped coffee. The Hats hogged the living room. They babysat Morty Bendish.

The office was air-cooled. A sliding door supplied privacy. We sat in matching wing chairs. Parker laid on the lawyerese.

Monroe, the kidnap job, and the "Sicko Psycho" string comprise a triumvirate. Fox is a "presumptive point of convergence." He fears the "degree of evidence obtained by illegal surveillance" and "the degree to which all three jobs are wholly assumption and speculation."

Gates said, "The 'Sicko Psycho' file runs to six big boxes. I lugged it over to Intel late last night. Leffler and Meadows kept assiduous reports, and they dotted all their *i*'s and crossed their *t*'s. Leffler's dirty, okay, I believe that—Freddy made the point in that report he filed yesterday. Sid's a worker, though—and Meadows is a comer. He's got a law degree, he's California Bar–licensed, and he's got a future with us. The important thing is that the file is jam-packed with dirt that Morty can use in his series."

Parker said, "The *Mirror*'s a dirt rag. We'll get Morty to ladle it on. Especially as it pertains to Monroe. Morty will drag her through the mud like there's no tomorrow."

I said, "I talked to Bob Kennedy. He's up-to-date on the 'Sicko Psycho,' and he's conversant on the overall plan. Here's a good lead that may cinch Monroe to the first six break-ins. Leffler and Meadows submitted *all* the letters the Psycho left at the first six crime scenes, and I submitted a paper scrap of the letter I found at the Monroe house. Ray called the paper and letter stock in all *seven* samples 'visibly archaic.' If we push him, we might get a confirmed evidential match on the paper, the glue, and the cut-up magazines that shitbird used. On top of that, I froze a semen scraping from the smut pix I found that night. I submitted that to Ray, and Leffler and Meadows submitted all their jizz samples."

Parker spiked his coffee. Old Overholt. It's the Breakfast of Champions.

"We've got to lay off of Fox. That approach is wildly untenable. It's based solely on our unprovable assumptions that the place is a fount of criminal endeavor—when all we've got is key-party and mail-drop bullshit, most of which derives from Federal postal infractions."

Gates sipped coffee. "Freddy's grand jury plan is a winner. It permits us to present sealed testimony with the assurance that the testimony will not result in indictments, and that the guilty parties who testify will receive immunity—but will remain municipally indictable should they break silence on our cases, most notably the kidnap job. It may also serve to scotch any plans Miller Leavy might make to burn Freddy and the Hats for the Danforth job."

Parker lit a cigarette. "Danforth, Dawes, Dewhurst. Who is this guy? He's 100% clean, nationwide. Let's go through those BHPD burglary files. There has to be dirt we can pull."

I said, "Morty's series will provide your basic numbskull reader with a Monroe-job solution that will engulf any and all Monroe/Kennedy rumors that might surface. *And* it will serve to convince Bobby K. not to go for indictments on me and my boys. *But* we need to conclusively ID the kidnappers, pop them, and convince them to testify, for an assured waltz on all kidnap and related charges. So far, I'm fairly certain that Gwen Perloff and possibly Paul Mitchell Grenier were in on it—but it's all instinct and no proof."

Gates laughed. "Perloff, Grenier, one unknown male Caucasian, one probable male Latin. Maybe they'll resist arrest—and Freddy and the Hats will have to toast them."

Parker swirled his drink. "Have the boys bring Morty in. I'm due downtown."

Gates got up and slid the door wide. The Hats ushered Morty B. in. I pulled a chair out. Red Stromwall sat him down.

Parker said, "The 'Sicko Psycho' will henceforth be known as the 'Sex Creep.' You will author a sensational, multipart, ongoing series on the

Sex Creep in the *Mirror-News*. We will apportion information to you, and you will deploy it to our exact specifications. Lieutenant Otash and the Hat Squad are taking over the investigation into the Sex Creep's first six West L.A. burglaries. Your brother-in-law, Officer Leffler, and his partner, Officer Meadows, are out as of now. Again, we will tell you what to write. In consideration of your efforts, all of the Federal and municipal mail-fraud charges filed against you will be dropped."

Morty stood up. He did a little heel-click/*Jawohl, mein Führer* number. It garnered big laughs.

"I'll do it. But where's this series of mine going? What's the *furkakte* punch line?"

I said, "Don't be dim, Morty. The Sex Creep murdered Marilyn Monroe."

Skull session. The Hats and me. We've planned a detailed read-through.

We've got occurrence summaries, lab sheets, record checks, and field interrogation cards. We've got field-interview reports. Leffler and Meadows *worked* the string. They weren't Burglary-desk cops. They were night-watch felony-car detectives. The complainants called West L.A. station. Patrol cops responded. Leffler and Meadows were dispatched, pro forma. They viewed the crime scenes, hot and fresh. They took extensive notes. They maintained a crime-scene photo file.

I redid my cubicle. I took down my "Monroe" and "Kidnap" corkboards and taped a plastic-sheath wall map in their place. The map spanned the northern section of West Los Angeles. It covered Brentwood, Mandeville Canyon, the Santa Monica Mountains, and Pacific Palisades. I grease pencil–marked it: "Sex Creep 459 locations."

The Hats showed. I shoved my desk into a corner and bought us sitdown room. They brought straight-backed chairs. I passed out grease pencils and mimeographed copies of the six occurrence reports.

We formed a chair circle. Max and Red passed out coffee and ashtrays. We jumped on the work.

459 #1: 11/18/61. (DR #63882, 1 of 6). 13821 Corsica Drive, Pacific Palisades. Complainant: Marcia Maria Davenport/WFA/DOB 6/12/19. Twice divorced, lives alone. Lives off trust fund. Complainant's call to station: 9:49 p.m. Suspect pushed up half-cracked window and entered house. No items stolen. Suspect dumped lingerie drawers, kicked over furniture, scattered barbiturate sleeping pills taken from medicine cabi-

net on bathroom rug. Suspect masturbated and ejaculated on lingerie-drawer items. (Semen sample to lab). Suspect left note composed in cutout/pasted-on magazine letters in lingerie drawer. Both magazine letters and paper backing appear to be significantly dated. The note reads "I saw you hiking at Will Rogers Park. Do you remember the moment you pulled your blouse out to scratch your back? I do."

I checked the map. I X-marked the address. Local geography. Corsica Drive adjoins Riviera Country Club. Will Rogers Park is one mile northwest.

459 #2: 12/4/61. (DR #63882, 2 of 6). 12242 Marlboro Street, Pacific Palisades. Complainant: Leona Jenks Hagedohm/WFA/DOB 4/16/28. Once divorced, lives alone. Math teacher at Paul Revere Junior High School. Complainant's call to station: 11:18 p.m. Suspect reached through pet-access flap and unhooked kitchen door. No items stolen. Suspect dumped lingerie drawers, dumped furniture in fireplace, slashed guest-bedroom mattress, masturbated and ejaculated on photographs of complainant in complainant's 1946 Santa Monica High School yearbook. (Semen sample to lab). Suspect left note composed in cutout/pasted-on magazine letters in lingerie drawer. Both magazine letters and paper backing appear to be significantly dated. The note reads "I like your way with the kids at Paul Revere. Are you too frigid to have kids of your own?"

I checked the map. I X-marked the address. The Sex Creep's creeping west. He's still south of Sunset. Marlboro Street is two blocks south of Paul Revere. The Sex Creep peeped Victim #2 as she walked to work.

459 #3: 12/16/61. (DR #63882, 3 of 6). 1545 Monaco Drive, Pacific Palisades. Complainant: Wanda Jean D'Allesio/WFA/DOB 1/9/30. Twice divorced, lives alone. Alimony recipient. Complainant's call to station: 10:04 p.m. Suspect vaulted in pushed-up window and entered house. No items stolen. Suspect dumped lingerie drawers, kicked over furniture, dumped and burned family photo albums in the living room fireplace, dumped barbiturate pills in the master-bathroom toilet, masturbated and ejaculated on a snapshot of complainant and first husband in swim attire. (Semen sample to lab). Suspect left note composed in cutout/pasted-on magazine letters in lingerie drawer. Magazine letters and paper backing appear to be significantly dated. The note reads "Two husbands is nothing. Carole Landis had four, and she died younger than you, even if I kill you tomorrow."

I checked the map. I X-marked the address. The Sex Creep's creeping back northwest. He's escalating. He's getting more agitated and more violent. The Carole Landis reference clinched it. The Sex Creep creeped the Monroe pad. Monaco Drive is one-half mile from the Landis pad on Capri Drive.

459 #4: 1/19/62. (DR #63882, 4 of 6). 10116 Mandeville Lane, Brentwood. Complainant: Arden Jane Brownleigh/WFA/DOB 5/21/32. Once divorced, lives alone. Alimony recipient. Complainant's call to station: 11:31 p.m. Suspect picked lock on rear service porch and entered house. No items stolen. Suspect dumped lingerie drawers, disconnected and overturned basement appliances, shattered glass-encased wedding photos of complainant and ex-husband, stuck pins in their faces and nailed the frameless photograph to the living room wall. Suspect masturbated and ejaculated in lingerie drawer. (Semen sample to lab). Suspect left note composed in cutout/glued-on magazine letters. Magazine letters and paper backing appear to be significantly dated. The note reads "You think you look like her. You fashion yourself after her. You're nowhere near."

I checked the map. I X-marked the address. The Creep's creeping east. He's into Brentwood now. He's veering toward Fifth Helena Drive. I checked the file photo of Arden Jane Brownleigh. She's got that vapid blond/Monroe look.

459 #5: 2/29/62. (DR #63882, 5 of 6). 10110 Highwood Street, Brentwood. Complainant: Lorraine (NMI) Smith/WFA/DOB 10/25/27. Twice divorced, lives alone. Alimony recipient. Complainant's call to station: 9:29 p.m. Suspect used glass cutter and entered bedroom window. No items stolen. Suspect dumped lingerie drawer and formed a tableau, consisting of soggy bathroom towels, dumped cigarette butts, pages torn out of complainant's address book scattered on random bookshelves. Suspect masturbated and ejaculated in lingerie drawer. (Semen sample to lab). Left note composed in cutout/glued-on magazine letters in lingerie drawer. Magazine letters and paper backing appear to be significantly dated. The note reads "You're like Cape Canaveral. You're my launching pad to greater things."

I checked the map. I X-marked the address. The Creep's creeping close. It's 2/29/62. I sense *this*.

He's already prowled the Monroe house. She's set to move in within two weeks. The trades reported it. He's been inside her prior cribs. He knows how she cultivates sloth and disarray. He's anticipating the sloth and disarray at Fifth Helena Drive. The creepoid Creep's on the hunt—

459 #6: 3/12/62. (DR #63882, 6 of 6). 2802 Fourth Anita Drive, Brentwood. Complainant: Dorothy Dilys Trent/WFA/DOB 7/21/33. Once divorced, lives alone. Registrar at University High School. Complainant's call to station: 12:41 a.m., 3/13/62. Suspect kicked in bedroom window. No items stolen. Suspect dumped lingerie drawer and formed a tableau, consisting of dumped soggy towels, dumped cigarette butts, torn pages out of complainant's address book scattered on random bookshelves. Suspect masturbated and ejaculated in lingerie drawer. (Semen sample to lab). Suspect left no note. Suspect left 1948 nude morgue photograph of actress Carole Landis in lingerie drawer.

I checked the map. I X-marked the address. *Sex Creep! Sex Creep! Sex Creep!* His internal shit's imponderable. He plays suicidal. He does not play homicidal. So what? Morty Bendish will twist established facts to spell *MURDER ONE.* We'll track the Sex Creep down and corner him. He'll try to escape. We'll shoot him dead and indict him for the Monroe snuff, posthumous. The lurid art of it will outcreep any and all Monroe-Kennedy rumors.

Max said, "Off the top of my head, he's no killer."

Red said, "Yeah—but Morty needs a punch line for his series."

Harry said, "He's in jail for some other sort of offense. That, or the nut bin. That's why he stopped in March."

Eddie said, "Not March—he was B and E'ing the Monroe crib in June and July. Remember? Marilyn was talking it up to her friends on Freddy's phone taps. It has to be the same guy—but Marilyn didn't report the break-ins. The Creep stiffed calls to three of the six victims. I read ahead to the follow-up reports, so that's how I know that. Remember? Marilyn told her friends she got breather calls."

Red said, "I heard those tapes. Her account of the break-ins played kosher, but the breather-call bit came off like a fabrication."

I lit a cigarette. "She kept the smut pix he jizzed on. I know her. She was a sick twist who craved sick attention. This fucker is nothing but sick drama, and that's the kind of shit Marilyn got off on."

The Hats dispersed. They had a mimeo file copy and took it to Vince and Paul's Steakhouse for a nosh-and-read. I read and chain-smoked in my cubicle. I tipped to one aspect, fast.

The Sicko Psycho/Sex Creep string was Sid Leffler's baby. He got seduced and worked it with and without J. T. Meadows. The Burglary-desk cops wised up and tossed him the string. The sex shit must have jazzed him. He studied under Paul de River. *That* meant *this:* more case lines and dubious headshrinkers constellate.

Leffler and Meadows worked it. They studied FI cards. They were submitted by night-watch patrol cops on the six break-in nights. Leffler and Meadows braced twenty-seven male Caucasians and three non-Caucasians out strolling Brentwood and the Palisades. They called in warrant checks and rap-sheet checks and got zero. Nobody popped up and shrieked *"Bust me!"* They roused known westside burglars and registered sex offenders and got zero squared. Print men dusted all six 459 locations. They got smudges/smears/the complainant's prints off exemplar sets and rubber-glove prints that indicated a small-handed man. Leffler schmoozed Ray Pinker into a favor. Ray did a walking portrait in the 459 #4 living room. A flat-weave carpet retained foot depressions. Ray tagged the Creep as a small-footed man. His stride was short. He walked heels out. He ran antithetical to the tall/big-foot man who tracked through the Monroe pad on 8/4/62.

A photo crew snapped all six 459 locations. I Man Camera'd the pix and merged sight and savvy. Leffler and Meadows canvassed the immediate neighbors. They described all six complainants as lonely divorced women. Said women spent most evenings alone. They played Broadway show tune albums and juiced. Neighbors said they heard songs from *Camelot* and *The Fantasticks* blasting on the break-in nights, *during the break-in time frames. The complainants were out of their homes and the Sex Creep was plundering. That* meant *this:*

He cased his intended victims. He cased their homes. He learned their habits. He surveilled them and pounced when they split for the evening. He observed their attire and extrapolated dates and social engagements. He calculated time spans. He broke in and spun disks. It sound-covered his ransackings. I skimmed crime-scene photos. I saw hurled furniture and jizzed-up lingerie. I played "Soon It's Gonna Rain," "Try to Remember," and "If Ever I Should Leave You" in a separate brain vault. It ran my Man Camera stereophonic. I went through the photo stacks. I saw the soggy towel/dumped ashtray tableaux. I saw the scattered address-book pages. I saw the cutout/glued-on magazine letters. I played those mawkish show tunes concurrent. A brain chant cut through my sound track:

Lonely women, lonely women, lonely women.

Leffler and Meadows milked the string dry. They set the Hats and me up for a shit-kicking reprise. Add Morty B.'s print barrage. Plus possible radio and TV. Something had to give.

I called Ray Pinker. I told him to rush-job the six semen scrapes. I told him to run cell-isolate tests on my Monroe-pad scrape. Ray said he'd work late tonight and do it.

I called Miller Leavy. He was barely civil. I told him to write to Lowell Farr's parents and goose my interview request. Leavy said he would. I told him to stiff a formal interview request to Albie Aadland. Leavy snarled and said he would.

I called Nat Denkins. I told him to goose his spot tails on Deedee Grenier and run them full-time. Nat squawked and called me a slave-driver. I pledged double pay. That brought him around. I called Phil Irwin and told him to rent a phone truck. Park it on Miller Drive, north of Gwen Perloff's pad. Hold down high-up/look-down surveillance. Eyeball the front door. Let's see who visits Big Gwen.

Daryl Gates cruised by. He said the Chief's monthly lunch with Sheriff Pitchess was inked in for tomorrow. Pete has some "hot" Black Muslim footage. He wants to sell it to Intel. "I'm looking for a quid pro quo, Freddy. A favor the Chief can lob at Pete."

I said, "Have the Chief ask him why Motel Mike Bayless transferred out of SHIT at the exact moment of the Perloff snatch, only to transfer back to SHIT in the immediate wake of the snatch, with only rudimentary work on the job completed. I'll get you a contact mike to attach to the table, so I can gauge Pete's answer."

Gates agreed and bopped back to his office. I called Eddie Chacón and urged him to lean on BNDD. Shelley Mandel was a big Zionist. He funneled black-market meds to the Irgun and the Haganah. I'm impressed—but get me Doc Shelley's current whereabouts.

Red Stromwall cruised by. He said the Hats were still matching phone bills and address-book listings from the Bev's Switchboard raid. He scheduled an interview with that Fox hairstylist. One of the swinger women from the raid called her three times. Eddie Benson jammed that woman who ran the housewife prosty ring. He said she's a wash—she don't know shit from Shinola.

Red scrammed. My cubicle was wicked hot. I goosed the AC dial and aimed a vent at my balls. Aahh—that's good.

I file-hopped. I jumped LAPD to BHPD. Both files denoted 459 PC—burglary/residential.

Five occurrence reports with missing-item lists. With station-house mugs but no print cards. The jobs occurred in the wake of cater-waitered parties. "Cater waiter" is a suspect occupation. It sustains bad boys between 459's, fruit hustles, and gigolo jaunts. I dumped the photo sheaths. Ronald Dewhurst smirked up at me.

He's aka Rick Dawes. Marilyn Monroe and Gwen Perloff knew him. I knew him as Richie Danforth. It was brief. Here's our denouement. Max Herman says, *"Sink him, Freddy."*

I crossed myself and dumped the print manifests. The squad lieutenant included a cover note. He wrote "Smudges, smears, partials and elimination-printed latents found at all locations. In addition, two different sets of rubber-glove prints were found at all locations. (Note photo blowups)."

I dug through the print sheath and pulled out the photos. "Differentiated?" That's dead-on. I studied the print card. I noted *this:*

Individual prints. Plus full hand spreads pressed on touch-and-grab planes. Hands pressed to window ledges, doorjambs, and drawer pulls at all five locations. The big-hand man had spatulate fingers. I never noticed Richie Danforth's fingers. The small-hand man had short, slender fingertips, down to the flex digit. *These* glove prints looked familiar. I naked-eyed them, in tight. They resembled the rubber-glove prints from the Sex Creep jobs.

The Intel darkroom featured a twin-lens microscope. I bundled up the BHPD print pix and the Creep manifest. I hit the darkroom and worked them.

I rigged the slides. I grabbed an X-Acto knife and excised representative print close-ups. I got a right-index-finger doorjamb from Sex Creep Job #3 and a window ledge from BHPD Job #5. #3 went under the left slide. #5 went under the right slide. I adjusted the eyepieces and dialed the lenses in identically tight.

Way tight. Near-*cellular* tight. Count the pixels, the microdots, the stretch flaws in taut latex.

Squint now. Cover your right eye and squint left. Note those three crosshatch dots. It's a subcellular cluster. You've got it memorized.

Now squint right. Cover your left eye. Squint down. *There's something like those same crosshatched dots.* Stressed latex meets hard surface. It's representative. It's not a match.

My eyes watered. I wiped them on my coat sleeve. I covered my right eye. I adjusted the left-hand slide and squinted left. I saw a big fat rubber-glove seam from BHPD Job #5. I saw a minute fissure near the digit flex. I switched eyes. I covered my left eye and adjusted the right-hand slide. I squinted right. I saw the same fat rubber-glove seam from the Sex Creep's Job #3. There's that same fissure near the digit flex.

It's a match. It's pure forensic gospel. The Sex Creep did the divorcée 459's solo. The Sex Creep doubled up with the Beverly Hills burglar. Said burglar might or might not be Richie Danforth/Rick Dawes/ Ronnie Dewhurst. It's not courthouse-valid evidence. Who gives a shit? Richie/Rick/Ronnie's dead and the Sex Creep's a newspaper casualty and X-marked for a lynch mob.

I shitworked past dusk. I reread the Sex Creep file and the BHPD burglary file and memorized small details. I reread the Sheriff's kidnap file and annotated inconsistencies. I called Nat Denkins. He reported: Deedee Grenier was shacked with a lezzie bar pickup. He'd resume the tail, tomorrow. Maybe she'd lead him to Paul Mitchell. I called Phil Irwin. He said his crane surveillance paid off, quick.

Darryl Zanuck showed up at Gwen's pad and stayed inside three hours. Pops left at 3:05 p.m. Phil tailed Gwen to Bullocks Wilshire. He followed her up to Ladies' Wear. She purchased a nifty black dress. She told the saleslady she was wearing it to a party Sunday night. It has to be the wife-swap bash. I'll be there. With "wife" Babs Payton. Harry Crowder will be there. With "wife" Lila Leeds.

I got cabin fever. The all-day shitwork stint compressed me. I split the PAB and cruised twilight L.A.

It was a hot summer night. I cruised with intent. I broomed out to West Hollywood. I dropped by the Jaguar, the Tradesman, the Falcon's Lair. I chatted up the lads. I gleaned zero leads per Paul Mitchell Grenier. I forked out ten-spots and phone-number slips. Call me if Paul Mitchell returns to Planet Earth. I pay C-notes for solid leads.

I drove by Bev's Switchboard and parked outside. No perverts, call girls, or call boys appeared and grabbed their mail. I split and buzzed out to the Palisades. I zigzagged residential streets and looked for the house Monroe sketched on 6/22/48. I saw nothing close.

I pulled up to 13821 Corsica Drive. Divorcée #1 lives here. Marcia Maria Davenport/current age forty-three/twice divorced, lives alone. Let's prowl the perimeter, let's peep windows, let's channel the Sex Creep and *PEEP.*

I did it. Sycamore trees enclosed the property lines on both sides. I hunkered low and popped up to scope lighted windows. I caught the living room first. Marcia Davenport paced and smoked. Her hi-fi belched samba music. Marcia popped her hips and sambaed wall to wall. She had bleached-blond Monroe hair. She wore it in the Monroe flip style. She grabbed a glass off an end table and sipped as she sambaed. It looked like straight gin.

The Sex Creep dug Marcia. She vibed experience. He perved her, he peeped her, he pursued her. He learned her routine and desecrated her home. I grokked it. I got the gestalt.

I drove to 12242 Marlboro Street. It's two blocks south of Sunset. Divorcée #2 lives here. Leona Jenks Hagedohm/current age thirty-four/once divorced, lives alone. It's a white Spanish job. Palm trees provide peep cover. I got out and strolled the perimeter. I caught Leona in the kitchen. She was wearing a panty-and-bra combo and nothing else. She chugged off a highball glass. She sudsed up her arms. She had short blond hair with dark roots. Two divorcées down, two dye jobs noted. The Sex Creep's got a type.

I cut out. I drove to 1545 Monaco Drive. Divorcée #3 lives here. Wanda Jean D'Allesio/current age thirty-two/twice divorced, lives alone. It was a stucco ranch spread. It lacked tree cover. That didn't matter. Wanda Jean sat on her front porch. She wore a frayed pink shift and chain-smoked Kool filter kings. She tried to read a magazine, it bored her, she tossed it. She had long brown hair. The Sex Creep dug her. He did not exclude brunettes. *I* dug her. She had that pent-up/caged-tigress look that always gassed me. Hey, Creep—this chick's ring-a-ding!

I split and cruised the Palisades commercial strip. I got a flash. The Sex Creep lives nearby. He walks to his B and E's or walks a dog to appear prosaic. He brings the dog inside his target pads. He's got access to real estate and/or court records and studies his target women. He simmers his lust to a boil. He breaks, enters, and peeps.

It was 10:00 p.m. I cruised the Palisades Village. I saw late sidewalk diners and Pali kids out trolling. I caught a line outside the Bay Theater. It's make-out-date central for Pali High libertines.

I parked on Sunset and strolled. I scanned kid cliques for Lowell Farr and didn't spot her. I saw a sidewalk art show, set up outside the Bay. An old lady hawked amateur stuff. She mimed Left Bank Paris. She featured oil paintings on easels. They were god-awful dreck.

I browsed my way through. I saw seascapes, mountain vistas, Will Rogers Park in bloom. Then jarring colors and a face cut into squares—with the eyeballs, nose, and mouth rearranged.

A woman's face. Marilyn Monroe's face. A companion oil to Lowell Farr's wall art. Note the "L. Farr/'62" daubed in the lower left corner. I peeped the wall art from Natasha Lytess' rooftop. Vandals painted over it. *That* painting torqued me then. *This* painting torqued me more.

Monroe's mouth grew out of her forehead. Two husbands and John F. Kennedy were trapped inside. DiMaggio, Arthur Miller, Mattress Jack himself. They screamed. Marilyn's mouth enclosed them. They were recognizable. Lowell did good detail work. Shattered music clefs poured from Marilyn's right ear. Scrabble letters poured from the left. They spelled "a life in discordance." Sharp fangs grew out of her hairline. Lowell scalped her. Nembutal capsules formed a bright yellow wig.

The painting was up for sale. It was a steal at fifty bucks. I gave the cashier a hundred. She almost plotzed.

I was itchy, antsy, adrenalized. The painting torqued me. The rubber-glove match torqued me more. I hit Sunset east and cut north on Benedict Canyon. I wanted to prowl unit 208 at the Tiki-Torch Village apartments.

I brain-screened flashbacks:

Saturday, 5/19/62. I tail Monroe to the Valley. I blow the tail. I scrawl parked-car plate numbers and misplace the tally sheet. I find the sheet belatedly and learn *this:*

Gwen Perloff parked her car two blocks from the Tiki-Torch. Likewise, Monroe. *Back on 5/19/62. At the same time of day.*

Cut to:

8/4/62. Monroe dies. Gwen Perloff is kidnapped. *She's rescued. At the Tiki-Torch apartments.*

I crossed Mulholland and downsloped to the Valley. The heat index spiked. Ranch pads devolved to swinger-pad blocks. I parked outside the Tiki-Torch. The courtyard was lit bright. Shrieks and pool-splash noise carried. The sidewalk reeked of chlorine.

The front gate was unlocked. I ambled on in. I shined on the water sports and the poolside tiki bar. I took side stairs up to unit 208.

I dug the Tiki-Torch. This sin pit aspired to class. The poolside view was a perk. 208 was a boss perv perch.

I peeled off the Sheriff's crime-scene tape and jammed a #4 pick in the door lock. Two twists right, two twists left. The door popped wide.

I stepped inside and shut the door behind me. The living room reeked of carpet-lift solvents. I flipped a wall switch. Recessed track lights threw a glow. The room had been cleaned out. A purple deep-pile carpet remained.

It was blast-oven hot. I flipped an AC switch and circulated cold air. A clipboard in-and-out log was propped by the door. It was big-crime de rigueur. Police personnel signed in and out for the job's duration.

I picked up the clipboard. One notebook sheet was clipped in. One entry was logged. Sergeant Michael J. Bayless signed in and out. He was here from 2:15 to 3:00 p.m./Sunday, 8/5/62.

Anomaly. Inconsistency. I'd read the Sheriff's task list for the snatch. The lab crew and photo crew had been here. The list reflected the pro forma shitwork decreed by kidnap jobs. The job went *pffft* then. Here's the big question. Did it go *pffft* from dearth of leads or cosmetic design?

More cops should have traipsed through here. Curious patrol cops. Canvass cops beating the heat. Cops hot to scope the chicks and make the scene.

I lit the pad and strolled the pad. It was cheese-luxe, all the way. The walls had been print-wiped. The task list noted that. The snatch men knew their shit. I checked the closet where the geeks stashed Gwen P. Gwen said they stuck an AC hose under the door to keep her cool and refreshed. I saw gouge marks at the bottom of the door frame. The hose would have fit right there.

The closet bit played *half* credible. It felt *almost* cop-contrived. I checked the two bedrooms. They were pristine. I checked Bathroom #1. It was pristine. Bathroom #2 was not quite pristine.

In the medicine chest. On the third shelf. There's a small X-Acto knife. There's purple fiber gack stuck to the blade.

The gack matches the purple deep-pile carpet. Additional fibers match a gray carpet pad.

It's an oversight. The toss cops shined the knife on. Somebody's been futzing under the living room rug.

I walked back to the living room. I pulled up the carpet and tossed all four corners to the center of the room. I saw a gouged-in pocket at the dead middle. Somebody fashioned a quickie stash hole.

I reached in. My hand brushed warm metal. I pulled out two padlock keys. They were stamped "208/storage."

We've got pool-courtyard apartments. There's an underground garage. The storage lockers would have to be—

There.

I tried not to run. I relocked the pad and walked to the main stairwell. I took the stairs down three at a time. The stairwell led straight to a fume-choked garage.

It was monsoon hot. The Tiki-ites favored flash rides. Vettes, T-Birds, 409 Chevys with lake pipes and cheater slicks. They vibed repo bait. Leaky pipes dripped dark ooze. They spattered off cherry paint jobs.

There it is. Up against the north wall. A steel door marked STORAGE.

I slid through car rows and dodged dripping ooze. The large key opened the large door. A wall switch lit the space. I clocked four walls with two locker rows per. 101 was just off to my left. Even numbers sat on top, odd numbers sat below. I beelined to the 200s and counted eight lockers over.

The small key fit. The door creaked open. I saw one fat newspaper stack.

That's it. There's nothing else. What the fuck is—

I started at the top. They were all *Herald*s. The *Herald* was L.A.'s Hearst rag. It ran threadbare compared to the *Times.* I pulled out the top three. They were dated Wednesday/Thursday/Friday/—8/1, 8/2, 8/3/62.

It was the ramp-up to the Monroe OD/kidnap convergence. I scanned all three issues. I checked every page. I indulged notions of microdots and dead-letter drops. I got old news and ink-smeared hands.

I dug out the bottom issue. It was dated 5/1/62. That induced hotbox chills. 208 was rented out that day. An obese lady rented it. She also rented the backup pad on 6th and Dunsmuir.

I saw *convergence/confluence/conspicuous design.* I scanned every page of the 5/1 issue. It was unscrawled and unscribbled. It was void of maildrop shit.

I pulled *Herald*s and read my way up to mid-May. Papers were consecutively stacked and unannotated. Yes—but hoarded toward what end?

I read my way up to Saturday, 5/19/62. I tailed Monroe here that day. She blew my tail. She split this location and caught a noon charter flight to New York. Her Madison Square Garden gig was set for that night. She was set to sing "Happy Birthday" to Big Jack.

I flipped to page two. The *Herald* ran a puff piece on the prez and his birthday girl. I flipped to the next fold and saw *this:*

A red-lipstick-scrawled heart. A red arrow piercing it. *"MM here today!!!"* scrawled within. It's an androgynous scrawl. Maybe an arty man/maybe a butch woman. Tiny pinholes pierced the heart. They dripped red-ink, ballpoint-pen blood.

I drove back downtown. I was beat-to-shit depleted and concurrently hopped up. A long day triggered a long flashback roll.

The Beverly Hills 459's. Danforth/Dawes/Dewhurst, partnered up with the Sex Creep. Rubber-glove entries/forensic crossover leads. The divorcées. Unit 208 at the Tiki-Torch. The storage bins. The newspaper scrawls. It proves *this:*

Monroe worked the kidnap job.

Convergence /confluence/conspiracy.

It was 1:00 a.m. I parked in the PAB lot and elevatored up to the lab. Ray Pinker's work bay was lit up bright-bright. His desk was sixteen-by-sixteen and fluorescent-lamp lit. He displayed the evidence I requested. It was multidiscipline and all Sex Creep.

I scanned left to right. I saw the magazine-letter notes left at the divorcée pads. I saw the note the Creep left at the Monroe pad. Plus glue-sample bottles and binders filled with exemplars of magazine type-faces and paper stock. Plus seven photo blowups of male ejaculate cells.

Ray walked in. He said, "It's all one guy. He's a type-AB secretor, so we've got a line on his blood. It's a rare type, so that should help you eliminate would-be suspects. California driver's licenses displayed blood type and thumbprints up to '56, so you should be able to get some eliminations or confirmations there. The paper backing is '46 to '50, cheap bond, chemically treated to adhere to the binding of the cheap men's magazines of the era. The cutout letters were clipped from *He-Man Adventure, Calling All Rogues, The All-Man Danger Digest,* and *Calling All Rogues Presents Filmland Femme Fatales.* The glue utilized in all seven notes is present-day Elmer's Glue-All, which was also widely used back then. The femme fatale rag only ran for two issues, but both featured Carole Landis. The note the Creep left Monroe utilized letters from an issue that featured a spread on poor Carole's suicide."

40

Morty Bendish delivered. I played paperboy.

The Hats and I staged a coup. We took over the West L.A. DB. The squad lieutenant was out golfing. We bootjacked his office and snatched his desk jug. Sixteen detectives evil-eyed us. They scoped the newspapers I dropped on their desks.

"Sex Creep Stalks Westside!!!" "Tuff Task Force Assigned!!!" "Vixen-Victim Marcia Davenport Resembles Soiled Sexpot Monroe!!!" "Cops Ponder Malevolent Monroe Connection!!!"

The *Mirror-News* delivered. It's the Chandler dynasty's down-market daily. It's the mongo kid brother of the mighty *L.A. Times.* Morty's column is tagged "Bendish's Back-Page Beat." It's subtitled "The Lurid Local Lore We Live For." The city editor moved Morty up to page three. Bill Parker pulled strings.

The headlines packed punch. The text tattled Marilyn's "nympho nook" in "bring-the-brisket Brentwood." It portrayed Divorcée #1 as a "lithe look-alike." It laid out B and E #1, sans jack-off and jizzed undies. It employed scare tactics.

"Will the Westside wither and warp into Tijuana North?? Are the Klubb Satan and its deranged donkey show soon to come? Is the Sex Creep the hellhound harbinger of horrid events on the horizon? The Westside has been a warm womb for wounded but still dishy and delectable divorcées. Trouble bodes—but if DA's Lieutenant Freddy Otash and the LAPD's hard-charging Hat Squad nail the Sex Creep, the Westside will remain safe and sane!!!!!"

The squadroom cops read the piece. The squadroom cops snickered and glared our way. Sid Leffler glared, J. T. Meadows glared. Max kicked the office door shut.

"Well, we've got Ray Pinker's call. It's all one guy."

Red said, "Jesus, and the Creep was out pulling 459's with Richie Danforth or whoever he was. This whole deal is a cluster fuck, but Freddy's pulled glove prints from both strings."

I lit a cigarette. "Phil Irwin called me an hour ago. He was up in his surveillance crane, early this morning. He saw Mike Bayless drive up Miller Drive, in his civilian car, straight toward Gwen Perloff's place. Bayless sees Phil, who's ex-Sheriff's, and drives right on past. He's dirty, and he's dirty with Perloff on the kidnap caper."

Max said, "That deal gets stranger and stranger. Witness those newspapers Freddy found last night."

Eddie said, "I forgot to mention that hairdresser at Fox. We're buying her lunch at Ships. She did Marilyn's hair on *Got to Give,* and she says she's got the latest and greatest. Also, she said that woman we popped at Bev's is a *puta,* and she's got no truck with her, other than styling her hair."

The desk jug went around. We all glug-glugged.

Harry said, "Let's get back to the Creep. We've got twenty-seven FI cards to go through, and we need to run reinterviews. Likewise, the registered sex offenders Leffler and Meadows hauled in."

I said, "I've read through the RSOs' statements, and I've checked their rap sheets and mug shots. They all seem too young to me. I've got the Creep pegged as older. He had to be—at least—an adolescent back in the late '40s, when all his sex shit started percolating. The old magazines, his Landis fixation, all of it. *And,* there's *got* to be some Landis paperwork *somewhere.* I want to see if there's anything to indicate she was hassled by peepers, breather calls, or psycho fans."

Red went *Nix.* "Her PD files have been picked clean. Every cop scrounger on God's green earth has had his snout in the files and nicked mementoes. Three of our divorcées got breather calls after the break-ins, and they all told Leffler and Meadows that the guy did not sound like some young kid looking to pull his pud."

I said, "Monroe ran her breather-call number on some friends of hers. I think it was all fabrication."

Max lit a cigar. "Yeah, of the woe-is-me variety."

Harry spun the desk jug. It skittered into his lap.

"I'm inclined not to toast the Creep, pro forma. Look what Richie Danforth got us. Look who's out to nail us for that one."

Edna Medina was eager to yak. She was forty-five or -six. She wore a floral-print muumuu and white tennys.

Max and I bought lunch. Harry, Red, and Eddie cranked it back at the DB. They were building a new Sex Creep file. The chore should protract. They'd be there all night.

We hogged a corner booth. Traffic boomed on La Cienega. Edna cocked her head and smiled at Max. She craved yak-yak more than lunch.

Max said, "This is a follow-up to that phone chat you had with Officer Benson, ma'am. You told him you did Marilyn Monroe's hair for *Something's Got to Give.* I'm sure you recall the conversation."

Edna poked a bread basket. "I recall it, too. I told him Miss Monroe was nice, but she was *loca.* And she talked a blue streak, which was *loca mas.*"

I said, "How so?"

"Well, she's an actress. So, she plays to her audience. She sees that I'm Mexican, so she starts working me. She tells me Mexico's her favorite country. I say, 'Try living there,' and she tells me she's a secret courier for bearer bonds, and she's working with a noted reformer to rebuild the Mexican economy. I told you, *loca mas.*"

Max signaled me: *You respond.*

I said, "And you replied?"

Edna said, "I told her this bond thing was a shuck, and who's this 'reformer,' he sounds like a dope pusher to me. So, Miss Monroe laughs and says, 'Well, he is.' She says she goes in disguise, and some old Russian lady fakes documents, and so she couriers bonds and sometimes dope, but dope should be legal in Mexico and the United States, so it can enchant people and turn them into revolutionaries who hunt down fascists. I told you, *loca mas.*"

The reformer is José Bolaños. The forger might be Natasha Lytess. She might have lied to me. She said Monroe was out of her life. Gwen Perloff peddles bearer bonds. That's established fact. She's a professional. She's the only one. She's in with deluded amateurs—up to and including Marilyn Monroe.

Max said, "Did Miss Monroe tell you the reformer's name?"

Edna sipped coffee. "José Bolaños. She said he had a big *chorizo.*"

I said, "Okay. You said she's *'loca mas.'* I'm betting she fed you crazier stories than that."

Edna poked the bread basket. "She said she had the goods on President Kennedy, and she said she was going to make him divorce Jackie and marry her. She said she and some other woman had a deal in the works to take over Fox, so that they'll make nothing but movies that glorify real people. I said, 'Will I get a raise then?' Miss Monroe said, 'No, but you'll get paid in Mar-Gwen preferred stock, which is more valuable than pure platinum.' Like I said, *loca mas.*"

Mar-Gwen. There you go. The confluence extends.

The swing creaked. The stars twinkled low. The lobster salad wilted. Our easy talk flatlined. We hooked our legs up and plopped them down on the room-service cart.

We sprawled on the swing. Lois and I run telepathic. She spins at my own warp speed. I called the convergence "All Of It." She deciphers my brain-waves.

"I know what you've been doing. People live to confide, you know. And I've developed a source."

I said, "Who?"

"Pat Lawford. Confidante of guess who? You said they tell each other everything. They're brother and sister, so I don't quite consider it unseemly."

The ground dipped. The sky dropped. The lights across Wilshire glared extra bright.

"Where'd you meet Pat?"

"She was sitting on your front porch. I came over to do just that thing. We acknowledged the pathos of it, and introduced ourselves."

I rolled my eyes. "She saw you in *Hot Tin Roof.* You recognized her. Bobby keeps her updated. I've got no secrets left. Half the world knows my shit."

Lois lit a cigarette. "We're going to Mass and brunch tomorrow."

I mock-groaned and nuzzled her. We laced hands and sideswiped a low star. I saw a *Twist Party Stakeout* script on a lounge chair. Lois annotated it. She marked up most of the pages.

"Sid Leffler. Have you met him?"

"Two days ago. He's desperate and ingratiating, and not quite as smart as he thinks. He invited me to Palisades High to catch his 'Officer Sid' show. Do you want to go?"

I said, "Yes."

"He told me he knows you."

I smiled. "Talk to your source, or read today's *Mirror*. It'll put you current on Sid Leffler and me."

Lois said, "I met Pat, and it embarrasses you. It shouldn't, though—given that we're both married, and you're not."

Call sheets were stacked by the scripts. I picked one up. Lois said, "We're shooting on Soundstage Six at Fox, and then we're moving to a house in the Palisades. Maury wants to shoot the party scenes there."

I scanned the sheet. It listed twelve "party dancers." Party Dancer #4: Georgia Lowell Farr.

41

The wife-swap party. It's on as of *NOW*.

We're swappers and worse tonight. We're the new depraved. We're sickniks up for cheap enchantment. We're the fuzz. We're party crashers out to quash the party.

West Hollywood. Havenhurst, south of Sunset. A big Spanish court-yard complex. The party's across the forecourt. 216's a boss duplex. We're up in 423. It was empty and offered up for lease. It's ours for tonight. Bill Parker pulled strings.

There's ten of us. We came to infiltrate, peep, and scrounge leads.

That's Babs Payton and me. Plus Harry Crowder and "wife" Lila Leeds. We're kicked back in 423 and gassing on the wide forecourt view. Phil Irwin's shooting infrared film. He's zeroed in on the 216 doorway. He's notching zoom-lens shots. Daryl Gates has binoculars fixed on the door. He's jotting descriptions of the guests.

Four men worked the outside slot. That's Nat Denkins, Red Strom-wall, Eddie Benson, and Max Herman. They're scrawling plate numbers and Minox-snapping the arrivals. It's one big effort geared toward one goal. ID Fox-allied libertines and fast-buck entrepreneurs.

ID them/brace them/squeeze them dry. Monroe/the kidnap job/the Beverly Hills 459's. The Sex Creep and all interconnected linkage.

Lila and Babs smoked and sipped flask juice. They wore their carhop outfits, sans skates. They're Stanislavski-ites. They're proletarian. It's their fashion statement. They're playing themselves. They're ex–film notables reduced to schlepping burgers and malts. Harry and I radiate *Fuzz*. That's okay. I'm here in my Shit Magnet guise.

I was nerve-knocked. Bill Parker and Pete Pitchess had their monthly lunch today. Daryl Gates slipped a contact mike under their table at

Mike Lyman's. I played the tape. Pitchess passed Parker some film that SHIT shot. I'd seen it before.

It's early May, this year. There's a big Muslim protest, outside the PAB. Select officers overreact.

Parker passed Pitchess three thou. Parker popped the question:

"Why would a SHIT supervisor quick-transfer to the West Hollywood squad just in time to crack the Perloff kidnap job, then immediately transfer back, leaving a major felony case untended and unresolved?"

Pitchess said, "I don't know and I don't care. The job's dirty, we both know it, and I don't want to see Freddy O. and the Hats get nailed for sinking that guy—despite Miller Leavy's hard-on to slam them. Motel Mike Bayless is a law unto himself, and I figured he transferred to West Hollywood because he had a girlfriend stashed nearby."

Spot-on, Pete. The girlfriend's Gwen Perloff. Motel Mike bossed the kidnap job. That's evident now.

Gates walked up. "You, Harry, and the wives should head out. The Chief wants you to know that you may hit a certain wrinkle, and if you do, he trusts your ability to extemporize."

I winked. Gates winked back. I grabbed Babs. Harry grabbed Lila. They wore carhop pedal pushers and tight white tops. Plus Naziesque peaked hats with the Stan's Drive-In logo. It's trendsetting couture, all the way.

We split 423 and elevatored down. We linked arms four across and strolled toward 216. The front door spilled light. A big guy worked a reservation log and collected money. We beelined on over. I dropped our pseudonyms: Freitag and Crawford, plus two. He scanned his list and went *Yup*. I passed him four C-notes. He ogled Lila and Babs. He said, "Those outfits really work. Call me weird, but I've always dug carhops more than stews."

It roused some yuks. The girls curtsied. Samba sounds drifted over. Cool school. Music to perv by. We drifted inside and drifted apart.

Your wife or mine? If you don't swing, don't ring.

I circulated. I orbed the living room. It was furnished on the come. Cheap butcher-block furniture. Beanbag chairs from the Akron. Hi-fi hookups, upstairs and down. They played synchronous *and* discordant. Stan Getz and Astrud Gilberto. Gerry Mulligan's low sax. Music to subsume talk and promote fuckee-suckee.

Cigarette smoke. A wet bar. Two Filipino barmen. A late '30s/early

'40s crowd. They were half-assed good-looking. They were trim. No porkers allowed!!! Here's the demographic. I'm in with moderate-affluent squares. Film-biz folk. Executives and overpaid blue-collar. There's no shitkickers/no white trash/no Valley-tract types.

I made people I'd seen on the Fox lot. I saw two Foxites make me. I saw a switch-hitter cat who packed the pork to Roddy McDowall. And—I saw *her*.

Gwen Perloff. Alone. Out on a railed-in terrace. Wearing her glasses. Smoking a cigarette. Quaffing a martini. Wearing that black dress Phil Irwin saw her buy.

I walked straight toward her. She turned and saw me. Her heels put her up at my height. She wore no makeup. She eschewed all affect. Her hands were as big as mine and her eyes just as dark brown. She was pale. Her dark brown hair veered to black. Her shag haircut worked. Her random gray streaks worked best.

I felt unprepared and underdressed. I resisted an impulse to crowd her. She spoke first.

"Let's skip the introductions. I know who you are, you know who I am. I know about the raid at Bev's, and I figured you'd show up here. You've been staking out my place, our eyes met once, it wasn't remotely romantic. You tossed a man off a cliff last month, and don't think I'm not grateful. Does that cover the amenities?"

Icebreaker. Go in innocuous. See if she laughs.

"I saw *Spawn of the A-Bomb*, back in '56. I've enjoyed your work ever since."

She doused the cigarette in her martini. She tossed the glass out in some shrubs.

"You saw *Spawn of the A-Bomb* at the Wiltern. You were casing me."

She stood very still. I stood very still. We sustained skirmish-line distance. My legs trembled. I flinched first.

"I heard your voice on a wiretap call, a few months ago. You were impersonating a cater waitress named Eleanora. You called Peter Lawford and pumped him for information on a cater waiter named Rick Dawes. You said he might be a fruit hustler or a pad burglar. Marilyn Monroe knew Rick Dawes. I've got his name on a paper scrap, in her handwriting. I pushed a kidnap suspect named Richie Danforth off a cliff the night Marilyn died, and his face matched a BHPD mug shot of a man named Ronnie Dewhurst."

She moved toward me. Her dress rustled. I felt her breath on my face. "It's like that, is it?"

I said, "Yes."

She said, "I came here to circulate, and to discuss certain things with certain people. We should go somewhere and discuss certain things, and we should feign some sort of rapture as we walk out."

The Glenarms Motor Hotel. Way east in Pasadena. The doorman slipped us the key. He was impressed. We were the first swappers out the door.

We caravanned. I got there first and ran a bug sweep. The suite was pristine. The décor was low-rent medieval. Throne chairs and coats of arms nailed to the walls. I closed off the bedroom. A pay icebox served canned martinis. I popped for two. I poured them into water glasses. Gwen Perloff walked in the door.

I locked it behind her. She grabbed her drink off the TV set and resituated the chairs. She allotted five feet between us. I handed her an ashtray and kept one for myself.

She said, "What are you looking for in all of this?"

"'All Of It' is what I call all of this. It saves time. I'm looking into Marilyn Monroe's activities in the months preceding her death, your kidnap, a string of house burglaries in Beverly Hills, which may be attributed to Ronnie Dewhurst, who you may have known as Rick Dawes. There were some crazy housebreakings in Brentwood and the Palisades between late '61 and early this year. That's 'All Of It.'"

She crossed her legs. Her hemline draped decorous. She didn't vamp me. I didn't stare.

"You'll have to be more specific."

I said, "*Cleopatra*. Fox in the dirt. Tattle that I picked up on the same wire line I was running when I heard you impersonate 'Eleanora.' Overlapping vice scams, bond trades, and dope deals. Separate factions within a general confluence, only one of which, Foxtone Services—has been identified as of this time. You yourself have been rumored to courier bearer bonds to Mexico, presumably to trade for foreign currency to finance narcotics deals."

She sipped her drink. It was rotgut booze. She did not react.

"Bearer-bonds-for-cash trades are not strictly illegal, but narcotics deals are."

I lit a cigarette. "I think the kidnap deal derives from the general criminal atmosphere at Fox, but as something more contained, more sophisticated, more—"

The door crashed in. It flew flat off the jamb and sheared off all the hinges. It slammed to the floor. It made large noise. Eddie Chacón ran in. Three Justice cops crowded up behind him. They body-blocked the throne chairs and knocked both of us to the floor.

They muzzled us with handkerchiefs and cuffed us behind our backs. They dragged us outside. Two Fed sleds hot-idled by the doorway. The back doors stood open. They tossed me in the lead sled. They tossed Gwen in the follow car. Code Three lights and sirens kicked on.

They dragged her. I saw blood where her legs scraped the ground.

The Feds gave good cell. Sturdy bunk. With a mattress, pillow, blanket. Entertaining wall graffiti: *Chuey Bites the Big One* and *Mondo y Yolanda por vida.* Eddie Chacón tucked me in and winked.

I was the sole dink in the men's tank. Gwen was up on the women's tier. The bust was a ruse. The bust was a scare tactic. Bill Parker and Ratfuck Bobby dreamed it up. Eddie and the stooge Feds are hard-nosing Gwen right now.

I tried to doze. I ran brain sweeps on *All Of It.* I unstitched and revised my points of connection. I traveled back to Hollygrove '37 and jumped back up to now. It was all supposition and assumption. I fed Ray Pinker Sex Creep/Monroe leads. I turned the Creep/Rick Dawes/rubber-glove lead. *Burglary* pervaded all of it. *Burglary* raged definitive.

Eddie Chacón walked up. He unlocked my door. He said, "Go home, *Señor* Freddy." He passed me a telefax sheet.

I read the note. Eddie ambled out. The note read *"Continue to extemporize with Miss Perloff. All best, WHP."*

I walked off the tier and upstairs. It was 1:00 a.m., Monday. The Fed building was dead. I traipsed office rows and the lobby. A night guard opened the door.

The night was clear. Gwen Perloff stood just outside. She was smoking a cigarette and counting low stars.

She said, "I need a drink. Take me someplace."

Kwan's Chinese Pagoda. Cops rule the roost here. I finagled us a dark back booth.

It was dark. The back booth cocooned us. We drank mai tais. Gwen futzed with her paper umbrella.

I said, "How did they play you? What did you tell them?"

"They asked questions about what you call 'All Of It.' They wanted to know who I know and did the kidnap really occur."

"What did you say?"

Gwen looked at me, through me—

"That's as specific as I'm going to get."

She bought the ruse. It might buy me time.

"Let's start over. 'Gwen, this is Freddy. Freddy, this is Gwen.' Isn't this a swell party? Do they really swap wives here? I like that samba music. Would you like to dance?"

Gwen deadpanned it. "They cut me loose, but they'll come around again. I know why they're buzzing me. I know they're buzzing you on the kidnap deal and what you and the Hats did to Richie Danforth, but I need to know how far you're in on the rest of it."

I said, "I was working a bug-and-tap job on your old Hollygrove chum, Marilyn. That was from April up to her death. I heard things, and I put things together. She had a coin stash, for making pay-phone calls. You've got one in your car. You've got a thing going with Motel Mike Bayless. On a good day, I can tell up from down. To quote you, 'That's as specific as I'm going to get.'"

Gwen stood up. She said, "I'm sure we'll speak again," and walked out.

42

Here's Pat. We're at my place. We're under the sheets. It's crowded down there. I've got visitors.

Lois rags Pat. *She's married, and she doesn't really love you. Kennedys don't love, they use and collect.* Gwen Perloff's present but mute. She'll play it just as close the next time we meet.

Pat said, "You're about ten thousand miles away, and you have been since I walked in the door. You saw Lois Saturday night, so I'll allow for a little distraction, but this is just too much."

I stage-yawned. It always ticked Pat off.

"Tell me about Mass and brunch. You and Lois, I still can't believe it."

Pat kicked the sheets off and stretched. I kissed her underarms and made her laugh.

"We went to Saint Michael's, in Santa Monica. We talked more than we prayed, because that's the kind of girls we are. We drank brunch more than we ate it, and we talked about you at some length. No, we failed to come to any conclusions."

I lit a cigarette. "I never know what you're thinking, and what conclusions you've come to. I know that Bobby will drop the hammer, sooner or later. 'Pat, don't you think this has gone far enough?'"

The AC spiked and frostbit the room. Pat ducked back under the sheets.

"I started keeping a journal, right after I met you. It was V-J Day, plus one. Our night together was my impetus, and I wrote down everything that I saw, did, and thought, up until February 19, 1951. It's a *read,* and you certainly spiced it up, at least for a little while."

I said, "Will you let me read it?"

Pat said, "Maybe."

Her tone bugged me. Ditto the context. We were kids then. I have duties now.

"Bobby's here in L.A. a lot. He's spending more time with me than I warrant, given that he's got Eddie Chacōn to take care of the help."

Pat bristled. "I know most of it, or all of it, so I could see why the attorney general and the president would want to keep track of your progress."

I poked her. "When Bobby's not telling me what to do, or holding subpoenas over my head, he's being too nice to me, like he's patting my head because I'm running through my hoops like a good dog."

Pat poked me back. "For a man who levied extortion against the future president of the United States in 1955, you're not doing so badly in 1962."

I laughed. The poke hurt. She was right. Fuck the Kennedys sideways.

"Go home. It's coming up on rush hour. Tell me you love me, whether you mean it or not, and get back to your brood."

Pat sat up. The sheet slid off her breasts.

"Shit, I just recalled something you should know. I . . . um . . . eavesdropped on Bobby calling Eddie Chacōn. They discussed something about 'unloading' bearer bonds, and from the way they talked, I could tell it had something to do with what you're working on."

I shrugged. "It sounds logical. Bearer bonds are all over this deal."

Pat hugged a pillow. "Here's what I just recalled. Peter's always ogling a group of stewardesses who play volleyball on Saturday mornings, two doors up the beach. There's always some stews in uniform, watching them play. Last week, I saw him key on a big blond girl in a Mexicali uniform. He gave her a wad of cash, and she handed him a flat manila envelope. I asked him what it was. He said 'Bearer bonds. They're the new coming thing.'"

Mexicali stew. Big blond. Ingrid Irmgard. She had that tattoo—El Manny and crossed boxing gloves. Mexico, bond schemes, dope. José Bolaños. Edna Medina cites Marilyn's smuggle-in-disguise rant. The Foxtone card in Marilyn's basement. The Bev's raid. "Your wife or mine?" "Investment opportunities."

43

The Hats snoozed in my cubicle. They deserved a nap. They got paper-blitzed last night. Check my desk, the shelves, the floor. A paper tidal wave just hit.

DMV kickbacks/Teletypes/R&I green sheets. NCIC kickbacks on the dinks from the Bev's Switchboard raid. Paper on the plate checks at the wife-swap bash.

The Hats wore sleep masks. They were flopped-over pages from today's *Mirror-News*. Morty B. delivered Part 2. Horror headlines popped out:

"Sex Creep in Savage Second Assault!!!" "Sexy Divorcée Monroe Look-alike!!!" "Sex Creep Desecrates Home and Marks Triumph in Animalistic Ritual!!!"

The *Mirror-News* constrained Morty. He couldn't write *jizz, spurt, semen, jack off, squirt*. He went with "globulous evidence of his lust." Sid Leffler and J. T. Meadows got big attaboys. They were the original IO's. I told Morty to ballyhoo them. We might need them for clue-clown work.

I was agitated. Albie Aadland's lawyer rebuffed Miller Leavy's interview request. Dorothy Denton Lowell rebuffed Miller's request to interview Lowell. Her kiss-off note temporized: "Maybe, when the fall semester is in full swing, and Lowell's studies have improved."

Agitation/frustration. I terminated Phil's stakeout on Gwen Perloff. She'll contact me before too long. I know that. She'll want to carve an exit deal. She'll want prosecution waivers and money. My grand-jury strategy would cover all that.

I had breakfast with Daryl Gates. He and Eddie Chacón grilled Gwen at the Fed building. Daryl ran it down.

Gwen held in strong. I know nothing about the kidnap. I *was* kidnapped. Yes, I knew Marilyn at Hollygrove. Yes, I knew Paul Mitchell Grenier. No, I haven't seen him in a dog's age. Money scams, emanating at Fox? I don't know what you're talking about.

Daryl ran down the ruse. The ruse threatened Gwen Perloff and implied that we know All Of It. It suggested the wide parameters of the All Of It. It stressed their interconnectedness and political import. It implied our lack of concrete proof and a dearth of leads on the Fox folk involved. Gwen heard them out. She flinched once. Eddie mentioned my work on the Jimmy Hoffa op. Gwen flashed an *aha!* look. She just figured out why a Fed *and* a city cop braced her. It pertained to the Hoffa/Bobby K. *mishigas*. It was a *very* well-known feud.

I watched the Hats sleep. I oozed agitation/frustration. I had to find Paul Mitchell Grenier and beat the truth out of him. Agitation/frustration. I wanted to nail the Sex Creep and jack him up on Pentothal. Perverts always motormouth under dope and duress.

Daryl Gates walked up. I pointed to the Hats and went *ssshhh*. We walked back into the squadroom. All the Intel cops were reading Morty's latest. Most of them yukked outright.

Gates handed me a sealed envelope. It was marked "General R. F. Kennedy." It felt like six or seven pages.

"The Chief wrote it. It's an extended précis on the Sex Creep investigation, and a detailed report on our efforts to get at the truth of Miss Monroe's death. The Chief goes on to laud your grand-jury strategy, and does a lawyer-to-lawyer bit on its efficacy. The Chief closes with an entreaty. He asks General Kennedy not to seek indictments on you and your men for the Hoffa op, and he asks him to yank Miller Leavy off of you and the Hats. He makes the point that indictments in those matters would taint our grand jury's findings, and he's right. The General is out at the Lawford house. The Chief wants you to hand-deliver the note to him and watch him read it."

William Henry Parker III. Accept no substitutes.

I cut north on PCH. I heard chopper thump off to my left, on the beach side. Sunbathers and lolling surfers pointed up, up, *up*. Two choppers hovered into view. They hovered low. I saw the U.S. presidential seal. Jack returns to Jack's Shack. His arrival's raising a stir.

People ran down the beach. They chased the choppers. They waved and squealed. Two women doffed their bikini tops and flashed their goods. The choppers pulled ahead and out of view. I heard *"We love Jack and Jackie"* chants. The volume grew and feathered out.

Three black sedans zipped by me. They were Secret Service, for sure. They cleaved toward the land side of PCH. I saw a '61 Impala, parked bluffside up ahead. The sedans surrounded it. Agents jumped out and plopped warning cones all around the sled.

Heavy traffic nudged me rightward. The Secret Service cars blew out, northbound. There was no way to cut into the traffic flow. I braked and pulled up behind the Impala.

Eddie Chacón stepped out. He motioned me over. I squeezed out my passenger door and walked up. Eddie held his door open. I slid into the front seat.

Jack Kennedy said, "Freddy, you cocksucker."

He wore khakis and a polo shirt, beat-up deck shoes and shades. He lit a cigar and blew smoke in my face.

I said, "Hey, Jack. What's shaking, baby?"

He said, "So much for decorum. You extorted me, you camel fucker. I should nuke Beirut just to put you in your place. You're lucky my brother has work for you—because, believe me, it could have gone the other way."

I lit a cigarette. Jack smiled. His tantrums ran in six-second spurts. I passed him the manila envelope.

"It's an update on the work we've been doing. It's from Bill Parker to the General."

Jack hocked and spit out the window. He was too thin, he looked frail, he ran six feet and 145, tops.

"I've got a date. Peter set it up. You've seen her on TV. She's been on *Perry Mason* and *Naked City*. Eddie suggested the car switch. He'll take this lemon, and we'll go somewhere in her car."

I said, "I wish you luck."

Jack said, "I don't need luck. I don't need more power and more women. I need to get to a safe place where the world can't crawl up my ass."

Amen, brother.

Jack blew smoke rings. "I like this guy, the Sex Creep. He reminds me of Eddie Chacón. Bobby's drawn to psychopaths. It explains his fondness for you and Eddie. Maybe Bobby will put the Creep through law school and get him a Justice appointment."

I laughed. Jack was spritzing now. Book him at the Losers—he'll draw big.

"I like the kidnap girl, Gwen what's-her-name. I saw a horror picture she was in, back while I was a senator. I asked Harry Cohn to set me up with her. Harry said, 'I heard she's trouble with a capital *T*.'"

A woman walked toward the car. Jack was right: I'd seen her. Two agents escorted her. They hugged the bluffside and made straight for the prez.

Jack said, "Mayor Yorty told me a good one. 'A lion is fucking a zebra. The zebra looks over his shoulder and says, Oh, shit, baby—I see my husband! Quick, pretend that you're killing me!'"

44

I got five minutes with the Kahuna. Big fucking deal. Ratfuck Bobby read
Bill Parker's note. Big fucking deal. He said, "Keep up the good work on
all fronts." He said, "Yes, Freddy's grand-jury play still looks good." He
said, "No—I'm still considering the possibility of prosecuting Freddy
and his thugs."

Ratfuck cited my evidential paucity. The wife-swap party was an
evidential bust. The paper chase turned up jackshit. Zero per the plate
checks. Zero per the green sheets. Zero suspicious phone calls. Zero
per employment checks. Nobody worked at Fox. Fox-allied swappers
and pervs stayed away. I knew why. My Foxtone-cards-under-the-
windshield fuckup warned them off.

The Hats worked the Sex Creep file. They've finished their restruc-
ture. Morty Bendish is three divorcées into his Sex Creep sextravaganza.
He lays on pulsing prose, scare tactics, pop-off-the-page paranoia. He
utilizes numerous euphemisms for *semen*. He hammers the divorcées'
"resemblance" to Marilyn Monroe. I edit Morty. I tell him what to write.
Grind the suspense, Morty. It's nothing but a dry hump until the Creep
snuffs Marilyn.

The *Mirror* ran slam-bam photo spreads. Dumped furniture. Slashed
heirlooms. Medicine-chest debris. Red devils and yellow jackets dumped
on bathroom floors. I edited the pieces, I read through the pieces, I
thought through them as I read. I told Morty to crank the divorcée
angle. Divorcées connoted desperate sex and ennui. They were nymphos. They lived in upscale nympho nooks. Marilyn lived in a nympho
nook. I thought through the nympho-divorcée bit. I conceded hyper-
bole. I pondered common denominators. Did the women know one
another? *How did the Sex Creep get hip to those specific women?*

The *Mirror* reported a 16% circulation spurt. The Sex Creep show was hot ink. Creep calls swamped the West L.A. station switchboard. Westside stiffs were outraged and scared. They demanded enhanced police protection. Nat Denkins flogs the Sex Creep on his nightly radio show. Creep-O-Mania scorches L.A. TV/radio ham George Putnam stokes the fear. "Inexorably, the Sex Creep's creepiness moves us ever closer to Marilyn Monroe."

No shit, Sherlock.

The Sex Creep investigation proceeds. It's the pulse of the Monroe/ kidnap/BHPD burglary jobs. I work All Of It. It's tail work and brainwork. I search for Paul Mitchell Grenier. He's a night bird. That entails night work. I brainwork in my cubicle. I put in eight-hour days there. I stare at my bulletin boards and file sheets and *think*. I stare at file photos and *think*. I plumb theoretical lines, case flank to case flank. I repeatedly reread the BHPD file. I've memorized the Dewhurst/Dawes/Danforth notes slipped inside. BHPD staked out Caviar Catering. They ran R&I checks on dicey young men and women employed there. Ronnie Dewhurst came up clean. Some cop snapped mug shots, regardless.

"Sink him, Freddy." The long drop and big smash. Ronnie Dewhurst as Richie Danforth.

BHPD's burglary string. Five jobs, altogether. Two sets of rubberglove prints at all locations. One large-finger man, one small-finger man. Near-identical glove seams on prints at the Sex Creep and BHPD jobs.

They're perfect eyeball matches. They're not quite courtroom-valid. Defense lawyers could twist the matches twelve different ways. So what? This job's not going to court.

Link the throughlines. Link the case flanks.

Take the Sex Creep jobs. The spotlight's on glove prints and jizz stains. We know his blood type. He's a type AB-negative secretor. Harry Crowder stiffed a call to the state Adult Authority. He's scrounging data on paroled 459 men, going back five years. Ditto data on freaks with masturbation MO's. Max and I are going over every FI card for the full Creepoid time frame. We'll pounce from there. We'll stretch all latenight prowlers/loiterers/nocturnal riffraff who vibe *wrong*. We'll read through the PD's apprehended burglar file and see who vibes *wrong*. We'll recanvass the six Creep locations, with *this* in mind:

Is the Creep a local Palisades or Brentwood guy? Does he live within his target area and covet women he sees routinely? Is he Palisades/ Brentwood affluent? Does he have access to house-deed records/estate-probate records/divorce records? Has he dream-cultivated a sisterhood of solitary women who drive him ever closer to a Creepoid consummation with Marilyn Monroe?

All Of It. All case flanks lead back to Marilyn Monroe.

I had Lowell Farr's Monroe portrait matted and framed. It now hangs on my north cubicle wall. Lowell portrays her pal Marilyn as pure disorder and disjuncture. Marilyn's eyes are her own eyes. They look back at Marilyn and judge her insane. The painting reflects the perv art of Weimar Berlin and Monroe's penchant for urban-grotesque photography. Lowell's perceptive. She sees through Monroe now. I peeped her as she slapped paint on Monroe's living room wall. That portrait was the run-up to *this* portrait. *This* portrait drove me back to the Sex Creep's six divorcées.

I'd already peeped divorcées 1, 2, and 3. I swung by the homes of 4, 5, and 6 on full-dark summer nights. The Creep's moving east. He's into Brentwood now. He's planned hot dates with Arden Jane Brownleigh/Lorraine (NMI) Smith/Dorothy Dilys Trent. He's escalating. He broke a glass-enclosed photograph of Brownleigh and her ex-husband. He stuck pins in their faces. He left Lorraine Smith a note: "You're like Cape Canaveral. You're my launching pad to greater things." He left Dorothy Trent a morgue photo of Carole Landis.

I extrapolated. It was 3/12/62. Monroe had just moved into Fifth Helena. Trent was a morgue-photo dry run for Monroe.

I observed Brownleigh, Smith, and Trent. Brownleigh cultivated the vapid Monroe look. Smith and Trent did not. I caught all three women at home alone. They evinced loneliness and agitation. They smoked and drank to excess. They tried to watch TV and read racy books. They tossed the books and flipped from baseball games to sitcoms. The Leffler-Meadows paperwork did not reveal interconnected relationships among the six women. How did the Creep key in on *these* six women? They were film-star surrogates in his mind. Landis and Monroe bookended his madness. The divorcées were avatars of prosaic sexuality and dashed wedlock. They were more than random and less than essential to him. Their divorcée status struck a chord in him. He saw them and gassed on them. He peeped them over time and developed a lust jones. He didn't ponder the chord they struck. Landis and Monroe were movie stars. They struck everybody. *They were safer.* The Sex Creep did not know why he did the crazy shit that he did. The divorcées took him deeper. He did not acknowledge this.

I stare at my bulletin boards. I stare at Lowell's portrait of Marilyn. I think. I think about women. The divorcées. Lowell, Pat, and Lois. Gwen Perloff, most of all.

She hasn't contacted me. I want her to read me wrong and sense that I'm all about the money. I want her to tour-guide me through Fox in duress and tell me how All Of It coheres.

I need to interview José Bolaños. He's holed up in Mexico. It might be impossible for now. I need to interview Lowell Farr. I've got a strong hunch here. Where are Marilyn Monroe's stash of everyday letters/love letters/fan letters/further communiqués from the Creep? She didn't bank-vault them. They weren't in her basement. Her lawyer had no idea. They weren't listed in the Coroner's Office inventory of her house. I think she gave them to Lowell Farr.

I need to reinterview Ingrid Irmgard. She lied to me. She sold Peter Lawford bearer bonds. Her boyfriend Juan Manuel Salas has a burglary sheet. He got popped in '54. He was at Chino concurrent with Paul Mitchell Grenier. He had a dumped 459 beef in '57. His PO thinks he's clean. He's an ace TV repairman these days.

I need to reinterview Natasha Lytess. I need to reinterview Del Kinney, Roddy McDowall, and Timmy Berlin. I need to hit them with *this:*

Tell me what I need to do to find Paul Mitchell Grenier. I want to put the screws to this psycho sack of shit. I want him to set some things straight.

Nat Denkins and Phil Irwin leapfrog-tail Deedee Grenier. She goes to Rancho Park Golf Course, Jeanne Carmen's pill parties, and Linda's Little Log Cabin. She avoids Norm's Nest. She steers clear of Paul Mitchell.

I've haunted the Klondike, the Falcon's Lair, the Jaguar, the Tradesman. Nobody's seen Paul Mitchell. So, I *think.* So, I *read.* My new favorite author? It's Paul de River.

I've read *The Sexual Criminal* eight times. The Doc inspired Monroe's final idiot immersion. I know he's giving a talk at the Wilshire Ebell, three days hence. I'll be there. I'll salt the audience with my boys and bring an Intel camera crew. We'll induce fear and consternation. We'll get the old quack all shook up.

Sid Leffler studied under de River. He's written true-detective rag pieces. He notched walk-through tape recordings at the six divorcée sites. He described the physical details and laid down verbose critiques of the Sex Creep's motivations. Leffler's florid prose style mimes de

River's. Leffler: probable de River obsessive. Monroe: certain de River obsessive.

I run out of brain steam around 3:00 a.m. I brain-screen women's faces then. Lois, Pat, Gwen. I imprint details until their features merge and my mind goes blank.

45

The summer postlude. It's jungle hot in L.A. It's "Saturnalia Saturday" at the Tradesman. That means half-price drinks and much whoop-de-do. The boys screen toga flicks on a wall-pinned bedsheet. Raucous laughs and wolf whistles ensue.

The boys know me now. I'm the chump detective. I dispense ten-spots and pursue Paul Mitchell Grenier. They hate Paul Mitchell. He defames the rough-trade imprimatur. They sniff ten-spots and swarm me at the door.

I dispensed twenties tonight. The boys oohed and aahed. One guy said, "He might be making a movie."

I said, "Where? What studio? What kind of movie?"

One guy said, "Paul Mitchell's got his own studio, but I don't know where it is. He's a live-on-the-fly, catch-as-catch-can sort of guy. And if I know Paul Mitchell, he's making dirty movies there."

They fed me fourth-hand lowdown. I've heard it all before. I split the Tradesman and drove west. I craved Brentwood and the Palisades. It was sea breeze–adjacent. It was the home of dishy divorcées and sex creeps on the hunt.

I'm a sex creep. I peep windows for profit and kicks. I booked west. The temperature dropped. I went by Fifth Helena and the Lytess house. The Monroe place was dark. The Lytess place threw light. Natasha's old Ford clogged up the driveway.

I cut loose for the Palisades. I looped quiet residential streets north and south of Sunset. The Sex Creep prowled here. He knew this turf. He 459'd the Palisades first. He worked up to Brentwood. Monroe was his denouement. The Palisades cradled him. He knew it. He coveted women here. He worked up to 459 PC with malicious intent. It all started right here.

I cruised random streets. I looked for that moderne house. Monroe sketched it in June '48. I cut over to Capri Drive. I cruised the house Carole Landis died in. She died in July '48. It was a big château/ranch job. Landis married a rich man. Hubby #4 owned the spread outright now.

Carole Landis, divorcée. Marilyn Monroe, divorcée. A distant kid marriage. That makes one. Plus Joe DiMaggio and Arthur Miller. That makes three.

Westside L.A. The recurrent number 48. That brain chant drove me batshit. I split east and found a phone booth on Bundy.

A directory dangled on a chain. I looked up Del Kinney. He lived at 1081 South Orlando. That's right off Olympic. I looked up Timmy Berlin. He lived on Charleville in Beverly Hills.

Kinney nudged me more. He was a brooder and a bachelor. He was career L.A. fuzz. He knew everybody. He did favors. He met Gwen Perloff in 1937. That's twenty-five years back.

The address was a peach stucco duplex. Kinney had the low floor. I rang the bell. It was 10:14 Saturday night.

Kinney opened up. He wore faded Sheriff's khakis with the emblems excised. His big cop hands dangled. He'd had a few. I smelled it.

He said, "It's Lieutenant Otash. It's late, and he's got questions. You'll note I didn't besmirch your rank or your expedient appointment."

He said it friendly and gestured me in. The front room was done up with nature prints and movie-set chairs. He pointed to one. I sat down and grabbed an ottoman. Kinney walked to a sideboard and fixed two highballs. I reached for mine. He plopped down facing me. He pulled up his own footrest.

He knew the drill. It's a drop-in chat/interrogation. It veers both ways.

I said, "Bill Parker called me this afternoon. He told me to lay off the Fox lot. That stunt I pulled with the Foxtone cards backfired."

Kinney cracked his knuckles. "By all means, stay off the lot. I know full well that there are cabals perpetrating outrageous schemes in the hopes they can circumvent the *Cleopatra* disaster, but under no circumstances will I divulge names or details."

I sipped my drink. It was very old/very strong bourbon.

"You should waltz, and resettle somewhere. You've got service pensions up the wazoo, and I'm sure you've got savings."

Kinney sipped sour mash. "I've been offered a very nice job. Could you see me as the sheriff of Monroe County, Wisconsin?"

I said, "Take it. Get out of here. Start over someplace clean."

"Do you think Gwen Perloff could adjust to the move and be happy as a sheriff's wife?"

It sandbagged me. "It's like that, huh?"

"On my end, it is."

I lit a cigarette. "I can't advise you there. She's in the shit, and under no circumstances will I divulge names and details."

Kinney lit a cigarette. "I'll have to accept that, then. I know you're dying to discuss Gwen, so let's get to it."

I said, "I keep thinking of Hollygrove, back when you first knew her. She met Marilyn Monroe and Paul Mitchell Grenier there, around the time her little sister disappeared."

Kinney shut his eyes. I orbed the room. I saw a framed religious print. Prayer hands and *"Lord, Thou seest me."*

"Well, Marilyn's and Gwen's lives kept crisscrossing. They met at the Grove—and, okay, Grenier was there with them. Then Gwen went back to foster care, and on to Le Conte Junior High and Hollywood High. Marilyn went to live with some nutty relatives, then went on to schools in Westwood and the Valley."

I coughed. I counted to ten. Kinney was a don't-tread-on-me type. He kept his eyes shut. I was half there.

"Nothing you tell me leaves this room, sir. I have it that Gwen and Marilyn reconnected in the late '40s, and worked as call girls together. They fell under the sway of a well-intentioned but dicey psychia—"

"Sheldon Mandel. A long-term Treasury informant, whereabouts unknown. He was a VD doctor. That was how he got next to all sorts of good-looking young women. You recall the postwar VD epidemic? Mandel talked turkey to the girls and saved them from a lot of grief, despite the obvious fact that he was a lecher at heart."

I said, "As in?"

Kinney opened his eyes. He put on wire-rimmed glasses and blinked at me.

"Doc Shelley was a scenester. The way I see it, he figured his good deeds licensed him to indulge his nasty side. He hung out at party pads, jam-session pads, fuck pads, and upscale call pads, and dispensed penicillin and prophylactic kits to the girls. He included intimate physical exams, free of charge. It gave him more time to schmooze up the girls."

I sipped bourbon. It was depth-charge stuff. It ran at least 140 proof.

"Isn't Mandel credited with inventing the so-called 'fuck deck,' and establishing it as an investment opportunity?"

Kinney sipped bourbon. His hairline popped sweat. It was depth-charge stuff. He craved that quick push out of the gate.

"I've heard the rumor, but Gwen would have told me if she and Marilyn had gone the deck route. And I'd rather move on to other topics, if you don't mind."

I said, "Mitzi Perloff. I'd like to get your overview."

Kinney cracked his thumbs. "The whole investigation and search was centered in Hollywood, up near the Immaculate Heart school and Ferndell Park, where the poor little girl liked to pick flowers. We thought of it as a body-dump case at the start. We got one eyewitness lead to the contrary, but it never played out. Mitzi was spotted on a westbound Wilshire bus on the day she disappeared. It's the bus route that commences in Hollywood, cuts south to Wilshire, then goes north through Westwood Village and out to the beach."

The westside jumps again. The westside pervades All Of It.

Kinney said, "Gwen was not quite eleven, but she walked a skirmish line through Ferndell Park, right beside my deputies. I have never seen such courage and composure. She found a little doll that Mitzi dropped or someone else threw away, and she did not falter, not for one instant."

Charleville ran one block south of Wilshire. Timmy Berlin's address put him right off Linden Drive. It was a mini-mosque triplex. Minarets and spires topped with gold-flecked paint.

Berlin had the downstairs unit. It was 11:40 p.m. His lights were on, his shades were up, his French doors were cracked wide.

I knocked twice. A peephole slid back. Somebody undid bolt locks and opened the door.

It was Timmy Berlin. He was fully dressed. Slacks, guayabera shirt, and tire-tread sandals. He held a pair of scissors. A Moviola was clamped to a lowboy table. He was cutting film.

I said, "I know it's late."

Berlin stepped back. I stepped inside. The living room was four-wall Monroe. Posters for *Niagara*/*River of No Return*/*The Prince and the Showgirl*/*Bus Stop*. Berlin looked mortified.

"I can't escape her, and I don't want to. I enjoy it more than it hurts. Freddy Otash knocks on my door at midnight, so it's got to be about Marilyn. There's coffee in the kitchen, and I was about to take a break."

I followed him back. The kitchen was space-age chromium. I squeezed into a breakfast nook and popped two Dexedrine. Berlin worked a hammered-tin contraption and cranked out two espressos.

He squeezed into the nook. "Okay, it's about Marilyn. Big surprise. The question is, 'Marilyn and who else?'"

I tossed my espresso back. Let's level out Del Kinney's home brew.

"Let's start with Natasha Lytess. I'm dealing with two versions here. Miss Lytess told me she hadn't seen Marilyn since '56. A backup witness said an old Russian woman fixed Marilyn up with forged travel documents, just recently. The backup witness has no reason to lie, while Miss Lytess might well have."

Berlin said, "Natasha lied. She's got cancer, and she's on her way out, so she's entitled. Also, she was unrequitedly in love with Marilyn, so I give her a pass there out of sheer empathy."

His spiel said *Coax me.* I tossed out some bait.

"Darryl Zanuck and Marilyn treated Miss Lytess quite shabbily. They terminated her employment and tossed her off the Fox lot. She rented a house near Marilyn. She was looking for some kind of solace during her last days."

Berlin said, "Natasha was a clinger. Mr. Z. hates clingers, and Marilyn hated to be clinged on. Believe me, I know. But, to return to your question, she lied. I saw Marilyn and Natasha lunching at Frascati, early in April. I saw them, but I was seated behind a wall fixture, so they couldn't see me."

I coaxed him. "And they spoke in stage whispers, as film people tend to do?"

"Yes. Marilyn pressed Natasha for tips on being less attractive, and more anonymous in public. Natasha recommended collagen facial injections to give herself a fleshier appearance. Then they discussed forged documents. Marilyn knew that Natasha utilized forged papers to escape Germany and emigrate in '38 or '39. The Aadland brothers smuggled lots of Jews out of Europe then, which tips their karmic balance back to the good side, in my view. Marilyn told Natasha she needed diplomatic papers to allow her to travel, in disguise, in and out of Mexico, without being searched. Natasha said she'd call Hersh Aadland to discuss it. Frankly, I think Natasha was having her on."

The dexies hit. I zoomed straight to snap judgments.

A "wheezy-voiced woman" called Darryl Zanuck and ratted the kidnap gig. It was Lytess. Natasha, la couturier. Monroe in disguise at civil rights rallies. The autopsy showed collagen deposits under one earlobe. Lytess again. Here's the big snap judgment. Lytess shaped Monroe's final immersion.

I lit a cigarette. "Paul de River. His book *The Sexual Criminal*. Was Marilyn a fan of de River? Was she ever headshrunk by him?"

Berlin went *Oh, yes.* "She was practically a de River devotee. She read all his books and monographs, and she kept telling me she wanted to hook up with him for some shrink sessions."

Berlin was clamped tight and dish-frenzied. He was popping his rocks.

"Albie Aadland. Do you know him? If so, what can you tell me about him?"

"Albie? There's either not much there or *lots* there, depending on who you talk to. He's the much-younger, nonhoodlum brother. Everyone agrees on that. He lives alone in a big house in Cheviot Hills, and he's got no love or sex life. That's accepted as gospel. There's a rumor that he dabbles in chemistry, pharmacology, and so-called radical psychology, but I don't know how accurate it is."

I'll buy it. Don't jive me on the brothers. Fuck their philanthropies. Albie Aadland shares their blood and their taint.

"You've got me het up on Albie, Mr. Berlin. What else can you tell me?"

Timmy Berlin screwed up his face. He's miming deep reflection. He wants to spiel.

"Well, he was briefly in Hollygrove with Marilyn and Paul Mitchell Grenier. And I just read in *Variety* that Gwen Perloff was there then, as well. You know Gwen, right? Recent kidnap victim and Mr. Z.'s illicit girlfriend?"

Oh, yes. I know Gwen.

"Keep going, please. Your Hollygrove information is all new to me."

Berlin lit a cigarette. "I've been around Fox since '50, and I've picked up a lot of lore. Albie's parents had died, years before. His brothers raised him and gave him gofer-type jobs. They made him a 'test pilot' for dope compounds cooked up by rogue chemists, back in the '30s.

The cops learned of all this, and they had Albie placed in Hollygrove. He got tight with Marilyn, Paul Mitchell Grenier, and a Mexican boy who lived in that crappy part of lower Hollywood near the Grove. The boy belonged to something called the 'peewee corps' of the Nite Owl gang, which was primarily a group of boys who pulled house burglaries. Paul Mitchell told me that he and Albie went out on 'several raids' with those boys."

Depth-charge. The brew, the pills, the snitch spiel—

"Also, I only just learned that Gwen had been in the Grove, because I read that piece on *Hard Luck Girl*. Marilyn told me that she, Albie, Paul Mitchell, and a Mexican boy who wasn't in the Grove used to climb a high tree on El Centro and watch movies being made on the RKO and Paramount lots. Marilyn said it was the beginning of a 'big actress fixation' for her and the other girl."

Kids together. Monroe. Gwen Perloff. Albie Aadland. Paul Mitchell Grenier. Who's the Mexican boy?

"You know, Freddy—when Marilyn and I escaped you and the other fools during the 'Wrong-Door Raid,' it convinced Marilyn that she could be a criminal as well as any man. That's when she told me that Paul Mitchell wanted to do a smut film about the raid, with Marilyn playing herself."

I chained cigarettes. My bloodstream swelled. I glimpsed Hollygrove and the kid clique as *ALL OF IT*.

"During your relationship, what did you and Marilyn do for kicks, outside the bedroom?"

Berlin crushed his cigarette. "Mostly, we read her fan mail and psychoanalyzed her fans. She said they were predictable, and that there was always a declension in fan crushes. Weird-o guys started out crushing on Carole Landis, then crushed on Jane Russell, and ended up crushing on her."

Landis preceded Monroe. She hit in the early '40s. Russell and Monroe hit roughly concurrent. Landis suicided in '48. The Sex Creep clipped letters from '40s magazines. He employed '40s bond paper. "Declension of fan crushes." The Creep deployed Landis-era props to bedevil Monroe in '62.

Berlin said, "Penny for your thoughts."

I said, "I'm having a hell of a time trying to locate Paul Mitchell. Do you have any ideas?"

"Well, there's his so-called studio. It's a little apartment on Kerwood, near Fox. Hillcrest caddies live in the building, mostly. I think Paul Mitchell sleeps there, on and off."

I stood up. Timmy Berlin went bereft. He could have snitched all night.

It was 1:12 a.m. I swung left off Olympic and slow-cruised Kerwood. It was a run-down cul-de-sac. Fox and Hillcrest CC were due south. I spotted the Belleview Apartments. It ran two floors and eight units, tops.

It was right at the hook of the cul-de-sac. Country club caddies are lowlifes. They're career boozehounds, hopheads, and track fiends. This must be the place.

I parked six dives north of the Belleview. The cul-de-sac was dark-dark and hushed. It was recessed. Two streetlights burned dim.

I got out my penlight and evidence kit. I pulled out rubber gloves. He might be there. If so, I'll roust him. He might not be there. If so, I'll forensic his crib.

I walked up and flashed the mailbox. It listed seven single men. Plus "PMG Studios, Ltd." in unit six.

I counted the units. It's probably upstairs. 1,2,3,4—down. 5,6,7,8—up. Nothing but dark windows. The Belleview's sleeping it off.

I unbuttoned my coat and freed my belt shit. I lugged my evidence kit upstairs and bit down on the penlight. I counted door plates down to six.

I knocked on the door. Little love taps. Night crawler Grenier. He receives late-night visitors. They'd knock that way.

No response. I waited a full minute and love-tapped again. No response. I got out a #3 pick and popped the door lock. I stepped inside and locked myself in.

The place reeked. I ID'd the musk. Butch male cologne and exertion. I flashed the interior. It was narrow and cramped. I laid down my kit and ran a premises check.

Movie cameras/Moviolas/boom mikes/arc lights. Four boxes stuffed with French ticklers, dildos, and S and M shit. A scuzzy mattress propped against one wall. A corkboard nailed to one wall. One piece of paper pinned to it. Note the legible hand scrawl.

"*Wrong-Door Raid!!!* A Paul Mitchell Grenier production for discerning and high-class adults. Starring Marilyn Monroe as Herself and Paul

Mitchell Grenier as Ace Hollywood Private Eye Freddy Otash. The roles of Frank Sinatra, Joe DiMaggio, Phil Irwin, Timmy Berlin, and the Old Lady to be cast soon. Filming begins October 10, 1962. Invitation-only premiere. The same day that box office dreck *Cleopatra* is released."

A kitchen adjoined the north wall. I grid-flashed it—a full 360 degrees. It was grimy and double-cramped. I checked the icebox. It was stuffed with vodka short dogs and amyl-nitrite poppers. A toilet sat out in plain view. Ditto an uncurtained showerhead and a medicine chest. I popped the door and saw *this:*

Four shelves lined with dental prostheses. It's a sex biter's trove. Dracula-fang dentures. Three upper plates with razor-blade teeth. A plate with "PMG" embossed. Dentures with ID tags attached: "Panther," "Jaguar," "Bengal Tiger," "Jackal," "Grizzly Bear."

The Jackal teeth pinned down a paper scrap. I pulled it out and read *this:*

"No. Ask for more $. This is just our opening salvo. Quit thinking of it as a one-shot deal. Mar-Gwen's future depends on it."

I recognized the scrawl. Marilyn Monroe wrote the note.

My heartbeat red-lined. My tach outrevved seven thousand.

I worked my way back through the dump. I penlight-strafed it, inch by inch. I saw a copy of *The Sexual Criminal,* crammed behind a film-reel stack. The pages were bitten and gnawed. Prosthetic choppers mauled and thrashed the book.

Grenier pen-marked the dentures he wore: "Jaguar," "Jackal," "Bengal Tiger." He bit through pix of noted sex fiends Harvey Glatman and Stephen Nash. He slipped snapshots of the Wrong-Door Raid building between the pages and bit them with his PMG teeth.

I opened my evidence kit. I got out my hand vacuum and futzed with the brush gears. I ran the nozzle between the dumped cameras and lights and picked up rug grit. The kitchen floor was chipped linoleum. I sucked up nameless gack and floor grit. I dumped the vacuum-bag yield in a plastic bag and dropped it into my kit.

Think evidence. Think latent prints. Hit touch-and-grab surfaces. This film equipment serves your designs. It's all touch-and-grab planes.

I got out my brush and tape-transfer strips. I dusted long arc-light poles and Moviolas. I pulled up smudges/smears/partials and a left-hand latent spread. I tape-transferred the spread and taped the corners to a black cardboard sheet. Red powder, black cardboard. The contrast offset the prints. I shot two Polaroids and dropped them in my kit.

I picked through camera debris and grabbed a long tripod. It was all touch-and-grab. I dusted one leg, two legs, three. I worked close. I saw something by the top bolt housing.

Rubber-glove prints. A full right-hand set. A *small-hand set*. It *seems* familiar, it *looks* familiar, it *might be* familiar and ring all the bells.

Squint. Naked-eye it. Study loops and whorls. There's that familiar glove seam. There's the applied pressure marks.

Count comparison points. Get your valid courtroom ID.

I counted slow. I hit twenty-four. I nailed loops, whorls, and tented arches. I doubled the required number and then some.

It's a match. The set matches the small-hand sets at the Beverly Hills break-ins. The set matches the sets at the divorcée break-ins. The Sex Creep was in this room. The Sex Creep touched Grenier's film gear.

I trembled. I flushed hot and cold. I stood in the dark and gulped air. I heard a key-in-lock sound. The door swung open. I saw the Biter Beast, backlit.

I attacked him. I pulled my sap and slammed him in the head. He squealed. I kicked his legs out from under him and kicked the door shut. He hit the floor. I stepped on his neck and pinned him there.

He gulped and went mute. I hit a wall switch and lit Grenier full-on. He wore blue jeans and a jean jacket. He wore pointy-toe fruit boots. They were pop-up-switchblade boots. Don't veer too close.

I eased off his neck. He looked up at me. I kicked him into a pile of cameras and lighting stands. I pulled my piece and aimed it at him.

He rubbed his sap-gouged head. He said, "At least you spared my teeth."

I said, "Let's start with some dirty Polaroids I saw. You and Marilyn, before you put your mark on her. I'm thinking they were outtakes from a fuck deck. Tell me if they were or they weren't."

Grenier went *Comme ci, comme ça*. "Yes and no, daddy. For one thing, the decks were a postwar phenomenon, and Marilyn and me shot those Polaroids sometime in '59. I considered the fuck deck bit, but it was stale bread by that time. Although, I have to say, Marilyn was there at the fuck deck inception."

I said, "With Shelley Mandel?"

Grenier rubbed his neck. I bore down and left heel imprints. They trickled blood.

"Mum's the word, dad."

"The kidnap. Lay out the personnel."

"Not tonight, sahib."

I said, "The Sex Creep. You've seen the *Mirror*, so you know who he is. He left glove prints in this very room, and he was sending Marilyn crazy notes and pictures, right before she died."

Grenier rubbed his sap wound and licked the blood off his fingers. Grenier stroked his crotch and grew a hard-on.

"I've read the *Mirror*, but I don't know what you're talking about. And Marilyn is passé. My new bitch du jour is Barbara Bouchet. You know how I know that? Every time I get the urge to rape and kill an actress, she hits the big time."

I said, "Dr. Paul de River?"

Grenier said, "I'm a Buddhist-existentialist. I don't believe in doctors."

"I saw Marilyn's note. 'Just our opening salvo.' 'Quit thinking of this as a one-shot deal.' What did she mean by that? Did the note refer to a ransom demand?"

Grenier said, "Marilyn who?" Grenier pulled out an amyl-nitrite popper. He waved it and popped it and took a huge sniff.

His face went red-red. He jumped up, fast on his feet. He pulled something from his coat pocket and jammed it in his mouth. He growl-roared low in his throat.

Tiger teeth. His spare set. Big fangs and flat lowers to gnaw meat. He growl-roared and lunged at me.

I fired point-blank. I blew his mouth and his neck cords out. A severed ear flew. His tiger teeth exploded. I powder-scorched his eyes down to the sockets. Muzzle flash set his hair aflame.

PART 7
HOP DREAM

(SEPTEMBER 9, 1962)

46

Opium.

My pallet at Kwan's. The tar, the pipe, the match. I'm a Chinaman. I fell off my camel and landed in Kowloon. There's two long pallet rows. My fellow Chinamen seek enchantment. I'm here to conjure All Of It in a safe dope habitat.

Nobody heard the gunshots. Somebody heard the gunshots. I'm fucked or I'll get away clean. I picked up the ejected shells. I dropped Monroe's note in my evidence kit. I stole the gnawed-on copy of *The Sexual Criminal*. I stole the smut-film-announcement page pinned to the corkboard. I poured film-cleaning solvents on the rug. They ate through the bloodstains and half-dissolved the foundation boards. I excised a large carpet patch and wrapped Grenier up. I hauled him out to my car and dumped him in the trunk. Nobody saw me, the whole world knows what I did.

I hit the San Diego Freeway and the Ridge Route north. I buried Grenier in a rock pile off U.S. 99. The dump site was a half mile from the roadway. I dropped heavy rocks on Grenier. They hit loud. Bones broke audible. I turned around and drove back to L.A.

The dump job took five hours. I'm safe here now.

Maybe I'll dream.

MAN CAMERA
RECALL/IMPRINT/REWIND—

I saw faces, I saw microphones, I heard denials overlap. Smoked-up committee rooms. Ratfuck Bobby badgers Jimmy Hoffa. Gwen Perloff hucksters Jantzen swimwear. Gwen and Motel Mike exit the Tiki-Torch. There's synchronicity there.

The Sex Creep. Face unknown. He's a shape-shifter in black. He did 459's with Dewhurst/Danforth/Dawes. "Sink him, Freddy." Dear beloved Lord, I repent.

A mail truck dumped letters in my lap. I read illegible inscriptions. Monroe, Bolaños, Ingrid Irmgard. Dope couriers. Natasha Lytess, forged docs conduit.

An envelope fell in my lap. A flashbulb blip lit me. Lowell has Marilyn's fan letters. Imagery equals fact.

I saw Hollygrove. I framed establishing shots of El Centro and Vine. I added '30s cars and period extras. I regressed the key players and saw them as children. Marilyn, Gwen, Albie Aadland. Paul Mitchell Grenier, reborn. Who's the Mexican kid? He's a Nite Owl peewee—

Jump cut. I'm out of my trance. Fucking burglary pervades this whole thing.

I smoked opium. I saw Lois and Pat naked. I saw them at Mass. They prayed for me and lit altar candles. Dear Lord, I repent.

Jump cut. Postwar L.A. street scenes. Hollywood Boulevard by night. I worked the Santa Claus Lane parade. Carole Landis was slated for grand marshal. The parade was in November. She died in July.

C words bombarded me. Conjecture/confluence/coincidence/convergence/conspiracy.

I saw exemplar fuck decks. Merry Christmas. Shelley Mandel's got script-pad stocking stuffers for YOU!!! Marilyn and Gwen work the call-girl circuit.

Marilyn sketches a house. Marilyn's got dirt on future Prez Jack. Postwar L.A. runs libertine. VD, be-bop, fuck decks, fuck pads, boomtime, boomtown, something happened right before Carole Landis popped those—

A typewriter fell in my lap. A blank sheet of paper was rolled in. I heard four key taps. I saw 1,9,4,8.

PART 8
RED LENS

(SEPTEMBER 10–16, 1962)

47

It was a good dream. The dream sent me to '48 and told me *Look Here.* It was a good snooze. I felt revitalized. It was a good purge. I killed Paul Mitchell Grenier and escaped his horror hutch. Grenier was Satan Incarnate. He just *had* to go.

I knew I'd waltz on it. I went by West L.A. station and checked occurrence sheets for Saturday-night-into-Sunday-morning rumbles. There were no shots-fired or unknown-trouble squeals for that patrol sector. It felt like a skate, all the way.

I brainworked in my cubicle. I orbed Lowell Farr's painting every half second. Red Stromwall was right. The Landis file had been raided. I found a folder in the "Suicides/1948" drawer at Homicide. The bio sheet ran threadbare. I knew most of it going in.

Her feature debut: *I Wake Up Screaming,* 1941. It was cranked out at Fox. *Moon Over Miami,* '41 and Fox again. Produced by old man Zanuck. Fox, resurgent. Fox, ubiquitous. She's in and out of Fox through the war years. She slips to postwar B roles. She wrote a memoir, *Four Jills and a Jeep.* It rehashed her USO-girl stint. It was serialized in *The Saturday Evening Post.* Fox filmed it in '44. It made money. She married four times. The last guy had gelt. He bought that big crib on Capri Drive.

I put the bio sheet down. It was stale news. I sipped coffee and scrawled notes.

Who's the Mexican kid? He lived near Hollygrove—'36–'37.

Shelley Mandel. Have Bill Parker hard-brace BNDD. Where is this hump?

Brace Albie Aadland. Re-brace Ingrid Irmgard. Devise a strategy. Gain access to Hollygrove today.

Interview Jane Russell. Quiz her on crazy fans, circa '50.

I segued back to Landis. The bio sheet droned on. It's 7/5/48. The maid arrives. Hubby's off on business. "Sexy Rexy" Harrison arrives. He lets himself in and finds the body. Landis left a note. Suicide Attempt #4 succeeds. Rexy's top-lining *Cleopatra*, right now.

Fox, ever-present. Fox, prosaically repetitive. Fox, under my itchy skin.

I was antsy. Paul Mitchell Grenier intruded. I smelled cleaning solvents and his brain residue. The Hats would say *Where Were You?* I had to concoct a good lie. Gwen Perloff intruded. I've called her service four times today. I called Nat and told him to double his efforts on the find-Grenier front. It was pure subterfuge.

I called Miller Leavy. He told me Albie Aadland hired Grant Cooper to rep him. Cooper was the best in the biz. There's a meeting tomorrow. 11:00 a.m. at Miller's office.

I sipped coffee and segued back to Landis. I hit a one-page "Known Associates" list.

Names, occupations, and relationships to Landis. There were seventeen names. Most were male. There were "actors," "friends," "ex-husbands." I skimmed down the page. I recognized no names. I hit Name #14. It screeched at me.

Marcia Maria Davenport/WFA/6/12/19. Twice divorced, lives alone. She was Carole Landis's "personal assistant," '47–'48. She's Divorcée Victim #1, 11/18/61. The Sex Creep kicked his string off with her.

I booked out to West L.A. station. The squadroom hummed. The day-watch guys knew me now. I got stray looks and no more. The Hats plus J. T. Meadows worked at partner desks. They shot me *Where Were You?* looks. I pulled a chair up.

They studied FI cards. J.T. passed me a stack. I went through them. They ran typical. Lone men on foot. Street stop-and-frisks. 10:00 p.m. to 3:00 a.m. Palisades Village to Brentwood Village. Hinky-type men. Loiterers. The unkempt. Guys with downscale westside addresses. Guys with bench warrants out. All jive offenses. Child-support delinquencies, drunk driving, D and D.

They "just felt like a walk." That's the standard peep-and-prowl rationale. They were riffraff. They stood out in the Palisades and Brentwood. Hey, Studley. What are *you* doing here?

J.T. passed a card around. It was dated 1/19/62. I skimmed it. It clicked with Divorcée Job #4. The victim's Arden Jane Brownleigh/10116 Mandeville Lane, Brentwood. The cardee is:

Preston Winslow Fong/Male Chinese/DOB 8/11/24. Address: the Beachglade Motel, PCH. Caddy at Riviera Country Club. Stopped at 10:49 p.m., Wilshire and Barrington. That's one mile from Arden Jane Brownleigh's. Fong was skunk-drunk. He said he "went strolling for kicks." The patrol cops radioed R&I and quick-ran him. They got no wants, no warrants. The West L.A. drunk tank was full up. The cops told Fong to beat it. Catch the Wilshire bus and go home.

J.T. said, "Sid and I interviewed him the next day. He impressed us as harmless. He had a '54 California license. It gave his blood as O positive, so that exonerated him as a suspect. We deep-dipped him through R&I, and the kickback had him suspected of jewelry store smash-and-grabs, going back to '50. He purportedly clouted high-end wristwatches, which he purportedly laid off on the golfers and caddies at Riviera."

Max said, "We should grind him. Crowd him until he gives something up."

Red said, "FI cards wear me thin. He's got the wrong blood. He's not the Creep, so why bother?"

Harry said, "I'm making time with Lila Leeds. That wife-swap job was good for something."

I said, "Lila swings both ways."

Eddie said, "She's not the Sex Creep, so can it."

J.T. said, "I think he saw something that night, but he denies it. That warrants a reinterview, in my book."

I lit a cigarette. "I turned a KA sheet on Carole Landis at Homicide. Divorcée #1 was her assistant, back in '47–'48."

The boys WHOOPED—

We drew straws for the interview. J.T., Max, and I won. Red, Harry, and Eddie stood back. They're working the phones. They're scrounging leads from Realtors and divorce-court clerks. How did the Creep get creeped on these six women?

Marcia Davenport scored her pad in Divorce #2. It was a boss Hawaiian lanai. It showcased teakwood, little waterfalls, topiary shrubs. We parked and walked up. I rang the bell. Some hula ditty trilled inside.

Marcia Davenport opened up. Her gaze bypassed Max and me and zoomed to J.T. She remembered him. He interviewed her before. J.T. entrapped hookers on the job and entrapped lonely women routinely. Max and I flashed credentials. Miss Davenport waved them off and tossed the door wide.

We walked in. The interior was boffo. Sunken living room, teak furniture, tropical-fish tanks. I noticed a wall photo. Miss Davenport wore golf togs. She posed with three other women. They stood outside the clubhouse at Riviera CC.

She pointed us to lounge chairs. We sat down. Spongy cushions went *whoosh.* She said something about drinks and bolted the room. J.T. tapped his chest. *She digs me / I'll take the lead.*

She was gone fourteen seconds. She popped back with a tray crammed with frosty drinks. She carried the tray carhop-style. She hopped cars in her youth. The drinks were already made. She's a juicer. She exemplifies loose ends. I signaled J.T.: *Let me go first.*

I watched the tropical fish slither and glide. Miss Davenport dispensed drinks. She was inappropriate. She fed cops booze at noon. She was horny. J.T. magnetized her. She ignored Max and me. It was rude. I assumed the Sex Creep's perspective. *She's my kind of woman. I'll start my string with her. I'll trash her beautiful home. I'll fuck her up for life.*

She sat down beside J.T. I said, "We're not supposed to drink on duty, you know."

Max caught the toss. "But, as it happens, we're corruptible types."

J.T. caught the rebound. "She corrupted Sid and me, the first time we interviewed her. And she told us to call her 'Marcia' at the door."

She said, "I was about to tell your colleagues that very thing." She had a twang. It was Texas, for sure.

J.T. played emcee. "This is Lieutenant Otash and Sergeant Herman, Marcia. We had a few more questions about the break-in, if you don't mind."

"I don't mind. The *Mirror-News* doesn't seem to mind, either—given the benefit they've accrued from my misfortune. *Really,* that Mr. Bendish. How could he honestly state that I look like or style myself to resemble Marilyn Monroe?"

We ha-ha'd on cue. She's a southern belle. She played to us. We played straight back to her.

J.T. said, "You've redone your home beautifully, Marcia. It's as if the break-in never occurred."

"Aren't you the kindest to say that. And the handsomest, I might add."

J.T. blushed. Max laughed. I came in, abrupt.

"Marcia, would it be safe to call you a Riviera Country Club habitué? You play golf, play cards, go on symphony outings?"

"Well . . . I wouldn't say 'habitué.' Riviera's not exactly a dope den, you know."

"I'll concede that I know dope dens better than I know country clubs."

Marcia downed half her drink. "You're a sketch, Lieutenant. You surely are."

Max sipped his drink. "The lieutenant's leading up to a key question, Marcia. The other women who were burglarized. Did you know them from the club?"

Marcia went *uh-huh*. "Me, Leona, Wanda Jean, Arden, Lorraine, and Dorothy. We're all sisters in devastation, but I didn't know them from the club. They belong to the club, but I don't play golf or cards with them, and they certainly aren't friends that I socialize with. I think Officer J.T. and Officer Sid barked up that selfsame tree the first time they interviewed me."

Riviera. Divorced women. *C* for *constellation*. Caddy Preston Fong. The wrong blood type clears him. He may or may not circumstantially click.

I said, "Let's put your initial interview and the scurrilous and invasive *Mirror-News* series aside for a moment. I'm wondering if you recall an event or an occasion where you and the other five women may have constellated and given this horrible individual a good look at all of you?"

Marcia killed her drink and lit a cigarette. Marcia struck a thinking-cap pose.

"The Gay Divorcée dance at the club. It grew out of some chats a bunch of us unlucky-in-love girls had, and some gripes about how the club management slighted us. Me, Leona, Wanda Jean, Arden, Lorraine, and Dorothy. We all went to the dance and had a whopping good time. I can even tell you the date. It was October 9th, '61. I saved my table-setting card as a souvenir."

Eyeball clicks circulated. Max to me to J.T. and back. The break-ins kicked on the next month.

"Tell me if I've got this straight, please. Divorced women conceived the dance idea, and the word went out. Members—men and women—signed up, and a crew of Riviera waiters, cooks, and kitchen help worked the event. Is that how it went?"

"It sure is. And, I'll tell you, the concept drew quite a crowd."

Signals passed—J.T. to Max to me. Marcia slid something in J.T.'s coat pocket. Oh, shit—it's her phone number. *Call me, sweetie pie.*

"I noticed the way you slung that drinks tray, Marcia. I'll bet you car-hopped at one time?"

"Right with Eversharp. I hopped at Simon's drive-in on Wilshire and Fairfax, back during the war."

"Was that before you went to work for Carole Landis?"

Marcia coughed smoke. My changeup pitch worked.

She crushed her cigarette. "Poor Carole. I haven't thought of her in a dog's age."

"The Sex Creep left a nude morgue shot of her at the Dorothy Trent break-in."

J.T. cut in right behind me. "Marcia, we'd like to get your impressions of Miss Landis. It would be a big help."

Marcia said, "She was friendly to a fault, rather bright, and fixated on men in a surely ditzy way. She surely ignored her wedding vows, and her career was on the skids, and she took pills and went to parties, and she told me she went to a sort of 'speakeasy place' where there was always a party going on. She hinted that the place sometimes became obstreperous, but then she was surely obstreperous herself. Oh, and here's an interesting sidelight to her story. She met two young girls, who were looking for house-sitting work, at that party place. One was Norma Jean Baker, who later became Marilyn Monroe. The other was that actress who got kidnapped a few months ago."

48

Albie Aadland. The nebbish kid brother. Hersh, Ira, and Meyer were beefy and lurchlike. Albie was midsize and slight. He wore a navy blazer and gray slacks. He had that coat-hanger frame.

The DA cut loose his conference room. We sat at a long oak table. We faced off across it. I sat with Miller Leavy. Albie and Grant Cooper faced us.

Leavy kicked it off. "We're here to discuss the August 4th abduction of an actress named Gwen Perloff, along with a series of perhaps interlocking financial-crime, narcotics-crime, and vice-crime conspiracies emanating from the 20th Century–Fox studio, perhaps collateral to the drug-overdose death of Marilyn Monroe. Lieutenant Otash will serve as my chief interlocutor. The lieutenant, Mr. Cooper, and I have spent time together in court, Mr. Aadland. We play fair, but we play rough. That's all I have for the prologue."

Cooper smiled. He was deadly handsome and deadly quick.

"The recently credentialed Lieutenant Otash. Once known as the 'Hellhound Who Held Hollywood Captive.' Hi, Freddy."

I said, "Hello, Grant. Again, good morning, Mr. Aadland."

Aadland smiled. He directly mimicked Cooper and me. I assumed his perspective. He calculated the smile. He learned male bonhomie from his brothers. This is what brusque men do.

"Hello, Lieutenant. It's a pleasure to finally meet you."

Cooper said, "Ask specific questions, please."

Leavy said, "Let's move this along."

I crowded the table. Albie pulled his elbows back.

"Did you participate in the Perloff snatch?"

Cooper said, "My client declines to answer."

I said, "You, Gwen Perloff, Marilyn Monroe, and Paul Mitchell Grenier met at the Hollygrove home. Who was the Mexican boy—your pal, who lived off-site?"

Cooper said, "My client declines to answer."

"Are you involved in Mr. Grenier's pornographic-film racket?"

Albie twitched. Cooper said, "My client declines to answer."

"Were you acquainted with the late Richard Danforth? Mr. Danforth was also known as 'Ronald Dewhurst' and 'Rick Dawes.'"

Cooper said, "My client declines to answer."

I lit a cigarette. Cooper lit a cigarette. Mimic Albie took the cue. His right hand trembled. He fumbled his cigarette. It took three match strikes to light it.

"Are you involved in the passing of bearer bonds, both real and forged, and the trading of bearer bonds for Mexican heroin and other narcotics, with or without the cooperation of a Mexican man named José Bolaños?"

Albie twitched and laced his hands up. Cooper said, "My client declines to answer." I glanced sidelong. Miller Leavy studied me.

"The aforementioned criminal enterprises are currently being perpetrated by separate and differentiated cabals employed at 20th Century–Fox. The looming disaster of the film *Cleopatra* serves as a goad. The cabals are out to provoke a stockbroker revolt and depose the current studio leadership. Have you heard of Mar-Gwen Productions, as in Marilyn and Gwen?"

Albie wrung his hands. He caught himself and placed them flat on the table. Cooper said, "My client declines to answer." He glared at his client. I read him. He's thinking *There's some twisted shit going on here.*

"Are your known-criminal brothers the guiding influence behind the aforementioned criminal enterprises?"

Cooper said, "My client declines to answer." He's giving me free rein. I'm giving him a primer for his presumed courtroom case. Leavy's giving me free rein. He's got Albie pegged as a pervert. He hates perverts. Albie's under the hot lights. Gas Chamber Leavy loves it.

"Are your known-criminal brothers jungled up with Jimmy Hoffa in the aforementioned criminal enterprises?"

Cooper said, "My client declines to answer."

"What sort of aberrant behavior did you, Mr. Grenier, Miss Monroe, and Miss Perloff indulge during your years at Hollygrove?"

Albie's wilting. Cooper eyed him and kept it zipped. He's luring me in.

"Who was the Mexican boy you hung out with? He was allegedly in the peewee corps of the Nite Owl gang. They were primarily a burglary gang, and you and Paul Mitchell Grenier purportedly went on 'burglary runs' with them, in your early adolescence. I might add that Danforth/Dewhurst/Dawes was a burglar, as well. What say ye to that, Mr. Aadland?"

Albie pulled his elbows back. Albie dropped his hands in his lap. His jerky knees knocked the table.

"Do you read the *Mirror*? Have you read about the Sex Creep and his burglaries?"

Shaky knees—Albie's ashtray skittered.

Get him. Crush him now. He's had enough/you've confirmed enough/Cooper and Leavy will call it off soon/HE knows that YOU know.

"Have you heard of a bent headshrinker named Paul de River? Are you a homosexual? Are you familiar with the fuck-deck craze of the late 1940s? Are you aware that your cousin Shelley Mandel invented the fuck deck? While I have you, will you please offer insight on the abduction and probable murder of Mitzi Perloff in February of '37?"

Albie stood up. His chair crashed. He'd wrung his hands red. He hate-glared me and twitch-walked to the door. Cooper came up behind him. He's the lawyer/best pal. He eased Albie out to the hallway.

Leavy rocked his chair back. "You gave Grant a boatload of courtroom ammo. I should have stopped you, but I was too embroiled in the show."

I said, "It's not going to court."

"I'll pretend I didn't hear that."

I undid my necktie and stretched. Leavy said, "He's dirty all right."
No shit, Dick Tracy.

Daryl Gates cranked up the juice. I begged immediate favors. He complied. I knew why.

Bill Parker stepped on his dick again. He blasted "civil rights agitators" and "Comsymps within the civil *wrongs* movement." He gave a talk at the Jonathan Club. He was half-tanked. An *L.A. Times* man attended. Whiskey Bill's tantrum made page three.

The FBI-boss deal was one month and ten days old. Ratfuck Bobby read the newspapers and my summary reports. They were candid. I omitted the killing of Paul Mitchell Grenier and nothing else. Ratfuck understood the levels of my legitimate investigation and Morty Bendish's newspaper shuck. He was complicit in their perpetration. He understood that the LAPD brought big weight to both the shuck *and* my investigation. I was out to smother Monroe/Kennedy rumors. The bonus payment was Bill Parker's FBI appointment. Ratfuck could renege in a heartbeat.

I told Gates we should double down. I needed five Intel cops for phone shitwork, *now*. I needed drift on the Nite Owl gang and their peewee corps, *now*. Our clue clowns should ditz old Hollywood Division hands and get the what for. I need enhanced drift on the Mitzi Perloff snuff. I need it now. The Mitzi snuff popped at the chronological core of the '37 convergence. Gates said he understood and rounded up the men.

I crashed in my cubicle. The Albie interview drained me. Albie was dirty. But how, when, and who with—and to what degree? He was at Hollygrove in '37. He might have roamed the margins of the '48 convergence. Marcia Davenport's revelations now defined said convergence. Marilyn and Gwen. House sitters for Carole Landis. Here's my vibe: they turned call-girl tricks out of the pad in Carole and hubby's absence. Plus the divorcée dance party. It supplied a new Sex Creep suspect pool:

Riviera Country Club. Perved-out members and/or employees.

Exhaustion slammed me. I dozed in my chair. The clue clowns called and woke me up. They reported near-nil results.

The Nite Owls played obscure. Scant paperwork existed. Their peewee corps spawned none. Juvenile arrest and court records were either sealed or expunged. The clue clowns turned no gang-member names. The Owls bopped from the mid-'30s to the early '40s. Their turf ran from Beverly to Melrose, Vine to Van Ness. Hollygrove stood at the west border. The Owls were suspected of a dozen lower-Hollywood B and E's. They were lower-Hollywood boys, *todos*.

The clowns delivered on Mitzi. They ran retirement records checks and sideswiped some old ex-cops who worked the case. I got four confirmations of Del Kinney's spiel. Mitzi was spotted on a westbound Wilshire bus, the same day she vanished.

Here's the big new lead:

An enhanced eyewit account of Mitzi on the bus. The unknown eyewit states *this*:

Two boys seemed to be traveling with Mitzi. They teased her as the bus moved west on Sunset. One boy was about thirteen. One boy was a bit older. There was no further description. I could not track the lead.

Dead children. *Los* Nite Owls. I caromed back to the key question—who's the Mexican boy?

He lived near Hollygrove—check. He joined the Monroe/Perloff/Grenier/Aadland clique—check. I'm running hot today. I just hatched myself a brainstorm.

Intel kept a reverse-directory library. I raided it and grabbed the '35, '36, and '37 books. I scanned addresses and names in my cubicle. I kept a tally of Latin-type surnames. Martinez, Salazar, Sanchez. Arredondo, Guttierez, García, Abado, Contreras, and more. I matched the names to addresses. I nailed Gower, El Centro, Van Ness, Ridgewood, Wilton, Gramercy, Saint Andrews. I nailed Lemon Grove Avenue—and more.

I dredged twenty-seven names. They were mid- to late '30s names. It was a long time ago and a long long shot. It was pavement-pounder shitwork—

I wore my crepe-soled shoes and carried a notebook. I started at El Centro and walked a beat east. Ramon Ramirez on Gower was long gone. Ditto, Gus Mora on Waring. I dipped south. Bobby Gomez and Luis Chasco were long gone. I dipped north to the Orbit Lounge and refreshed myself. I hit a waitress up for her phone number. She told me to fuck off.

I trudged east. I got six straight not-at-homes and six straight jolts of incomprehension. *Man, I wasn't born yet. That's the Stone Age, Daddy-O.*

My feet hurt. I door-knocked sixteen cribs. I had eleven to go. Add on the not-at-homes. That made seventeen.

I door-knocked a wood-frame house on Lemon Grove and Saint Andrews. A man in bus-driver garb opened up. I noticed a fight poster on the back wall.

March 16, '52. Hollywood Legion Stadium. All local talent. Juan Manuel "El Manny" Salas versus El Tigre Flores—walloping welterweight tiff!!!

I badged the man. He acted bored. I asked how long he'd lived in the house. He said his dad bought the house back in the '20s. His dad was a grip at Paramount. It's right down the street. His dad made good bread.

I pointed to the poster. I dropped the "El Manny" moniker. The man said Manny grew up in this very house. He was a *vato loco*. He's his cousin Hector's boy.

49

I went in badge-heavy. The airport cops humored me. My credentials cowed them. They lent me a luggage cart and a stress room on the international concourse. Mexicali flight 291—Guadalajara to L.A.

Hello, Ingrid. Remember me? I soft-played you the first time. I've got corroborative witnesses now.

The airplane taxied up. It was a turboprop job. Festive sombreros were etched on the fuselage. I stood upside my cart, in plain view. Tech men rolled out the off-loading steps. The hatch popped from inside. A dark-haired stew clicked them into place.

Gringo tourists off-loaded. They were sunburned and looked sunsmacked. It was warm in L.A. It was hot in Mexico. The stews kept them lubed and pacified. The *mucho mas* margarita cart trundled the aisles nonstop.

The off-load took twenty minutes. The *turistas* weaved and lugged hand luggage toward the Customs-entry door. I pinned my badge to my left lapel and glowered. I'd see her, she'd see me, I'd gauge her reaction. She'd know it's a roust.

She was third down the steps. She shoulder-slung a garment bag and a big black suede purse. I hopped in the cart and wheeled over. I blocked off the steps. I motioned the pilot and copilot around me. I stood square in front of her. She squeezed the purse and planted her feet.

She held up the line. It was backed up into the airplane. I grabbed her arm and pulled her off the steps. Her feet dragged, she squeezed the purse, she tripped up onto the cart. I hung a U-turn and brodied us up to the Customs door.

Inbound *turistas* gassed the show. Two uniformed Customs men played escort. We bypassed the passport and visa lines and cut right. A Customs lieutenant jogged up and unlocked the door.

I eased Ingrid inside and plopped her down at the table. She squeezed her purse. I pulled it out of her hands and dropped it on the table. I kicked the door shut and hit a fan switch. Cool air blew.

I straddled the spare chair. I lit a cigarette and offered the pack. Ingrid took one. I lit her up.

"You were observed at a beachfront volleyball game. You were selling bearer bonds to your transient lover and Girl Book procurer, Peter Lawford. Your main lover, Manny Salas, appears to have taken part in a kidnapping last month. You told me that a 'queen-bee' cater waitress conceived the Girl Book idea. That was a lie. I asked you if you were running dope in and out of Mexico. You denied it. You denied running bearer bonds. I'm betting you lied there, too."

Ingrid smoked and futzed with her ashtray. I poked her purse and went *tee-hee*.

I flashed a Ronnie Dewhurst mug shot. Ingrid shook her head. I flashed a Gwen Perloff movie still. Ingrid shook her head. I flashed a Paul Mitchell Grenier mug shot. Ingrid shook her head.

She lies. She's quaking now. That's good. She clutched her purse extra tight.

"Burglary's all over this thing I'm working on. Manny went down for burglary in August '54. He went to Chino. He met a stat-rape man named Paul Mitchell Grenier there. I'd say they got tight. I'd say they stayed tight after they got out. Manny got popped for burglary in '57. You said it was a humbug deal, but I don't think so. I think you're fingering burglary scores for Manny, when you're not running dope and bearer bonds and posing for beaver pix."

Ingrid quaked. Ingrid squeezed her purse. I snatched it and dumped it out on the table.

Cosmetics, wallet, house keys, car keys, cigarettes, matches, loose coins. I poked through the wallet. She carried forty-two dollars. El Manny leered in photo sleeves. Driver's license, Mexicali ID card, a slip of paper stashed behind Manny Pic #4.

I unfolded it. It was blue ink–printed. It listed six addresses and eight-digit numbers, all on one line. *"Avenida"* and *"Calle"* meant Mexico. U.S. bearer bonds ran to eight digits. Snap call: Ingrid's got a delivery route.

Ingrid gulped, Ingrid quaked, Ingrid chained cigarettes. I felt the purse, all around. I brushed a lining bulge and pulled my pocketknife. Ingrid mewled and squeaked.

I slashed the lining. I hit an inset stash hole. A glassine bag was stuffed in. It contained white powder. I unfolded the bag and tasted the powder. It was high-grade cocaine.

I rewrapped the bag and tucked it in my back pocket. I pat-patted it. I held up the handwritten list.

"The dope goes with me. That list confirms that you're moving bearer bonds, so I'm honor-bound to inform Customs and the Mexican State Police. I'll give you two hours before I call them. Don't hide out or run, because it will only mess your life up that much more."

Ingrid sniveled. "I know *something* about burglary. It involves that kidnap girl, Gwen, but it was a long time ago. If the Customs guys think I'm playing ball, they might go easy on me."

I said, "Tell me. If I like it, I'll pass it along."

Ingrid chained cigarettes. "It was a long time ago, but it's got a movie-star angle. The Gwen chick knew Marilyn Monroe, from an orphanage they were in. Later on, they were call girls running wild. They used to do house-sitting jobs for rich people, and they fingered burglary scores."

I smiled. "Did you get that from El Manny?"

"No."

"You just heard it somewhere? You pulled it off the grapevine?"

Ingrid nodded—*yes, yes, yes.* Ingrid stroked the airplane wings on her chest.

"I like the tip, but I know damn well you got it from Manny."

Ingrid pouted. "What are you going to do with the *coca?*"

I said, "Sniff it or sell it. I haven't decided yet."

Gwen Perloff was due. She chose the restaurant. She called my service three hours back. "Villa Frascati/Beverly Hills/7:00 tonight."

I arrived early. I wore my best chalk-stripe and scored a tête-à-tête booth. Gwen would be prompt.

I sniffed the *coca grande.* It spurred a work binge. I called Customs and gave them Ingrid's particulars. They scheduled the grab for 5:00 sharp. I called Morty Bendish and laid down a phone edit. He was on to Divorcée #3: Wanda Jean D'Allesio. I told him to lean on the scare tactics, big. Emphasize hot-prowl hunk Donald Keith Bashor. He snuffed two women in '55 and '56. He burned in '57. Raid the *Mirror* photo morgue.

Run shots of Karil Graham, dead. Run a *BIG* shot of Bashor strapped in the Green Room.

Stress the Monroe connection. Monroe OD'd on yellow jackets. The Sex Creep dumped Wanda Jean's yellow-jacket stash in her off-the-boudoir toilet. Employ a *tick, tick, tick* motif. We're up to Divorcée #3. There's three more to go. Then it's August 4—and the Creep's hot date with Marilyn Monroe.

Morty pledged quick compliance. *Jawohl, Herr Freddy!* I rang up Nat and Phil. I dictated their scripts for Doc de River's gig at the Wilshire Ebell, tomorrow. Intel would film it. George Putnam would run it on his TV show, tomorrow night. Putnam was the Chief's favorite right-wing gasbag.

I wrote my daily summary and transmitted it. The Chief/Daryl Gates/ the Hats and Ratfuck Bobby received it. The El Manny/Ingrid leads should gas them.

I eyeballed the Customs grab. I parked across the street and down from Ingrid's stewardess flop pad. I saw El Manny's TV-repair truck parked at the curb.

Coca grande stimulated brainflow. I got a significant jolt. I theorized *this:*

Manny ran his own Monroe listening post. He was the kidnap clique's tech man. I found bug mounts on my 8/4/62 break-in. El Manny installed them and monitored the post. He watchdogged the ditzy Monroe—at Bayless and Gwen P.'s instigation.

I called Bob Kennedy. I begged him to issue a fed warrant on El Manny. El Bobby said, "Maybe." My plan? Serve the warrant and take El Manny someplace secluded. Kick the shit out of him and demand the whole tale.

The grab went down at 5:02. Three Fed sleds/six agents total. They quick-walked down the driveway and quick-walked back with Ingrid cuffed. El Manny followed them out. The Fed sleds laid tread. Manny blew his baby doll a fat kiss.

A maître d' walked Gwen up. She wore a fitted pearl-gray suit. I stood up. The maître d' pulled Gwen's chair out. She entered rooms. She was decorous. She inspired subservience.

I sat down and cut straight in.

"I've put something together. It's a work-up. Feel free to remark on the validity. One—you, Motel Mike, Albie, Paul Mitchell Grenier, and Manny Salas put the kidnap together. Richie Danforth and Buzzy Stein were off to the side. Marilyn was an errand girl, and supplied some *je ne sais quoi*. Two—you and Marilyn were call girls together. You were fingering burglary scores, back in '48. Some shit happened with you two and Carole Landis—but I don't know what it was."

Gwen lit a cigarette. "Paul Mitchell Grenier loves cats. He has a cat-access flap built into his back door, and he always leaves food and water out for them. I've been calling his service—from pay phones, of course—and leaving messages for the past several days. Paul hasn't called me back. I have my own key, so I went over to feed the cats myself."

I clamped down on my water glass. It shook and almost shattered.

"The place had been tossed. Certain paper items had been stolen. I saw traces of bloodstains where someone had applied solvents to dissolve certain stains. I found a fingerprint brush behind an editing machine, and I had a friend check your LAPD personnel file. You took a college forensic course in 1946, and you know how to lift, preserve, and identify prints. You had been quite pointedly looking for Paul Mitchell. I think he interrupted your toss, and you killed him."

The glass shattered. Water sprayed the table. I pulled a large shard out of my hand.

Gwen stood up. She said, "I'm sure we'll speak again."

She grabbed her purse and walked out. She turned heads all the way out the door.

50

The Wilshire Ebell. Home to chamber recitals and prep-school teas. Plus, Moral Rearmament and Ayn Rand study groups.

Eight hundred seats. A raised stage and lectern. The Hancock Park Ladies Guild invites speakers. Paul de River's due today.

His topic: "The Criminal Consciousness of Our Society."

I took an aisle seat. Nat, Phil, and Morty Bendish backstopped me. Nat brought his rowdy kid brother, Kareem. I paid twelve winos to mutter and belch.

It's a put-the-word-out scenario. It may be precipitous. Albie Aadland knows we know. Ingrid Irmgard knows we know. De River will know—if he's sentient and he plays in at all. Gwen Perloff knows we know. She's nullified my knowledge. She knows I killed Paul Mitchell Grenier.

Intel stood ready. Three cameramen and two soundmen rolled film at the back. The AC blew a fuse. The room broiled. Four hundred stiffs squirmed in their seats. They were pensioner age and dead bored. I'm here to furnish distraction.

An old girl walked to the lectern. She introduced "the learned and savvy Dr. de River." She dropped his résumé and ballyhooed his service to the "psychically ravaged" and the "So Cal cognoscenti." De River creaked onstage. I heard his bones pop six rows back. He pledged a fast-paced chat and a Q and A after. He cleared his throat and hocked into a hankie. He needed a haircut. He needed a whisk broom. Scalp gack dusted his suit coat.

De River launched. His faux-French accent dipped in and out. Big words proliferated. The winos sucked T-bird and evinced restlessness.

De River wandered off point. The talk went pity-party. The LAPD fired me/the State Med Board censured me/my Jap publisher owes me money. I support sterilization for habitual criminals and mental defectives. Don't look so shocked. I don't mean snip-snip.

The Doc cranked it and lost it. The emcee lady panicked. She held up an APPLAUSE!!! sign. The clap-claps ran lukewarm. An old lady trekked the aisles with a microphone. Morty Bendish called her over.

He grabbed the mike. "Doc, that criminal consciousness rebop lacks panache. Let's get down to the oooga-booga of crime in L.A. today. By that, I mean the Sex Creep, who's violated the homes of six luscious westside divorcées. I've been writing about it in the *Mirror-News*, and my series has created a burgeoning sensation here in the southland. I'm proud to mention that my brother-in-law, Officer Sid Leffler, put the Sex Creep case together, and he tags the Creep as the most dangerous psycho since Jack the Ripper. Hey, Doc—you know Sid, right? He took classes from you back in the '40s. And, you know, Doc—I'm pretty sure the Creep snuffed Marilyn Monroe."

The audience gasped, tittered, roared. The winos whooped and cheered. De River flushed. He torqued on "Leffler." Sid lied. He said he took the classes. That was it. He said he did not know de River warm and up close. Morty said they were tight. Morty should know. Now de River's clenched up, beaucoup tight.

Nat slid down Morty's aisle. The microphone lady scowled. Morty passed Nat the mike. Nat spieled off my script.

"I heard the Black Muslims put out a contract on the Creep, because they know he's out perving on Negro women."

More gasps, hoots, titters, stomps, cheers—

Kareem yelled, "The Creep's in with the Klan and the Birchers! I predict vigilante action all over the southside!"

Phil slid down Morty's aisle. The microphone lady plotzed. Phil snatched the mike from Nat. More stomps, whistles, hoots—

"Doc, a very astute cop named Jack Clemmons told me the Creep is 100% good for the Monroe snuff, and that Monroe was into some heavy-duty criminal stuff herself."

The emcee lady led de River offstage. A backup dowager pressed an oxygen mask to his face.

———

The caddy lot adjoined the caddy shack. Dirt roads and eucalyptus groves enclosed it. The clubhouse overlooked the course. It was '20s Spanish de-luxe. Capri Drive dead-ended at Riviera. Plumb line: the Landis spread was six blocks due north.

I parked between caddy junkers. Max and J.T. were due. Preston Fong was out on the course. He'd kick loose soon.

I tried to doze. Max and J.T. were late. I'd braced the dining room/ kitchen boss already. He recalled the divorcée dance ball. He didn't know no Sex Creep. The dining room manager hovered. I told him to pull his files on the male slaves who worked the gig. Get me their blood types. Chop, chop on this. He said he'd comply.

I dozed. Some geek knock-knocked my windshield. I opened my eyes. J. T. Meadows scooched into the car.

He just got laid. I know the signs. He grinned, slaphappy. All's right with the world.

"Wipe off that lipstick. Marcia Davenport was wearing the same shade three days ago."

He pulled a handkerchief and scrubbed his face raw. He checked himself in the rearview mirror and cracked a shit-eater grin.

"I picked up some leads, along with the rest of it. Marcia said Monroe and Perloff had no sense of boundaries. They went through the house, trying on Carole's clothes. Some jewelry went missing, or it might have been misplaced. Monroe and Perloff had gourmet taste. They sampled the caviar and the foie gras but ignored the tuna casserole."

Max pulled up. He got out and stretched himself loose. J.T. and I got out. Max said, "Who's this dink again?"

J.T. said, "Preston Fong. He's Chinese, and about thirty-five. His blood type clears him. He's technically clean, but he smash-and-grabs jewelry stores and clouts display watches. There's a bust and a no-file in his jacket, but that's way back in '50. Sid and I interviewed him. I think he saw something that night."

"That night." As in, 1/19/62. Leffler and Meadows braced him on 1/20. Fong was a night bird and a peep-and-prowl artiste. Brother Fong and me. We're *Kameraden* under the skin.

The dink walked toward us. He wore hand-me-down golf slacks and a pink Banlon shirt. He ran five-nine and 140. He sported a flattop. He looked alert.

We squared up to him. J.T. knew him. He kicked it off.

"Preston, this is Lieutenant Otash and Sergeant Herman."

Fong said, "Where's Sid the comedian? That guy was a sketch."

J.T. smiled. "Preston, you weren't entirely candid when we talked to you back in January."

Fong shrugged. "That was months and months ago. I told you, I was drunk. What's going on? There's all this Sex Creep jive in the *Mirror*."

Max lit a cigar. "Officer Meadows thinks you were up to no good, but nobody thinks you're the Creep."

J.T. said, "I think you might have seen something you haven't told us about."

Max blew smoke in his face. "So, we're back to run you through it again. You know how this shit works. We hassle you until you tell us what we want to hear."

Fong rolled his eyes. It was snotty. I stabbed his chest—hard.

"Listen, papa-san—you were a watch clouter way back when, and if you've done it since, we don't care. We're only interested in the Creep, and what you might have seen that night."

Fong pawed the ground. His golf cleats kicked up dirt.

"Okay. I was drunk, and I was looking to get back over to San Vicente. There used to be a jewelry store near that church on Bundy, so I thought I'd do some window-shopping. I was drunk, and I took a wrong turn somewhere. I saw a guy trying to slide up a side window on a really spiffed house. It was on Gretna Green, a big ranch style. He was a tall blond guy, and I knew he was looking to score."

51

The heat broke. Fall hit early. Pat shivered under thin sheets.

I tossed her a blanket. She bundled in and snatched her coffee off the nightstand.

"Jack's worried about the congressionals. It's all he talks about."

I stage-yawned. "I'm worried about your brother indicting me. It's all I think about."

"I'm going to Mass and brunch with Lois. The ten at St. Michael's, this Sunday. I'll be sure to fill you in."

The bed sagged. It held Pat, Lois, and me. Plus Gwen Perloff. Forget church. *They're* my un-Holy Trinity. I should evict Pat and Lois. They stand apart from All Of It. I need Gwen to tell me things.

Pat checked her watch. "The doctor told Jackie she'll have twins next time. She's playing catch-up with Bobby."

"I'm playing catch-up with Bobby. I need a Federal arrest warrant, and the go-ahead to thump a guy."

Pat pillow-thumped me. I squeaked. I mimed a rape suspect spitting teeth.

"Let me read your diary. You can watch me. I'm trying to sustain this thing of ours. It'll give us something to talk about—besides Jack's and Bobby's accomplishments, your shitty marriage, and all the shit I'm in."

Pat laughed. "It's the third time you've asked me. I think you're looking for something specific, and it has to do with some personal agenda you've got going."

She's right. Jack fell in the shit, back in '48. Monroe knew about it. Pat's diary covered that year. I'm in over my head. I'm a clue clown with leads and no conclusion.

———

Hambone Officer Sid. He puts on a show. He works the show. He kills the auditorium lights and runs slides. Sid crowds the lectern. Morty B. straddles a chair, close in. He's "my brother-in-law, the newshound." It's borscht-belt shtick.

Pali High. Packed with moms, dads, and kids. I sat with Lois. Lowell Farr sat three rows up, on the side.

She's got Monroe's fan letters. That means Creep letters. We're back in mid-July. Marilyn and Lowell. They mess around in Marilyn's basement. They come out dirty. Lowell sticks something in her handbag. It's those letters. It has to be.

Sid flashed car-crash slides. Multiple dead/tots thrown free/steering columns punched through chests. The audience gasped. Sid exhorted seat belts and conscientious low-speed driving. Motorcycle decapitation. *Eeeks* and *skreeks* reverberate. Sid segues to kids and dope.

I buttonholed Morty before the show. I *re*-pressed him on Sid and Doc de River. Morty *re*-stressed: they're tight city. Sid's been feeding the Doc LAPD reports for years.

Sid flashed before-and-after slides. Teenage girls in Kodachrome. Shown predope and in the throes. They were good-looking girls. They wore cut-low bikinis. They were nubile in the former shots, ravaged in the latter. They went glow of health to dissolution. Glazed eyes and shrunken limbs. Slack skin and glossy hair gone in tufts. Bikini girls. Always the bikini girls. Akin to the horror pix in *The Sexual Criminal*. Akin to the Weimar-era pix that Marilyn Monroe hoarded.

The lights went up. Some Pali lettermen chanted, "Sex Creep! Sex Creep! Sex Creep!"

Sid pointed Morty to the lectern. Morty ambled up. He said, "Here's a preview of the next installment in my series. I've been in serious consultation with an eminent headshrinker here in the City of the Fallen Angels, and he told me the Creep is living through a 'declension of fan crushes,' which is to say that he crushed on the late Carole Landis, then went on to crush on someone like Jane Russell, then went on to the crush object of the era—the late Marilyn Monroe."

Pali cheerleaders chanted, "Two, four, six, eight!! He's the man we love to hate!! Sex Creep! Sex Creep! Sex Creep!"

"Declension of fan crushes." Timmy Berlin said Marilyn coined the concept. She cited Landis and Russell. "Eminent headshrinker" equals Paul de River. The

Doc shares the concept with Leffler. The Sidster feeds it to Morty. It affirms one thing. De River counseled Monroe as she trucked with Timmy Berlin. It infers de River's criminal designs.

A Pali boy raised his hand. Morty pointed to him. The kid said, "How often do these pervert B and E guys graduate to murder?"

Morty said, "Take this to the bank, junior. The Creep snuffed Monroe. 'Easy come, easy go'—right, kid? 'That's the way, if love must have its day.' Now, in general, Sex Creep types only murder out of jealousy—if they feel that their crush object has betrayed them with a close friend or lover."

Sid bowed. Morty bowed. The audience erupted. They gave the Sid and Morty Show a big standing O. Fan types stormed the stage and waved today's *Mirror*. The headline read *"Creep-O Mania Hits L.A.!!! Cops Investigate Murder Link!!!"*

Lois said, "What a crock of shit."

I scoped the stage. Sid Leffler passed out business cards. Not to adults or male students. To Pali coeds exclusive. He leaned too close as he spoke to them. He brushed their hair every time.

A quickie gig fell on me. The revived Eddie Fisher at the Losers. Four sets, in and out. By invitation only. The club named Eddie "Loser Emeritus." Richard Nixon declined the award.

Nat and Phil worked the rope line and bopped home. I told them to leapfrog El Manny Salas and call in three times a day. Eddie was boffo. He sang his big hits and spritzed his signature self-loathing. Liz gobbles *schvantz* on the Via Veneto. Liz and Dick hatch a mongoloid love child. The full house cracked up.

It was late. Eddie and I yakked in the greenroom. Bo Belinsky raided the pill jars. He craved a nap. Take a pink one and a green one, Bo. You'll doze for sixteen hours. You'll awake refreshed. Take a red one and a blue one then. You'll revitalize.

Bo took a pink one and a green one. He said, "I've got it bad for Liz. Come on, Eddie. Give me a one-night-only pass."

Eddie popped a red one and a blue one. Eddie chased them with Vat 69.

"That's my wife you're defaming. She's the Whore of Rome, and *Cleopatra*'s the sack of Rome, and when Fox pulls production, the Italian economy will tank."

Liz fan-danced me. I recalled old Roddy McDowall dish. It was *Confidential* slush-pile skank.

The late '40s. Teen-star Liz. Roddy was older. He squired Liz around L.A.'s low hot spots. Donkey shows and beyond. Black-white sextravaganzas. Young Liz orbs wild shit. Plus, *this:*

Liz might know wild shit per Fox in duress.

Bo said, "Freddy's thinking and scheming. He's in a trance."

Eddie said, "Freddy's a schemer. It's how he's survived this long."

Bo dozed off. Eddie dropped his cashmere topcoat on him.

"He's pitching today. 2:00 p.m.—the Angels versus the Orioles. He'll sleep right through it."

I sipped Vat 69. "I need some skank Liz might be privy to. She's in L.A., on hiatus—and I want to ease her into the sack with Bo. He'll get me the skank, he'll get laid, and I'll shoot infrared film. It's a *mitzvah*, Eddie. The film proves adultery. It'll cut your alimony nut way down."

Eddie said, "I'm in. The Loser Emeritus has eaten enough shit."

I pulled up to the Pico gate. It was pushing 2:00 a.m. I wanted to brace Roddy McDowall. Bill Parker had ordered me off the lot. Del Kinney had confirmed it. Roddy haunted the costume bins. He was costuming his *Cleo* fuck spoof. He'd be here. I had questions. He needed production bread. I paid good gelt for good answers.

Monroe's fan mail. Riff it for me. Give me Jane Russell's phone number. "Declension of fan crushes." Did Monroe talk that shit up to you?

I approached the guard hut. A late-model DeVille dipped in front of me. Three big men got out.

They blinked and covered their eyes. Well, now. It's the Aadland brothers.

My headlights nailed them. Hersh, Ira, and Meyer. They're russet-haired and blue-eyed. They're Albie A. built full scale and mean.

I dimmed my lights and stepped out of the car. The Aadlands stepped close. They wore cut-trim Sy Devore suits. They ran six-three and 260. The Devore look tanked on them.

Meyer said, "You're working up a derogatory profile on poor Marilyn. It's not exactly a secret, you know."

Ira said, "There's a payoff that our friend Jimmy H. would like to avoid."

Hersh said, "We like Mr. Hoover. We'd hate to see Bill Parker get his job."

Meyer said, "Your profile for Parker and the Kennedys sounds just like the profile Jimmy had you prepare."

Ira said, "Please desist. Please leave Albie alone and stay off the lot—which Bill Parker himself has told you to do."

They were deep-red sclerotic. They radiated ill health.

Meyer said, "Would a large sum of money persuade you?"

I said, "No."

Ira said, "May I ask why?"

I said, "I've got a bug up my ass. I'm not for sale on this one."

52

Lunch in the Palisades. The Canton King Terrace. Lowell Farr, Lois, and me. I blew off the parental-consent note. Lois and Lowell were film-set pals. Lois cast my role and set up the meet.

I was a DA's lieutenant. That's true for now. My queries pertained to Marilyn Monroe. Lois coaxed Lowell and reeled her in.

We sipped green tea. Lois and Lowell critiqued *Twist Party Stakeout*. I studied Lowell and fought off All Of It frustration.

She wore a madras shirtdress and Weejuns. The Aadland approach wigged me. Gwen P. was all stalemate. Phil and Nat tailed Manny Salas. He made nine pay-phone calls this morning. Preston Fong scanned mug books at the downtown DB. The blond B and E man was a likely suspect. Lowell towered over Lois. She'll top six feet, easy. The divorcée-dance-lead dipped sideways. Ray Pinker blood-tested the waiters and kitchen help assigned to the gig. Their blood types cleared them. None was blond. They were R&I and NCIC clean. Daryl Gates got me a phone date with Jane Russell. Hey, Jane—what's this "declension of fan crushes" shit?

Our food came. Lois and Lowell dug in. I pushed my plate away.

Lowell said, "My mom thinks I made up the friendship with Marilyn. None of my friends believes that I actually knew her. You two and Officer Sid believe me, but try convincing my mom."

Lois speared a shrimp. "The people at Pali seem to love him."

Lowell studied Lois and me. She buzz-bombed most everybody. Monroe was like that.

"He grovels for love. I think it's unseemly. He's a stage ham, but he's very insecure."

I said, "Would you call him 'handsy'? Would you say he has a bent for underage girls?"

Lowell twirled her soup spoon. "I'd say he verges on inappropriate. He asks girls their bra size and when they started to develop. A twelfth-grade girl I know says he probably masturbates to excess."

Lois gagged on her soup. She grabbed her napkin and staved off a hurl. I laughed, Lowell laughed. Lois leaned into me. Lowell caught the move. I read her. She thinks we're doing it.

I said, "Lowell, did Marilyn give you a stack of her fan letters, that day you were digging around in the basement?"

She was gobsmacked. She did a broad double take.

"Well, yes she did. How did you know about—"

"And who did you tell about it?"

"Just Officer Sid. He was the only one. I said I hadn't read them—and he seemed to be relieved about that. Then he said I should consign the letters to him, which I did."

Lois said, "What did he intend—"

"He said he intended to sell them, and he said he'd use the money to start a research fund to help out kids with cancer."

Lois rolled her eyes. I said, "Did he tell you who he intended to sell the letters to?"

"No—but he told me he knew a 'rogue psychiatrist,' who was his mentor, and that the man might find them valuable as a research tool."

Rogue shrink de River/Sid, you perved-out piece of—

Lowell said, "There's one other thing. I heard Officer Sid talking to Mr. Bendish at the aud call. Mr. Bendish called his Sex Creep series a 'moneymaker,' especially if he brings in Jack Clemmons to put a 'political spin' on it. Does that make any sense to you?"

Morty knows from opportunity. So do I. I coined the phrase "Opportunity is love."

Bo lived at the Ravenswood. Rossmore, right off Melrose. His digs showcased a wide view. Vine Street by night bedazzled. The pad bedazzled. Living room, two bedrooms, two baths. Black leather furniture and purple-flocked wallpaper. Lava lamps and kooky Kandinsky prints.

We got lucky. Bernie found an interior wall crawl. It bordered the living room and master bedroom. A hinged panel opened on a hallway.

The space was twelve feet long and three feet wide. It was crammed with bunched wires and AC-DC outlets. The bedroom wall was flocked velour. Bo shot us a work sample. We could mount the peephole and sustain a mid-shot of the bed.

It was a four-man/all-day job. Bernie disconnected the wire clumps. We bought off the manager and hogged a freight elevator. Eight trash-cart runs got our gear up. Bernie discovered the wire clumps. Nat and Phil shot Polaroids of the reconnection points. Bernie rewired the crawl space. We wore masks to squelch sawdust inhalation. I installed mikes under bedside lamp shades and Day-Glo wall tapestry. Nat and Phil built a camera box with a floor swivel. I drilled and gouged a hole through the bedroom wall straight through to the crawl space.

We mounted the camera and loaded in infrared film. The floor swivel gave us wiggle room within the static frame. We cocooned the crawl space. We tacked on acoustical baffling as a sound muffler. I fixed a two-way mirror to the interior-bedroom wall. The camera lens peeped straight through to the bed. Specially tinted glass served to magnify the action. Liz and Bo would expand in big-screen Fuck-O-Scope.

We worked. I shitworked and brainworked. I talked to Jane Russell this morning. I laid out the Sex Creep deal and Monroe's "declension of fan crushes" theory. Miss Russell said *this:*

Something like that happened to her. It was '51. She was on The Las Vegas Story *in Vegas. Somebody tossed her suite at the Flamingo. The furniture was dumped and rearranged. She got a mash note in the mail. The dink pasted magazine letters to coarse paper backing. It expressed his deep love. It admonished her not to go the Carole Landis route.*

Jane Russell indicts the Sex Creep. It's a good lead. Here's my backup revelation:

"Declension of fan crushes." Purportedly Marilyn Monroe's concept. She shared it with Timmy Berlin, circa '54.

Marilyn Monroe wasn't smart enough to concoct it. She wasn't prescient. She lacked the brain cells to ascribe the concept to Landis and Russell. The Sex Creep did not creep Monroe's divorcée surrogates until 1961. He did not creep Monroe's new digs until 1962. "Declension of fan crushes" is pure de River–speak. That means this:

Monroe bopped with and gassed on de River. The initial relationship was brief or sustained. It commenced in 1954 and resurrected this year.

Natasha Lytess. She's jungled up with Doctor Paul. The Doc palsied when I mentioned her name. She injected Monroe with collagen. It augmented her big-

girl immersions. She abctted the kidnap gang. Marilyn debuted her obese self at political demonstrations. LAPD footage exists. "Declension of fan crushes." It was Paul de River's mid-'50s construction. It might mean that he knew or knew of the Sex Creep years before the Creep's divorcée break-ins and Marilyn Monroe's late-in-life transit of criminal behavior.

We finished up the hot-wire job. We cleaned up and spot-checked our mess. We packed up our gear and showered in Bo's bathrooms. We put on clean clothes.

The haul-debris-out job took two hours. Monroe/Lytess/de River. I was still shaking inside.

I drove back to Intel. I wanted to screen more Monroe surveillance film. Her immersions. Let's track them backward. The collagen injections. Let's ascribe a time frame to the Monroe–de River bond.

The squadroom bustled. Preston Fong scanned mug books. The Hats and J. T. Meadows chatted up false confessors. The *Mirror* series drew creepy crawlers. The West L.A. squad interviewed the first wave. The second wave engulfed them. Intel caught the overflow. I scanned faces. None of these guys was tall and blond. None fit the thirty-to-forty age profile.

I ducked into the film vault/projection room. I pulled Nat and Phil off their Manny Salas stakeout and told them to poll high school coeds. Make the rounds. Hit Pali High, Santa Monica High, University and Hamilton High. Secure the gist of Officer Sid Leffler. Nat called me an hour back. Dig: Sid was pawing half the girls on the SaMo pep squad.

I hit the AC switch and cooled the room off. I troubleshot the projector and scoped the reels and feeder housing. I checked wall clipboards. Monroe had her own dated index. I caught something, straight off.

The film-can list. Always thirty-two single-spaced pages. It's down to fourteen now. The Monroe shelves were half-depleted.

I saw a penciled-in addition. *"Muslim protest footage/outside PAB/ 4/30/62."* It was the Hoffa-op time frame. That tweaked me. I recalled my daily work sheets. Monroe was not spot-tailed that day.

I orbed shelves and found the film can. I removed the reel and coiled it on the spool. I secured the splice and doused the room lights. Let there be film.

It was black and white. There's Los Angeles Street and the PAB, full-on. The shot fed me the approximate numbers. That's two hundred picket punks on the sidewalk. There's no sound. The geeks jab picket signs. The camera zooms in. They shout and gesticulate. It's uncanny. Wide-open mouths make no noise.

The camera scanned, north to south. I read signs: FREEDOM NOW!/ F——— THE FUZZ!/BLUE FASCISM MUST GO! I read faces. Beatniks, colored priests and nuns, college kids on a lark. I squinted. I trolled for obese shapes. I saw three porky men and—

I recognized a floral muumuu. I'd seen it in her bedroom closet. It's *her*. She's done up Big-Girl-Plus. She's jabbing a F——— THE FUZZ placard. She's been injected. Her face shows it, plain.

She's walking toward a man. He's tall. He's wearing biz attire. He's not a protest type. He's got no grievance and no sign. He's limping. It's a slight hitch-and-walk limp. It's a *left-leg* limp. Marilyn hugs the man and talks to the man. It's Motel Mike Bayless.

Man Camera. Boomerang cut. We're back at 8/4/62.

Marilyn's dead. I enter her house. I note the mashed-down carpet impressions and photograph them. Ray Pinker does a walking portrait. The man's 6'1"/190/big feet/slight left-leg limp. That's Motel Mike, definitive. He's chatting up Marilyn, 4/30/62. He's in her pad the night she died, 8/4/62.

Kwan's was cave-dweller cool and underlit. I killed two hours there. I sipped ginger ale and doodled. I scrawled names and drew connecting arrows. I drew question marks beside them. I did not extrapolate, assume, or surmise. I got out and walked back to the PAB. I saw a Fed sedan parked at the curb.

Eddie Chacōn stood beside it. He waved me over and cracked the back door. I slid inside. Ratfuck Bobby passed me an envelope.

"It's a Federal grand-jury subpoena for Juan Manuel Salas. I'm going forth with your brainstorm, but I'm not ready to impanel the jury yet."

I sniffed the envelope. It smelled good. *Opportunity is love.*

"Max Herman and I will pick up Salas, within the next few days. We'll lean on him and debrief him."

Ratfuck rolled a cigar. "I would expect no less of you."

I said, "The Aadland brothers crowded me last night. They told me to desist, offered me money, warned me off the lot, and said Jimmy would very much appreciate my compliance. I told them no."

Ratfuck lit the cigar. "You have my word that I will not seek indictments on you and your men for the Hoffa op. I'm setting other traps for Jimmy, and they do not include his Monroe incursion. Additionally, I've told Miller Leavy not to take action on you and the Hats for your misadventure with Richard Danforth."

I said, "Thank you, sir."

The AG passed me a cigar. "What else do you need, as of right now?"

"I need Eddie for a black-bag job on Paul de River. He's eyeball-deep in this whole thing."

"How close are you, as of right now?"

"You and Jack are squeaky-clean. The Sex Creep killed Marilyn Monroe. That's the official version. The American public will eat it up. Piddling versions of desperate phone calls and White House adultery don't stand a chance."

Ratfuck blew smoke in my face. I stepped out of the car.

The missing Monroe footage gored me. I walked straight to Daryl Gates' office. Gates pointed to a chair. I sat down and eased the door shut.

"The Monroe film-can index has been reduced, at least 50%. I need to know what you know."

Gates moved his in-tray and dropped his feet on his desk. He dipped his chair and laced his hands behind his back.

"It's a cash trade with the Sheriff's. Pete Pitchess wants his department covered if this whole Monroe publicity craze extends, and if Morty Bendish's series fizzles out, and the public starts getting an itch for new answers. Pete wants *his* department to be the one to leak the word on Monroe as a Commie, so that he can buff his anti-Red credentials and look like he was wise to Marilyn's subversive shit from the gate."

I said, "I get it—but there's more."

Gates said, "There is, but let me start with a disclaimer. I will not in any way seek to circumvent the Chief's FBI-boss deal, or the PD's suborning of your Monroe-Kennedy incursion. That said, I'm backing Pitchess for the FBI-boss job."

I flinched. For one half second. The gestalt hit me then.

Gates sighed. "Bill Parker is losing it. I don't think he'll last much longer. The booze, the bum ticker, the way he blew the Muslim deal, the way he keeps shooting his mouth off. I don't think he'll *live* until Jack Kennedy's reelection. To top it off, Sam Yorty's gunning for him now. The Chief ordered Intel to shoot surveillance footage of Mayor Sam in plain sight. He'll step on his dick once too often, and Sam's promised me his job if the Chief dies, or gets the FBI nod, or does something so egregious that the City Council votes to can him."

I crossed myself. Bill Parker, double-dealt. Bill Parker, self-complicit. Bill Parker—I owed him and honored him—which Gates damn well fucking knew.

"I want you to keep quiet about this."

Gates said, "Okay."

"The Hats and me. We need to put the boots to Sid Leffler. He's dirty up the ying-yang."

Gates said, "Okay."

"When the time's right, I want Pete Pitchess to deliver Mike Bayless into LAPD custody."

Gates said, "Okay—but what do we get out of all this?"

I lit a cigarette. "Bobby K. pledged a no-file on my Hoffa op. He told Miller Leavy to desist on Richie Danforth. He's going with my grand-jury proposal. The sealed testimony, the whole deal. We're going to bury all of it."

Gates clap-clapped. "That's nothing but good news. But it rather implies that Jack and Bobby are dirty within the All Of It, because the Kennedys only look after themselves."

53

The crawl space broiled. Bernie and I worked in our skivvies. Bo and Liz dined at La Scala. Bo dialed his home phone ten minutes back. It rang three times. That meant *We're on our way.*

He memorized his script. He knows what to dig for. We're filming it in Fuck-O-Scope. The camera's packed with infrared and aimed at the bed. The two-way mirror enhances the picture. We've checked the mike feeds five times. We're on go, go, *go.*

It's fifteen minutes to blastoff. The kids are en route. Beverly Hills to Hollywood. Thin Sunday-night traffic. Beverly to Rossmore and north. Bo drives fast—he's got a '61 Vette.

Bernie said, *"Oy."* We couldn't smoke. We dripped sweat on the camera box and tripod.

I heard the front door creak. I heard keys jiggle. I heard *clump, clump, clump, clump.* They've kicked off their shoes. The microphones magnified sound. A hallway light hit the bedroom doorway. I checked the viewfinder. The camera field glowed pink-red.

Bo: "I can't believe this is happening."

Liz: "Relax, doll. It's Camelot, or haven't you heard? We've got a license to swing."

They entered the bedroom. Zippers *skreeked.* Foot scuffs approached the bed. They've entered the frame. Bo turned on a nightstand light. It clarified the pink-red. Bernie adjusted the zoom lens. Their star faces popped—identifiable-plus.

They full-body clinched. They stood by the bed and peeled. They're in the buff. They tumble. Bedsprings *creak-creak.*

Bernie dethrottled the lens. He framed a full-bed shot. They foreplayed on a tufted duvet. They moaned and said stupid shit like "Fuck" and "Oh, baby." The foreplay protracted. It was all pink-red legs, backs, breasts, and asses. Bernie jiggled the lens upward. He nailed key facial footage.

The *Oh, baby*'s escalated. There's the missionary capture. The *Fuck*s and *Oh, baby*'s garbled, pitched, and went monotone. The mattress creaked in sync. I timed the ride off my wristwatch. It ran seventeen minutes and fourteen seconds.

Silence. Liz lights a cigarette. The smoke plumes pink-red. They're supine now. They mime the French Nouvelle Vague. It's the postfuck languor shot.

Liz *re*-sparks. She motormouths. It's defamatory small talk. Richard Burton's hung like a light switch. He never washes it. Joe Mankiewicz is a crypto fag. Lassie's replacing her in the role of Cleopatra. Really, cupcake—it's that big a dog.

Grab the opening, numbnuts—she just tossed you one.

Bo: "I know Fox is in the shit, and that there's rumors floating around. Fox has turned into a real hornet's nest, what with all the vice and money-crime stuff that's supposedly happening. See, the people there are trying to protect themselves and build nest eggs in case Fox goes in the tank."

Liz: "Yep, and 'vice' doesn't even begin to describe it. How's this sound? Two-week wife-swap parties in Jamaica, with cheap charter flights piloted by unlicensed pilots. It's called 'Fox Tail Airlines,' because you've got all-nude stewardesses who wear these fake fox tails, so you can pull them when you want more cocktails or more peanuts. If that's not your scene, how about boy's-night-out weekends in Tijuana, with visits to the Chicago Club to catch the donkey show, plus all the pills you can gobble, and Mexican State Police escorts all the way. Also, you've got to gas this. The guy who put all this together is a hunky Mexican cat named José Bolaños, who is not only a Communist but was the late Marilyn Monroe's lover."

Bo: "Wow. Marilyn Monroe's lover, huh?"

Liz: "*Es la verdad*, cupcake. José's a piece of work. He's allegedly mob-connected, here in the States. As in, Jimmy Hoffa and the Aadland brothers, who still have some clout at Fox."

Bo: "Wow. Marilyn Monroe, huh? She had a thing with this beaner, José?"

Liz: "Roddy McDowall spilled the dish to me. Marilyn was José's slave. She ran heroin in and out of Mexico for him, in disguise yet—with fake passports, the whole megillah."

Bo: "I've always heard Marilyn wasn't that bright. She must have had help with the documents and disguises."

Go, Bo, go! You've got Motormouth Liz primed to talk!

Liz: "You hit it on the head, doll. Marilyn always had a coterie of sycophants, brown-nosers, and quacks calling the shots for her, and telling her she was a genius. She was hooked on this quack shrink, who palled with this dyke drama coach of hers, and they shot her up with collagen, to pudge her up in the face. She moved into a house near Marilyn, to coach her. I swear it's all true! Marilyn told Roddy, and Roddy told me!"

It's confirmed. Doc de River and Natasha Lytess—all jungled up.

Bo: "Wow. This Roddy guy sounds like a sketch."

Liz: "I love Roddy. We were kiddie stars together, way back when. He got shafted on *Cleopatra,* but now he's getting his revenge. The A brothers are financing a series of gay smut films that Roddy's directing. And, dig—they're all *Cleopatra*-themed, with costumes from the actual film!"

Bo: "Wow. All this studio-scam stuff sure is interesting."

Liz: "How's this? This accountant at Fox—he's actually an Aadland—is planning guided sex tours to Haiti and the Dominican Republic. The A boys have got connections with the dictators down there, so everything is safe, and chaperoned by the Tonton Macoute and Dominican State Police goons."

Bo: "Wow. What about this bearer-bond racket I've been hearing about?"

Liz: "It's all true! This hack actress, Gwen something, knows forgers who concoct consecutive-number bonds that look like the real thing, and they don't get found out until later, when the stupes try to cash them in. It's crazy! I bought two bonds, just for kicks."

Bo: "Wow. These guys the A brothers have supposedly deep roots at Fox. I'm an East Coast guy, so hoods have always intrigued me."

Liz: "They go back to the '30s at Fox. If it's illegal, they're entrenched in it."

Bo: "They've got a cousin who's legit, though. He used to be my Uncle Sol's doctor, back in the '40s. Shelley Mandel. My dad said he was a mensch."

Liz: "Dr. Shel was as bent as bent gets. The Fed Narcotics Bureau has been monitoring him since the late '40s, for supposedly peddling illegal penicillin, when, in fact, he was giving it away to all these call girls he was obsessed with, and to these hard-nosed Israeli guys. He did his bit during the big VD epidemic, and, boy, did he ever overprescribe! I got my first Benzedrine and Demerol from Shel."

Bo: "He sounds like a swinger. What's he doing now?"

Liz: "He's a recluse. He's hiding out at some sort of chemical lab at the beach. The BNDD keeps track of him, sort of halfheartedly."

Bo: "He must have swung too hard for too long."

Liz: "Shel was a Renaissance cat, and he was tight with the A boys. They owned a string of fuck pads back in the '30s, and Shel bought the one in West L.A. off of them after the war. Here's something wild. Roddy took me to it, when I was something like sixteen. Anything goes, cupcake. I couldn't believe my young virgin eyes. It must have been the summer of '48, because Carole Landis was seen at the place right before she suicided."

Tilt/bingo/three-cherry jack—

Bo: "You and Roddy were both pretty young then, and that fuck pad sounds like a pretty rough place. I hope you had someone who knew the ropes showing you around."

Liz: "We had two storm troopers for escorts. Real Gestapo types. A motorcycle cop named Norm Krause, and a younger guy named Jack Clemmons, who'd applied to the LAPD. You want to hear something ironic? He was the cop who caught the dead-body call on Marilyn Monroe!"

Bo: "Wow. That is some ironic shit."

PART 9
BLACK BAG

(SEPTEMBER 17–28, 1962)

54

Late stakeout.

I was banned. I had no Fox-lot access. I parked outside the north parking slots and peeped in.

It was late. Roddy worked late. His '54 Skylark stood by itself. He worked in Soundstage #22. Wide-open doors let light out and cool air in.

Roddy had all-lot access. The A boys pulled strings. Roddy worked for them now. Roddy, the smut-film kingpin.

Roddy knew the score. I paid hot bread for hot tattle. We've trekked that road before. I knew his MO. The bars closed at 2:00. He'd leave soon or work all night.

He rolled at 1:12. He padlocked Stage 22 and remote-controlled the north gate. I rolled right behind him. He shagged the Skylark. He cut to Olympic eastbound and north on Crescent Heights. I was right behind. Roddy's got a yen. It's the Jaguar or the Tradesman tonight.

I drop-tailed him. I laid back and kept my headlights short of his back bumper. He cut east on Santa Monica and U-turned up to the Jag.

The Jag was rough trade. Roddy jumped out of his sled and into the perv pit. I ticked seconds off my wristwatch and followed him in.

It was old movie night. A bedsheet served as a screen. The projector ran off track. Grainy footage and German voices revealed the plot. It's a Nazi bunkhouse flick. Fritzie types strutted in jockstraps and peeled from there.

The boys wore pajamas and lounged on sleeping bags. Slumber party—the humps would ogle and hoot until noon.

Roddy stood at the bar. He saw me and three-syllable groaned. He rubbed his fingers and went *So?* I said, "Lots." He hooked my front belt loops and bitch-led me out to the alley.

The temperature dropped. We leaned against an old VDub and lit cigarettes.

"I want to invest in your *Cleo*-spoof series. If the Aadland brothers are investing, it must be a high-yield deal."

Roddy sighed. "Who told you? Which hunky centurion did you extort the information from?"

I said, "Liz Taylor told me."

"That fat twat. I rue the time I've put into her, lo these many years."

I pulled out my flash roll. I peeled off twenty C-notes and fanned them. Roddy crunched my hands and pried the bills loose.

He said, "For starters, you realize. I'm taking Dirty Cleo Productions public, but I'm giving you this early investment opportunity, in light of our long and collegial relationship."

I tossed my cigarette. "Lay it out. You were showing Liz around some local hot spots, circa '48. I need to know how Carole Landis and Shelley Mandel might fit in. Follow my lead here. Fuck pads, fuck decks, two cop escorts named Norm Krause and Jack Clemmons, and two call girls named Monroe and Perloff in the vicinity, house-sitting for Carole Landis, who's in some sort of final tailspin."

Dirty Roddy. He stuck a hand in my pants pocket and removed my cigarettes. He lit up and blew high smoke rings.

"Carole was desperate, sad, and wild to the core. How many times can one marry without glimpsing the essential emptiness of the act? She posed for a deck with the prodigious 'Captain Hook.' He was a smut legend of the postwar era. It was shot at Shelley's fuck pad on the Palisades-Brentwood border, although I can't recall the look of the house, or the address. Orson Welles manned the camera. There's one for *cinéastes*, worldwide. I retained a copy of the deck, for my investment portfolio."

I said, "More on Landis. Chop, chop—you're stringing this out."

"Reminiscence is an art, and I refuse to be rushed. But I will work toward brevity here."

"Roddy . . ."

"All right. Carole was on her fourth husband, and concurrently in love with Rex Harrison, and a Junior League type. She was always falling in love and always trying to live straight—but she always went for the momentary thrill every time she got bored, like so many of us. Krause and Clemmons? They chaperoned studio biggies and visiting-

L.A. notables on junkets to gay bars, drag balls, black-and-white tryst spots, fuck pads, dope dens, and the live-sex pits down in T.J. Krause had an in with Chief Worton—the interim man between C. B. Horrall and your pal Bill Parker."

I rolled one finger. *Come on / I'm paying you / pick up the pace.*

"All right. *Yes,* I knew Marilyn and Gwen house-sat for Carole. *Yes,* but you have to consider the fact that Gwen was and is nothing but a criminal—so if *she* was working a house-sit gig, there had to be a money angle somewhere."

A '57 Chrysler rock-rock-rocked on its struts. Four male feet poked out a back window.

I said, "Shelley Mandel."

Roddy shrugged. "I always liked him. I think he got too far embroiled with the Aadlands, and it unnerved him a bit. The last I heard, he had retired to Terry Lux's dry-out farm. He's got his own lab there, and he screws around with microscopes and blood cells."

The Chrysler rocked on overdrive. The bare feet flailed. The S and M flick blared Wagner. The Jaguar boys had taste.

55

Terry Lux. Noted plastic surgeon. His farm had legs. His farm hid out and dried out Nazis on the run and big film folk. Terry cut rich Japanese to look Chinese and saved them from the World War II internment. Terry treated rare diseases and soaked rich stiffs dry. Folks lived at the farm. Terry catered to xenophobes/remittance men/fugitives from government committees.

The farm was gated and patrolled by goons in golf carts. Evil mastiffs abetted them. I turned east off PCH and climbed the Malibu bluffs. A gate guard met me. I'd called ahead. I dropped my name and Hersh Aadland's. It worked. The guard told me to park. It was cart turf the rest of the way.

He wheeled me through a bulb-lit tunnel. We went under PCH. Car traffic hummed four feet above us. We exited on the beach side. We hit a paved road and passed two guard huts. I saw bungalows up ahead.

We passed them. I was antsy. Lois gave me a reel of *Twist Party Stakeout.* "Second-unit director" Sid Leffler shot it. I projector-screened it at Intel.

It was sound-dubbed. Pali High girls gyrated to the beat of the "Twist Subversives." They wore low-slung bikinis. They dirty-dogged it through the "Sexaholic Twist." Lois said Sid wrote the song. Lowell Farr twisted among them. Her bikini top dipped half off.

It gored me. It stutter-looped through my head. It left me unhinged. Then Gwen called my service. She was peremptory. "Frascati at 8:00."

We blew past the bungalows. We turned down a frontage road shrouded by date palms. I smelled brewed chemicals. I saw two small stucco buildings. Residence and lab. Skulls and crossbones were stenciled on both.

I hopped out. Dr. Shel stood on his porch. He was fifty-five. He was tall, lanky, and sunburned. He wore a lab coat and Bermuda shorts.

I stepped up on the porch. The cart U-turned and brodied off. Dr. Shel said, "Federal or local? I get visitors sometimes."

I said, "Local."

"With questions pertaining to?"

"No sore subjects. I know you never sold black-market penicillin. You gave it away to lovely young women, which I laud you for."

"Don't forget Israel. I gave most of it to Israel. I'm a son of the diaspora, and my humanitarian efforts for Israel more than compensate for my efforts to woo those 'lovely young women.'"

I smiled. "Israel and women. You're preaching to the choir here."

Dr. Shel steered me inside. His front room was beach-motel kitsch. A wood-paneled den opened up behind it.

"You're not Vice? You're not going to roust me for conceiving a certain kind of playing card? For once owning a property rather indecorously known as a 'fuck pad'?"

I torqued him. "No, but I'd like you to give me the address of the place."

Dr. Shel said, "11868 Pavia Place. It's an upscale address where some admittedly downscale activities took place."

Pavia Place crosses Capri Drive. Carole Landis lived on Capri. Riviera CC adjoins Capri. The Landis house and the fuck pad sit one third of a mile apart.

"Hell, Doctor. You were a young buck then. Your good deeds have more than compensated for your indiscretions."

Dr. Shel showed me into the den. It parodied all dens. The knotty-pine walls. The black-and-white fan glossies. All signed to "Dear Dr. Shelley." All ascribed thus:

"Thank you for your good work in helping me to overcome the malady too embarrassing to name."

Identical inscriptions. Familiar faces. Local politicos, film stars and athletes. Many good-looking and anonymous young women.

Along with:

Jeanne Carmen, Lila Leeds, Barbara Payton, Deedee Grenier. No Carole Landis and no Marilyn Monroe.

Dr. Shel laughed. "I told them all to write the same disingenuous and innocuous thing. I hate to see people incriminate themselves."

I said, "I don't see Marilyn Monroe or Carole Landis."

"That's because they weren't similarly afflicted."

I turned and stepped toward the front room. I saw two unin-scribed photos. They sat atop a TV set. They were pride-of-place/ off-by-themselves.

Robert F. Kennedy and Gwen Perloff. They were in their early twen-ties then.

"Well. There's our new attorney general, and a very lovely woman. I'm guessing they weren't afflicted, either."

Dr. Shel deadpanned me. I felt All Of It contract and expand.

I slow-cruised Pavia Place and found the house. It was a '20s-vintage Spanish Colonial. It was a hell-bent fuck pad in 1948. It's a square-ass-family home now.

Jungle gyms and water slides cluttered up the lawn. A sign was staked in the frontyard grass. It announced the location shoot of *Twist Party Stakeout*.

11868 Pavia Place.

Marilyn Monroe sketched this house. She signed the sketch and dated it: 6/22/48.

I arrived at Frascati early. I sat in *our* booth. In *our* private nook. I brain-screened the two photographs. I did not ascribe meaning. It would blow all prior meaning sky-high.

I was fried. I worked my cubicle phone for three hours straight. I called Lois and asked her who picked Pavia Place for the *Stakeout* loca-tion. Lois said, "Sid Leffler." I called Morty Bendish and buzzed him per Sid, sotto voce. Morty restressed:

Doc de River feeds Sid all his highbrow cop perceptions. De River fed Sid all his highbrow Sex Creep riffs. Sid and the Doc talk at least once a day.

I called Red Stromwall. Red beefed the fake confessors swarming the PAB. Morty's *Mirror* series set off an avalanche. Preston Fong's still scanning mug books. The downtown DB logs forty-six books, total.

Harry and Eddie are *re*-bracing registered sex offenders. J.T.'s steer-ing them through. It's a thankless job. They've cleared these geeks already. It's major-case shitwork at its worst.

I called Del Kinney. I told him to buzz his old pals at the ABC. I want to raid Norm's Nest. It's ultradirty. The Grenier sibs are running badger games out of there. Norm Krause and Jack Clemmons are dirty. They're embroiled in a right-wing-nut group called the White Dog Bund. Del was skeptical. I pulled out the stops and punched him in the heart.

"I'm working angles to pull Gwen out of the shit on the kidnap job, and crunching Krause and Clemmons is one of them."

Del said, "Okay, Freddy. I'll try."

She wore a gray twill suit tonight. Plus new gray hair and new tortoiseshell glasses. I memorized her DMV stats. I was four years, two months, and five days older than her.

I stood up. *Our* waiter pulled her chair out. He signaled a drinks waiter. He brought the martinis.

We sipped them. We lit cigarettes. I conjured Doc Shel's photographs.

Gwen said, "I talked to Del a few hours ago. He told me there might be a chance for certain people involved in what you call 'All Of It' to walk away clean."

"I'll get to it. I had a question first."

"As to?"

"Your criminal career."

Gwen crushed her cigarette. "It's blunt, but I'll play. I keep a list of criminal offenses, and calculate the exact day the statute of limitations elapses."

I said, "For instance?"

"For instance, I fingered a house burglary on June 11, 1948. The statute expired on that day, seven years later."

Landis. The house-sitting job. She indirectly tweaked me.

"Don't stop there."

"I set up a payroll heist on February 9, 1950. That's it for now."

I leaned close. Our arms brushed. Gwen did not flinch.

"You could waltz on the kidnap job and everything else you're involved in. That goes for your partners, too—as long as they haven't crossed some lines that the Feds and Bill Parker can't live with."

Gwen leaned close. Our fingers brushed. I stifled a flinch.

"You're the one who's crossed the line. With Richard Danforth and Paul Mitchell. I can live with Danforth, but Paul Mitchell's something else."

"Why Danforth? What's your grievance there?"

Gwen said, "I'm not telling you."

I coughed. "I'll lay the deal out for you. There'll be no loopholes and no surprises."

"Tell me. And tell me why you specified the Feds when you first mentioned it."

I said, "You were right, at the gate. It's a buyback deal initiated by Bob Kennedy and Bill Parker—and that includes the Sex Creep buzz in the *Mirror*. It's all about squelching Marilyn-and-Jack rumors, and your kidnap fiasco, and all the scams at Fox got crammed in, along with my Danforth blunder. The initial plan was to bury all of it with a Federal grand-jury play, secret testimony, blanket immunity, and heavy punitive measures for any and all public exposure of sworn testimony. But—as of right now—I'm thinking the AG will let all the would-be testifiers off with sworn and sealed testimony, and no courtroom appearances."

She did not blink. Not at "Federal." Not at "Bob Kennedy."

Gwen said, "I'll think about it."

I said, "I know a woman. I keep asking her if she loves me. She always says, 'I'll think about it.'"

Gwen not quite smiled. I leaned close.

"I read your sister's file, at Hollywood station. I found a corroborative eyewit statement, and I doubt if Del Kinney's seen it."

"Tell me."

"Two boys were with Mitzi on the bus. They were teasing her. One was about thirteen, the other a bit older."

Gwen stood up. She said, "I'm sure we'll speak again," and walked out.

56

Leffler was due. Max called him and set up the meet. Phil and Nat submitted briefs. Sid stands accused. We had him for stat rape and coerced oral cop. Nat and Phil turned nineteen complainants. They posited a hundred felony counts. Sid had skeeved westside girls since '50-something.

The downtown May Company. 10th and Broadway. The rear parking lot. Harry and Eddie picked the spot. Red set up the space.

An abandoned storeroom. Located just inside. One chair and one bright lightbulb. *We have some questions, Sid.*

We packed palm-weighted sap gloves. Stitched-in buckshot jacked the heft. J. T. Meadows was home with his wife and kids. Or out poking Marcia Davenport. J.T. and Divorcée #1. They got a thang going on.

Leffler showed. He cut in off Broadway and hit his brights. Red yanked the service door up. Leffler idled up. We walked into his lights.

That's right. It's five guys. You thought Max came alone.

Red and I worked the door. Leffler went all doe-in-the-headlights. Red pulled him out of his sled. I snatched his belt gun and dumped the shells. He thrashed. I arm-barred him and frog-marched him inside.

Harry kicked the door shut. Eddie cuffed him to the chair. I said, "You've got suspect relationships. We're here to discuss them. You had a long run with the girls, Sid. That's why we're going this route."

Leffler popped sweat. His glasses slid down his nose. We stood over him. Max and Eddie kicked the chair slats. We pulled on our gloves. Leffler pissed his pants. Note the lap lake.

I love-tapped him. Leffler's head snapped. He bit his lips and drew blood. I double-stuffed my gloves. Buckshot *and* ball bearings. They doubled the heft.

Max said, "We're going to run some names by you. You hear the name, you acknowledge it, you tell us what you know. That's the drill here. Prompt answers will serve to spare you pain."

I said, "Marilyn Monroe."

Leffler said, "Dead movie star. Killed by the Sex Creep, if I'm any judge of my brother-in-law's dramatic designs."

I cuffed him. His head snapped. The thump induced reverb. Leffler yelped and popped tears.

"No smart answers. You hear a name, you answer one of two ways. You say, 'I don't know any more than you do,' or you say, 'I have information.'"

Leffler went *Yes yes yes.* "I don't know anything you don't know. Come *on*, she's Marilyn Monroe."

I said, "Gwen Perloff?"

Leffler went *Yes.* "I don't know any more than you do. I've never met her, I've never dealt with her on the job, I've read about her, and that's it."

Red said, "Richard Danforth. Aka 'Ronnie Dewhurst' and 'Rick Dawes.'"

"The same answer, you fucking sadists. You're beating on a brother officer here—and guys like you always pay in the long run."

I cracked him. Leffler yelped loud. I ripped an eyebrow loose. Blood dripped in his eyes.

Leffler *shrieked.* "No, no, no. I don't know."

Eddie said, "Juan Manuel Salas? Aka 'El Manny'?"

"I don't know him. I don't know any more than you do."

He blubbered it. He gnawed his lips and stained his mouth red.

I said, "Paul Mitchell Grenier."

Leffler went *Yes yes yes.* "Him, I know. But he's just a punk I've seen around the Fox lot. His kid sister Deedee filed a missing-person report on him yesterday. He's a *faigelah,* and some sort of fly-by-night."

Harry said, "Albie Aadland?"

Leffler spit blood and squirmed in his chair. He was tight-cuffed. Cuff ratchets gouged his wrists raw.

"Albie's a jock-sniffer. He collects tough guys like regular guys collect baseball cards. His idea of kicks is visitor's day at Chino."

I said, "You worked guard gigs for the Aadlands in the '30s and after the war. You were a fuck-pad habitué. Give us something there."

"What's to give? It was an 'anything goes' scenario. I kept my eyes shut and my head down most of the time."

Max lit a cigar. "Carole Landis, Shelley Mandel, Norm Krause, and Jack Clemmons. Plus a rackets surge at Fox, right now."

Leffler coughed. "You dumb bunnies dumped a kidnap suspect, and now there's hell to pay. I can spell *buyback* as well as the next guy. How long do you think Morty can keep up his jive series before people get bored? Does *Der Führer* Parker honestly think his deal with Bob Kennedy is anything less than an open secret? He's too old, he's too drunk, his health's in the shit—"

I bitch-slapped him. I split his lips and tore a nostril loose. My glove stitches popped. Buckshot and ball bearings blew wide.

Leffler screeched. That one hurt. He bucked his chair. His legs spasmed.

Eddie said, "High school girls. We've got nineteen complainants. They'll swear out perv-one warrants."

I said, "Lois Nettleton and Lowell Farr told me you've got a type. Lowell said you cherry-picked the cast of your twist-party flick."

Leffler bleat-laughed. A loose tooth dropped in his lap.

"I don't need to grovel for young cooze, and I don't need to break the law. I'm in the Industry, bubi. I've got carte blanche. I always make them crack out some ID. Show me you're legal, kid. I'm a policeman, and I know the law."

I lit a cigarette. "That house on Pavia Place. Why'd you choose it for the film location?"

"It was a fuck pad back in the ice age, but I knew the new owners rented it out for shoots. I'm an auteur. I know my shit. I'm a pro in a world full of amateurs, so—"

Harry cut in. "Paul de River. Give us the drill on that quack."

Leffler spit blood. It hit Harry's shoes. Leffler played kamikaze. He called up punk bravado.

"He's ten times the man, with twenty times the intellect, of all you fascist slugs. We've been tight since before the PD canned him. I feed him all my best file dirt. He pays me twice my salary, and he reveres me."

I gut-punched him. I heard ribs crack. Leffler shrieked.

"This is straight from Lowell Farr. Monroe gave her her fan mail for safekeeping, but you talked her out of it. You said you intended to sell it—so who did you sell it to?"

Leffler coughed. He upchucked two teeth and a slice of his tongue.

"I sold it to her shrink, Ralph Greenson. I didn't even read the letters. My pal Dr. Paul's her radical shrink. He said he didn't even want them.

He already knew this Sex Creep guy, and he figured half of the fucking letters were from him."

Sheared ribs pierced his shirt. Dark blood bubbled out.

Looks traveled. The Hats to me and back. *He can't take much more. Let's dump him at Georgia Street.*

Max uncuffed him. Harry and Eddie stood him up on his feet. He weaved and puked gastric bile.

Red said, "You're fired. That's straight from *Der Führer,* himself."

57

The grand jury's impaneled. They're strictly rubber-stamp. They want Manny Salas *NOW.*

They want "All tools and electrical articles, paraphernalia and electrical devices, as obtained from Mr. Salas' workplace. Plus all articles of electrical gear that might prove efficacious in the practice of illegal surveillance."

Witness warrant/search warrant. Max and I worked for Ratfuck now. Manny always clocked in at 9:15. We sprawled in a prowl sled and skunk-eyed the back door.

The Repair King shop. Brentwood's one and only. San Vicente, right off Bundy. It's a half mile from Fifth Helena. Manny ran the listening post. It's a valid presumption. Manny was the man to squeeze *now.* He linked Hollygrove '37 to Brentwood *now.* He was a burglar. Gwen fingered a 459 on 6/11/48. I think Manny did the job.

We surveilled the alley and back door. We covered Manny's parking slot. We were dead-ass exhausted. We cleaned Sid Leffler up and hauled him to Queen of Angels. We fed the intake docs a line of shit per his wounds. I called Customs and the Mex State Police. Ingrid Irmgard remained in custody. Customs agents studied her delivery list and popped six Mex nationals with forged bearer bonds. The Staties APB'd José Bolaños. They ran an all-Baja dragnet. José vaporized. The Staties doubled down and kept looking.

Max dozed. I dozed. Something Leffler said ditzed me awake. Leffler, on Albie Aadland: "His idea of kicks is visitor's day at Chino."

Manny pulled in. He parked two slots down from us. We got out slow and jumped quick. He sensed heat and whirled around. We sandbagged him. I banged his head on the roof ledge. He slumped, knees-first. Max kicked him in the balls and cuffed his hands behind his back. I ran into the shop.

I went through the back door. I crashed the workshop. I ID'd Manny's workspace, easy. He'd tacked Ingrid Irmgard nudie shots above his bench.

A salesman ran up to me. I shoved the warrant at him and shoved him away. I pulled drawers, I dumped drawers, I dumped a tool kit. There's the shit, right—

There.

Bug mounts/condenser mikes/bundled bug loops. Manny hot-wired Fifth Helena. This gear replicates the Monroe house gear. It's a courtroom-valid grab. Ratfuck would cream his jeans.

The table, the chairs, the standard see-thru mirror. The Fed setup mimed the LAPD's.

Manny's a federal witness now. He's hanging insouciant. He should evince more fear.

I kicked his toolbox. "It's evidence, Manny. You ran a listening post out of the Repair King basement. You had Marilyn Monroe hot-wired, and I'm wondering why."

Manny scratched his right-arm tattoo: *Manny y Ingrid por Vida.*

"Everybody wants to get next to Marilyn, right? I was planning to offer her a part in my next picture. It's about my days as a stumblebum welterweight, before I went to TV-repair school and learned a trade."

Max lit a cigar. "Well, you certainly share a history with Marilyn, given that you grew up less than a mile away from Hollygrove. You, Marilyn, Albie, and Paul Mitchell Grenier. You were a tight little clique."

Manny made the jerk-off sign. "So you say. But I say I learned a trade. If I felt like calling Marilyn, I would have done it. I wouldn't have to hot-wire her crib."

I lit a cigarette. "You were in Chino with Grenier. That was in '54 to '56. You were in for 459, and he was in for stat rape. Albie Aadland loved a good Chino visit. I'm guessing he visited you and Paul Mitchell. Can you think of anyone else he visited there?"

"He visited me and Paul Mitchell. That's all I know."

Max drummed the table. "The Monroe wire job. Give us some details."

Manny said, "No comment, and don't think you can phone-book me, because there's that *Cubano* Fed standing outside the door."

I went *tut-tut*. "Your girlfriend Ingrid, José Bolaños, bond scams, dope, Mexican runs up the wazoo."

Manny combed his hair. He had killer hair. It was thick and combed straight back. He pulled out a hairnet and tugged it in place. Max haw-haw-hawed.

"Chino. You and Paul Mitchell intersect. Albie comes to visit. Give us a few tidbits."

Manny patted his pompadour. He wore khakis and a Sir Guy shirt. He dressed classic *vato loco*.

"Chino was kicks. Me and Paul Mitchell drank pruno and poked sissies. Albie visited us, and soaked up the atmosphere. He got his rocks off talking to psychos and hoods. He was a chickenshit, you dig? He wasn't evil and committed to wild shit, like his brothers. That's all you're getting from me, so don't bother me with any kidnap shit, Marilyn shit, or Fox-rackets shit, because I don't know shit, and I wouldn't roll if I did."

I sighed. I'm forbearing Uncle Freddy. You're in a jam, son. I want to help.

"Here's what we're dealing with. You, Gwen, Paul Mitchell, Albie, and Motel Mike could waltz. As in, you present sealed testimony before a Federal grand jury, or you depose in writing. You receive total immunity. We're dealing with a certain level of official embarrassment, and some guys with clout would rather not be embarrassed. *But,* here's a rub. There's burglary all over this thing, and you're a reformed burglar. So, I'd like you to stretch your memory way back, to before the statute of limitations on some 459's expired. *Comprende?* Give us an oldie, so we can tell the jury foreman, 'See, El Manny knows at least some of the personnel in this mess.'"

El Manny combed his eyebrows. Fluorescent lights toasted his hairdo. It melted his Brylcreem.

"Remember that other blondie cooze who killed herself? Carole Landis? It must have been '48, sometime. Marilyn and Gwen were house-sitting the Carole cooze's place, and Gwen tipped me to a jewel stash in a wall safe. Okay, I found the combination in a desk drawer, and I clouted the jewels. The cooze never reported the theft, because she was schizzy, and then she killed herself. The punch line is that I found a fuck deck in the safe, but I left it there. It was Carole and this big-dick guy, Captain Hook, doing it in fifty-two variations. Marilyn and Gwen were there, and Marilyn had this enchanted look on her face. She said something like 'Wow, what a nifty blackmail tool. If you're willing to pose yourself, if you find the right mark, if you're willing to wait.'"

58

Greenson met me at his office. I sent a note and requested an interview. I explained why. He responded at once.

I sat in the waiting room. Jack and Jackie beamed up from *Vogue*. They laid out their summer vacation. Jackie called Biarritz yummy. They had suntans. The grapefruit/amphetamine diet kept them thin. They wore resort clothes *c'est bon*.

The receptionist buzzed me back. I knew the way. Greenson stood behind his desk. He said "Lieutenant" and gestured to a Saarinen chair. I sat down. He set the clock. The fifty-minute hour clicks in.

"Yes, I did purchase Marilyn's letters. I was tempted to read them, but I resisted the urge. The provenance rather intrigued me—Marilyn to young Lowell to Officer Leffler. But the officer impressed me as an unstable man with an agenda, so I thought it best to burn the letters and be done with it."

I believed him. "Unstable" nails Leffler. *Desperate* nails him best. He was a big name-dropper. He rivaled Monroe there. He dropped Paul de River's name the most.

I said, "I've spent considerable time on this now, and I've concluded that Marilyn met Paul de River, and that he sought to mold her in the manner of the many psychopaths in his charge."

Greenson tugged at his cuff links. "They met in the early '50s, I believe. Marilyn's orphanage chum, 'Gwen'—a criminal, frankly—introduced her to de River. Over the years—intermittently, at first, and far more pointedly as she unknowingly entered the last stage of her life—Marilyn came to believe that she could take her native acting skills and develop an entirely differentiated persona—in the manner of Gwen, who was very much stronger than she was, and whom Marilyn flat-out idolized. Marilyn divulged very little information as to her new 'criminal metamorphosis,' but she spent great portions of our sessions analyzing Gwen's character, and marveling at how Gwen—who had suffered the same neglect and privations as she had—had emerged as someone resolute, clear-minded, and able to live in the real world with far greater grace than she ever had. And Gwen went after what she wanted with deadly resolve—which Marilyn admired more than anything else."

The Gwen-Marilyn riff took me back. Dope fiend Marilyn sideswiped me. '48 to '62. Fourteen years. Marilyn's pill habit. She crossed "Norma Jean Baker" off a barb vial in '48. She crossed "Marilyn Monroe" off a barb vial in '62. All Of It constellated in '48. The dumped-pill aspect torqued me. Fourteen years elapsed. Marilyn does now what she did then.

I said, "Doctor, where did Marilyn get the pills that killed her?"

"I don't know. She took the pills I prescribed her, or she dumped them, as she did with the pills her internist prescribed. She told me that she received pills from her friend Jeanne Carmen, and she followed the same pattern there."

I kicked it around. My brain gears click, clicked.

59

Jeanne Carmen. She peddled pills to the L.A. underground and always dealt fair and square. Greenson's office to Jeanne's place—just a ten-minute hop.

I took Wilshire to Doheny and cut north. I replayed the mobile stake-out on Manny Salas.

Red laid it out. The stakeout kicked on last night. The Feds cut Manny loose. He caught a cab. Harry and Eddie tailed him to Albie Aadland's house. They held down surveillance. Albie and Manny burned paper stacks in the backyard bar-b-q pit.

I was restless last night. I perched by the phone and willed Gwen to call. She didn't call. I drove to Frascati and sat in our booth. Gwen did not show.

I talked to Max, an hour back. He said the Creep job slogs on. The RSO's have been cleared. The fake confessors, likewise. Preston Fong's still scanning mug books. Morty's up to part 5 in his series. He awaits Freddy's next phone edit. The record checks have fizzled out, dead.

I parked on Elevado and hopped out. I leapfrogged the stairs and rang Jeanne's bell. She yelled, "It's open!" I let myself in. The living room doubled as a practice tee. Jeanne putted golf balls toward a coffee cup.

"Hi, Freddy. What's shakin', love?"

I said, "Who's got the most extensive collection of fuck decks that you know of?"

Jeanne sunk a long one. "Either Roddy McDowall or Sam Yorty."

"Put aside Greenson and the various doctors that Marilyn might have been blowing. Who can you think of that might have been sup-plying her with pills?"

Jeanne said, "Santa Claus."

I said, "What?"

Jeanne leaned on her putter. "Some anonymous fan of hers. He leaves her yellow jackets, wherever she's living. That's on New Year's, Easter, Thanksgiving, and her birthday. Marilyn buries them in her garden, wherever she happens to be living, and only digs them up when she's desperate."

I went out the door. Jeanne yelled, "It was too brief, baby!"

I made Fifth Helena in near-record time. I parked behind the house and vaulted the backyard fence. I went straight to the garden and pawed through loose dirt. I pulled out two empty pill vials. They were unmarked. It surprised me. I thought *this:*

She moved in in March. That's pre-Easter. Her birthday was on 6/1/62.

I dug further. I found six yellow capsules. They resembled Nembutal. They were *not* manufacturer-marked. I pulled a capsule apart and tasted the medicine. It played off-kilter. I examined the plastic coating. It was hand-stamped "TCS Pharmacy." That played phony.

Trust your instincts. Make the leap. You're on to something here.

The Sex Creep. He's got a lab. He brews his own dope. He's a crazy autodidact. He's a rogue chemist—wild-ass and self-taught.

60

Chino. The soft joint. It housed first-time felons and career deadbeat dads. It's forty miles southeast of L.A. That's out in the scrub hills and gimcrack subdivisions. Dorms replace cellblocks. Wired enclosures replace The Walls. WPA-style buildings flank the grounds.

Admin Building #2 housed a file room. I cut past some picnic tables and found it. I set up the trip yesterday. I talked to a deputy warden and ran down my request. He said he'd pull the Grenier and Salas files.

He checked a visitors index. He said Paul de River never came to Chino. Albert Aadland did. He came with the Friends Service Committee. His visits began in '49. They stopped a heartbeat after Salas and Grenier were granted parole.

I parked beside the building and walked in. A trusty pointed me to the file room. The deputy warden delivered. He fixed me up with a table and chair. It was stacked with folders, pencils, and scratch pads. Plus a thermos/coffee setup.

Files were stacked floor to rafters. They bulged up wall-to-wall shelves. The basement was steam-heated. I took off my suit coat and dug in.

I skimmed visitors logs back to '50. I brought my FI card/RSO list with me. I ran it through the logs and got no matches. Albie visited Chino seventeen times with the Friends Service Committee. Those visits ran from fall '49 to spring '54. Salas arrived in June of '54. Grenier arrived in August. Albie visited them as a "personal friend." His visits ran through to their late '56 paroles.

Albie was here. Salas and Grenier were here. Did the Sex Creep pass through here? Was he locked down here? Did Salas and Grenier know him? Did Albie visit him here?

Nine hundred burglars and sex fiends passed through Chino from the late '40s to '56. The names started with Aquino and ended with Ziegler. The Creep's rare blood type was a now-useless ID device. I'd have to skim nine hundred infirmary files. It would take at least two fucking weeks.

I read through Salas' and Grenier's complaint files. Manny guzzled pruno and beat up hapless inmates. Paul Mitchell bit a dorm queen and made him his bitch.

An old-hand guard drifted by. I poured him a cup of coffee. He said, "Are you the lieutenant that's got that big interest in that strange one Albie A.?"

I nodded. I had paperwork eyestrain. I saw three of everything.

"Well, I've worked Visitors since the war, and I can't name anybody specific that Albie visited, except his pals Grenier and Salas, but I do remember how he was always lugging psych texts around with him, giving the cons little quizzes and taking notes, and acting not at all like the other Quakers did. He was always name-dropping some headshrink named de River. He was sure enthralled by that guy."

I extrapolated. I surmised.

De River. Albie cultivated prospects for de River. HE RECRUITED for de River. He sought out prospects to send on perverted practice runs—

The guard said, "There's one other thing."

"What?"

"I always had Albie pegged for a short eyes. You know, we've got outdoor visiting here, and I'd always see Albie giving little girls these weird looks."

61

The raid's on.

We mobilized outside Norm's Nest. Del Kinney yanked chains and made the deal *GO.* Three ABC men packed shotguns. Max and I went with sidearms and saps. Del stood with us. He packed my Ithaca pump. Red, Harry, and Eddie crouched by the back door. Two Sheriff's matrons hunkered in the rear parking lot.

The preraid stakeout concluded. We know who's inside. It's Norm Krause, Jack Clemmons, and Deedee Grenier. That's our target group and no more. Del cued the intrusion. He squawked on a duck-call gizmo —quack, quack, quack.

Let's roll.

Del blew the front door off. He triggered a spread at the center mass and took it down in one go. It slammed hard. It outslammed the shit-kicker music on the jukebox. It stunned Norm, Jack, and Deedee. They spilled drinks and toppled their stools at the bar.

We ran in. The matrons grabbed Deedee. She pulled a rat-tail comb and stabbed at their eyes. They kicked her legs and proned her full on the floor. Max and Red grabbed Norm Krause. He played it taciturn and eschewed resistance. I grabbed Jack Clemmons. He carried a belt gun and a flat sap. I frisked him and tossed them behind the bar. Jack feared me. He complied, meek-meek.

It went quick. It was all blunt force and loud affect. Deedee looked straight at me. She said, "I know what you did."

The ABC ran a branch office in Burbank. Muster room/squadroom/sweat-boxes/jail.

I sweatboxed Jack Clemmons. Max and Red took Norm Krause. Harry and Eddie handled Deedee Grenier. The matrons hovered and measured Deedee for a strip search.

Jack and I sucked flask juice. I spiked it up. 151/hashish chunks/*coca grande* from Ingrid I's stash.

"Your relationship with Mike Bayless predated Marilyn Monroe's death. He put you in the sack with Gwen Perloff and extorted you out of the Sheriff's race. Here's my question. Did he tell you to expect an auspicious station call on the night of August 4?"

Jack was a Georgia boy. He knew from home brew. My shit sandbagged him.

"I figured it pertained to the kidnap. Something like a callout. You know, a big roundup to beat the bushes for the girl."

The room was hot. I flicked the AC switch. Cold air flowed.

"The raid was a shuck. It was nothing but your wake-up call. You and Norm get a walk on any stunts you might have pulled recently. I'm only interested in you and Norm, back in '48. You were shepherding bigwigs and film people through the westside dive circuit."

Clemmons sucked jungle juice. "It was Norm's gig, more than mine. I didn't come on the PD until '50. Norm and me had similar political interests, so we became pals. Somebody—maybe on the PD or in the DA's Office, something like that—was worried about naïve movie-biz kids getting in trouble at homo bars, dope dens, fuck pads, and the like, so Norm and me got paid to be escorts."

I sipped juice. My scalp prickled. I reprised Deedee: *"I know what you did."*

"Were there any other policemen working this sort of gig?"

Clemmons belched. He wore a short-sleeved shirt. His White Dog Bund tattoos gassed me. Evil bull terriers snarled.

"Just Sid Leffler. He'd stop by this fuck pad on Pavia Place, and I knew that he had a history with the place, going back maybe ten or eleven years, because the A brothers and this fool Dr. Shel owned the place, and he always said this particular pad was haunted, but he never said why."

I got chills. They were jungle-juice indigenous. They felt good. You got sweat pops and ice jabs inside one second.

"Tell me about the bigwigs and movie folks you escorted."

Clemmons said, "Well, Orson Welles. He was always taking dirty pictures and shooting dirty movies, and you had Sam Yorty, back when he was a congressman. He collected these smutty decks of playing cards, and I think Welles was the guy who took the pictures."

I lit a cigarette. "Roddy McDowall and Elizabeth Taylor?"

Clemmons shrugged. "I'm not sure. I was usually zonked, so a lot of that time was a blur. Ask Norm. He's got a better memory than me."

Clemmons waltzed. Krause replaced him. He knew from jungle juice. He took measured pops and licked his lips.

"Jack said you asked him about Liz Taylor and Roddy McDowall. Okay, we showed them around. So what? Why are you so hipped on all this ancient history?"

"You caught the state comptroller, Tom Kuchel, blowing a young kid. That was in '49. You tried to extort Kuchel, after the station captain kicked the beef. Somehow, you walked on Extortion One. I think you must have had a favor on the books, with a ranking PD man or a heavy politician. Why don't you elaborate on that?"

Krause wiped his face. He sweated up his handkerchief. He had cold blue eyes. They put out fifty thousand volts.

"I did favors for Chief Horrall, before the grand jury sacked him. I did some favors when Bill Worton came in. I pulled a couple of wheels out of the shit in the summer of '48, and Worton remembered that when I stepped in the shit with Kuchel. And that's all I'm giving you, you A-rab piece of shit."

The raid was a bust. Krause was intransigent. Clemmons was addled and aphasic. Deedee got kicked out early. She ambled off somewhere.

I walked through the ABC lot. I was fried. It was 2:16 a.m.

Something jumped out behind me. Something pounded my back. Somebody jabbed a lit cigarette in my face. I heard *You killed my brother*/*"It has to be you"*/*"Your goons tailed me"*/*"Who else could it be"*/*"You killed my—"*

It was Deedee. She jabbed the cigarette. She missed my eyes and scorched my neck. She clawed my back. She raked through my shirt and drew blood. I tried to grab her, she pulled away, I caught her hair and slammed her against a parked car. She cracked then. She just sat there and sobbed.

62

Frascati.

Gwen didn't call me. I'm here anyway. I got dressed up to eat alone. People used to run from me here. They thought I bugged the tables. Illicit lovers saw me here. They split in opposite directions.

I messed with the bread basket and chained cigarettes. I teethed on Pat's diary and her now-empty house.

Her '45 to '51 diary. That means summer '48. She surely mentions her siblings. The Kennedys are tight-knit.

The house is empty. Pat, Peter, and the help are down in Laguna. It's an easy B and E. I've done it before.

Gwen walked up. She dodged the headwaiter and made tracks to me. She wore a russet-flecked suit.

"I forgot to call. I just assumed you'd be here."

I smiled. A waiter brought two martinis. I tried for a comeback and faltered.

"You've been frightening some friends of mine."

I said, "It's a walk-away for all of you—unless Parker, Leavy, and the AG learn something about you kids they can't live with."

I dropped "AG" to tweak her. She did not tweak.

"I'm more circumspect than the 'other kids.' And I can't vouch for their criminal activities as far back as you seem to be probing. And I still have a hard time picturing you as a front man for such powerful figures."

I said, "We're united in common cause. I'm out to dodge indictments and spare them embarrassment. Buyback deals always play out along these lines."

Gwen sipped her drink. "Without admitting any sort of active complicity or complicitous knowledge, how will the alleged vice and financial crimes allegedly conceived at Fox be legally dealt with?"

I lit a cigarette. "Through cease-and-desist orders, issued by local, state, and Federal agencies, under threat of a studio-wide internal audit, and individual IRS audits on all the conspirators involved."

Gwen lit a cigarette. "It unnerves me that you're looking into my sister's death."

"We're dealing with convergences. 1937. Your sister disappears, and you meet the kids at Hollygrove. And I've learned some things that I kick around while I wait for you to get off the dime and tell me what they all mean."

Gwen said, "Not just yet."

I said, "Tell me about *Hard Luck Girl*."

"There's nothing to tell. I wrote a crummy script, I'm a crummy actress, and I broke it off with Darryl, so he pulled the plug on it. I'm really just a bait girl emeritus who's considering her options, so if you have any ideas, please let me know."

I touched her arm. "Sit still and let me put some things together."

The house smelled different. Her suite smelled different. Her closet smelled like cedar blocks rescented or replaced. The diaries were here. Pat said they were. I didn't see them out in plain sight. B and E is tactile and olfactory. Scent enhances color. It spurs my efforts to work in the dark.

Seven volumes. 1945 to 1951. Red leather-bound. She kept our V-J Day photo here. Why aren't the diaries here?

I smelled boot polish. I smelled it on the floor and on the boot mats. That particular scent belonged. I tweaked and caught a subscent. An antiqued polish scent. I reached behind the boot mats and pulled volume one out.

There it is. The red leather has been polished and buffed. Pat spine-marked it: *"P.K., 1945."*

I penlight-flashed pages. January 1 to August 15 were totally blank. She began the diary the day she met me. She drew a circle around "Marine MSGT F.O." She's an aging bubblegummer with a pricey Mont Blanc pen. Twelve lines of *X*'s and *O*'s followed. They indicated our two days. They stopped at my LAPD Academy address and the recruit-line phone number.

I flashed more blank pages. I put volume one aside. I reached blind and pulled out volume four. It was spine-marked *"P.K., 1948."*

I bit down on my penlight. I skim-read one hundred pages on Jack's second congressional run. January, February, March, April, May. *"Jack seems to be spending a good deal of time in L.A."* We're into late June '48 now. Pat writes: *"Where's Jack? Mother and Dad are worried."*

I flashed into July. I hit 7/3/48. Pat writes, *"Bobby. Abrupt flight to L.A."* 7/3/48, again. Pat writes, *"Reserve airport car."* I hit 7/5 and 7/6/48. Pat writes, *"Chief Worton helpful with escorts"* and *"Bobby says considerable pain."*

I wasn't shocked or surprised. I'd seen Shelley Mandel's Wall of Shame.

63

Ratfuck Bobby said, "Good morning, Lieutenant."

I stood up. "Good morning, sir."

Eddie Chacōn called me in, impromptu. He said the boss needs ten minutes. Go to the U.S. Attorney's Office. Camelot beckons. You must be punctual. The Kennedys demand that.

Bobby went *Sit.* I perched on a schoolboy chair. Bobby sprawled in the U.S. Attorney's recliner.

I notched phone time this morning. I badgered airline and rent-a-car drones. They gave up their summer '48 flights and airport rentals. *I'm 76.8% sure now.*

Ratfuck said, "I've given it a good deal of thought. I've read through your summaries, and I've decided to go with sealed depositions and sworn-secrecy documents."

I'm 83.4% sure now.

"Yes, sir. I think that's prudent."

"Eddie's wondering if you've picked a date to get your black bags together."

I said, "Tomorrow night, sir."

"Good. I'll tell Eddie. Oh, and while I have you. I'm hosting a dinner for some State Assembly people. I need to reserve a nicely cloistered room in a restaurant. I'm thinking of Beverly Hills, say at 7:30. Can you recommend a place?"

I said, "You can't beat Frascati, on Wilshire. I know a guy there. He'll set it up."

It was a dumb kid play. Their paths won't cross. I sat in Frascati anyway. Gwen did not propose a meet with me. She might or might not show. The AG runs punctual. It's kismet or it's not.

I eyeballed the front door. I sipped Old Crow and snarfed Dexedrine. I spent the afternoon sacked out with Lois. She asked me who burned my neck. I said, "An angry lesbian golf pro."

Lois said, "Why?"

I said, "She thought I killed her brother."

Lois said, "*Did* you?"

I said, "Yes."

Lois went *whoops*. Lois recovered quick.

"Bobby told Pat to dump you, and she told me. He said people have started talking. Your expiration date has come and gone, and now's the time to cut it off."

I said, "I'm sure you'll stay friends with her. And, for what it's worth, she was never you."

Lois squeezed my hand. "Do you love me?"

I said, "I'll think about it."

Pat, Lois, Gwen. They're my un-Holy Trinity.

I watched the door. The headwaiter inked the reservation for 7:30 sharp. It was 7:28 now.

The front door opened and closed. The AG walked in. He slouched and tried to appear anonymous. People checked him out sidelong and tried not to stare.

I saw him. He didn't see me. I planned it that way.

Gwen walked in.

She saw Bobby. He saw her. They held *This Look*. Their hands reached out and brushed. It was brief but emphatic. I saw it. Nobody else did.

64

Black-bag job.

We crouched in a Fed surveillance van. We deployed sign language and ran checklists.

Ten days presurveillance. *Check.* De River leaves his office at six sharp. *Check.* There's no on-premises guard. *Check.* The address is not silent alarm–rigged. It does not plug to Hollywood Station. Phil Irwin confirmed it five times.

Nat and Phil are out cruising the neighborhood. They're two-way radio–equipped. There's no hinky broadcast traffic. They're running wide perimeters. Oakwood to Fountain/La Brea to Fairfax and back.

We parked across the street from de River's building. The downstairs neighbors were off in Saint-Tropez. We ran inventory checks:

Power drills. Crowbars. Dissolving solvent. Wheel-fitted hand trucks. Flashlights. Penlights. Lock picks. Rolls of acoustical padding. *Check*— eight times over.

Our gear is stashed in reinforced duffel bags. Double-check *that.*

De River's living room adjoins his file trove. A reinforced door provides access. The file trove is there. His files might be coded. They will be boxed. This *will* take time.

Eddie brought powdered nitro. He knew how to rig controlled blow-outs. De River kept a narco safe. We decided to blow it and split the contents. He planned to donate his cut to the Free Cuba Committee. I planned to stick my cut up my nose.

We hauled the duffel bags out of the van. We quick-marched them across the street and up the steps. We reconnoitered on the second-floor landing. Eddie fumbled picks at the door lock. *Shit*—none of them fit.

I removed a power drill and jammed in a steel-cutter bit. I bored the keyhole and derailed the inner-lock mechanism. The front door popped open. We blew our undetected-entry shot.

We got in fast. We shut the door. The bore noise ran minimal. We bit down on our penlights. We walked to the steel-plate door and quadrant-flashed it.

It looks impregnable. That's tough fucking shit.

It's two-side milled. On both sides. It pushes in off two fulcrums. There's a left-side hinge and a right-side hinge. It requires two firm shoves.

I took the left. Eddie took the right. We created a noise-deflection shield. We cut strips of acoustical padding and taped them to the flanking walls. We slapped on four full layers. We mummified the file-room enclosure. We went in with power drills and crowbars and took the door down.

It took twenty-seven minutes and twelve left-side and right-side bores. I did not posit an internal alarm system. The files were surely all criminal. De River would never risk police or security-company scrutiny.

The door *wiggled*.

The door *shimmied*.

The door *caved*.

It listed backward. We got behind it and put all our weight up against it. We slow-slow-slow eased it down to the floor.

We're inside the file trove. It's eight feet deep. There's shelves filled with manuscript boxes. They line the walls shoulder-high.

I caught my breath. I said, "Look for a simple number-substitution code." Eddie went *Sí—yo comprende*.

We hauled down boxes. I checked three for prototype distinctions. The boxes were marked by eight-letter or fourteen-letter designations. That meant "Sessions" or "Correspondence." That meant tape boxes for "Sessions" and envelopes or folders for "Correspondence." Substitution-code numbers would be scrawled above that. They marked the patients' names.

I confirmed my theory. "Sessions" meant tape reels inside. "Correspondence" meant letters or printed matter inside. The boxes were heedlessly marked and stacked. As in "Box 1 of 3, 4, 19, 12" et al.

We hauled down boxes. I looked for seven-number first names and six-number surnames. They would designate "Marilyn Monroe." The *M*'s should be supplanted with two number thirteens. M was the thirteenth letter of the alphabet. Eddie worked the same motif for "Albert Aadland." Six letters, seven letters, two number ones to capitalize.

We hauled down boxes. We went at it. Hours crawled by. I scored four hours and seven minutes in:

"Marilyn Monroe/Sessions/Box 1 of 3." Eddie scored nine minutes later: *"Albert Aadland/Correspondence/Box 1 of 4."*

We rounded up our seven-box swag and placed them on hand trucks. We packed our duffel bags. We scoured the apartment. The narcotics safe was tucked behind a sliding wall panel.

Eddie dragged it out. We donned face masks and worked in asbestos gloves. We daubed and brushed liquid nitro at the hinge points and dial backings. We quadruple-wrapped the safe in acoustical baffling and tapped the charge flush against the dial mount. We set the charge and stood back. The door popped. The box lurched. We filled four paper bags with the best shit on earth.

We off-loaded our gear and the file boxes. We made three trips out to the van. We were stone gone at 6:04 a.m.

65

I worked at home.

Code work vexes me. I studied it in the Marine Corps. It confused me then and confuses me now. I tapped my safe stash and mixed a powdered Demerol and bourbon cocktail. It juked my brain cells and helped me concentrate.

I tried word-replacement and Bible codes and failed to link scriptural texts. There were no live tapes in the Monroe boxes. They were all copied transcriptions. I scanned text pages. I quick-skimmed the Monroe and Aadland boxes. I could not decipher one simple word.

I worked on my living room floor. I compiled proper-noun lists and plucked words that might pop phonetic. It was all word gobbledygook. I could not locate one single name.

We hid the van and our gear in Phil's garage. Nat and Phil were staking out the de River place. They'll be there when Pops spots the chaos. They'll gas on the old geek's response.

I worked up a Bible-verse code. It backfired. Every Old and New Testament verse raked me. They excoriated my sinfulness. They called me to repentance. They prophesied my eternal rot in hell.

The doorbell rang. I got up and cracked the door. It was Max Herman and J. T. Meadows. They were shaky and pale. J.T. weaved on his feet.

Max said, "Lowell Farr's dead. Two patrol guys found her in some bushes. She was dumped in a pocket park, north of Palisades Village. She'd been shot four times."

———

We took Sunset straight out. I don't remember the drive. I saw gargoyles and heard tape spools of Old Testament injunctions. I saw the living Lowell and Lowell's Monroe painting. They stutter-looped nonstop.

Traffic bottlenecked at the village line. Max pulled up on the north sidewalk and tooted pedestrians off the bricks. We hooked north at the corner and around to the right.

We hit Linda Place. Little benches lined the sidewalk. Shrub mounds pressed up behind them. Cops huddled. Polaroids popped. Overlapped arc lights burned bright. The street was all jammed-up prowl cars. They ran their gumball lights full.

The lights were up, the rope was up, four patrol cops moved looky-loos out. Max and I pushed our way into it. We lodged our first peep. It was close-up and in tight.

Lowell lay supine. She wore a green paisley dress and brown flats. A brown leather handbag was off to one side. Big-bore entrance wounds scorched the green fabric and soaked it black-red.

Twenty cops hovered. J.T. huddled up a canvass crew. Max and I crowded close and studied the scene.

The setting was too quaint. Linda Place was a pocket park and pastoral cut-by. Benches, leaves, eucalyptus trees. A faint sea breeze.

Two patrol guys jabbered. The girl's bag had been tossed. They found a ticket stub for last night's show at the Bay. They ran *Sayonara* and *No Time for Sergeants*. Mom and dad were off downtown. They went to Mike Lyman's and the Philharmonic. They got home at 1:00 a.m. Lowell's bedroom door was shut. They figured she was asleep.

Max and I swapped looks. We knew from make-out dates. Pali boys and girls hid out and made out at the Bay. Lowell told Marilyn. I picked it up on my tap feeds. The Bay was "a motel room for nice kids."

Preset make-out dates. Lowell described the scene. She indulged the practice. She confided in Monroe. I eavesdropped on my feed lines.

The Sex Creep killed her. It has to be him. It wasn't Sid Leffler. He's beat-to-shit at Queen of Angels.

Max cleared a space. We stood by the body and bootjacked the job then and there. I dug through Lowell's handbag. I found her car keys. They sat atop a neat pile of purse junk—cosmetics, comb, wallet, hairbrush. The house keys were jammed at the bottom of the bag. The house keys played anomalous. I thought *this:*

Lowell strolls by Linda Place. The Creep confronts her and shoots her. He dumps her in the bushes. He grabs her house keys and goes to the Farr house. He lets himself in. He wants Monroe's fan letters. He thinks Lowell has them. He doesn't know that Lowell sold the letters to Sid Leffler. He tosses Lowell's bedroom. He doesn't find the letters. He walks back to the dump site and jams the keys back in her handbag.

I caught a glint on Lowell's skirt front. I knelt and up-closed it. I ID'd the glint:

They were spent silencer threads. *That* meant *this.* The piece was suppressor-equipped.

I flashed back. I cut to Sid's Pali gig. Morty Bendish costars. The Q and A spawns a Sex Creep brouhaha. Sid and Morty reference a Doc de River paraphrase:

Passive pervs sometimes escalate and kill. IF the crush object develops a real-life love interest or deep friendship. The Creep glimpsed the burgeoning Lowell-Marilyn bond. It sent him batshit.

I said, "All the crazy shit this fucker has pulled, and now he kills a young woman. It's got to be him."

Max said, "Leffler sold Monroe's letters to Doc Greenson, instead of de River. If de River already knew this Sex Creep guy, and if he figured that half of Monroe's letters already came from him, then why buy a stack of pricey letters for no new information?"

The squadroom lieutenant showed. He gathered up clue clowns and described his stint at the Farr house. He talked to Lowell's parents. He'd went through Lowell's address book. It was packed with Pali boys' names. Some were marked with hearts and arrows. Lowell's mother ran down the Bay Theater/"make-out date" custom. A neighbor woman fed her the gist. Lowell would *never* do such a thing.

I shook my head. The lieutenant motormouthed.

"We've set up a command post in the Pali auditorium. Lowell had eleven make-out dates marked in her address book, including the one last night. We need two-man teams to round up those boys and bring them to Pali. We're going to interview them consecutively, in the boys' gym. We'll be working all day and most of the night."

Max said, "It's the Creep. All this horny-boy shit is futile."

I said, "I agree."

Max said, "What do we do now?"

I said, "We go back to what we were doing. We try to ID the Creep."

The canvass cops and squadroom guys dispersed. Morgue jockeys sheet-draped Lowell's gurney. I stood by Lowell and bumped the wheels, accidental-on-purpose. I studied the crime scene. I saw work-boot tracks. I saw mud and blood caught in the heel cleats. The boots were non-LAPD.

The cleat prints tracked off, northbound. They hit clean cement and cut away from Linda Place and the crime scene. They moved due north. They tracked toward Will Rogers Park and the Santa Monica hills.

I saw Bible typeface. I saw my code doodles. I tasted Demerol and bourbon. I saw Lowell shot four times. Homemade suppressors popped and leaked threads. I saw her blood douse the heel prints. It glowed weird colors. It bubbled. It blasphemed Lowell and me. It contradicted the Bible. That meant it was wrong.

I reached into a prowl sled and grabbed a 12-gauge pump. I tracked the boot prints *away* from the crime scene.

It was easy. I sighted *down*. Lowell's blood sluiced into more weird colors.

I tracked the prints up a commercial block. I entered the park. The temperature dropped. Trees grew out of nowhere. They looked wrong and smelled wrong. A breeze fluttered branches. The sound echoed shrill. It brought Lowell back to me. I smelled her blood merged with parkland scents.

I jacked a round in the chamber and aimed at the sound. I blasted through the sound, shredded limbs, and mulched tree trunks. Somebody screamed behind me. I whirled and triggered a spread. A man yelled, *"Hey!"* A man yelled, *"What the hell—"*

Rustles and foot scuffs came at me. I shotgunned them. Seedling trees vaporized. Four big men slammed into me and hoisted me. They tossed me and carried me over their heads. They went through my pockets. They shoved yellow jackets into my mouth and made me gag them down. I saw Lowell in a paint-smeared smock.

I came to standing up. The Hats crowded around me. Harry and Eddie arm-clamped me. I was weavy and zorched. I thought I saw Lowell. I saw a snapshot of Marilyn and Lowell, propped on an end table.

It was Lowell's bedroom. Print techs dusted scattered envelopes on the floor.

Max said, "It's the Creep. Ray Pinker found ripped glove seams in Lowell's correspondence drawer. That places him at the BHPD 459 scenes, the divorcée scenes, and here. That means he's good for the snuff."

My belt line felt light. The boys snatched my piece, my sap, my knucks. Max said, "You gave us a scare, son."

I pulled my coat wide. Max replaced my shit. Harry and Eddie walked into the living room and soft-braced the Farrs. Dorothy Farr harped on Lowell's pretend friendship with Marilyn Monroe. Eddie soft-rebuked her. Lowell was surely Miss Monroe's best friend during her last months alive.

Dorothy Farr sobbed. I scanned the bedroom. Marilyn sketches covered the walls. I clocked the provenance of the painting that I now owned.

A wall mural depicted President Monroe's inauguration. It was a cut-and-paste job. Lowell scissored up a big *Life* spread. She decapitated JFK and glued Monroe's face atop his. Speech squibs played the mock prez for laughs.

It was sicknik humor. President Monroe lets it all hang out.

She announced her new cabinet. Big Dick Dave will tend to her carnal needs and run the Supreme Court. Peter Lawford will be secretary of poontang. Lois Nettleton will run the National Endowment for the Arts.

Red Stromwall walked in. "We're due at Pali. Daryl Gates is running the interviews with the make-out boys."

I was still half-zorched and weavy. Max and Red arm-clamped me and led me outside. They tossed me in the back of their prowl sled. I felt a weeper fit coming on.

The run up Temescal Canyon took five minutes. Eleven boys cluttered up the bleachers off the basketball court. Daryl Gates walked boy to boy and asked polite questions. He knew it was a humbug deal. It was geared to mollify mom and dad.

I sat on a courtside bench and watched. The boys gave me some last moments with Lowell. They extolled her wild-but-good character. She was "kooky," "wiggy," and "out of sight." But she'd always take your paper route at a moment's notice. "I was afraid to ask her to the prom, because she was so much taller than me." "She told me all these lies about Marilyn Monroe. I said, 'Lowell, you're the world's worst fibber,' but I loved her anyway."

I couldn't take any more. I bolted the gym and sat up against the back wall. A cold breeze raked me. I shivered. Lowell ran through the parkland with me. I knew she was up in heaven. She came down to make sure I was okay.

I shivered and sobbed. Somebody tossed a handkerchief in my face.

I looked up. Max Herman said, "Stop that shit. Let's go find him and kill him."

I stuck to my pad. I laid off the narco stash. I messed with letter codes, book codes, and word-substitution codes. Lois called me. I ignored the call.

I went back to the Bible. I read through the Old and New Testaments. I looked for code-breaker clues and discovered prayers for Lowell instead.

I screened dance outtakes from *Twist Party Stakeout*. I did it just to see Lowell alive. I saw Lowell half-clad. It racked me. God censured me. I hurled the projector at the wall.

66

The Hats plus Freddy O. We indulged a show-the-flag run. It was all out in the open now. We decided to finalize it.

We scheduled a find-the-Creep session at Intel. Gates knew some pro code breakers. I told him to give me one more shot. Give me a last crack at it. I'll jump back to pure brainwork then.

We crammed into a prowl sled. We hit El Manny's pad in Echo Park first. Manny was out. We cut west and drove by Albie Aadland's spread in Cheviot Hills. Albie's boss Mercedes was parked in the driveway.

We got out and posed. Max ran the two-way radio. I goosed the volume. It raised a staticky roar.

Albie walked out. He carried a briefcase. He walked past us and got in his Mercedes. I said, "Albie, it's over."

Motel Mike ate lunch at Kwan's every day. He always dines with good-looking women. Motel Mike and a boss brunette sipped soup at a dining room table. We pulled chairs up. Their nice-lunch vibe crashed. I said, "Mike, it's over."

Mike stood up. He cranked a hard right hand and launched it. Red sidestepped the punch and grabbed Mike's neck. He smashed Mike's face into his soup bowl and held it there. Mike glugged for breath. The brunette snatched her purse and vamoosed.

We waltzed out to the parking lot. Max said, "Let's brace Gwen Perloff."
I said, "I'd rather not."
Harry said, "She's the linchpin of the whole deal."
I hemmed and shuffled my feet. Eddie said, "Freddy's in love."

The Hats plus Freddy O. We shitworked at Intel. J. T. Meadows wedged an extra desk in. The Creep escalates to Murder One. It mandates a reassessment. That means we reread and rediscuss everything.

We were backlogged. Forty nut confessors clogged the hallways. Morty's Creep series soared. The *Mirror* ballyhooed a new sales spike. *"Sex Creep Slays Pali Coed!!! He's Public Menace #1!!!"* Nat Denkins was hosting a Creep-O-Rama show on KKXZ tonight.

We huddled up. We shitworked.

J.T. was grouchy. Marcia Davenport was feeding him grief. She wanted J.T. to divorce his wife and marry her. The Hats and I ran a fever. We couldn't see past it. We read informant sheets and double-checked our ordnance. We loaded shotguns with *triple*-aught buckshot and slugs.

Daryl Gates stepped into my cubicle. He waved a Telex sheet.

"The dining room boss at Riviera just called me. He said he made a mistake about the men he had working the divorcée dance, and he said he realized that he brought this guy in from a temp agency. He's a Charles Douglas Schoendienst, DOB 6/12/23, blond, six-two, and 190. I ran him, and he's got a perv jacket. There's two burglary falls in Utah, a dismissed rape beef up in Santa Clara, *and* he's AB negative."

I stood up. "Preston's got a motel-room flop on PCH. Let's run this by him and try for a match."

Max, J.T., and I rolled. The beach run took an hour. Sunset was bumper-locked with surf wagons and hitchhiking freaks. They saw the fuzz-mobile stuffed with big shorthairs and flipped us off covert.

The Beachglade was up on the land side. It was a horseshoe-shaped auto court, circa '35. Preston bunked in 121. We parked and door-knocked him. He opened up quick.

It went fast then.

I saw the shelves. I saw the watches and the table. I saw the vats and the beakers. I saw the measuring scale and spilled powder. I saw the mock yellow jackets. I saw headlines:

Calling All Rogues Presents Filmland Femme—

I saw Manny Salas. He stepped out of a backroom pissoir.

I pulled my piece. Preston pulled his piece. We stood in tight and felt the air buzz. Max pulled his piece. Preston shot J. T. Meadows. He double-tapped two gut shots and blew out his ribs. I shot Preston in the face and neck. Manny Salas pulled a piece and fired wide of the doorway. Wood chips exploded. Max shot him three times. I shot him four times. We severed his right arm and blew him straight through the rear wall.

PART 10

FUCK DECK

(SEPTEMBER 29–OCTOBER 12, 1962)

67

Max and me. We did it. We blew up Sex Creep Preston Fong and Manny Salas. Fong killed J. T. Meadows. *"THERE'S THREE DEAD IN BEACHFRONT-MOTEL SHOOT-OUT!!!!"*

The papers had at it. The *Mirror* soared out front. Bill Parker fed Morty Bendish prime dirt. The story scorched local and national TV. Adjunct police agencies took it from there.

U.S. and Mexican Customs squads formed a task force. They wrung it dry. They enhanced the breadth of All Of It. They worked off my theories. They supplied the verification that I failed to get.

Preston Fong was not Preston Fong. He was a Chinese-Filipino man named Terry Jay Aquino. I recalled the name Terry Jay Aquino. He was on a paroled-burglar list I saw at Chino. Aquino served time concurrent with Paul Mitchell Grenier and Manny Salas. The guard I talked to at Chino saw Aquino's photo in the *Herald*. He called me and said, "Albie Aadland visited *that* guy, as well as Grenier and Salas. Albie visited him most of all."

Aquino split the Philippines in 1943. He was nineteen. He booked to Mexico. He had already earned a chem degree at Polytechnic Institute. Ray Pinker forensic'd Aquino's room at the Beachglade. Ray compared his Nembutal compounds with the "Santa Claus" compounds I dug up in Marilyn Monroe's yard. The bond-componentry was identical.

Terry Jay Aquino committed the Beverly Hills 459's. He partnered up with Rick Dawes/Ronnie Dewhurst/Richard Danforth. The Hats and I killed Dawes/Dewhurst/Danforth. Ray found the ripped-seam rubber gloves that Aquino wore at the Beverly Hills jobs and at all six of the divorcée break-ins. They perfectly matched the print manifests from those crimes. They perfectly matched the ripped-seam prints from Lowell Farr's bedroom and the Bev's Switchboard mailbox.

I read the LAPD file on Manny's dismissed burglary charge in '57. Identical ripped-seam rubber-glove prints were found at the house Manny was accused of B and E'ing. *That* meant *this:*

Terry Jay and El Manny were old B and E partners. It explained Manny's presence at the Beachglade Motel.

Mexican Customs agents state *this:*

Terry's mother divorced Terry's father in 1945. Terry's father sent Terry's mother obscene notes clipped from magazine pages. Terry watched his father prepare the notes. Terry's father urged him to ejaculate into his mother's lingerie and put a Sex Hex on her. The Sex Hex would assure that Terry and his dad got lots of sex and that Terry's unfaithful mama would die from VD.

Terry purchased "Preston Fong" identification in T.J. It was 1947. He bought the fake ID from Hersh Aadland. *That* fact strongly suggests *this:*

Terry Jay Aquino knew *Albie* Aadland well before his Chino jolt. And well before Albie's prison-visitor work with the Friends Service Committee.

Terry's forged ID included a Mexican passport, driver's license, and Federal ID card. Terry altered his true AB blood type to the far more common O.

"Preston Fong" entered America in late '47. He gravitated to West L.A. and the beach. He caddied at the Hillcrest, Bel Air, and Riviera Country Clubs. He found a permanent caddy home at Riviera, early in '48. Riviera adjoined the home of Carole Landis and the Pavia Place fuck pad.

Preston perved on fine wristwatches. He snatched them from jewelry store windows. He was "suspected" of the jewelry store jobs, and was popped on suspicion in the spring of 1950. He was never arrested or convicted. He carried his old Aquino ID on the odd pad-prowl-just-to-be-there-and-look-around jobs. He got popped in the summer of '54. He was sent to Chino as Terry Jay Aquino. He'd just acquired a California driver's license. It listed his blood type as O positive.

That's Terry Jay Aquino. It's the official cop version. There's also the Albie Aadland-to-Paul de River version. I'm marking it accessible now.

I cracked de River's code and concluded my stint of code transcription. It wasn't difficult. I made it difficult. I castigated myself with biblical screeds. I stepped aside from that self-laceration. I detected a simple number-replacement code and took it from there.

"*Albie Aadland Correspondence*"/"*Marilyn Monroe Sessions.*" I read the Albie shit first. It was *one-way* correspondence. The file did not include de River's coded replies.

Albie's letters revealed *this:*

De River was Albie's intellectual big brother and deranged confessor. De River saw all and condoned all. They shared an urgent curiosity for all things sexual and criminal. Albie was a volitional celibate and a drug-dabbling voluptuary. His brothers got him hooked on rare compounds synthesized and manufactured in Mexico. Hersh knew a Filipino youth, now masquerading as Chinese, under false credentials. The boy had an outré childhood not unlike Albie's own. He compounded drugs. He test-piloted them—just as Albie test-piloted dope for his brothers and for Doctor Paul himself.

Albie's letters were undated. I think de River's Albie file was chronologically arrayed. One letter arrived in the spring of '48. I'm sure of it. In it, Albie asks de River *this:*

"*Is your Filipino-cum-Chinaman a golf caddy? My brothers retain an interest in a fuck pad—and the newly credentialed Chinaman shows up quite a bit. The FP is near the Riviera Club, so I wonder. And, he accurately laid out the synthesis of an amphetamine/opioid pill he popped on the premises. I'm sure he didn't compound the formula, because I know who did. In other words, I find Le Chinois very interesting.*"

The next run of letters ran banal. Albie gasbagged on the Leopold-Loeb case and the Albert Dyer child murders. He asked, "*Are volitional celibates who resist adult female advances more likely to become child molester–killers than other men?*"

Two more banal letters followed. Albie was a camp follower. He extolled sex slasher Otto Stephen Wilson and wondered who killed the Black Dahlia. Then, Albie wrote *this:*

A highly rambling letter about the "Haunted House" his brothers and their doctor cousin shared a percentage of. It started up as a prohibition speakeasy. It catered to the "westside crowd." Albie called the place a "precursor" fuck pad. The place tanked in '38, and resurrected after the war, on the "exact same" westside lot. It drew a "slumming celebrity crowd," "Negro hepcats," "jazz cats," and "anyone with a lively wit, a good line of patter, and the common sense not to stare at the famous faces engaged in what the squarejohn world considers to be contemptible acts."

The letters went banal again. They remained banal for several years. They were all prurient psych ponder and babble. Red Light Bandit

Caryl Chessman: "He keeps beating the Green Room." That places the letter in '53 or '54. Aquino/Fong's in Chino now. *Now,* Albie asks de River terse little questions:

They pertain to "Our Charge." They pertain to "J.R." As in Jane Russell. They pertain to M.M. As in *Guess Who?*

The terse questions extend. Albie fawns and queries de River, per:

459 PC/hot and soft prowls. "Our" monitoring process and "your" monitoring process. Albie's *BIG* question: "Can inner-outer directed psychopaths also be third-party directed?"

I think *this:*

They got cautious then. They committed nothing to paper. They went to untappable pay-phone communiqués. Just like Marilyn and Gwen. Just like Who Else in '62?

I completed my Albie file read-through. One question tweaked me. How and when did Aquino/Fong meet Dawes/Dewhurst/Danforth— his future B and E partner?

I decided I should start with Gwen Perloff. Thus, it's '37 again. Gwen's almost eleven. She's acting up at her foster home on De Longpre and Wilton. She's shoplifting clothes out of Hollywood shops and selling the threads to Le Conte Junior High kids. It was just a hunch, *BUT—*

I drove to Le Conte and badged the principal. The man let me peruse the '37–'38 Le Conte yearbooks. *And*—there he was, at age thirteen.

Roger Alan Denfrey. He's a B-9 Class member. He's one of those good-looking-with-a-mean-streak boys. He'd grow up to be a burglar and a fake-kidnap man.

I killed him. I killed him on a cop-sanctioned whim.

I checked R&I. I checked nationwide police files up the ying-yang. Roger Alan Denfrey. No wants, no warrants, no criminal record. Did Gwen Perloff meet him in 1937? The odds rate overwhelmingly *YES.*

On to Marilyn. Her coded sessions file delivered. I got verbatim-transcribed Q and A here. The sessions had been tape-recorded and code-transcribed by de River himself. Marilyn consulted him from '52 to mid-'54. De River coined the phrase "declension of fan crushes" at that time. It preceded her coupling with Timmy Berlin and her own attribution of the phrase. De River used Carole Landis as an example of a "neophyte crusher's crush." Marilyn said, "Oh, I knew Carole all right. There's stories I could tell you."

De River bloviated. He cited the great courage it took for creative people to engage the world on its own cruel terms and overcome the self-pampering of the artist. He discussed the importance of disguise, of deliberately denuding one's good looks, of establishing covert means of communication. He cited the Russian theater masters who lived their own versions of cult and criminality under the threat of Stalin's show trials and the head Red's capricious will to slaughter. The perpetration of revisionist art led to official censure, torture, and death. American artists had it soft. Cultivated criminality could work for them—but only if they committed properly bold crimes.

De River excoriated MM. He considered her to be shallow, vain, impetuous, peremptory, whimsical, usurious, and driven by infantile exhibitionism. The only way that she could successfully revise and shape an all-new persona would be for her to go anonymous and cultivate risk in the real world. And revel in the risk of exposure and punishment. Marilyn cited her "bit actress" friend Gwen. She had accomplished just that.

Gwen was Marilyn's age. They shared a room at Hollygrove. Gwen had taken on The Life. They played girl sleuth games at the Grove. Gwen said The Life meant going native. She set up burglary scores and scored bitch-seductress film roles. She comported with burglars, armed robbers, and flimflam men. She started stealing young. Her kid sister had been abducted and certainly snuffed. It *induced* her to go native.

De River told Marilyn that he already knew Gwen. She had been referred to his Sex Offense Bureau at LAPD. She engaged in group therapy under his direction.

De River was starting to *bore* Marilyn. De River fixated on the bold Gwen at the expense of the grasping "dim bulb" Marilyn. Marilyn talked up Gwen. She was her alter ego, doppelgänger, and amanuensis. Gwen carried the symbolic and metaphysical weight that Marilyn could not hoist to her own frail shoulders. Why mince words? De River packed a torch for Gwen and wrote off Marilyn as "stale goods." She emitted a stale stench of desperate fear and put her own artistic success above all moral considerations. She could not inhabit any role other than the role of herself, at the risk of grave psychic peril. Marilyn's first shot at radical therapy pooped out. She reconvened with de River earlier this year. She said she'd re-clicked with old friends. They'd planned a caper. She needed to develop impersonation and survival skills. She needed makeup and wardrobe. De River recommended their mutual friend, Natasha Lytess. Marilyn responded, *"Oooohhhh—I just love Natasha!!!"*

That was it. De River stopped recording his Marilyn sessions. He was dispensing hard criminal advice now. He went from shrink to gang lord. He *had* to be Preston Fong/Terry Jay Aquino's old mentor. Albie

Aadland hooked up with old pal Marilyn and old pals Manny, Paul Mitchell, and *La* Gwen herself. *They* formed their fake kidnap cabal.

Then Jimmy Hoffa appeared and started some shit rolling. Jimmy, and his pals the A boys. They had deep and crazy roots with the Mar-Gwen gang. Then I tossed a man off a cliff.

The services ran back-to-back. Sam Yorty planned it that way. It lubed the press and kept things moving. James Thornton Meadows and Georgia Lowell Farr. 1929 and '45, up to right now. It was all too brief, kids.

Protestant ceremonies. Adjoining hillsides at Forest Lawn Glendale. The Meadows' show ran first. It was a big PD send-off. It featured bagpipers and Navy choppers scattering mums. J.T. was line-of-duty and mandated the splurge. Lois stood with me both times. She refused to touch me or look at me. She told me why walking in.

"This is on you, Freddy. J.T. and Lowell. You thought you could score, so you cooked something up. You put together a group of your playmates, and this is how it panned out."

Bill Parker showed up for Meadows. Ditto, Daryl Gates. The full Intel Division showed. Miller Leavy showed. Ranking cops wore their dress blues. The LAPD rolled out one thousand plus. Parker consoled Meadows' widow and three children. I consoled a half-crocked Marcia Davenport. The service attenuated. The sun bore down. Parker gave the cutoff sign at an hour and fifteen minutes. His glad-hand line ran twice as long as the ceremony.

The Farr gig was nearby. It was an easy stroll for those inclined. The mourning circle was intimate. Family, friends, a few classmates. The Hat Squad, Nat and Phil. Speakers cranked Lowell's favorite jazz chart—the Gerry Mulligan Quartet with "My Funny Valentine." The pastor read from the Old Testament.

"I know that my redeemer liveth, and that he shall stand at the latter day upon the earth. And though this body be destroyed, yet shall I see God, whom I shall see for myself, and mine eyes shall behold, and not as a stranger."

Lois ditched me at the moment of interment. I nicked a memory card. Lowell wore her red beret. She wore it the night she painted Marilyn Monroe, while I watched.

68

I woke up scared. Something pressed upside me. I guzzled cold coffee and reached for the phone.

I called Gwen. Her service took the call. I left a "Call me" message.

I called Lois at her hotel. The desk man said she checked out last night. I called Maury Dexter on the *Twist Party* set. Maury said Lois bailed on the picture. The Farr girl messed with her head.

Gwen didn't call. Gwen hadn't called. I ate alone at Frascati, four nights straight. The depositions are prepped to go. Morty Bendish concluded his Sex Creep series. All Of It runs long on theory and falls short of resolution.

I called the night nurse at Queen of Angels. She debriefed me on Sid Leffler. He's heavily medicated. The pain is bad. He talks in his sleep. He rants about a haunted house.

I called Del Kinney. Del picked up, one ring in. I said, "It's Otash. I've been thinking about something."

Del went *Aw-oh*. I said, "Ollie Hammond's in an hour. Come on. We're both awake."

"I'll be there, but you're buying me breakfast."

Ollie's was deadsville. Service was quick. We noshed T-bones and hash browns.

I lit a cigarette. "I'm teething on Mitzi. I found some old paperwork, and I turned a second eyewit to Mitzi on the bus."

Del sipped coffee. "I know about that lead. Gwen told me you told her. Mitzi's on the bus, and this eyewit says she was being teased by two boys. One was about thirteen, the second boy was a bit older."

"That's correct. And the big question is, 'Have you got a name on that eyewit?'"

"No. And the lead is twenty-five and a half years old."

Del eyeballed my steak. "Well, there you are. The original IO's out of Hollywood station were all old guys in '37, so I'm fairly sure they're all gone now. I do know that the West L.A. squadroom guys ran bus-route checks on that Hollywood-to-the-beach run for a good two weeks, after they got that first lead. You know how this works. They buzzed the regular riders on Mitzi and who she might have been with, and what stop she might have got off at. Nothing came of it, or I would have heard. If there's file notations anywhere, they'll be in the sludge room at the West L.A. station."

"Who ran it for the West L.A. dicks? Can you give me a name and a pedigree?"

Del said, "Arthur McCall. He died on Guadalcanal, but he was sure as shit a fine detective while he served. His widow's still with us. She lives out in Glendale, and I've got her address. You never know. She might have kept some of Arthur's old pocket notebooks."

I shut my eyes. I craved more sleep. It was 4:00 a.m. Shitwork runs loomed.

"'Teething on Mitzi' means 'teething on Gwen.' Don't fall in love with her, Freddy. If she's anybody's, she's mine."

The sludge room. Old files, dead files, nonfiles. Non sequitur paper slips. Petrified rat turds. Old cardboard boxes, banged up for years.

'40 back to '16. No '37 box. *That* box was missing. I triple-combed the sludge room. A conclusion slammed me. The '37 box had been snatched.

An early bird patrol cop watched me. He was a nib-snout type. I said, "I'm looking for the '37 box. I can't find it anywhere."

The guy picked his teeth. "Mr. Clean went on a kick, about a month ago. He said, 'We're looking at twenty-five years now, so I'm giving these old chestnuts the heave-ho.'"

I said, "Who's Mr. Clean?"

He said, "Sid Leffler. I know you know him, and I know you and the Hats put him down for the count."

I tossed an empty box at him. He laughed and flipped me off.

Mrs. McCall trimmed hedges by the driveway. I parked at the curb and walked up. She saw the box of candy I brought and fluffed out her hair.

She was sixty-something. She was fit. She read me in one glance.

"I don't need a road map, if that's what you're thinking. You've got better manners than most, and you're too young to have worked with Arthur. I'm sure it's either old case files or Arthur's old pocket notebooks. Please don't tell me I'm too far off."

I passed her the candy. She popped the lid and plucked a nougat concoction. I grabbed a plain chocolate and snarfed it.

"It's the old notebooks, isn't it? Let's walk over to the garage. Arthur was meticulous in everything that he did. He kept everything in boxes marked by date and year."

We ambled over. The boxes were clumped on a shelf above some pruning shears.

They were grease pencil–marked. I eyeball-trolled the shelf. There it is: "1936–'37."

I hauled it down and balanced it on one knee. Mrs. McCall popped chocolates and observed me. The box was packed with file folders. Meticulous McCall. He arranged his boxes by month. I finger-walked straight to "2/17/37, *Perloff, Mitzi*." I dug out a pocket-size notebook.

It was marked:

"Bus-route canvass, 3/4 to 3/7/37."

I flipped pages. 1, 2, 3, 4, 5, 6, 7, 8—penciled-in names, addresses, and cross-outs. I hit Page #9 and saw *this:*

"Mrs. Bernice Rhoden/WFA/DOB 11/2/92. 11892 Temescal Canyon/GL-8992. States she can't recall date, but girl (assumed to be MP) got off at Mandeville Canyon stop. Confirmed that boys were teasing MP and that they alighted from bus at same stop. Did not overhear teasing but sensed it. Boys were desc. as 12 to 14, one tall, one short. Taller boy had 'lighter hair.' Shorter boy, possibly younger, had Harold Lloyd–type round eyeglasses."

I sensed it. I looped Le Conte Junior High to Intel and back west again. I checked old phone directories and the new white pages. Mrs. Rhoden was sixty-nine now. She still lived in Temescal Canyon. I called her and ID'd myself. I said I'd like to drop by and show her some pictures. They pertained to that missing girl and those two boys on the bus. Mrs. Rhoden recalled the incident. She told me to come out.

Hollygrove was close by Le Conte. Some Grove kids went to school at the Grove, some kids went to Le Conte. They knew me at Le Conte now. I ID'd Dawes/Danforth/Dewhurst as Roger Alan Denfrey. I worked off a Grove-to-Le Conte hunch.

The principal humored me one more time. He let me desecrate a run of '35 to '37 yearbooks. I ripped out pictures of Roger Denfrey and a boy with Harold Lloyd glasses.

I drove to the PAB and hit the Intel squadroom. I raided a stack of juvie mug books. I plucked six Roger Denfrey–look-alike mugs and six shots resembling the glasses kid. I pasted them to a shirt cardboard and added the yearbook pix. I concocted a twelve-boy mug run. Mrs. Rhoden would scan it and go yea or nay.

The mug shots and yearbook pix covered two shirt cardboards. I broomed back to Temescal Canyon. Mrs. Rhoden lived in a neat Craftsman house. She perched on her porch.

I jammed to the curb. I leaped steps up to her. Mrs. Rhoden eyeballed the mug shots and pix. She did not equivocate. She did not stall or hem and haw. She pointed straight to Roger Denfrey and Albie Aadland.

69

Miller Leavy called me in. He sat me down. He said, "Open your brief-case." Miller's flying high. Bill Parker told me why.

I popped my briefcase. Miller displayed four grand-jury subpoe-nas. They were Federal. They dunned Natasha Lytess, Sidney Leffler, Michael J. Bayless, and Gwen Perloff. I went *Load me up.*

Leavy dropped the papers in. He hooked his thumbs in his vest. He did a cock-of-the-walk routine.

"The AG anointed me. I'm officially 'Kitchen Cabinet' now. It may have been your original brainstorm, but I'm the one charged with its implementation."

"Congratulations, boss. You're the perfect man for the job."

Leavy hopped in his desk chair. He plopped his feet on the desk and wiggled them at me.

"Bill Parker wants you to serve and debrief Mike Bayless in LAPD custody. He's paying Pete Pitchess off in Intel files for the privilege. Max and Red are escorting him from the Sheriff's DB to the foyer of the PAB. The press will be there. Mayor Yorty plans to be there."

I laughed. "Tell true, boss. You're getting a Federal judgeship out of this."

"And you and the Hats are getting a skate on Murder One or Man-slaughter Two, or whatever else I could have wangled. Don't play me blithe, junior. I'm out of your league."

I said, "There's no subpoena for Albie Aadland."

Leavy coughed. "Well—he's an Aadland—and Grant Cooper's rep-resenting him. That merits consideration."

I adjusted my necktie and shot my cuffs. I indulged a quick primp. It ate five seconds up.

"I've been thinking, boss. You haven't had a good murder case in a dog's age. I mean a real gas-chamber bounce."

Leavy *harumphed*. "Don't I know it. And I don't mind telling you that I'm salivating for one."

I lit a cigarette. "I'm working on something. It's a juvie sex snuff, and it's twenty-five years old. It's a no-body deal, like your Ewing Scott case."

"I'm salivating already. Female victim? Tell me we got lucky. Females engender the most sympathy."

I winked. "I'll tell you more, once we've got these depositions out of the way. It's a headline banger."

They put Motel Mike through it. They manhandled him. They subjected him to ridicule. They strolled him through downtown L.A.

Here's the route: the Hall of Justice to the PAB. East on Temple and south on L.A. Street. It's about a half mile. He's handcuffed behind his back. He's hard-clamped by Max Herman and Red Stromwall. They're moving him out. He's half off his feet.

They're three men on a stroll. Newshounds and TV camera trucks track them. Flashbulb pops plague them. Looky-loos tag along. They razz Motel Mike. They dispense jabbery contempt.

I bird-dogged it. Foot traffic veered into the street. Max and Red came on resolute. Motel Mike wilted and weaved between them. They hit the PAB lobby. Flashbulbs popped exponential. The lobby was quadruple-packed. Max and Red stiff-armed politicos and cops off to one side. The jail elevator cranked wide. They shoved Motel Mike in.

I saw Sam Yorty. He waved me over. We hobknobbed by the cigar stand. Crowd noise engulfed us. We had to shout.

Mayor Sam went in close. "Parker's got a mean streak. Putting a jazzy guy like Mike through something like this is unkosher."

I shoulder-draped him. "He's got the true skank on Mike—trust me on that."

"When Mike sorts all this grief out, he'll need work. I'm going to hire him on as my bodyguard."

I laughed. The lobby roar abated. I tossed a wild pitch, in tight.

"Mr. Mayor—who do you think has the best fuck-deck collection, you or Roddy McDowall?"

Mayor Sam went *oooh-la-la*. "Roddy's got me licked on sheer volume, but I've got the king deck, the one with the provenance and the resale potential. You can't beat the participants, and Orson Welles took the pictures. Fifty-two 'poses,' with the ace of spades triple-signed."

"Who'd you buy it from?"

"A bent motor cop named Norm Krause. He was a dirty trickster for old Chief Worton, back when men were men and sheep were scared."

I yocked. Mayor Sam saw DA McKesson and beelined on over. I walked to the jail stairs and jogged down a flight.

Newsmen swamped the check-in desk. I ducked down to attorney-room row. Room #B was preprepped to go.

I stepped inside. *Mike, you've earned it. You won't be here long. You know I work for effect.*

The jailers laid out a small table. Plus two slat-wood chairs. The centerpiece *worked.* They plopped down a fifth of Old Crow and two shot glasses. *Mike, I've got no gripe with you.*

Max and Red walked him in and uncuffed him. They about-faced and walked straight back out. Motel Mike rubbed his wrists. I cracked the jug and poured two shots. I dropped the subpoena on the table.

"No testimony. All records sealed. You attest to me and a few others. You're enjoined to secrecy, under threat of prosecution. You're immune from this moment on. No state, municipal, or rogue local agency can touch you. You walk on all your misdeeds."

Motel Mike flipped his chair and straddled the slats. Motel Mike downed Shot #1.

"Gwen told me something like this was in the works, so who am I to scoff? You know Gwen, right? You're the man who knows everything and everyone, so I'd be surprised if you didn't know her."

I downed Shot #1. "Parker's kicking you loose in two hours. You're off the Sheriff's, but you keep your pension. You'll attest in a private room at Ollie Hammond's. It'll be me, Daryl Gates, Parker, and Miller Leavy."

"You're the Welcome Wagon, right? I get the show of force, and Mr. Shakedown himself smoothes my feathers."

I downed Shot #2. "You were in Marilyn Monroe's house on the night she died. It's an OD, and I'm not trying to prove anything else. The lab made you off a walking portrait. I've got one question here. What were you there for, that night?"

Motel Mike twirled the jug. "The snatch had gone down. Natasha Lytess, Marilyn's wardrobe mistress, got antsy when the first radio reports hit. She knew where Richie Danforth and Buzzy Stein were holed up, and she called her pal Darryl Zanuck, who was about to get tapped for two hundred grand. She ratted the deal, and Zanuck called Bill Parker. So here come you and the Hats to fuck it all up."

I said, "*And?*"

"*And* the snatch team was the late Manny Salas, the missing and perhaps late Paul Mitchell Grenier, and the ever-diffident and wimpy Albie Aadland. Manny was running the listening post on the Monroe-home feed. Marilyn was stone batshit crazy, and she was mouthing off all sorts of injudicious shit to her new sidekick, Lowell Farr. Marilyn required surveillance, and Manny provided it. He ran the post out of that TV shop where he worked. He was on the wire that night, and he heard Marilyn playing a radio report on the snatch, and how you and the Hats bumped Richie Danforth. She got on her horn to the Farr girl, out of her mind and about half coherent, and pitched all this shit about this man whose death she caused. Manny *was* listening, and he called me and told me to get over to Marilyn's place and calm her down. Brentwood to Pacific Palisades calls are no toll, so you never got to review any calls to the girl on Marilyn's phone bills. Okay, I drove over to Marilyn's place. I broke in, and I was about to start pulling bug mounts, when I found Marilyn dead. Then Peter Lawford showed up, and I shimmied back out the window. Then *you* showed up, while I was half a block away, watching you lug an evidence kit and pull your pud."

Man Camera. Instant flashback. I recalled *this* moment *that* night.

"The radio was right by the bed. I turned it on. It was fine-tuned to an all-news station. An announcer mentioned an earlier report. Marilyn must have heard that one. It stressed the dead suspect, by name. It laid out the Hats and me, by name. Then, she called Lowell, then she took the pills."

Motel Mike leaned in. He smiled gleeful. He tapped my head twice. *Mr. Shakedown. Nobody ever said you're not quick.*

"There you have it. You killed a man, and Marilyn got all weepy. The Lowell girl failed to console her. Marilyn got weepy on her best of days, but this was too fucking much. So, who's the one packing the guilt here? You tell me."

70

Summons server. Errand boy. Factotum.

I drove to Brentwood. I brought Natasha Lytess a three-dollar bouquet. Motel Mike's indictment banged through my head.

Phone work. I spent last night shagging calls. I stared at news pix of Lowell Farr and Mitzi Perloff. Nat and Phil reported in. Nat said a carting truck arrived at Doc de River's place. Four workmen removed the Doc's file boxes and dumped them in the back. Phil tailed the truck to an incinerator landfill. A workman passed the landfill boss a wad of Doc de River's money. The workmen off-loaded the boxes and dumped them in the on-site pyre. Phil watched them ignite.

That meant *this:*

No de River evidence. No further Albie Aadland drift.

I've got my Albie-to-de River correspondence. I hoard it with deadly intent. I want Miller Leavy to utilize it. I want him to deploy it as only he knows how. I want him to put Albie down.

I've developed a plan. It's a two-hand play. I'll sweatbox Albie and Miller. The mirror walls and sound speakers will broadcast the show. I'll stand there with Gwen Perloff.

Eddie Chacón called me. He reported *this:*

José Bolaños vanished in Mexico. The *pendejos* on Ingrid Irmgard's bearer-bond list declined to press charges. Customs cut Ingrid loose. She's back in L.A. "Hey, *Señor* Freddy—you and Max blew up her *puto* boyfriend!"

Max and Red are serving backup subpoenas. They're hitting Norm Krause and Jack Clemmons today. They might or might not be deposed. Harry Crowder and Eddie Benson lockstep Albie Aadland. The surveillance serves one purpose. They're out to make Albie squirm.

Ratfuck Bob Teletyped me. He told me to do *this:*

Craft a final summary. It should supplant and enhance the issued subpoenas and backup paperwork. Lay out your actions from 4/9/62 up to this moment. I expect and demand complete candor. This document will survive in the vacuum of just you and me.

I Teletyped a reply. I stressed my compliance and pledged prompt delivery. I pledged full candor. I said I'd include detailed notes on the '37 and '48 combustions that triggered the full chain of events.

I pulled up behind Natasha's old Ford. I heard her coughing—way back in the yard. I took the driveway back, slow. I coughed myself. It preannounced me and gave her time to compose.

She sat in her chair. She caught some good morning rays. I coughed again. I worked for kicks and grins. She said, "Don't you start doing it."

Her eyes were pinned. She'd lost more weight. She sipped tea and pointed to her spare chair. I dragged it over. She snatched the depo and bouquet.

"Gwen called me. She told me to expect you, and played to my vanity. She said the oral deposition will occur in a private room at a nice restaurant. What more could someone as stage-addled as I ask for?"

I said, "Give me a sneak peek. Tell me how you met Paul de River, and how the two of you directed Marilyn's performance."

It was a vividly theatrical performance and a peerless feat of breath control and stage savvy. She anticipated my one question and memorized her lines in advance. She was determined not to exceed her stage manager's brief and spoke to the point at all times. The point was not her feckless love for Marilyn Monroe. It was something altogether more sinister.

The Fox lot, '49 into '50. De River was a tech consultant on Otto Preminger's crime lox, *Where the Sidewalk Ends.* He riffed motivation to auteur Otto and star Dana Andrews. She was a dialogue coach on the film. They were both hipped on Russian theater and criminal psychopathy. De River considered actors to be a morally deficient species. She agreed, in full. She audited a few group therapy sessions at de River's Sex Offense Bureau at LAPD. Marilyn's old friend and amanuensis Gwen Perloff was in the group. Her participation spared her a jail knock for soliciting. Miss Lytess learned that Miss Perloff was an orphanage *confrère* of the emergent actress Marilyn Monroe. Miss Lytess knew Marilyn from *The Asphalt Jungle.* Miss Perloff was a dangerous criminal. Miss Perloff wanted to be an actress. Marilyn Monroe possessed a broad, if rudimentary, talent. Miss Perloff possessed no talent. Marilyn was craven to her core. Miss Perloff was strong to her core. And Marilyn wanted to be a criminal.

'51 into '52. Marilyn began spewing outlandish criminal fantasies. She entered therapy with Dr. Paul, '53 to '54. She left therapy abruptly. It was too rigorous. She was too diffuse. She had succumbed to the idiot notion of being Marilyn Monroe, movie star and worldwide sensation. She sustained her friendship with Gwen Perloff. Their métier was the impromptu late-night phone call. Marilyn went publicly crazy for all the world to see. Gwen Perloff did not seem to mind. She told Marilyn real-life criminal stories. Marilyn dished ripe criminal fantasies in return. Marilyn held her fantasies to be real and brooked no contradiction. She believed that she owned the world but was not of the world and comported within this perilous schism. Criminal fantasy consumed her. She sought professional criminal counsel and reentered therapy with Dr. Paul early this year. He suggested that she spend yet more phone time with Gwen Perloff. Dr. Paul contacted Miss Lytess. He told her that Marilyn needed their help in crafting a real-life criminal persona—and that there would be a good weekly paycheck for the work.

Thus:

Miss Lytess met Motel Mike Bayless, Manny Salas, Paul Mitchell Grenier, and Albie Aadland. She remet the astoundingly self-possessed Gwen Perloff and transferred the full force of her tortuous crush on Marilyn to Gwen.

The cabal decided to stage a publicity kidnap. And perhaps invest a small portion of the money in the racket schemes percolating on the Fox lot.

Marilyn's lunacy kept pace with her Fox-in-duress fears. She remade herself as a criminal mastermind. She concocted scheme upon scheme—each more ridiculous—up to and including a studio takeover by Mar-Gwen Productions.

Gwen Perloff was a part-time bond courier. She ran real bonds and forged bonds, crafted by consorts of Albie Aadland's elder brothers. Gwen set Marilyn up with a man named José Bolaños. The Fox Rackets Conspiracy burst to life and imploded all at once.

It shouldn't have. Marilyn's grandiosity made it all happen. It was supposed to be a fake kidnap score. They'd be in and out. With a reasonable ransom demand and an equitable cash split. Gwen wanted a stake. She wanted to blow off her acting career and split L.A. forever. Motel Mike wanted a stake. He wanted to set up college funds for his kids. Albie wanted to wax bold and impress his big brothers. Manny wanted a stake. He wanted to set himself up in his own TV-repair shop. Paul Mitchell wanted a stake. He wanted to set himself up as a director of high-class smut films starring Marilyn Monroe. The straight kidnap gig might have worked—but Marilyn wanted *MORE*.

Gwen tried to control Marilyn. Miss Lytess and Doc de River crafted her zaftig-girl-hide-in-plain-sight persona. Marilyn performed adroitly. She couriered bonds and dope bravely and successfully. She lived within her disguise. She redressed the deranged-movie-star role that was killing her.

This cabal enjoyed the surcease. It was short-lived. Fox dumped Marilyn off *Got to Give*. Marilyn went on an anti-Kennedy kick. She said she planned to blackmail the president. He would divorce Jackie and marry her. Marilyn blew her mind. It was permanent. Miss Lytess knew it. Manny and Paul Mitchell blew their minds. Paul Mitchell bit Manny once. Miss Lytess feared for Marilyn's safety. She called Darryl Zanuck and ratted the kidnap gig off.

She paused and coughed. She sipped tea and popped two pain pills.

"We all loved drama, at the cost of our souls. Even Paul Mitchell and Manny were crazy for movies. Gwen described it as an 'idiot enchantment.' Why is it that the more sentient of us could fail to see how wrong it was? We were all so jejune. All our artful notions were pure ignorance and arrogance. That's what appalls me the most."

71

The postmidnight oil. I'm burning it, white-hot.

Ratfuck Bob demands a summary. I'm 214 pages in now. I've put a lens to my crazy summer of 1962. I've confessed to the murder of Roger Denfrey and shifted the blame off the Hats. I've confessed the murder of Paul Mitchell Grenier and directed the Feds to the dump site.

I've been at it for nine hours straight. I've taken breaks to call L.A.-area drugstores and check their summer '48 sales records. I located two penicillin scripts filled by Dr. Shelley Mandel. It confirmed my key summer '48 throughlines.

I concentrated on Sid Leffler then. Daryl Gates served Leffler's subpoena at Queen of Angels last night. I dug up Sex Offense Bureau records in a Headquarters Vice storeroom this morning. I pulled group-therapy attendance sheets from '49 to '52. Leffler audited two dozen sessions that Gwen Perloff also attended. The sessions were conducted by Sid's close pal, Paul de River.

Leffler. Sid, the linchpin. Sid, the old-timer. Sid knew the Aadland brothers in the mid- to late '30s. He ran errands and tossed stink bombs for them. He's been mumbling *"haunted house"* in his sleep. Four duty nurses have confirmed it. The haunted house is most likely the Pavia Place fuck pad. It shut down in '37 or '38 and resurrected after the war. The Aadland brothers and cousin Shelley Mandel held profit points.

Leffler worked chump jobs at the '30s fuck pad. *Why did it shut down?* Leffler was a doormat-stooge at the postwar pad. Leffler lied about Albie Aadland. He said he only glimpsed the young Albie during picket-line dustups on the Fox lot. Leffler dumped the '37 file box at the West L.A. station.

Leffler cracked under duress. He said he tried to sell Marilyn Monroe's letters to Paul de River. De River nixed the offer. De River told Leffler that he already knew the Sex Creep and stated that half of the letters surely came from him. Leffler revealed this before I read the coded Albie letters to de River. The Sex Creep was a postwar fuck-pad habitué. Leffler surely sideswiped him at that hot spot.

I'm going to predepose Leffler at 9:00 a.m. I'll type out a prepared list of questions and insert spaces for his handwritten replies. His signature will certify his plea bargain with Miller Leavy. Leffler stands accused of a hundred-plus counts of stat rape and forced oral cop. The nineteen complainants are all westside high school coeds.

I watched the fucker sleep. I nicked a get-well card at the nurses' station and stuck my query sheet inside it. I left it beside Leffler's water cup.

The guest chair gouged my ass. I chain-smoked and scratched my balls raw. Late-sleeper Leffler—it was 9:29 a.m.

I saw him stir. He couldn't see me. I set the window drapes just so.

He stirred and stretched. He reached for his cup. He saw the get-well card and pulled out the query sheet.

I said, "Hey, there. You're a sleepyhead."

Sid Leffler screamed.

Miller Leavy established a protocol. Leffler would rat Albie Aadland within precise legal guidelines. His 3-to-5 sex crime sentence would be suspended. He would instead receive a jive-public-service slap on the wrist. Lieutenant Freddy O. would tape-record a precise Q and A. Leffler would respond to my queries and write in his replies. We would both initial the responses. Only two individuals would read the rat sheet. They were Leavy and Gwen Perloff.

Leffler was malingering at Queen of Angels. He was milking his rest cure before a return to his fucked-up life. He withstood a good shitkicking. The kicking did not justify this indolent cure. We didn't thump him to oblivion. He got off easy.

He worked in bed. I sat in my ass-gouging chair. He spoke and then inked his answers to my questions. The room was quiet. A window cooling unit hummed. My portable recorder spooled tape. We hand-annotated the typescript after each Q and A. The finished document reads like *this:*

FO/Q: "When and where did you meet Gwen Perloff?"

SL/A: "In 1950, at the Sex Offense Bureau at LAPD."

FO/Q: "In what specific context?"

SL/A: "Group therapy. Gwen got popped for soliciting, and she had to attend these sessions, to dodge jail time. Doc de River ran the groups. He gassed on Gwen, I could tell."

FO/Q: "What personal business did Miss Perloff most frequently bring up at these sessions?"

SL/A: "The disappearance of her kid sister, Mitzi, in February of '37. Everybody figured some kiddie slasher did her in. Gwen was convinced that a Le Conte Junior High boy named Roger did it. He was a mean kid, and he bragged about killing little girls."

FO/Q: "Where were you working in February of '37?"

SL/A: "At . . . well . . . the Aadland brothers owned a party house, on Pavia Place, in the Palisades. I served drinks and ran errands."

FO/Q: "Did a Le Conte boy named Roger Denfrey, and Albie Aadland—the much younger Aadland brother—habituate this establishment?"

SL/A: "Yes."

FO/Q: "And on a particular February night, did Roger Denfrey relay some disturbing news with regards to Albie Aadland to you?"

SL/A: "Yes. He said that Albie had been fondling Mitzi under the Le Conte bleachers, back in Hollywood, and that he talked her into taking a bus ride to the beach with them . . . and . . . they were teasing her on the bus, and they brought her there to the party house, and he disappeared with her into an upstairs bedroom, and Roger went up to see what was going on, and he saw them naked, and Albie was strangling Mitzi and shoving a washcloth in her mouth."

FO/Q: "What did you do then?"

SL/A: "I went up and saw the body, and then I called Hersh Aadland and told him what happened."

FO/Q: "What did Hersh Aadland do?"

SL/A: "What do you think, asshole? He bundled up the body and dumped it someplace."

FO/Q: "Did Roger Denfrey participate in the murder?"

SL/A: "No. He was listening to a radio show downstairs when it happened."

I eyeballed Gwen's building. I sat in my car and kept precise track of the time.

It was 9:34 p.m. Gwen was at home. She's burning her living room lights. I saw her car tucked in her parking slot. I slid the Q and A under her front door. It was 8:34 p.m. then. I included a personal note:

"Consider all of this. Tell me how you'd like me to proceed."

Her shades were yanked tight. Living room lights burned behind them. The front door did not budge. Time decohered. I waited for Gwen to call me in.

I talked to Miller Leavy, four hours back. He read the Q and A and revoked Albie's immunity deal. He said he did not intend to inform Rat-dog Bobby of the Leffler/Mitzi offshoot of our cases. He said he intends to file Murder One on Albie and try him as an adult. February 17, 1937, is twenty-five years, seven months, and nineteen days ago.

Time decohered. I sat in my car and plain yearned. I kept my windows down. The night was near warm. I couldn't will sound into sight or—

I heard a high-pitched sound. It came from upstairs and off-right. It went from whine to woman's shriek. I heard crash and thud sounds off-right. I saw cloaked window-curtains shimmy and heard glass break.

I piled out and ran. I heard all the sounds all at once and all with the sound increased. I ran upstairs and paused. I saw loose doorjamb mounts and shoulder-punched the door in. I tripped inside and saw *this:*

Gwen. She's throwing things at the south wall. Straight-back chairs, soft chairs, glass shelves, and bric-a-brac. They're piled up at the foot of the wall. She's gouged the wall past the paint and foundation boards, and still with that *shriek*—

I tripped again. I got to her and behind her and threw myself at her. I got my arms around her and wrestled her loose. We bumped heads and tripped sideways and clipped shelves and kicked rugs up and fell into a leather couch as she flailed.

We got our heads turned around. Her face was dry and dark red–blotted. There were no tears.

We paused. We caught some breath. She didn't tremble. She didn't sob. She gnawed at her lips. We paused again—so I kissed her.

We fell into it and stayed with it. I kept my watch facedown on the nightstand. We kept our clothes off. Nobody called in a noise beef. No deputies rolled out and banged at the door. Time went someplace. We stayed close. We said things. We didn't want to lose the fit. Gwen said,

"I should tell you first. I don't want to tell it in a roomful of men and stenographers, and lose it because we didn't walk through it first."

She stated it. She didn't ask me. She walked into the living room and walked back with a tape rig. She plugged it into the wall and laid it down on the sheets.

All right, then. Tell me.

It was the Grove, first and always. It was Gwen and Norma Jean Baker, the incipient Marilyn. It was the gang. Gwen and Marilyn lorded it over Albie, Paul Mitchell, and their pal from outside—Manny Salas. They were movie-mad kids. *Little* kids—eleven, twelve, thirteen. There were long days up in that tree on El Centro. The Grove offered long views. They had a big view of Paramount and RKO. There were extras in costume and movie stars on parade.

They were little kids with big imaginations. Gwen and Mitzi lived in a foster home at De Longpre and Wilton at first. You could see the kid versions of who they'd all become. Paul Mitchell was mean. He liked to bite and fight. El Manny was a house burglar and amateur boxer. He was a Nite Owl peewee and loved to futz around with electrical things. Albie was studious and withdrawn. He hoarded dirty pictures. His big brothers forced him to commit minor crimes and test-pilot dope. Marilyn was ambitious and sweet-natured, up to a point. Gwen was not that way. She was calculating to the nth degree.

Mitzi vanished. The Sheriff's and L.A. police investigated. Gwen ran wild. She boosted threads from Hollywood shops and peddled them to kids at Le Conte Junior High. Albie went to Le Conte and came back home to the Grove. Gwen met a Le Conte boy named Roger Denfrey. Roger strutted tall in the ensembles that Gwen stole for him.

The foster home expelled Gwen. The girl was just too wild. She got lucky and got sent to the Grove. Gwen and Marilyn played girl-sleuth games. They fantasy-solved Mitzi's murder a thousand times over. Gwen suspected Roger Denfrey. He told Le Conte kids that he wanted to become a pimp and sex-slash little girls. He harped on this. He told all who would listen.

The late '30s. The early war years. The gang comes of age.

Manny Salas goes off to high school and trade school. Manny fights professional. Paul Mitchell fights and bites and becomes a boss jocker at Georgia Street Juvenile. Albie attends Occidental College. Marilyn tears through foster homes. She endures boarding stints with distant relatives and endures a kid marriage. Gwen becomes a semipro shoplifter and late-teen lingerie model. She's kept up with Manny. She sucks up to rich men and sleeps with them on occasion. She targets their homes for El Manny's 459 prowls.

The war ends. The swinging postwar-L.A. era kicks on. El Manny's a pad burglar. Paul Mitchell's a grip, bit actor, and part-time fruit hustler. Marilyn and Gwen are starlet manqués and fledgling call girls. They haunt studio casting offices and scrounge bit parts.

It's now '48. Marilyn and Gwen reconnect on the L.A. nightlife circuit. Gwen's heard of a wild joint on Pavia Place. It's way out in the Palisades. It's a party house. Such places are commonly known as "fuck pads."

You've got men and women—all good-looking. There's nifty film folk and inspired squarejohn types out to *HOWL*. You've got booze and dope. *Oooh-la-la*—there's private compounds and the best prescription shit of the era. You have Dr. Shelley Mandel. With his script-writing largesse and his cautionary VD spiels and free-flowing penicillin.

Orson Welles habituates the fuck pad. Visiting celebs pass through. Gwen sees Roddy McDowall and Liz Taylor on several occasions. Marilyn and Gwen become fuck-pad regulars. Dr. Shelley becomes Marilyn's personal physician. Random rich boys pass through the fuck pad. Plus noted politicians. They're often escorted by an L.A. cop named Norm and an almost-cop named Jack.

The fuck pad swings *HARD*. Local weird-o's pass through. An unknown trumpet virtuoso. This weird Chinaman who steals watches and may or may not cook dope. A cop named Sid Leffler provides security. He's a longtime Aadland stooge.

There's jazz combos. There's jam sessions and impromptu smut-foto sessions. Orson Welles is quite the shutterbug. There's orgy action in plain sight. *And* there's Doc Shelley's invention—the fuck deck.

Dig:

Get your jollies in the moment. Pose fifty-two times over. Orson's a fuck-deck enthusiast. So's the Queen of the Fuck Pad:

Carole Landis. Real star/perhaps fading star/on her fourth marriage. She has a big house four blocks off on Capri Drive.

Carole did a fuck deck with a jazz horn called "Captain Hook." He possessed a foot-long curved schlong. Carole's married. So what?

Carole's got a thing going with Brit heartthrob Rex Harrison. Carole's got her eye on rookie congressman John F. Kennedy. He digs passing through L.A. and scrounging strange woof-woof.

Marilyn digs Jack Kennedy. Gwen observes it, plainly. Marilyn *hates* Carole. She possesses everything that Marilyn does not.

It's now late June '48. Gwen, Carole, Marilyn, and Jack Kennedy are on the premises. A girl named Marcia Davenport works as Carole's assistant. She hires Gwen and Marilyn to house-sit Carole's place when Carole and hubby dip out of town. Gwen and Marilyn enjoy momentary luxury. Gwen tips Manny Salas to a safe full of jewels. He 459's Carole's house and gives Gwen a cut of the fence money.

It's June 28, '48. Carole's out of town. Marilyn and Jack Kennedy are ensconced at the fuck pad. They're zonked on opium and cocaine. They take the plunge and go the fuck-deck route. Orson Welles shoots them in fifty-two sizzling positions. Orson, Jack, and Marilyn sign the back of the developed fotos. Doc Shelley does the technical work and gets the pix turned into a prototype deck.

Who got the deck then? Nobody knows.

It's now coming up on Independence Day, '48. Jack K.'s on a fuck-pad toot. He's comatose in a back bedroom. Carole's back in town. She's heard the rumors: Jack and Marilyn went the fuck-deck route. Carole's distraught. Rex Harrison won't leave his wife. Her career's in the tank. Her fourth husband's a dud. Jack Kennedy's a heartless no-goodnik.

Gwen and Marilyn walk Carole back to her house. It's just a few blocks away. That weird-o Chinaman seems to be tailing them. He's eavesdropping on the riff that Marilyn's laying on Carole:

No man is worth the trouble that you're putting yourself through. I've got red devils and yellow jackets. Go home, have a snooze, and call your shrink in the morning.

Carole went home. She took Marilyn's pills and killed herself. Jack K. remained conked at the fuck pad. Norm the cop and Jack the almost-cop are waltzing a bigwig pol through the pad. They get spooked by Jack K.'s condition.

Norm called Chief Worton. Chief Worton called Robert Kennedy in Boston. Young Robert was twenty-two. He had pressing travel plans. He wanted to scope out postwar Europe and soak up bebop and existential-ism. He flew out to L.A. instead.

Chief Worton had Norm the cop and Jack the almost-cop rescue Congressman John F. Kennedy from the fuck pad. Bobby K. backstopped the rescue operation. Bobby met Gwen Perloff at a little park down Pavia Place. He was rubbed raw by brother Jack's suicidal tomcat ways. Gwen was rubbed raw by Carole's suicide and Marilyn's take-a-nap-sweetie riff. The attraction went heart-deep for six days. Bobby and Gwen. Six days in July '48. Gwen gave Bobby the clap. Doc Shelley prescribed penicillin. Pharmacy records existed. Travel records existed. The Jack-Marilyn fuck deck *still* exists somewhere.

Bobby and Gwen broke it off. It was terminal at the gate. They both knew it. Gwen passed a dose to Robert F. Kennedy. Bobby said he forgave her. Gwen didn't believe him. Bobby took Jack back to Washington. *Gwen and Bobby?* Cole Porter said it best: "It was just one of those things."

Time schizzed. Marilyn became MARILYN MONROE. Gwen jumped into The Life. She fingered scores and got popped for soliciting in '50. A judge sentenced her to a stint with Paul de River's Sex Offense Bureau. She attended group therapy sessions. All the crime talk torqued her. She teethed on Roger Denfrey as Mitzi's killer. She remet Sid Leffler at the group gigs. It was "Hi, Sid," "Hi, Gwen," and no more. She met a young Sheriff's cop named Mike Bayless. He was auditing group sessions. Gwen became his longtime lover and informant. Motel Mike began a longtime search for Roger Denfrey.

Denfrey had no criminal record. Not *anywhere*. Mike saw him as a fringe figure. He was *possibly* quite dangerous. Mike did not make him for specific sex offenses. Gwen said she *knew*. She was stronger than Mike. She told Mike to find him and let her kill him. Mike said he would.

Time schizzed. Gwen went to the Pasadena Playhouse. She did swimwear ads and got contracts at Universal and Fox. Marilyn became that much more *Marilyn Monroe*. Marilyn began to deteriorate and decohere. Gwen got costar roles in horror flicks. She ran into Paul Mitchell and Albie at Fox. They had Manny in tow sometimes. She ran into Marilyn at Fox. She had dinner with Marilyn, Paul Mitchell, Manny, and Albie two or three times a year. She introduced them to Mike Bayless. He was *still* searching for Roger Denfrey. Mike and Marilyn had an affair. Mike grokked her crime fixation and tattled it to Gwen. Paul Mitchell and Manny were Chino ex-cons. Scholarly Albie was crime-fixated. Gwen began and sustained an affair with Darryl F. Zanuck. Gwen acted in B flicks and schlepped bearer bonds for Zanuck, Hersh Aadland, and other big studio guys. Mike chased Roger Denfrey. Marilyn started pressing for a publicity kidnap. Marilyn bewitched Mike Bayless. She had him out looking for the MM/JFK fuck deck. No real leads ever surfaced or popped.

Marilyn remet Senator Jack in 1954. He didn't connect her to his old fuck-deck pal. *Really.* Was she *that* unmemorable? Marilyn and Jack had once-a-year quickies, up and through his inauguration as prez. Marilyn wanted to *own* that deck. It might prove useful. She might decide to replace that lockjawed stiff Jackie as First Lady.

Marilyn is losing it. She's boozing more. She's gobbling more pills and jumping more gas-station jockeys and pizza-delivery boys. She's plotting a takeover of 20th Century–Fox. The studio is besieged by money woes engendered by King Lox *Cleopatra*. Albie Aadland tattles Marilyn's takeover shit to his brothers and Jimmy Hoffa. They like the idea and tell Albie to stay in touch as this *Cleopatra* grief evolves. Mike Bayless tells Gwen that he's tracked Roger Denfrey to the name Rick Dawes. "Rick Dawes" is a sometime cater waiter and possible Beverly Hills house burglar. Gwen gets a cater-waitress gig and starts tracking Dawes/Denfrey herself. Manny's got his swinging stewardess girlfriend, Ingrid Irmgard. She's moving bonds for the A boys. The boys want to co-opt Marilyn's takeover plan. Gwen spots Manny and the weird-o Chinaman from the fuck pad. They're going over floor plans for a burglary job. She spots them at a diner near Fox. Gwen and Mike hatch a plan. They'll lure Roger Denfrey into their kidnap gang. They'll lull him down and set him up so that Gwen can kill him. Analysand Marilyn is tattling her criminal plans to Paul de River. He brings Natasha Lytess into play. She signs on as drama coach and wardrobe mistress. Marilyn wants to courier dope and bonds? Natasha will provide appropriate disguises and motivation. Mike finds Roger Denfrey and suborns him into the gang. Mike tells Gwen what Roger told him. He's committed a string of Beverly Hills 459's with a Chink named Preston Fong. Crazy moneymaking schemes proliferate at Fox. Jimmy Hoffa hires Freddy O. for his Marilyn/Jack the K bug-tap extravaganza.

Gwen pushed the rig OFF switch. Tape hiss stopped short. She went *So?* I said, "Tell me what you want to do."

She touched my leg. She said, "Let me think about it."

72

I worked at home. I sat at the living room table and waited for Gwen to call. I typed up my concluding summary to Robert F. Kennedy. Carbon copies would go out to Bill Parker, Daryl Gates, Miller Leavy, and the Hats.

I would delete Gwen's account of the fuck-deck shenanigans. It would not sully the carbon copies. Ratfuck Bobby was there at the start. Only *he* got the full lurid ride.

He earned it. I earned it. Gwen earned it. Nobody else did.

I underscored Sid Leffler's account of the Mitzi Perloff murder. I went back and underscored my account of Paul Mitchell Grenier's death. Now you know where I dumped him. He just had to go. All justification stops there.

I took breaks and sipped coffee on the porch. Gwen buzz-bombed me. She might call, she might not. We left our end point unestablished. I woke up and found her gone. She'd cleaned up her living room. It was spick-and-span. I slept through it all.

She's got me thinking. I thought of the prez and the AG and the spring of '55. I pulled Jack out of some shit with a call girl. I presented the bill. Jack high-hatted me. Fifty grand might have been grandiose. Twenty grand would have been swell. The K boys are cheap. That's my final perspective on the brothers Kennedy.

My summary topped out at 421 pages. I ran the carbons downtown. I told Eddie Chacón to telefax the AG. I dropped off copies at the PAB and the DA's Office. I drove home and went to sleep.

Gwen didn't call. Parker and Gates called. I lobbied them on Gwen's behalf. Don't make her depose. Let her play the tape instead. They agreed. We argued endgames and conceived *this:*

Leavy files on Albie for Murder One. It's not a gas-chamber bounce. Albie was a juvie back in '37. It's a no-body job. All we've got are the admissions of a rapist ex-cop. Let Miller *have* at Albie instead.

Bust him and delay his lawyer's phone call. Put Albie in a sweatbox with Miller. Maybe Miller can shake loose a confession or induce a psychic collapse. Maybe he can rig Life Plus 99 Years or something equally harsh.

Parker and Gates liked it. Parker said he's run it by Miller. Gates said he'd invite the Hats. I said I'd invite Gwen.

Miller called me two hours later. He said it's on. Max and Red were set to haul Albie in. Buff the look-see mirror and fine-tune the hallway speakers. Albie's overmatched.

The deposition gigs went down. We scheduled them, one per night. We deposed Natasha Lytess in a private room at Kwan's Chinese Pagoda. Natasha played Belle of the Ball and charmed the shit out of Parker, Leavy, and Gates. She was sickly and dying. Her last Monroe stint ran felonious. She inspired admiration in four vindictive men. We dined and boozed until 3:00 a.m. We had a blast.

Motel Mike Bayless deposed in a private room at Ollie Hammond's Steakhouse. He held forth candidly and confirmed Gwen's recorded statement 100%. He expressed surprise per one thing. Terry Jay Aquino/aka Preston Fong/aka Sex Creep. *That* fucker as a 459 accomplice of Manny Salas *and* Roger Denfrey?

I said, "It all goes back to Albie and the three convergences. The fuck pad in '37 and '48, and Chino in '54. Albie cinches up the whole deal."

We deposed Sid Leffler in his hospital room. It was loathsome work. Miller Leavy's *eyes*? You've never *seen* such contempt.

The Leffler depo induced an aftertaste. I drove home and conjured Lowell Farr and Mitzi Perloff, alive and grown-up. I got restless and called Roddy McDowall.

We shot the breeze for ten seconds. Roddy invited me to a sneak peek at Jeanne Carmen's place. I asked him if he had the Monroe/JFK fuck deck. He said no—the best he could do was Carole Landis and Captain Hook. He was strapped for bread and sold the King Deck to Sam Yorty.

That's not bad. Mayor Sam's always liked me.

Gwen called at 4:00 the next morning. She said, "Yes," and hung up the phone.

73

The wall mirror projected a blur. It framed Leavy and Albie off-kilter. It distorted colors. Miller's suit and Albie's hair beamed out garish shades.

The hall speakers worked A-OK. Miller cleared his throat to announce the launch. Gwen jerked and brushed against me. Bill Parker went *Whoa*. Daryl Gates and the Hats twitched.

Gwen. I knew her clothes now. She'd worn the dark gray suit before. It complemented new gray hair. Her black-frame glasses offset her face in bold contrast.

She'd been respectfully brusque. We went through the introductions in six seconds. Max and Red picked Albie up and drove him downtown in his own Mercedes. A lab crew was tossing his sled in the basement garage. A second crew was tossing his house. They won't find jack shit. Albie and El Manny torched all his paper.

Miller coughed and launched. Gwen stood close and brushed my fingers.

"Your fellow kidnap conspirators have been granted immunity, Mr. Aadland. Yours has been revoked. You facilitated the criminal actions of Terry Jay Aquino, also known as Preston Fong, also known as the Sex Creep. You met Aquino at Chino in 1954, and went on to coach him in felonious endeavors, abetted by Dr. Paul de River. The Creep went on to kill a girl named Georgia Lowell Farr, and a policeman named J.T. Meadows. I intend to see you indicted as a coconspirator."

Albie smoked and fretted his cuff links. Max thinks he popped tranquilizers back at his house. Albie said, "This is a humbug deal." His voice was gravel-raw.

Miller said, "Additionally, you murdered a minor child named Mitzi Perloff in February 1937. You were a child yourself at that time. The one eyewitness, Roger Denfrey, is now dead. My one living witness, Sid Leffler, is a thoroughly disgraced ex-cop. A paucity of witnesses and a lack of physical evidence will not impede the actions of the L.A. County grand jury. They will issue a true bill for first-degree murder. At trial, I will call your three brothers and Paul de River. They will vividly describe your boyhood perversions and related criminal activities, in an effort to dodge suborning indictments themselves."

Albie said, "*So?* I've got Grant Cooper. He's better than you. He'll get a phone call sometime in the next hour. 'Grant, this is Albie. They've got me at the Detective Bureau. They haven't hosed me yet—but they might. Get down here, all right?'"

Miller feigned a yuk. Here comes the leap. Miller laid it out before the pickup. Sidelong looks traveled. They ran Parker to Gates to the Hats and me.

Gwen stared straight ahead. Her jaw flexed some new way. I wanted her to touch me. She gripped the window ledge.

Miller said, "I will now ask you a series of hypothetical questions, which will not be courtroom admissible. My hope is that I might gain theoretical knowledge of the one known homicide that you have committed, and that such knowledge will serve to mitigate my absolutist stance in court."

Albie said, "You're a ham. Always the big words, but you're headed for a trouncing."

Miller said, "Yes or no, Mr. Aadland? I know you're anxious to call Mr. Cooper."

Albie sighed. "I was raised to be accommodating, so I'll play along until I get bored."

JML/Q: "If you were to have killed Mitzi Perloff, what would your motive have been?"

AA/A: "Sex, I guess. She was little, and she wasn't a dish like her big sister. She had something, though, and who can account for taste? Also, I'm the altruistic type. If I did what you said I did, I'd be breaking her in for the unlucky guy she'd marry some dark day."

Gwen squeezed my hand and pressed it into her leg. The Hats passed a flask.

JML/Q: "Did you get what you wanted, in that upstairs bedroom—if, hypothetically, you got anything at all?"

AA/A: "If I did it, if I was looking for anything, it was a measure of relief from my status as an Aadland who couldn't hack The Life, and had to eat shit and test-pilot dope that scrambled my brain. As in rape clear's a man's pipes and allows him to compete in this shitty competitive world we live in."

JML/Q: "Was the act itself pleasurable?"

AA/A: "Not really. It was more a case of any old port in a storm. I'm squeamish, and all the blood and ooze put me in a state of postcoital regret. You know, like those Frenchy films where the lovers lay around, smoke cigarettes, and discuss how life's this doomed proposition."

It went telepathic. Albie paused and lit a cigarette. It gave the gallery a pause to drift and breathe clean air. Parker/Gates/the Hats. They walked away from Gwen and me. They walked toward the Homicide squadroom.

Gwen. With the tears now. Pooling up behind her glasses.

I took her arm and walked her toward a stairway landing. We went through the door. We stood on metal stairs that nobody used. To our left: sweatbox row. To our right: the connecting door to the elevator bank.

We stood there. Here's the wait. I stuck my handkerchief in the out-looking door crack. The door looked out on Sweatbox #3. I held Gwen and pulled off her glasses. She rubbed her face on my shirtfront and blotted her tears.

Time schizzed. I held her up against the stairway wall. She spasmed as the wait dragged. It went almost an hour. The door crack fed us the view.

Miller and Albie walked out the #3 door. They walked away from us and toward the squadroom.

Gwen knew the drill. She pushed herself off the wall and walked ahead of me. We went through the elevator-bank door.

The lift down was shut. Red arrows lit up. I pushed the down button. The door slid open. We stepped inside. I pushed the basement button. The lift lurched straight down. We stepped into the PD's garage.

Albie's Mercedes. It was two car rows back. The lab guys were gone. I pointed to a wall stanchion. Gwen walked ahead of me. I flipped a blower-fan switch at eye level. A noise wave hit the basement.

Gwen pulled on cloth gloves. I 459'd Albie's house last night. I stole a .357 Magnum revolver. Albie is left-handed. He'll start the car with his right hand. He'll rest his left arm on the door sill. It's a natural posture for a—

The freight-lift door clanked open. A little sound device dinged.

Gwen and I stood behind the stanchion. Albie walked to the Mercedes and opened the driver's door. His left arm is right where it should be.

Gwen walked up to the car. She pulled the Magnum from her hand-bag and gave Albie a beat.

He saw it and knew it. I know that. Gwen put the gun to his head and pulled the trigger. Albie convulsed. The wad-cutter load blew through him. It took out half his skull and tore out the passenger-door panel.

Gwen dropped the piece on the ground. I know suicide blowback. I told her just where to drop it. The blower fan covered the noise.

Gwen walked back over to me.

74

I stared down my phone. Nobody called last night. It wasn't on the TV or radio news. It didn't make the p.m. papers yesterday or the a.m. rags today.

I drove Gwen home yesterday. She told me she was shucking L.A. for good tomorrow night. Del Kinney took the sheriff's job in Wisconsin. They were going to get married. She might drop by Jeanne Carmen's place and say hi.

That stood as our good-byes. We did it. We didn't discuss it. We'd know the price sometime today.

We did it. Parker and Gates knew we did it. Miller Leavy knew we did it. They might nail us. They might indulge us and let us waltz. They might kick it up to Bob Kennedy and let him decide. It could play out twenty ways. We risked that. We'd know the price sometime today.

I stared down my phone. Gwen didn't call. She was packing up to ditch L.A. for good. Leavy didn't call. Likewise Parker and Gates. No cops door-knocked me. I was shit-sheared. I was bughouse/no-shit scared.

I stared down my phone. I willed it to ring and got no response. I smoked thirty cigarettes. Eddie Chacõn called at 4:20. He fed me an update.

"It has fallen on *Señor* Bob to make the call on you and Miss Perloff. He hasn't decided yet."

Eddie hung up. I forced myself to eat half a sandwich. I puked it back up ten minutes later. I gargled Old Crow and put the plug in the jug.

Gwen didn't call. No reporters called. No TV crews assembled outside. No cops knocked on my door.

Eddie called back at 5:19. I jumped on the phone.

"*Señor* Bob is letting it slide. *Señor* Leavy was outraged, but *Señor* Bob beat him down. *Puto* Leavy wants to file Manslaughter Two on you for *La Gran Puta* Grenier. Once more, *Señor* Bob prevailed."

I went to a party. Something was racking up inside of me. It was big and ugly, dirty and strange. I wanted to divert myself. I wanted to get blitzed and hold it down.

Del Kinney broke the word at Fox. It was his last official duty. He did an all-lot mail drop.

All this criminal shit stops now. The City Attorney's set to run a studio-wide audit and personal audits on all your bank accounts. The IRS is now auditing your Federal tax returns. Cease and desist immediately. You're nullified, as of now.

Roddy McDowall got an exemption. One of Del's guys leaked Roddy the word early. Roddy could shoot his *Cleopatra*-spoof fuck film. Hence, the party tonight.

Jeanne's living room was jam-packed. It was a film-biz demimonde scene. You've got Babs Payton, Lila Leeds, and Jeanne's bit player/call girl neighbors. Nat and Phil showed. Some Sheriff's squadroom guys made the scene. Eddie Fisher and Bo Belinsky made quite an entrance. Eddie spritzed unleavened joy. Liz cut his kid-support nut in half. He squeezed Liz with the Liz/Bo smut reel.

Gwen wasn't there.

The night was borderline balmy. I wedged the door open for sight lines on Gwen or No Gwen. I ate two pizza slices and kept them down. I recognized the delivery boy. It was Monroe's old squeeze, "Big Dick Dave."

Jeanne owned a cheap-o projector and pull-down screen. Roddy had redubbed real *Cleopatra* footage with gag dialogue. I grabbed a chair and set it to keep a bead on the door. A Sheriff's guy doused the room lights. Roddy did a *Roll 'em* bit. Jeanne rolled film.

It was sound film. Roddy intoned a camp prologue:

"All hail the demise of a once-proud motion picture studio!!! Because this flick is the Dog of Dogs and Lox of Loxes!!!"

The kids roared. Roddy cut to dreary shots of Roman processionals. The camera swooped wide of the set. It panned a '60-vintage shopping center, outside of Rome. *Bambinos* licked ice-cream cones. Bedraggled moms lugged shopping bags.

The kids hooted and cheered. Roddy cut to a series of shots in Cleo's throne room. The shots reduced to close-ups. Redubbed Richard Burton and Liz Taylor traded Roddyesque quips.

Redubbed Richard said, "Give me some pussy, you fine Egyptian motherfucker!"

Redubbed Liz said, "You better be a good muff diver, because I heard you're hung like a light switch!"

The kids *re*-roared. It was funny shit. I faded out of it, fast. I looked out the door. People passed on the walkway. Nobody was her.

The reel rolled on. The projector spool glitched and killed the show halfway in. The kids threw out stage groans. Lila Leeds turned on the room lights. The brightness burned my eyes.

That racking thing took me over. It doubled me over and made my eyes burn. I wiped my face and nailed the source. It was a brutal wave of love for Robert F. Kennedy.

The party dragged on. I sat in my chair and talked to people. I looked out the door. The party slogged on. My wait felt like an all-night surveillance. It was my last shot at something. I couldn't forfeit the look-see.

I didn't mark the time.

Then she was there.

The doorway framed her, the walkway lights backlit her.

She winked and blew me a kiss. She lip-synched *I love you* and stepped out of the frame.

75

Mayor Sam allotted me ten minutes. We crashed in green wing chairs. His secretary served eye-openers. She built 100-proof vodka mimosas. They were revered by the City Hall set.

Mayor Sam said, "Motel Mike signed on as my bodyguard. What's a little kidnap caper between friends?"

I laughed and cut to it. Let's not prolong this. Mayor Sam could get brusque.

"Fuck decks. I know you've got the big one, and I'm willing to pay."

Mayor Sam did not blink. He rubbed his fingers together and went for the gist.

"Twenty grand. That's the number. Anything less—*sayonara*, baby."

I said, "Ten grand and a wall-peek film of Liz Taylor and Bo Belinsky. It's high-resolution infrared, with good sound quality."

Mayor Sam said, "Shit, that's a good deal."

The beach displayed all the signs. Cars were triple-parked on PCH southbound. Numbskulls jumped on their hoods to sneak views. Fans jammed up the sand, street to wave line. I heard *"They're here!"* and *"He's here!"* and *"Maybe we'll see Jackie!"*

Eddie Chacón called my service. He told me to be prompt and park in Mrs. Lawford's garage slot. The door was up and Pat's Bonneville was missing. I drove straight in.

I got out and hooked down the north pathway. I smelled his cigar smoke. He was out by the pool. I pulled a lounge chair up beside his.

He wore sunglasses. That slayed me. He traveled incognito. I stifled a laugh.

"Hello, Mr. Kennedy."

He doffed his shades. Bright sunlight made him blink.

"Hi, Freddy. Eddie said you've got something for me."

I passed him Mayor Sam's fuck deck. It came brown paper–wrapped. This ghastly object. I did not strip the paper and peek.

He tossed me a paper bag. It was heavy. Heads popped over the fence line. *"Oh, gawwd—I saw Bobby!"*

"Fifty grand. Jack says thanks. He concedes that he stiffed you in '55, but he's compensating you now."

I said, "That means it's over."

"That's right."

"And it was nothing but a cover-up from the gate."

He tossed me a cigar. It bounced off my chest and skittered close to the pool.

"I knew you'd take it all the way. '48 would have sufficed, but you took it back to Gwen's little sister, and did some good there. I told Jack, and that's why he kicked out the bread."

I said, "Loose ends out in the world. You wanted me to identify and curtail them. Jack's the big guy, and you'll move in when he's done."

He said, "Well put, if blunt. I also wanted to see who else you'd reel in and how much you'd find out."

"Hoffa? The Aadlands?"

He blew smoke rings. Two old girls jumped above the fence line and waved. He waved right back.

"Hoffa's deal with you was another cover-up. That's why he folded so quick when Marilyn died. He put you out as bait at Fox, to see what you could detect about the scams he and the Aadlands were putting money into. You're a whizbang detective, and Jimmy's a numbnuts. He bought all of Marilyn's crazy notions and thought they were moneymakers. Star power. He was up for some enchantment, and fell for it. Eddie's bracing the Aadlands tomorrow. He's turning them as informants. They'll testify against Hoffa in my jury-tampering case in Tennessee."

I laughed. "Bill Parker. Does he get the FBI gig?"

"No. He's too intemperate and juiced up. Pete Pitchess is only marginally better. Jack and I are looking at John Doar. He's a Justice lawyer, and a civil rights man. He's got a New Frontier look to him."

I grabbed my brown bag and stood up. Kennedy stood up. We exchanged bone crushers. He winced first.

"You're not as bad as you used to be, Freddy. You can take some pride in that."

I plumbed a line due east. There was nothing to do and no place to go. There was nobody to extort or intimidate. There were no opportunities disguised as love.

Loose ends.

That plumb line due east.

I U-turned onto Sunset. I saw Pali High—home of the Dolphins. I saw the Farr house and the Bay Theater. A jog north took me by Fifth Helena. A jog south took me back to Sunset and east to the Strip. Gwen's place stood empty. The living room had sustained damage. The dutiful Sheriff's wife will forward a check. I cruised by the Chapman Park Hotel and reversed course. I drove by Hollygrove and scoped that big tree.

I drove to the run-down house on Dunoon. Natasha's junker Ford was gone. She's off at the drugstore or the market. She doesn't roll anywhere else.

I'm an eideteker. I see things and imprint things that no one else sees. Natasha's front door has a built-in mail chute. It's long and wide. I brain-screened the dimensions the first time I was here.

A light rain kicked on. I walked up to the porch. I dropped Jack's fifty grand and a get-well card down the chute.

DRAMATIS PERSONAE

WHO ARE THE ENCHANTERS?

FREDDY OTASH: Tainted ex-cop, defrocked private eye, dope fiend, and free-lance extortionist. The hero-narrator of *The Enchanters*.

MARILYN MONROE: Film star and fledgling criminal. The idée fixe of *The Enchanters*.

ROBERT F. KENNEDY: U.S. attorney general. Jack Kennedy's hatchet man. A brooding presence in *The Enchanters*.

WILLIAM H. PARKER: LAPD Chief. Boozehound. Brilliant lawyer. A big cheese among *The Enchanters*.

LOIS NETTLETON: Much-honored TV and stage actress. Freddy O.'s in love with her. A luminous presence in *The Enchanters*.

JOHN F. KENNEDY: U.S. president. At moral risk in *The Enchanters*.

PATRICIA KENNEDY LAWFORD: The sister of Bob and Jack. Freddy O.'s lost love. Married to actor Peter Lawford. Addled by Kennedy privilege in *The Enchanters*.

PETER LAWFORD: Actor and Kennedy family stooge. Bombed out of his gourd in *The Enchanters*.

DARYL GATES: Lieutenant, LAPD. Future LAPD Chief. A cunning addition to *The Enchanters*.

ROBBIE MOLETTE: Duplicitous Freddy O. goon. A reptilian presence in *The Enchanters*.

ELIZABETH TAYLOR: Scenery-chewing Film Star. She's running the king-size lox *Cleopatra* over budget. She's played for laughs in *The Enchanters*.

DARRYL F. ZANUCK: Furious and impotent film mogul. He hemorrhages money in *The Enchanters*.

PETE PITCHESS: Power-mad L.A. County Sheriff. A seething shadow figure in *The Enchanters*.

CAROLE LANDIS: Minor '40s film star. A suicide in '48. She unlocks the many mysteries in *The Enchanters*.

BERNIE SPINDEL: Electronic-surveillance whiz. He lays wire in *The Enchanters*.

HERSHEL "BUZZY" STEIN: Two-bit hoodlum. An enigma in *The Enchanters*.

EDDIE FISHER: Noted crooner, fourth husband of Liz Taylor. He's howl-arious in *The Enchanters*.

DEEDEE GRENIER: Golf pro, police informant, low-rent criminal. She's dubiously employed in *The Enchanters*.

PAUL MITCHELL GRENIER: Ex-convict, psycho leather-bar biter. A tidal wave of slime in *The Enchanters*.

SAM YORTY: Mayor of Los Angeles. He cracks jokes and glides through *The Enchanters*.

JACK CLEMMONS: Sergeant, LAPD. Right-wing nut. Provides topical flavor to *The Enchanters*.

NATASHA LYTESS: Russian-born drama coach. Stupidly in love with Marilyn Monroe. She oozes sagacity in *The Enchanters*.

MAX HERMAN: Hard-charging LAPD detective. On the illustrious Hat Squad. He kicks brutal ass in *The Enchanters*.

RED STROMWALL: Hard-charging LAPD detective. On the illustrious Hat Squad. He kicks brutal ass in *The Enchanters*.

HARRY CROWDER: Hard-charging LAPD detective. On the illustrious Hat Squad. He kicks brutal ass in *The Enchanters*.

EDDIE BENSON: Hard-charging LAPD detective. On the illustrious Hat Squad. He kicks brutal ass in *The Enchanters*.

RICHIE DANFORTH/RICK DAWES/RONNIE DEWHURST/ROGER DENFREY: His evil vibe simmers in *The Enchanters*.

MARCIA MARIA DAVENPORT: Divorcée burglary victim. A pervert stalks her in *The Enchanters*.

LEONA JENKS HAGEDOHM: Divorcée burglary victim. A pervert stalks her in *The Enchanters*.

ARDEN JANE BROWNLEIGH: Divorcée burglary victim. A pervert stalks her in *The Enchanters*.

DOROTHY DILYS TRENT: Divorcée burglary victim. A pervert stalks her in *The Enchanters*.

WANDA JEAN D'ALLESIO: Divorcée burglary victim. A pervert stalks her in *The Enchanters*.

LORRAINE SMITH: Divorcée burglary victim. A pervert stalks her in *The Enchanters*.

SHELDON MANDEL, M.D.: A hotshot VD doctor back in the '40s. An ambiguous riddle in *The Enchanters*.

RAY PINKER: LAPD's legendary forensic chemist. He puts together crucial scientific shit in *The Enchanters*.

J. MILLER "GAS CHAMBER" LEAVY: Hard-hitting L.A. prosecutor. He injects a note of probity in *The Enchanters*.

MILT CHARGIN: Bottom-shelf nightclub ventriloquist. He defines '62 L.A.'s raucous sense of humor in *The Enchanters*.

INGRID IRMGARD: Scando-fox, swinging stewardess, dope conduit. She's up to no good in *The Enchanters*.

MAURY DEXTER: Baron of the B flicks. He lends a populist sensibility to *The Enchanters*.

NORM KRAUSE: Ex-LAPD motor cop, extortionist, right-wing nut. He skeeves up *The Enchanters*.

PAUL DE RIVER, M.D.: Corrupt and corrupting headshrinker. Don't go near his couch! A sinister aspect of *The Enchanters*.

JOSÉ BOLAÑOS: Communist, dope peddler, exploiter of Marilyn Monroe's madness. Will he survive *The Enchanters?*

SID LEFFLER: LAPD squadroom cop, going nowhere. Possesses a twisted bent. He stirs Freddy O.'s wrath in *The Enchanters*.

GWEN PERLOFF: Orphanage pal of Marilyn Monroe. Hard-ass criminal. Freddy comes to love her in *The Enchanters*.

"MOTEL MIKE" BAYLESS: Sheriff's detective. Intelligence operator. Women crave his handsome ass in *The Enchanters*.

"NASTY NAT" DENKINS: Freddy O.'s #1 goon. He rocks steady in *The Enchanters*.

PHIL IRWIN: Freddy O.'s #2 goon. He rocks steady in *The Enchanters*.

JIMMY HOFFA: Mobbed-up labor leader. On the run from Bob Kennedy in *The Enchanters*.

HANS MASLICK: Homicide cop in Weimar Berlin. Part-time Brownshirt. Full-time dope fiend. Forensic visionary. Freddy deploys Maslick's vision in *The Enchanters*.

BO BELINSKY: Hunky pitching ace for the L.A. Angels. He helps Freddy set up Liz Taylor in *The Enchanters*.

EDGAR CHACÓN: Justice Department lawyer-investigator. Bobby K.'s pet goon. Cuban exile bagman. He's luridly alive in *The Enchanters*.

J. T. MEADOWS: West L.A. squadroom cop. Hot on the trail of a sex-psycho burglar. A classic dogged cop in *The Enchanters*.

MORTY BENDISH: Scurrilous scribe for the sleazoid *L.A. Mirror-News*. A vivid voice for the tabloid gestalt of *The Enchanters*.

GEORGIA LOWELL FARR: Palisades High School junior. Boon companion of Marilyn Monroe. An artiste in the making. She prophecies the simmering '60s in *The Enchanters*.

LILA LEEDS: Part-time actress, part-time carhop, part-time bait girl. She adds period verismo to *The Enchanters*.

JEANNE CARMEN: Pill peddler, golf trick-shot artist, onetime call girl. Dig her "pill-pillow parties" in *The Enchanters*.

RALPH R. GREENSON, M.D.: Marilyn Monroe's chief headshrink. Watch Monroe exploit him as he feeds off of her in *The Enchanters*.

RODDY MCDOWALL: Noted film and TV actor. Gay blade about town. Director of underground fuck flicks. Roddy's got aaallll the lines in *The Enchanters*.

HERSHEL AADLAND: Mobbed up. Corrupt studio labor facilitator. White slaver, head breaker, bad to the bone. He skulks through *The Enchanters*.

MEYER AADLAND: Hersh's brother. Mobbed up. Corrupt studio labor facilitator. White slaver, head breaker, bad to the bone. He skulks through *The Enchanters*.

IRA AADLAND: Hersh and Meyer's brother. Mobbed up. Corrupt studio labor facilitator. White slaver, head breaker, bad to the bone. He skulks through *The Enchanters*.

ALBIE AADLAND: Much younger brother of Hersh, Meyer, Ira. He will unlock the door to many secrets in *The Enchanters*.

JUAN MANUEL SALAS/AKA "EL MANNY": Ex-welterweight. Now a TV repairman. Ingrid Irmgard's lover. Is he a kidnap conspirator? Find out in *The Enchanters*.

BARBARA PAYTON: Ex-actress, ex–call girl, current carhop. She provides Freddy with good skinny on postwar L.A. in *The Enchanters*.

TIMMY BERLIN: Marilyn Monroe's circa '54 lover. He still packs a torch in *The Enchanters*.

DOROTHY DENTON LOWELL FARR: Georgia Lowell Farr's mom. She can't believe her daughter and Monroe are tight pals. She finds out in *The Enchanters*.

DEL KINNEY, JR.: Ex-Sheriff's, ex–Alcoholic Beverage Control. Current 20th Century–Fox security boss. He strikes up an alliance with Freddy O. in *The Enchanters*.

BEV SHOFTEL: She runs a storefront mail drop for sleazoid Hollywood types. Said types abound in *The Enchanters*.

EDNA MEDINA: She styles Marilyn Monroe's hair and gets an earful of Monroe's crazy shit. Monroe wears her thin in *The Enchanters*.

PRESTON FONG/TERRY JAY AQUINO: Riviera Country Club caddy. Rogue chemist. Hoarder of fine wristwatches. Out strolling for kicks in *The Enchanters*.

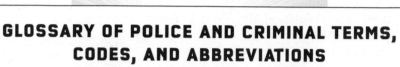

GLOSSARY OF POLICE AND CRIMINAL TERMS, CODES, AND ABBREVIATIONS

211: The California Penal Code designation for armed robbery.

459: The California Penal Code designation for burglary.

ABC: The California State Office of Alcoholic Beverage Control.

AD VICE: The LAPD's Administrative Vice Division.

ADW: The criminal charge of Assault with a Deadly Weapon.

AID: The LAPD's Accident Investigation Division.

BAIT GIRLS: Young women hired by sleazoid divorce lawyers and corrupt studio bosses to entrap cheating husbands and/or rope in business prospects.

BNDD: The Bureau of Narcotics and Dangerous Drugs.

CCW: The criminal charge of Carrying a Concealed Weapon.

CODE 3: A two-way-radio directive urging cops to run their red lights and sirens.

DB: Detective Bureau, headquarters or divisional.

DR #: A designation for the LAPD classification of Divisional Records.

FI CARDS: Field interrogation cards. Patrol cops stop suspicious pedestrians, run warrant checks, and FI-card the mofos.

GREEN SHEETS: Light-hued Teletype pages detailing a person's criminal offenses.

THE HAT SQUAD: LAPD Robbery Division, 1949–1962. Max Herman, Red Stromwall, Harry Crowder, Eddie Benson. The four very big men wear pearl-gray suits and white fedoras. They chase down the worst of the worst. Do not fuck with them.

HUAC: The Federal and individual state agencies charged with investigating subversive individuals and organizations.

INTEL: The LAPD's Intelligence Division.

KA SHEETS: Known associate sheets kept on suspected criminals.

THE LOSERS CLUB: A circa '62 West Hollywood nightclub. Name acts gig the joint. Said joint veers raw. Comics there work topical. A sign on the façade denotes the "Loser of the Week." It's the early '60s, baby. Losers are cool.

NCIC: The National Crime Information Center.

PAB: The Police Administration Building, at 1st and Los Angeles Streets.

R&I: The LAPD's Records and Information Division.

SHIT: An acronym for the Sheriff's Handpicked Intelligence Team.

THE "WRONG-DOOR RAID": A November '54 cluster fuck. Involved: Freddy Otash, Marilyn Monroe, Joe DiMaggio, Phil Irwin, and Frank Sinatra. This Mickey Mouse scandal alerted the California State Assembly to the corrupt practices of scandal magazines and the bent detectives they hired—chief among them, Freddy Otash.

A Note About the Author

James Ellroy was born in Los Angeles. He is the author of the Underworld U.S.A. Trilogy: *American Tabloid, The Cold Six Thousand,* and *Blood's A Rover,* and the L.A. Quartet novels: *The Black Dahlia, The Big Nowhere, L.A. Confidential,* and *White Jazz.* He is the recipient of the *Los Angeles Times* Robert Kirsch Award for lifetime achievement. He lives in Colorado.

Jacket images, left to right, top to bottom: (Marilyn Monroe) Archivio GBB/ Alamy; (Daryl F. Gates) George Brich/AP Images; (Patricia Kennedy Lawford) Magite Historic/Alamy; (Natasha Lytess) J. R. Eyerman/The LIFE Picture Collection/Shutterstock; (U.S. Attorney General Robert Kennedy) Glasshouse Images/Alamy; (Roddy McDowall) Getty Images; (Lois Nettleton) Getty Images; (Carole Landis) The Hollywood Archive/Alamy; (William H. Parker) Getty Images; (Fred Otash) Getty Images